BOSS LADY

LARALYN DORAN

A THREE DOGS DAY

BOSS LADY

Copyright © 2021 by Laralyn Doran.

For information contact Laralyn Doran at:
P. O. Box 234
Monrovia, MD 21770-0234
www.LaralynDoran.com

Book and Cover design by Deranged Doctor Designs
Photography: Lindee Robinson
Editors: Holly Ingraham | Elaine York
Proofreader: Katie Testa

ISBN: 978-1-7353474-2-4 (eBook)
ISBN: 978-1-7353474-3-1 (Trade Paperback)
First Edition: June 2021

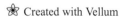 Created with Vellum

For Mom and Dad

LARALYN DORAN

1

SONOMA, CA

Harper

It was an unspoken understanding that when some Southern women said, "Well, bless your heart…" they meant, "You're an asshole."

Alright…that may be a loose translation—but it was times like these when I had to bite my tongue from saying it.

I stood on the infield of the Sonoma racetrack baking in the June California sun, listening to my father's friends talk around me as they discussed his latest strategy for increasing his stock car's team visibility. It was a side competition involving my best friend, Charlotte Jean "CJ" Lomax, the only woman racing at the Cup level, and Grady McBane, a charming Indy champion who was currently the *bane* of her existence and star of her fantasies, depending on the hour.

CJ and Grady were alternating races and the one with the best record at the end of the season would win the contract with our team, Merrick Motorsports, for the next season. They both needed the contract to save their careers, and the public was obsessed with following the drama it produced.

"I think it's so nice your Daddy is giving CJ this opportunity to race at the Cup level and against drivers of this caliber." An executive friend of my father's drawled as his slimy gaze blatantly traveled up and down my short-clad legs. "She's lucky to have such a beautiful friend and a family like yours in her corner to champion her career."

"Well, bless your heart, aren't you sweet..." I waved him off and graced him with the most pageant-worthy smile, thankful I still wore my mirrored sunglasses so he couldn't see the death rays I was shooting. I nodded. "Of course, my daddy knows talent, and the fact that she's won championships in all the other circuits she's raced had nothing to do with the fact that she's made it this far."

As her manager, it was up to me to see that she got a fair deal. But, in one of the most testosterone-filled sports industries in the world, it didn't matter who your daddy was, it was a hell of a challenge at each turn.

"Well, you must be proud of your brother—coming up with this idea of Grady and CJ competing for the contract—it's gained so much attention."

I'd lost the reins on my sarcasm and cynicism I usually kept tucked neatly away. I tapped his arm. "You know I *am*...so, so proud." My Carolina drawl came out thick, with a higher tone than I usually spoke and a smile so wide and so fake it could replace Harley Quinn's before she starts swinging her bat at people.

It was hot, I was cranky, and I didn't want to get into it with a misogynistic, old man.

I'd spent the last hour chasing my brother around this damn track in this heat because he couldn't even manage to keep his phone charged, and corralling *his* driver, Grady McBane, through his pre-race itinerary. On top of that, when Grady's equally disagreeable brother showed up unannounced, I had to run interference between them, all while managing to greet my father's friends and try to wrangle my own driver to keep her from making a major PR faux pas.

My father, seeing signs of me losing my renowned grace and coolness, attempted to redirect my ire. "Harper, honey. Why don't you go try to find Junior, again, so the boys here have a chance to chat with him and maybe wrangle up one of our drivers. If Grady is preparing to race, grab CJ."

My father gave me his wide-eye, with a tilt of his head that said, *Stop-being-rude, this-isn't-how-I-raised-you.* I stared down my father, a very defiant and rebellious move for me, but one only he would know was uncharacteristic.

"Fine." I gave my father a tight smile. I clutched my iPad to my chest as if it anchored my temper.

I whirled in a huff, grateful to make any type of escape before I said or did something I'd regret, and I didn't see who I almost ran over.

I was not a petite girl. Even without my heels, if I bumped into a man, there was a good chance we'd both go down. I stumbled over my unintended victim, braced myself on a hard chest and was able to right myself, and came face to face with none other than Mr. Cal McBane, Grady's disagreeable brother. I was introduced to him briefly in Grady's motorhome earlier today, when I intruded on the brothers' not-so-happy reunion. I quickly removed my intruding hand. "Cal—wow, I'm so sorry. I wasn't looking—"

"Hey, Harper, are you okay?" He surveyed me up and down, reaching out a hand as if to steady me.

I stepped back out of his reach and waved him off. "Oh, I'm fine. Just in too much of a rush. I need to watch where I'm going."

"Are you sure?" He flipped up his sunglasses, and...um, wow. He was handsome. More so than I'd remembered from our previous run-in inside the motorhome. I mean, I'd caught how striking he was earlier and noted it, but this close, I had a whole different appreciation.

In a male-dominated industry filled with testosterone, there were plenty of good-looking, confident men. Cal was a more commanding, when-he-enters-a-room-he-owns-it kind of handsome. He had the kind of broad shoulders you wanted to wrap your arms around, and his strong jaw was emphasized with brown scruff that was probably there no matter when he shaved. I noticed his hair was brown, but now in the sun there were waves of chestnut that ran through it. However, what had given me the wow factor this time, and left me momentarily stunned, was the undivided attention I was getting from his stare.

3

Earlier, I wasn't close enough to see how intricate the color of his eyes were. Now...they were mesmerizing. You could call them hazel, but they were really, a generous green, accented with flashes of amber through them. Good God, I wasn't studying his eyes with people milling around us. I was flat-out staring.

He took a half step toward me, reaching out as if to protect me from the people walking by. "I saw you from across the way and thought I'd come apologize for what you got caught up in—"

I shook my head, "No, it's fine. If there's one thing I get, it's pain-in-the-ass brothers." I was suddenly very aware of how bad I was sweating. Great. I ran my hand over my brow. "Although, not knowing you very well, I have to admit, I'm still Team Grady."

He let out a small laugh and the smile lit up his face. "Why don't you let me walk with you and I can try to change that?"

"Okay—now I see the brotherly resemblance—you're both charmers..."

He winked in response and strode beside me as I started to walk. "Where are you off to in such a hurry?"

I stopped and let out a sound of exasperation. "It's just been a hell of a day and the race hasn't even started." I threw my hand in the air. "I've been stuck dealing with my father, trying to keep your brother on schedule because my brother can't seem to handle that small task. Plus, I have to continue to run interference with our two drivers to stop them from either jumping each other or CJ killing him on national television."

He put his hands in his pockets, rocked back on his heels, and said, "So, in other words, you have time to show me around?" His tone ticked up as if leading me to say, "Yes, of course."

I smiled at his attempt and nudged him with my elbow, walking forward. "Come along and I'll walk you to the media tent. You can see your brother and CJ in action or my brother's attempts at trying to hog the limelight away from his own driver."

"How did you get roped into this—"

"Circus." I supplied the word and his brows rose.

"Well, I was going to say contest—but if that's the word you want to use, I guess it's telling."

We'd walked a bit toward the media tent when my brother came barreling out. "Harper, get CJ out of here!"

Oh, for heaven's sake. "Hello, Junior."

"I mean it, Harper. Go in there—" He pointed to the tent. "And drag her out or so help me—"

"What? You're going to run to Dad? Grow the hell up." I turned to Cal, who was witnessing this juvenile behavior. "I'm so sorry—now it's your turn to witness sibling drama." I turned back to Junior and motioned between the two men. "Cal McBane, this is Grady's manager and my immature brother, Everett Merrick Junior. Feel free to call him Jackass, though, as he answers to that as well."

Cal, to his credit, thinned his lips to hide the grin I knew was slipping through, and held out his hand. "Pleased to meet you."

Junior straightened immediately, shaking Cal's hand. "I'm sorry, Mr. McBane. Just dealing with a little internal issue with one of the drivers." My brother glared at me and then said, "Excuse us a moment." He yanked on my elbow, pulling me to the side. I relented because I didn't want to draw a bigger scene than he was already causing.

"This isn't her race. She's undermining Grady's first race—" He raised his voice like a petulant child, pointing at the tent. "You're her manager, so go in there and fetch her! Drag her out of there if you have to—"

"Excuse me." Cal stepped in between us. "Did you just tell Harper to 'fetch' a woman and drag her out...as if she were a dog?"

My brother straightened, his face was no longer petulant, instead waffling between indignant and embarrassed—clearly assessing Cal's opinion and what it was worth to him. "Today is your brother's debut race. He shouldn't have to share the media time with another driver."

Cal folded his arms over his chest. "Personally, I'd rather see my employees look out for the company—for the team—rather than piss around trying to establish territory. But, hey," he held up his hands in a shrug, "that's how I run McBane Industries, maybe you should go talk with your father—maybe he has a different philosophy that is more engrained in discrimination and nepotism."

My brother flinched. My father wouldn't take kindly to that assessment. "I don't see how any of this is your business," Junior muttered, and then literally turned his back on Cal. Pointing in my face because he thought I was going to be easier to deal with. "Get her out of there or I will."

I laughed him off and pushed past him, tossing a derisive, "I'd like to see you try."

My brother stomped off, muttering a string of curses, and I glanced over at Cal, embarrassed at what amateurs we must appear to him. "Sorry about that."

"Don't worry about—" he was cut off when in a quick move, Cal reached for me, pulling me close, and turned as he maneuvered around a rowdy group of guys, one, the size of a linebacker, stumbled over another, just missed flying into us, and faceplanted on the ground.

The guys helped their friend up and hooted and hollered how funny it was, taking off without realizing how close they came to taking me out.

I straightened, trying to get my bearings, and looked at Cal, who turned his murderous glare off the retreating men and down to me—his hands still around my waist. His face softened as he bent his head slightly to come eye-level with me.

Jesus, Harper, close your mouth before you start to drool.

His scent of cedar and sandalwood was such a welcomed scent after a day of beer, sweat, tires, and gasoline, and I was more than aware of every surface of me that was touching every part of him.

"Are you ok? Did I hurt you?"

"I'm fine." I stepped back, his arms fell from my waist, but one kept hold of my hand. "Really, I'm good." I glanced back up at him, realizing how close his face still was to mine. He was about four or five inches taller than me—which, for me, was perfect. Being a woman considered a bit on the tall side, I never considered myself someone who could easily be swept off my feet, but he seemed to do it effortlessly.

"Thank you—it seems you saved me from being flattened by frat boys." I forced a smile, but this time, it was because there were butter-flies doing laps in my belly, and when things grew awkwardly quiet between us and his gaze stayed on me, I think I may have stopped breathing.

He smiled a devilish smile. "I'd gladly come to your rescue, when-ever you need it."

Oh boy…the blush intensified.

"Yes, well. I'm not in the market for a hero, Mr. McBane."

"I'm not saying you are, Ms. Merrick. But sometimes, it's good to have someone there to catch you when you fall."

The words were out of my mouth before I even realized what I said. "I have no intention of falling for anyone."

2

INDIANAPOLIS, IN

Harper

There were times I regretted my Southern upbringing and envied CJ's penchant for beer, cut-offs, t-shirts, and foul-mouth temper. It seemed more liberating.

I sat at an outdoor hotel bar close to the track with my legs crossed, waiting for Aunt Sadie to show. Even in a soft yellow sundress, it was unseasonably warm for a September night in Indianapolis. After the long day I had at the racetrack, my empty glass of chardonnay was unacceptable. I waved down the server, giving him my best debutante smile when he approached to refill my glass. I snatched the bottle from his hand. "Thanks, hon. Just put it on my tab."

His brow furrowed as he paused, a bit perplexed, and then left.

Keeping CJ from castrating her nemesis—who was also the man she was in love with—and trying to figure out how to get my family's stock car team out of the PR quicksand my father had thrown us into was requiring chardonnay by the bottle, instead of the glass.

My father and brother were systematically making our family's stock car team the next family reality show. In the process of courting notoriety, they were tarnishing the company's image with a series of gimmicks, instead of marketing ourselves as a truly serious business. Where were we going to be after this season was over with?

They were going to be like a Top 40 song that got overplayed on the radio for weeks.

They were going to be a joke. Our company would be a joke.

The level of expectation would be so high for both our drivers that even a championship wouldn't be enough to reach the height of the pedestal people put them on, both individually and together.

I poured more wine and took another generous pull of the chardonnay. I wouldn't even kid myself into believing I was sipping it anymore.

My eye caught a group sitting caddy-corner to me in a cluster of chairs. I recognized some of them—a few executives from the Butler Corporation, a competing team that had been on the decline over the past few seasons.

One of the executives leaned back and shouted over. "Hey, Harper. Your girl looked good out there today. Glad to see she has her head back in the game and that pretty boy isn't distracting her so much." His smirk was goading and smug.

Yeah, screw you.

I smiled my best debutante smile and tilted my glass in acknowledgment of their taunt. "Thank you. She did look good. I'm so happy your boy didn't have engine trouble today." I raised my glass and the volume of my voice. "It must be such a relief to have actually finished a race."

That's when the crew chief suddenly darted up from behind the crowd, scowling. "It wasn't the car; it was the driver. Damn kids these days don't know how the hell to drive the cars without burning them out," the crew chief said. What was his name? Jeff…something.

I nodded and took another sip of my drink. Someone pulled on the guy's shirt until he sat back down.

Whatever.

George Butler's son, Bo, who was also one of his executives, came sauntering over, adjusting his belt buckle, a cocky expression on his face. Great. Time for him to try to be the big guy standing up for "his people" and put the little woman in her place.

I didn't bother to stand for two reasons. First, I was comfortable. Second, I didn't want to spill my wine, and third, I was taller than him, and that would just egg him on. Alright—that was three reasons. Maybe I should slow down on the wine...

"Your daddy's still humoring you and your pet project, huh? How long's that going to last?" he said, managing to stop leering at my legs long enough to check over his shoulder at his group for approval.

I leaned back, cocked my head, and gave a slight smirk. "Hello, Bo. Hadn't seen you in an age—you or Lisette." My smile widened. "How's she doing?"

Bo stiffened.

You want to play? Fine...

"It's been so long since I talked—oh." I sat up, my brows furrowing and my hand to my mouth faking a slight faux-pas, in a loud whisper, I said, "I'm so sorry, I forgot about...I'm so sorry, I didn't even know Lisette was interested in yoga. Good for her. I hear it can change your life."

His wife had recently left him for a yoga instructor—a female yoga instructor.

He adjusted his belt and cracked his neck, and with a sneer, muttered, "You are such a spoiled, pretentious bitch—"

That made me stand up quickly. I may be polite and gracious, but I didn't take insults sitting down. With my sandals, I was a few inches taller than him, and he took a few steps back as I straightened to my full height. One side of my lips may have tilted up at his scowl when he realized his concession. I didn't care if his fragile masculinity was tied up in his height or threatened by me literally looking down on him.

"Oh, well. I guess I'll call Lisette..." I leaned over him, "and offer my congratulations."

"Soon you and that friend of yours will be off the track and out of our hair for good."

He turned to stomp off.

I huffed at the back of his bad combover. "It doesn't seem you have much hair to worry about." I waved. "I can see you're busy. We'll catch up later. Have a good evening."

With that unpleasantness out of the way, I resumed my brooding.

"Hey, doll." Aunt Sadie attempted to pull a chair closer with one hand while the other attempted not to spill the cocktail, probably an Old Fashioned, teetering in her other hand and sloshing precariously to the sides of the highball glass. She wore navy slacks, one-inch sensible pumps, and a long, colorful tunic. Her bright red hair was perfectly styled and unmoving, make-up perfectly applied, and her jewelry was voluminous and the most noticeable thing about her. Large rings, multiple necklaces, big earrings. It was the whole package.

"What's Lil' Bo want with you?"

"Hi, Sadie. Just to cause trouble. Nothing I can't handle." I grabbed the glass. "Here, give me that. No sense in wasting a perfectly good cocktail." I mimicked her own adage.

As she dragged the heavy cushioned piece of furniture closer to me, a loud protesting groan came from it, and most of the surrounding patrons stared at us. Once she was settled, she leaned in even closer—her eyebrows reaching her hairline, anticipation blanketing her face.

"Pfft." She waved her hand in dismissal. "I know what's going to make that boy madder than a wet hen..." She snickered, leaning over, putting down her cocktail and rubbing her hands with glee, her rings and necklaces clicking and clacking with the enthusiasm that radiated from her face. "He's pissed. I overheard his father tell some people today that if the team doesn't start turning around, he's dumping it."

"Really..." I leaned forward, my elbow perched on the arm of the chair and chin cradled in my hand, almost like a baby bird with their mouth stretched open for a juicy worm.

Sadie leaned forward like the mama bird ready to feed me. "Supposedly, since Bo's taken over the team, they haven't been able to crack the top twenty and are plagued with financial problems as well."

"I knew they were having problems on the track—"

"Yes, well...the team is draining their resources, which is not something George can handle right now."

"Too bad for George. But I can't say I won't be sorry to see Bo

11

go." I leaned back in the seat, stared out at the bar, and drank more of my wine—weary and drained.

"Why the sad face?" Sadie settled in with her cocktail.

"I don't know what to do to get CJ and I out of this circus."

Sadie patted my knee.

"Any way I look at this, this season isn't going to end well. I don't see my father choosing CJ over Grady. The media won't allow it. Grady is too charming. The sponsors love him, the fans love him. I can't think of a team willing to drop their driver in favor of CJ. I'm supposed help steer her through all of this." I held out my hand, helpless. "What am I going to do?"

Sadie squeezed my knee. "I know, hon. I think Everett started off with good intentions, but I think the circus got out of hand, and now he's enjoying the frenzy of attention Merrick is getting too much to see the damage it's causing." She leaned back, taking a sip of her drink. "I heard Grady's brother was in town, maybe he could convince Grady back to Chicago?"

"Who, Cal?" I waved her off, just mentioning his name conjured the memory of our meeting I'd been trying so hard to forget. "No, that ship has sailed. No way Grady will return to the family fold now. Grady probably sent him packing already."

"That's too bad. Caught an eyeful of him earlier today…and it wasn't a bad view." She wiggled her brows. "Those shoulders and that—"

"Sadie, please…" I scolded her. I didn't need any reminder of his shoulders or any other part of him.

"Don't tell me you didn't notice. You may be going through an extreme dry spell, but you aren't dead."

Oh, I'd noticed. I heard he was at the track briefly today. I was disappointed we never crossed paths and regretted I hadn't nudged fate by possibly tripping into him again.

"It would be worth helping those brothers mend their ways just to see him around more." An approving hum came from her as she took another drink of her cocktail.

I wondered if I should cut her off.

"Well," she slapped her hand on the arm of her chair, "It's up to us to come up with something that will help our girl land on her feet."

My aunt stared at me—all trace of teasing was gone. "Besides the fact that I think it's time for you to break off from Merrick. I love my brother, but I see what's happening over there. You've outgrown Merrick, darling. Whether or not Everett realizes it, you must see it."

I pondered what she said as we sat in silence, sipping on our drinks in a bar that was filling up around us.

Boisterous noise and laughter came from over my shoulder in the direction of the Butler group. Sadie's eyes narrowed, and like a predator spotting new prey, she stilled. My aunt being still and silent was an unnatural occurrence, and usually a harbinger that had me on alert.

"What is it?"

She cocked an eyebrow and remained silent. She slowly lifted her highball to her mouth,

and downed the remainder of her drink. She waved her hand at me in the universal sign to finish up my drink. "I'm paying our tab. Let's go. I have an idea, but I don't want to discuss it here. Let's go back to my room and talk...and tomorrow I want to make a few phone calls."

She stood so abruptly she swayed a bit. "Whoa..." She paused, then stood as if perfecting a dismount—arms outstretched and smiling a triumphant, "I'm good! Let's go."

Confused at her sudden commands, I hadn't moved. "What's going—"

"Harper, shake a tail feather. We got planning to do—time to shift the world on its ass, girl." She waved her hands at me with impatience and then flagged down our waiter and started shoving money at him. She wasn't waiting for a check.

"Sadie—" I tried to grab her attention to get an explanation.

"Hell with it, bring the wine, then." She grabbed my wine bottle as if it were the carrot on the end of the stick that would entice me to follow.

Hate to admit it, but it worked.

3

LAKE NORMAN, NC

Cal

My brother Grady has the devil's luck.

Only he could walk away from a horrendous car crash this past weekend at Talladega Speedway with the woman of his dreams wrapped around him.

My mother hasn't been herself lately and the stress of this wasn't something she needed. She was about to run down here, but I was able to convince her to stay home after promising to come by and check on him after my scouting trip to Atlanta for an investment deal.

I'd arrived at his Lake Norman house early that morning and got the first-hand account about the drama—how he dueled with a menacing rival, participated in a crash that took out more than a dozen cars, ended the race on his roof with a wreckage scattered around him, and still managed to carry CJ away with all his limbs still intact.

"Well, we all knew you had a hard head," I said to him, sitting in his kitchen on a beautiful October afternoon, enjoying the renewed banter between us. Our fallout started with my brother's indiscretions with the engaged daughter of a competitor. My father, sick of his shit, kicked him off our company's Indy team, and he became persona non grata in the Indy industry.

We both made mistakes following his scandal, but it was my father who really made things worse. His inability to bend or listen to his own son—well, that part was an ongoing issue.

It all led him to stock car racing, Merrick Motorsports, and to the woman who changed his life, CJ Lomax.

"But seriously, you need to stop proving it and give that poor brain of yours a break. Your girlfriend is going to want something to go along with your good looks."

Grady raised his brows at me. "You admit I'm the good-looking one..." he grinned his trademark, cocky smile. He stood up. "Yeah, well, I'd have to be the smart one also, because *I*," he gave me a pointed glance, "have the best taste in girlfriends."

I dropped my head in anticipation of what was coming next.

"Speaking of better taste in girlfriends," he said as he walked out of the kitchen and into the family room. "How did you get Vanessa to allow you to come down here?" Grady stuck his hands in his pockets, rocking back on his heels as CJ came in the room and wrapped an arm around him. "You've been traveling a lot lately."

I walked over to the arm of their sofa and leaned against it. "Vanessa and I broke up."

"Hallelujah." Grady tilted his face to heaven in obvious thanks.

CJ smacked his abs. "Grady, that's a horrible thing to say. I'm sorry, Cal."

I rubbed my hand over the back of my neck to hide the tilt of my lips. I knew my brother would have this reaction. The tilt was not in amusement of my breakup, but at being thankful for having that familiarity back in our relationship—something I didn't think we'd ever get back.

"It actually happened a few months ago," I said, "before my visit to Sonoma." There was no love lost between my ex-girlfriend and my brother. It was one of the reasons we broke up—she didn't exactly support my attempts at reconciling, and I got tired listening to her bitch about him.

"Wow, you never said anything," Grady said, genuinely surprised.

"Well, you were busy yelling at me and telling me to fuck off." I tilted my head. "Would telling you I broke up with Vanessa have helped to shut you up?"

He shrugged his shoulders, "May have?"

"Yeah, you're full of shit." I said it with a teasing tone.

A horn blared from outside the house.

"That's Cooper—he's taking me to my doctor's appointment," Grady said. "Are you staying here?"

"Nah, I got a hotel reservation," I said.

"Well, stick around, I'll be back in a bit and we can go to dinner. Harper's coming over. I think Gus, also."

The mention of Harper's name was a jolt to my system.

I hadn't seen her since Sonoma, but she left an impression. Bold, sassy, and beautiful. Not beautiful...gorgeous. But in a way that was deep, not just her hair, eyes, legs, and smile. No—there was a lot to Harper Merrick I found intriguing.

CJ turned to me after Grady left—her smile was contagious. "They should be on their way over now. Let's get some things together and we can sit on the dock and have some cocktails."

I nodded, already feeling more relaxed than I had in weeks—maybe months. We went into the kitchen and began to assemble a cooler of drinks and snacks to take down.

The doorbell rang, twice in quick succession.

"I'll be right back. Grady keeps a pretty well-stocked kitchen. There are some cheeses in the compartment in the big fridge, and there is a wine fridge over below the island. Can you grab a bottle of chardonnay for Harper?" CJ said, while walking to the door.

My little brother seemed to have grown up—a fridge of wine and cheese instead of beer and chips. Mom would be shocked.

"Well, it's all going to hell in a handbasket before it's even gotten off the ground." A panicked female voice—not CJ's—boomed from the other room.

"Harper, what's—" CJ said.

Harper. I closed the fridge, the bottle of wine in my hand forgotten.

"You aren't going to believe this. That little prick." Anger and bitterness came from the sweetest voice. "That little scrawny, bitter, woman-hating prick convinced his father that he was underselling the team and Butler has backed out of our deal."

"What?" The tone of CJ's voice concerned me enough to put down the wine and walk to the doorway separating the rooms.

"Yes. Supposedly Bo found out about the meeting Sadie and I had with George Butler in Vegas and wasn't on board with his father selling off what he considered part of his legacy. He was more enraged when he found out he was selling it to me—to us. Selling to women. Can you believe that?"

Selling what?

I peeked around the corner and saw Harper Merrick pacing my brother's family room, her long legs no match for the small space. Her straight blonde hair appeared windblown, her cheeks had a bit of color —whether from her anger or the sun. Given the vibrancy of her blue eyes—I'd guess it was her anger. The vivid blue dress she wore conflicted with the mood she projected, but her flushed face, golden hair, and the energy she radiated reminded me of sunshine in a blue sky…beautiful enough to light your way or beautiful enough to burn you from the inside out.

"He couldn't fathom women buying a race team—women-owned, women-operated, woman-driven—oh, hell no! God forbid. The world may end, and his dick may fall off." She threw her hands up in the air. "Is it our fault his wife prefers women? Are we all supposed to be punished because she left him for her yoga instructor?" She threw out her long, graceful arms in exasperation.

I had to consciously hold back a laugh from her vehemence.

Her energy was…magnetic, and I was rooted in place just watching her.

"Harper—calm down, I'm not understanding—"

"He knows how bad we want it now—he sees the writing on the wall. He knows we are trying to leave Merrick and split off on our own and wants to squeeze us." She rubbed her forehead and emitted what seemed like an uncharacteristic, frustrated groan that grew into a growl.

"Goddammit!" she yelled. "We can't match his price—we don't have the money to buy the team." She dropped into the armchair in the family room.

CJ rounded it to face her and sat on the edge of the coffee table—her shoulders deflated.

"I thought it was a done deal or I wouldn't have gotten your hopes up." Harper's head hung low. "I'm glad we hadn't said anything to Grady or my father yet."

Crap. If Grady didn't know about this—clearly, I wasn't supposed to know.

CJ's head turned, she spotted me slinking in the doorway, and her mouth dropped open—she'd forgotten I was in the kitchen.

Harper's face remained in her hands as she continued speaking. "I'm not going to give up—I'll figure something out." Her back to me, she still hadn't seen me. She drew her head up and took in a deep, weary breath before standing. "We'll just wear George Butler down so much that he'll ignore his pig-headed son enough to want to dump at least one of the teams in favor of some cash flow. Maybe we don't buy the entire operation, at least not right away…"

I knew I was past the point where I should've made my presence known.

"Harper…" CJ stood slowly, lifting her hand to stop Harper from speaking.

"We'll just have to find another partner…or—"

Before I could even think about it, before it even registered that my feet were moving, I stepped into the room.

The two women turned to me—both with matching stunned expressions. Harper, however, almost fell over, grasping the mantel of the fireplace.

I held out my hands in a grand gesture and then clapped them together. "That sounds like a great idea. I'm in."

CJ's eyes grew round.

"What the hell are *you* doing here?" Harper said, regaining her balance. "You...you..." Then she shot a glare at CJ. "You should've said—"

"I forgot and then you wouldn't shut up!" CJ stood and held out her hands in defense.

Catching both women unaware gave me perverse pleasure that clouded the monumental mistake I was probably making of involving myself in an incredibly risky business venture with this group and it would undoubtedly displease my brother and definitely piss off my father—maybe that was a bonus.

I had no other explanation except I was caught up in the moment. It rarely happened. I'm not sure the last time it did—at least not sober.

Harper was so energized—so passionate. It was unavoidable. And the thought of being invested in something down here seemed...well, fun.

Jesus, I was going to invest millions of dollars in one of the worst investments in sports without seeing any type of business plan...all for fun. I needed my head examined. My father was going to lose his mind —well, that may be fun to see, also.

However, I was drawn to the idea—even if, at the moment, the venture was on the verge of failing already. I was confident I could contribute. My gut wouldn't let me do anything else.

I took a seat at the end of sectional, threw my hand over the back, and crossed my leg over my knee. "So, tell me all about it."

Harper became unstuck. She took a giant step toward me. "You weren't supposed to hear any of this. Shame on you for having such bad manners and eavesdropping."

I couldn't stop the flicker of amusement. She was chastising me. I loved it.

"Sunshine, people on the other side of the lake would've heard you," I said. "But now you've piqued my interest. You Charlotteans are some fun people." My smirk widened as I squinted my eyes. "It's becoming a wicked pleasure...and I want in." I opened my hands and motioned them on. "Please, tell me more."

Both women stood before me, as opposite in physical attributes as two beautiful creatures could be. Harper, long, lithe, and fair. CJ, petite, fit, and brunette. They had their arms crossed over their chests and glared at me—blue and brown eyes bored into me.

They were not amused or charmed, both speaking simultaneously over one another.

"Hell, no."

"Why in heaven's name would we want to partner up with you?"

"Grady spent the past two years running from your partnership..."

"You're the exact type of machismo that we are trying to avoid."

"We don't need another dominating male in our business."

I'm not sure who said what, and I'm not sure how long it went on, both of them spouting off all the reasons why they wanted me nowhere near their project.

"Ladies." I held up a hand. "Please."

"Condescending ass." That one was Harper. "Don't you give us a hand to be quiet, as if you were a king silencing his followers. What the hell?"

I stood, face blank, closed my eyes, and clasped my hands behind my back, waiting.

CJ continued to glare. "I thought I liked you."

Harper shifted on her feet. "Now what are you doing, ignoring us?"

"I am waiting for my turn to speak. Is it now?"

Harper's glare on me intensified. I took that as a yes.

"I can give you the money to buy the team. I can also offer to bridge the gap between Butler and you, because as much as it sucks, if this Bo guy is being a dick about selling to women, he may be willing to sell to me, instead."

"I wouldn't give him the satisfaction—"

"Well, now that is your first lesson, then." I stepped toward her. "Use whatever advantage you have to get the lowest price you can. As condescending as it sounds, as unfair as it sounds, it's just business. Do you want the team?" I stepped into her space. She flinched slightly but held her ground.

Staring up at me she gritted, "Yes. But—"

"No but...as long as it's moral and somewhat ethical, it's fair game," I said. "Let Bo believe he's selling to me. I'll lower the price."

"It won't be a McBane company. CJ isn't going to leave Merrick to drive for McBane. That defeats the purpose. Sadie and I wanted to start something new—something different."

I held up my hand and continued. "When the time comes, you sign the papers under whatever company name you want, and I will walk into the shadows. He won't breathe a word because he will look like the fool he is going to be."

"No, you will walk away—"

I put my hands in my pockets and rocked back on my heels. "Not if I'm investing millions of dollars in a team, darling. I don't care how vivacious and beautiful you are, I don't walk away from my investments."

"Oh, boy..." CJ muttered.

I didn't take my attention off of Harper. Calculation and shrewdness behind those beautiful cornflower blue eyes.

Still, silence reigned, waiting for one of us to blink.

"Staring at me isn't going to shake my resolve." My voice was serious, steady.

"Calling me beautiful doesn't make me swoon, and it won't deplete my brain cells until I submit to your whims. I still don't want you involved in my team."

"You won't have a team if I don't give you the money." This woman expected me to fork over money and walk away? Seriously. "Of course, I could just buy the team myself and give it to Grady—" the side of my mouth tilted up. I couldn't help baiting her, it was firing up my soul.

"The hell you will!" Harper's fists flew down to her hips, but at least it was better than flying at my face.

"Okay, okay, you two." CJ stepped up. "Back to your corners." She gave me a gentle shove before putting both hands on Harper's shoulders and pushing her friend to the armchair. Her face was beautiful, even with full anger blanketing it. Anger that intensified since I made my presence known—and I wasn't even ashamed of it.

CJ turned to me. "Cal, I don't have to tell you the tenuous relationship with your brother would not withstand you interfering by buying him a race team. The whole point of him trying to win this contract is to prove he can make it without the McBane name. That won't work."

She turned to Harper. "While I wasn't on board with the idea of taking on such a monumental challenge of starting a team, I don't think we'll ever get an opportunity to do something like this again. The more I've thought about it, the more awesome I think it could be." She sat on the edge of the coffee table again. "While Cal is still a loose cannon, we understand his motivations, at least, and we can set parameters—" She glared pointedly at me.

Harper stared out Grady's front window, and I could almost see her weighing her options and realizing she didn't have many. "I need to talk to Sadie," she muttered, but it was her body deflating that made me feel a twinge of guilt.

I casually sat on the arm of the sofa, and crossed my arms over my chest, drawing in a deep, cleansing breath and letting it out. "Listen, I do want to be involved. It wasn't a lie. I loved watching you and CJ this year and the energy that follows you both. I know you have a stellar business education and a family history in the industry, but I'm not going to dump millions of dollars in an industry that is renowned for being one of the worst returns on investments in sports and simply walk away."

"It's not like I don't know what I'm doing. I live and breathe this sport—" she gritted at me. "More than you would ever understand."

"Yes, but you've never run a company; you've never had the pressures or the challenges, especially in what seems to be a hostile industry. You haven't even bought the company, and you're already hitting opposition."

Harper flinched.

"I'm sorry if you think that's blunt or if you find me condescending."

I glanced at CJ to gauge how she was taking it. She gave the slightest nod, but then shifted to Harper.

"As far as anyone has to know, you could be the owner and I could be the silent partner—but darling, I won't be silent with you."

Harper stood and walked over to me, cocked out a hip, and

crossing crossed her arms over her chest. "Let's talk to Sadie." CJ came over and joined us. "For now, let's keep it between us...four..." She turned to CJ and pointed at her. "Do not tell Grady about this yet."

"Grady won't be happy about my involvement...you weren't wrong about that," I added.

"You can tell him when the deal is done," Harper said. "He's going to have to get used to there being things about the business you two can't share."

"Okay, but you—" CJ pointed at me. "You're telling him about your involvement. I'm not getting in the middle of that."

Great.

I set my sights on Harper. "Do we have a deal?"

"We need to pass it through Sadie, but..." We locked eyes on each other as if we were twelve and having a staring contest. I blinked and warmth lit up through me. "Fine. But we have a lot to discuss." She held out her hand and I took it.

She gave it a strong squeeze and she could've been holding any other part of my body and it would've had the same dizzying effect. "I never doubted it, Ms. Merrick. I'll always be available whenever you need to talk with me." All I did was let the smallest bit of amusement and happiness show on my face and her eyes narrowed.

Harper let out an exasperated sound and CJ threw up her hands, walking away and muttering, "Oh, Lord. Here we go..."

4

CHARLOTTE, NC

Harper

Adrenaline was coursing through my veins as if I were the one who hit the barrier wall at 180 miles per hour. We were walking out of Merrick Motorsports' executive buildings, having just told my father about our plans—about CJ and I quitting Merrick. It wasn't pretty—not that I was delusional, thinking it would be easy. In fact, it was the hardest thing I'd ever done.

The meeting started off bad and got worse.

"CJ won't be signing with you for next season."

My father halted and tilted his head, as if he needed better reception to hear me. "Excuse me?"

And dammit, I used up all my courage to get that sentence out. Now I had to dig deep to say it again—to find the power to inflict disappointment on my father.

"CJ and I are both taking positions with another team. Actually, CJ is taking a new position, I'm just resigning. I mean, I'm resigning and hiring CJ—"

It was close to the end of the season, and my father believed he was going to swoop in as the last-minute savior. He freed up a second car so he could keep both CJ and Grady—negating the entire need for the competition the year before.

I saw red.

I didn't handle it well.

"It's too late." I halted the discussion with the decisive slash of my hand through the air. "It's too late, Dad. CJ is going to drive for me."

"You?" I could've told him monkeys from Mars were going to hire her and he would've been less astounded.

"Yes, me. I am the co-owner of a new team Butler sold to me and my investors, and CJ was just signed as a principal Cup driver for next season."

"What the hell?" Merrick roared. "Where did you get the money to buy a team? Who would partner with a girl your age?"

Cue Aunt Sadie walking in the door in 3...2...1...

"She's partnering with me, Everett, and you'd be smart to realize who you were referring to as 'girl'."

"Are you okay?" CJ asked, as I relived the memory that would haunt me until my father's look of betrayal and the feeling that I just staged a coup left my emotional hemisphere.

I took in a deep breath. "I gave a lot to the company. I sacrificed a lot to come home after college...to join the company."

"I know," CJ said. "At the time it was for the best. You know that now."

I nodded but couldn't look at my aunt or CJ. I lost my relationship with Spencer over working at Merrick. We'd been college sweethearts, set on a future together. Spencer didn't want to stay in Charlotte, and I wasn't sure if I ever wanted to leave. Spencer didn't wait around for me to decide.

I built my life around Merrick. Now, it felt like a crash—both in adrenaline and in spirit.

I stopped outside the doors, drawing in deep breaths of air, and surveyed the campus before moving toward my Lexus. It was the last time I'd be there as an employee.

Sadie and CJ were speaking behind me as they walked out, but I only heard murmurs over the waves of white noise filling my ears.

My eyes burned. I refused to let the waterworks turn on. No. Not today. Tears weren't on the agenda. I blinked them away and took in one more deep, cleansing breath.

"Well, I'm glad that's over," Sadie said, coming up behind me and putting an arm around my waist, giving it a squeeze. "I'm sorry I was late, but it was better for you to do it anyway. He needed to hear it from you first."

I glanced down at my mini dynamo of an aunt. Her vibrantly dyed red hair reaching my cheek as I smiled at her. "You just wanted us to take the first shots."

CJ chuckled.

"And you—" I turned on my best friend. "Some big help you were. I don't know the last time I'd ever seen you freeze or remain that quiet."

She shrugged. "What did you want me to say? I'm just the driver. I go with whoever is going to pay for my car and my paycheck."

"You know you're more than just a driver."

She waved me off and looked away. "I felt bad, okay." She stared off. "Even with all that went down this past year, and as angry as I've been at Junior and your father, he's done a lot for me." She stared into the distant pines lining the parking lot. "He believed in me when other teams tossed me aside. I felt bad about walking out of there."

We all stood silent.

While we felt justified in breaking off from them and were excited about our new venture, today was painful—there was no way to disguise it.

I stepped out of Sadie's arms and opened my purse, rummaging for my phone. "I hope he eventually forgives me," I whispered.

"He will," Sadie whispered back. "His pride just took a hit. But he'll come around once he realizes it was *his* daughter who got the best of him—not some random opponent. That will balance the scales."

She straightened, and with a flip of a switch brightened. "Let's focus on the future. CJ, go home. Get our boys and let's go to dinner to celebrate Grady's birthday and our newfound partnership."

"Cal should be telling Grady about his involvement in the new team as we speak," CJ said, as we walked to her truck. "Given how new their reconciliation is, I hope this doesn't blow it. Crappy way to ruin a birthday. Hopefully, there isn't much blood shed and we'll get to the restaurant on time."

Cal McBane. Our new partner—silent partner. No one outside our immediate circle was going to know about it, for now. The announcement was going to be made that Sadie and I bought a small team from Butler, and CJ was going to be our principal driver. It helped that Cal was able to talk down his price. Staffing and day-to-day operations would be under my authority, but finances were between Sadie, Cal, and myself.

"Out of the frying pan and into the fire..." I said, walking toward my car. Not looking back at them, I added my biggest concern. "I hope we didn't just sell our souls to the devil for this dream."

5

CHARLOTTE, NC

Cal

The drinks were flowing, and CJ and Harper were dancing. Sadie begged off after dinner, much to Harper's relief and my disappointment, saying she had "other late-night plans."

Nonetheless, watching Harper move was entertaining enough. Who would've thought the latest CEO of a yet-to-be-named stock car race team could move so well? They needed to blow off some steam after dropping the bomb on Merrick about leaving earlier that evening. I was sitting back in a booth, nursing a Guinness, appreciating the view of CJ and Harper dancing, but not the noise.

I may be getting too old for this shit.

My brother approached the table and motioned to the outdoor balcony of the club that overlooked downtown.

I grabbed my beer and followed him, appreciating the fresh air and the marginally quieter atmosphere.

He surveyed downtown Charlotte when I approached him.

"Happy Birthday, bro," I said, tipping my bottle up to him as he turned around.

"So, tell me. What exactly are you up to now?"

"I thought we'd discussed this earlier while the ladies were at Merrick? Why do I need to be up to something? I'm helping out a friend. And from what it looks like, your girlfriend, too."

"And since when is Harper your friend?" He turned to me. "You don't do anything without a reason. And I know Dad didn't approve of this..."

I took a pull of my beer, also staring out over the skyline. Charlotte was a young city, growing by leaps and bounds. The energy was emanating from it—probably why I was so drawn to it. Chicago seemed to represent established age, and wisdom, and old money. Charlotte was the future and vibrance.

"So, what's in it for you?" Grady took a swig of his beer and returned to his question.

I leaned an arm on a railing and turned to him, studying him closely. "Are you happy here? Not just with CJ, but with what you have going on?"

He hesitated, and then his voice softened. "Yeah. I am."

I gave a slight nod. "You seem settled."

"Yeah."

"Ok." And I stood.

"You still haven't answered my question."

I gave him a small smile. "Yes, little brother, I have. If you are happy, and things here are settled. I'm good. I'm leaving tomorrow and will be out of your hair. I'm glad things are working out for you." I motioned inside to the dance floor where the ladies were twirling each other around.

"Why are you involved with Harper's team?"

I shrugged a shoulder. "She and Sadie had a good idea—an inventive idea that would get you and CJ out of a tough situation. They'd hit a wall and they were short on funding. We had the money from the sale of the Indy team after you left. Dad's also distracted, and I was able to get it by him." I grinned while taking another pull on my beer.

"Ahhh," he said.

"Trust me, it was not easy convincing them—at least convincing

Harper. She is a very stubborn and proud woman. But she's sharp and a visionary. I like her. I appreciate talent. Plus, I find it mutually beneficial—"

"She can keep an eye on me." He put the pieces together.

I glanced up at the sky as if to ponder the thought in jest. "Well, that's a perk. But really, I wanted to learn about the industry you are calling home now." That wasn't the whole truth.

I didn't even want to admit the truth.

The truth was I was envious. I didn't begrudge him his happiness, his freedom. I guess, when Harper said they didn't have the money, the moment I saw her dream slip through her hands, heard the tone of frustration in her voice…I saw a chance that I could catch some of that. A glimmer of being part of something special. Be a part of it.

It sounded ridiculous.

I had friends. I had wealth, power, connections. I could have practically any woman in Chicago I wanted—and that wasn't ego speaking. I didn't have a damaged past to recover from. I didn't have a sad soul that needed saving. But the sun seemed to shine brighter down here. I was drawn to it, and I don't think it was the warmth from being reunited with my brother, or of righting a wrong between us.

I wasn't sure what it was. I knew that down here I was able to breathe.

I couldn't tell him that.

Grady put down his bottle as he took a deep breath, stepped back, and put his hands on his hips. "When are you going to realize I'm not a complete fuck-up?" he said in a low timbre, not looking at me.

Damn. "Grady. Look at me."

He didn't turn his head, but gave me a side-eye glare.

"You're your own man. I get it." My voice dropped in tone. "I'm not spying on you. I was joking. It really wasn't about you. I liked the idea of their new team," I said, trying to lighten the mood, "If I really wanted to fuck with you, I'd buy out Merrick."

"He'd never sell to you."

I tilted my head, shrugged one shoulder, but tilted my lips in a tight smile, letting him know it wasn't out of the realm of things I considered.

"You're such an asshole." But his tone hinted at the slight amusement in my expression.

My focus slid to the girls who were garnering attention inside. The dance floor had cleared around them, and Harper was fending off a guy's advances. I began to approach the doors to sweep in to rescue her when CJ stepped up, all five-foot nothing of her, getting in the guy's face, or well, his chest. Her teeth gritted as she spoke. Her hands, down by her sides, were opening and closing as if she were an athlete warming up.

"Um, Grady, you may want to go get your girlfriend, before someone loses a body part, and we spend the evening bailing her out of jail for assault."

We were too far away, and it was too noisy to hear what was being said. But the stupid man was laughing, glancing over at his friends, and tilting his condescending glare back at CJ, not backing down. The glint in her eye, where her clinching hands were in proximity to the man's body, and the menacing excitement that lit her face didn't bode well for the man's genitals.

"Oh, Jesus!" Grady sprang and ran through the doorway just as CJ's hand moved. "CJ, not the balls!"

I pulled up outside CJ's bungalow, all of us still laughing at how CJ brought down a man almost twice her size and was able to get away with it because he was too ashamed to press charges.

"Man, Grady, you finally found a woman who can keep you in line. I think I'm a little afraid for you." A glance in my rearview mirror showed the way Grady was nuzzling CJ's neck, he wasn't listening, and he most certainly wasn't afraid of CJ's hands. At least not now.

"Hmmm…" Was the response I got. Harper and I rolled our eyes at each other as we pulled up outside CJ's bungalow.

Harper turned around in her seat to announce, "Alright, love birds, out you go."

CJ was giggling, which seemed as out of place as a nun at a rock concert, and the two of them ran crookedly into her house.

"Good thing I was designated driver tonight."

Harper laughed as she watched them fumble to walk in the door. "Probably." She sighed. "Although, it wasn't as much fun for you, I guess."

"I had a good time." I pulled back out onto CJ's street. "You'll need to give me directions to your building."

"Turn right at the next light and then go two blocks and make a left. We'll be on that road for a bit."

I nodded. "Did you have fun?"

She leaned back in her seat and sighed. "Yes, it's been a while since I've been able to relax. I don't think I realized it until tonight." There was a quiet pause as I drove.

"I've never seen you and Grady so congenial with each other. It must be a relief not to want to rip off each other's heads." Out of my periphery I saw her look at me, and I stole a glance at her light eyes in the darkness of the car.

I smiled. "Yes. We were once close."

"Do you think you could get that back?"

Our fallout was bad. A lot of things were said and done.

"I think we are on our way." And I meant it. We'd both changed, but we were brothers.

"Is that why you offered to help us? To get back in his good graces? Because I'm not sure if it was the right move?"

I smiled. "He's not big on me interfering. Actually, that was a gamble. No, he wasn't thrilled about me investing." I stopped at the next stoplight and looked over at her. "I wasn't lying when I said I was intrigued. I am. I want to see you all succeed. Not because of Grady... or because of CJ, but because I'm all about the underdog. CJ's talented and has underdog written all over her. I think deep down, you do too. Everyone thinks you are the golden princess up on the pedestal with the silver spoon, but I see you. You work hard for people to see past that."

Even with only the dashboard lights to illuminate the inside of the car, I saw the change on her face. Her face went soft.

"I know what it's like to be yoked with family expectation and a road laid out for you before you even know where you want to go." I turned back to the road as the light changed color.

I began to reach out to touch her hand but drew back. "I'm excited about our partnership, Harper. Please don't think of me as another person to fight with."

She went quiet. Her elbow on the armrest, her gaze out the window. "Turn right again up at the next intersection."

I went for levity. "Anyway, trying to keep CJ from being arrested is something to bond over, don't you think? It's like a team-building exercise. Although, I hope we can come up with ones with less severe consequences." I caught her dress inching up before I looked away. God, her legs were amazing.

"It's the silver building ahead on the right."

I pulled up to the roundabout in front of her building and saw a group of men stagger in. She started to get out of the car. "Thanks for the ride, Cal. I had fun—"

I put the car in park and turned off the engine. "I'm walking you up."

"What? Why?"

"I don't—" I motioned to the group waiting at the elevators. "I don't want you getting in the elevator with a bunch of drunk guys. I'll just take you up to your floor."

"Cal."

"Just humor me." She studied my face, as I studied the men turning toward us, and nodded.

Sure enough, as soon as the men saw Harper enter the lobby, they started to snicker, staring at her and elbowing each other. I put my arm around her waist, drawing her to me. When we walked onto the elevator, they followed. She stared up at me and I winked. *I got you.*

I pulled her in front of me, wrapping my arms around her in a hug

—cocooning her with her back to my front. I made a deliberate effort to keep my dick far, far away from her backside and focused my glare on the men who were having difficulty standing still, and continuing to snicker at whatever their inebriated brains found amusing.

The elevator opened to her floor and she moved forward, effortlessly transitioning to handholding when we stepped off the elevator. I didn't let go, and neither did she, until we reached her door and she had to get out her key. She unlocked her door and stepped in; I followed as if it were the most natural thing. As if I always watched her hips sway as she walked through the apartment each night when we got home.

She threw down her purse on the sofa and turned back around.

"Nice place." It was a two-floor apartment with an open concept— all done in white, gray, and taupe. Very clean, yet it still managed to be inviting and not cold. There was a deep, soft gray sectional off to the left, and a kitchen ahead with a dining area immediately after. Floor-to-ceiling windows ran the back of the wall in the living room, and a large, open staircase led to a second floor.

Her eyes were downcast, and she fidgeted as her steps faltered slightly, and it brought my brain cells back online long enough to catch her elbow. She was nervous.

"I'm sure those idiots are gone now. I should go." I realized she may think I expected something from her. That wasn't why I came up here. Damn idiot.

Yet, I didn't want her to be nervous with me. I gave her a small, reassuring smile as I reached for her hand and pulled her slightly toward me. God help me, she bit that full bottom lip of hers, and it was affecting me in ways that I knew I had to leave.

To give my lips something else to focus on, I gallantly kissed the top of her hand and appreciated her bewildered expression.

"It's been interesting, as always, Harper." I straightened but didn't release her, and we stared at each other—as if trapped by a spell.

Alright, I was lying. I did want something to happen—I really wanted to kiss her.

Which was why I let go, stepped back, opened the door, and got the hell out of there. I glanced back long enough to see she was a bit dumbfounded—lost. "Lock up behind me. Okay, hon— um…goodnight."

I waited for her to nod and close the door, and for the click of the lock, before I tore my hand through my hair and fled.

Oh, boy. Yeah.

So, that can never happen.

Leave it to me to complicate an already complicated situation.

6

LAKE NORMAN, NC

Cal

I was scheduled to head back to Chicago later that afternoon and to all that awaited me with McBane and my parents. My mom hinted at wanting to have dinner and "a talk." I dreaded the "talk" and wondered what it involved—undoubtedly me settling down or grilling me about Grady's life.

Today, however, I was going to Grady's house for a powwow about the unveiling and rollout of the new team. I wondered if I needed to strap on body armor or a cup for this, because I wouldn't sit in the corner and stay quiet, and that's the only thing Harper was going to want me to do.

Given the chemistry that almost ignited last night...Damn, I shouldn't have crossed that threshold—literally and figuratively. Because even though nothing happened, there was definitely enough of a moment where I know we both contemplated it.

I thought I'd imagined our chemistry in Sonoma. With this new partnership, there were too many lines, too many walls she erected and surrounded with contentiousness—so concerned that I was going to be another man trying to take control of her life. I really shot myself in the foot with that deal and locked the door on anything happening between us.

I walked in the house and was greeted by Sadie in a flowing burgundy tunic that clashed with her bright red hair. "Cal, darlin', good morning!"

"Hello, Ms. Sadie."

"What did I say about calling me Ms. Sadie..."

"Hello, beautiful..." I grinned at her.

She waved me off as she walked away, but she was smiling. "Come on in, flirt." I followed her into the dining room off the kitchen where CJ, Gus, Harper, and Cooper were sitting.

Grady came walking in carrying a tray of pastries and coffee, bright-eyed and grinning. "Hey. Good morning, bro."

"You've been...busy," I said, gesturing to the spread on the table. "I would've expected to find you still in bed this morning. Not up playing Martha Stewart."

"Don't be an ass and have a donut," he said, sitting down.

Harper was studying her phone, and hadn't looked up since I walked in.

Okay...not taking it personally. I mean, why would she look up at me?

I sat across from here, grabbed a Boston cream, and sat back.

Finally, Harper put down her phone, pulled out her laptop, propped it open, and grabbed everyone's attention with a simple, "Okay. Let's start."

Immediately, everyone stopped chatting and turned to her.

I ate my donut and also gave her my attention. The plainness of her black top helped the blueness of her eyes jump with the excitement in the tone her voice.

"To start, Sadie and I have settled on the name of the team." Sadie carried in a sign with the flourish of Vanna White. On it was written "Merlo Racing" in a simple graphic accented in a burgundy color.

"Mer-lo," I sounded it out. Clever," I commented, but not saying anything about how I hadn't been consulted on the name or on the logo. Mer-Lo…Merrick and Lomax. The color Sadie wore that I labeled as burgundy was designed to be the color merlot.

Harper was peering at me out of the corner of her eye, gauging my reaction. I gave none.

"Next. How are you announcing?" I asked, leaning over to take a bottle of water from the center of the table.

She leaned forward, a cock of an eyebrow. "CJ and I are taking a trip to New York to Racing Sports Update on Thursday to announce it with Tyler Wilson."

I nodded, contemplative. "That could work." I glanced over to Sadie. "You don't want to be part of the announcement?"

Sadie opened her mouth to speak.

"No!" Both CJ and Harper both shouted.

Harper held out a hand. "I think it's probably best we limit it to the two of us. Sadie can handle the coordination with the tracks and industry contacts. We can all have our respective responsibilities."

I leaned back in my chair, crossed my arms. "Oh yeah, and what responsibilities do I have exactly?"

Without batting an eye, she looked straight at me, shrugged a shoulder, and said, "Nothing…don't you have an entire corporation to run in Chicago?"

I stared at her and we defiantly locked eyes for a moment, so much being said without words exchanged.

"O-kay…" CJ, surprisingly, stepped in and attempted to deflect. She nodded a thank you at me, probably for not verbally challenging Harper in front of everyone. "So, we wanted to discuss our vision—our plans—so everyone was on the same page and knew what we were striving for."

I remained silent, wanting to see where she was going to go with it.

"First, the staff…" Harper stood and gave out presentation folders. "Enclosed are the lists of the current employees we believe will be staying—some already left or will be leaving because they want to or because we will ask them to. We will need to make some quick hiring decisions."

Everyone at the table flipped through the sheets.

"Main issues are the crew chief and engineers."

I glanced over at Gus. "You aren't coming?"

His head was low. "Nah. I've got a contract with Everett. Besides, someone has to stick around with this idiot." He threw a thumb over at my brother.

My brother threw up his middle finger.

"What are you doing about the crew chief position?" I asked.

"We are still talking with Jeff Brooks..." Harper closed her eyes briefly as if it pained her to say it.

"But wasn't the team losing with him?"

"Yes—" CJ said, picking at her nails.

"There were a number of reasons they were doing poorly," Harper said. "And we're exploring other options. Maybe Keith Peters."

I turned back to Gus. "Who'd you recommend?"

Gus glanced at Harper and CJ with trepidation before turning to me. "I don't think Keith's your man."

Harper bristled. I think it was the use of the word "your" when addressing me.

"Truthfully, even if Jeff stuck around, there is no way he and CJ would mesh," Gus said.

Without looking up, CJ commented, "He's a prick."

Gus caught Harper's death glare and said, "I'm sorry, but this is the shit we're supposed to be hashing out today."

"Alright..." I held up a hand and waited for alternatives. "Who else—"

"We're talking with a few people tomorrow." She knew I was leaving this evening. "We'll come up with something. Once we find the crew chief, the rest will fall in place. Next."

And I let her get away with it. I let her move on. Because they had bigger issues—ones I was really here for and would insist on being part of the discussion.

With a decisive smack, she turned the page to the next section in the folder. "Sponsorship."

She droned on about different companies Butler used to have sponsorship deals with, and what the likelihood was of continuing their relationships. None of them were full-year deals—mostly a couple of races at a time. "One of Butler's problems is he didn't put any money into marketing talent or sponsorship retention. We need to focus on that now."

I didn't say a word.

I didn't say that with a few calls I could have that locked up tight, and then they could focus on other things.

I didn't say that I could handle it. No problem.

But I wanted to.

"—also, I'm hiring Amara Chopra to come on and help with PR and also to expand our social media presence."

"Do you really think that's necessary?" Sadie asked. "Wouldn't you be better served to spend that on engineers and equipment?"

"We negotiated a separate alliance with Standard Stock to utilize their machinery and simulators—we can get by for the season. It's important for us to come out of the gate with a bang by enhancing our social media influence, marketability, and that would give the added power to draw sponsorship deals."

Sadie said, "Well, since I barely use Instagram, I'll leave that to you, darling."

"Right now we will be lucky to land sponsorships because of the exposure CJ drew from this past year. I don't doubt she will do well this year, given a decent crew. We need to capitalize on her popularity right now and ride that wave into next year."

"I just want to be a driver, not a social media influencer," CJ said, a bit annoyed.

"You are..." Harper turned to her. "You don't have to do much. Just be you."

"Oh boy..." Gus whispered, and CJ kicked him under the table.

I crossed my arms. "That sounds great. I agree with the idea of social media. But you still need sponsors—now."

It was the truth, because without sponsors she didn't have income to run the team.

And I may as well have rained on her parade. "Obviously. I am working on that."

"I'd like to see a list of possibilities by Wednesday. We can discuss them and what McBane can do to enhance the list."

Her hands went white knuckled as they gripped the edge of the table. "That won't be necessary."

"Let's take a look at the list Wednesday—"

Grady jumped in, "CJ, tell Cal about the initiative you and Harper told me about the other day."

He nodded to her, handing off the ball and giving her a nudge as if telling her to change the topic quickly.

She was staring between Harper and me. "Uh, okay—yeah. What you may not know is Merrick, even with all the complaining we've been doing lately, really saved me. I wouldn't be here if it wasn't for the interest he took in the young pain-in-the-ass kid I was, who had a lot of talent but not enough opportunity. It's why I was so conflicted about leaving. I'd like to pay it forward. Help other girls who didn't have a solid upbringing, maybe didn't have the opportunities or support I had to dare to dream.

"So—" CJ picked at her nails again, and Grady reached out and laid a hand on her forearm, encouraging her. She cleared her throat. "Harper, you tell him."

I crossed my leg over my knee and shifted my attention back to Harper, whose face softened as she stared at her friend and Grady. She swept over the table, landing on me—becoming stoic once again. "One thing that we wanted to do, once we get the team settled, is create a development program." She straightened her back. Bracing for criticism. "It may take a while. I know it can't be a top priority, but it means something to the core of what we are trying to create, so it will be something we want to put in place." She stared me down. "We want to offer opportunities for mentorships or internships to female drivers, those interested in STEM, things like that. Go into the community, maybe outreach to other areas over the summer—"

"I think that's a fantastic idea," Gus said.

"So do I…" Cooper added.

"I told you they'd like it," Sadie said.

Harper began to smile, gaining confidence before shifting her attention to me.

I tilted my head. "Driven Women," I said.

"I'm sorry?"

"I think that's what you should call yourself. "Driven Women—The Driven Women Initiative."

The smile she gave me could light up a hundred racetracks, and it was the warmth of that smile that I took with me as I flew home to Chicago.

7

CHICAGO, IL

Cal

As I walked barefoot into my kitchen wearing ratty jeans and a Nirvana t-shirt, I appreciated the stillness and the relief of not having the weight of expectation and intrusiveness that came with having a girlfriend—well, a girlfriend like Vanessa, at least. I wouldn't say I was against having a relationship. After watching Grady and CJ, I realized I'd done the right thing breaking up with her. What Vanessa and I had wasn't the kind of relationship I wanted.

I went to the fridge to complete my evening with a snack and a beer. There was a very important interview I wouldn't miss.

The calmness was a reprieve. Tomorrow, I was scheduled to have dinner with my parents, and even though my mother was trying to hide the stress in her voice, I knew it was not going to be a fun evening.

My phone buzzed in my back pocket. Grady's number appeared on the display. "Hello?"

"Hey, you watching Tyler's show?" my brother asked, as his way of greeting.

"Yep. Just getting ready. You?"

I walked toward my den and my wall-size television. "Wouldn't miss it. I thought you'd be there."

"Doctor won't let me travel yet." You could hear the sulk in his tone.

"Are they afraid you scrambled your eggs too much this time?"

"Something like that. Made the mistake of taking CJ to the last appointment with me and he freaked her out by announcing how many concussions I've already had. Supposedly, there is a limit to how much my brain can handle." He let out a beleaguered sigh. "So, I'm on lockdown."

"Poor Grady, does she carry your balls around in her pocket now?"

"Don't you worry about my balls...she takes good care of them."

I flipped on the television and turned to the sports channel. CJ, Harper, and Tyler Wilson were already on stage at Racing Sports Update, the talk show they agreed to appear on with the promise of a big announcement.

Tyler began, *"Our guests this evening are CJ Lomax and Harper Merrick. These ladies, while both legacies in the industry, are also making a name of their own as one of the two teams embroiled in Merrick Motorsports Madness, as the media has come to call it."*

"Welcome, ladies."

"Thank you, Tyler," they both said for the television audience.

"The girls look good—poised, confident," I said over the phone to Grady.

"Tell me, Ms. Merrick—"

"No need for such formality, Tyler—Harper, please..." Harper sat like a queen on a throne and blasted all of them with that weaponized smile.

"Yes, um, Harper...you and CJ have been friends since you were children. Your father, as an influential stock car team owner, could've had his pick from a pool of talented drivers in stock car and in other racing circuits. Why do you think your father went outside and brought in an Indy driver instead of pulling CJ, or one of his other drivers, up from the ranks?"

"Oh, boy. That didn't take long..." Grady muttered. "Bad move, Tyler, my man. CJ wasn't a fan of his to begin with."

"*Seriously? We are going down that road again?*" CJ's hands flew up in aggravation.

I caught Harper's hand as she touched CJ's feigning amusement. "*Well, Tyler...*" She leaned over toward him, his gaze landing on her cleavage, and I decided I was with CJ. "*First, have you even met my father?*"

"*Of course, you know I—*"

"*Because if you knew anything about my family, you'd know three things...first, the Merricks only employ the best—the best staff, the best engineers, the best crew, and the best drivers.*" Her brow quirked up.

"*Second, my father...no one can make my father do anything. Trust me, I was a teenage daughter growing up under his roof. And third—*"

My lip quirked at how calmly and thoroughly she was handling him. "*Tyler, that question is older than my long-dead grandmother. Seriously? Where have you been? Did you even bother to study CJ's record from quarter-midgets up until this past year?*"

"*Well—yeah. I mean, she's good. But what inspired your father to put CJ in a car? Why a woman? Was it at your urging?*"

CJ managed to bark out a laugh that was condescending as hell. "*Now, he's insulting your father's intelligence, Harper.*"

Harper, all humor gone, followed with, "*There are other women drivers, Tyler. Surely you've been to a track besides just on Sundays?*" She stood with all seriousness. "*Is there a producer around? This is a racing show, right? You do realize there are several circuits out there with women drivers, right? CJ isn't an anomaly?*"

"*I'd like to think I'm a valuable gem—*"

Grady started to chuckle. "He's going down now..."

"*Some may consider you an odd duck—*" Harper said.

"*A diamond in the rough...*" CJ volleyed.

"*Strange bird—*" Harper countered.

CJ shrugged. "*Maybe even a prodigy—*"

"And...Tyler just lost control of his show," I muttered, with a tinge of amusement.

"Let's face it, he lost it the moment they walked on the stage," my brother said, pride lacing his voice.

Harper then seemed to realize Tyler was still there. *"But my point is, Tyler...they've been around. Janet Guthrie, Shawna Robinson, Patty Moise, Jennifer Jo Cobb, Kenzie Ruston, Danica Patrick, all paving the way...and coming up the ranks now are women like Gracie Trotter, Toni Breidinger, Hailie Deegan, Natalie Decker... so you see, she's not one of a kind."*

"I resent that statement." Even I could tell CJ was having fun.

"Darlin', you know what I mean."

Tyler made another mistake—turning to CJ, he questioned, *"What did you get out of this season while racing some of the top men in the industry?"*

"I'm surprised they're tolerating this guy," I said to my brother.

"They're playing with him—like a cat with a lizard—although, my girl is already getting bored," he replied.

"Tyler, I think all drivers learn something from each other each year. I learned what it was like to be a rookie this year and have people gunning for you."

CJ tilted her head and glared. *"Hey, Tyler...I understand you've had other rookies on this week. Did you ask them that same question? What did they get out of racing me?"*

"You tell 'em, honey," Grady cheered.

"CJ, I think it's a legitimate question, especially how things were between you and McBane. With all the speculation and attention, the two of you got most of the media coverage this past season. Was it all a gimmick, a publicity stunt to repair McBane's image and to promote a female driver who was racing well above her level?"

"Ok—now I want to punch him," Grady said.

"Racing well above..." CJ sputtered as she stood, before Harper grabbed her arm and guided her back into her seat.

"I think we're entitled to ask what was in it for you, besides the relationship with

McBane—"

"So, you want to know what happened with me and Grady, do

you?" CJ's eye twitched, and there was an obvious glint that I didn't think boded well. But my attention was on Harper, whose face was set.

"I think the racing community deserves to know that truth about what went on behind the scenes this season at Merrick, and what the result will be going forward? Who will be racing for them next year?"

CJ tilted her head down, clenched her fists, and peered at poor Tyler from beneath her lashes. *"I tell you what, Tyler...I'll give you the scoop on me and Grady, and if you keep it up with these welcoming, non-judgmental questions, I'll tell you about what happened with this guy in Daytona."*

Harper grabbed her hand and held it. *"We're done here."* Harper's smirk at the camera was almost charming. *"Poor Tyler will need his balls intact so his producers can rip them off when they find out the scoop he just lost by being an asshole."* She stood, and with CJ next to her, she strutted across the stage with her head high. The cameramen were wise enough to follow them as they left. *"Pleasure as always, Tyler."*

"Well, that's my cue. I better go call her and calm her down. I'll catch you later. Are you coming down this way soon?"

"I thought you were coming home for Thanksgiving?"

"Yeah...I'm working on it."

"Well, I have a teleconference with the Boss Lady tomorrow, maybe I can ask her to put in a word with CJ."

"Not sure if it will help. She's a bit gun-shy. By the way, I wouldn't let Harper hear you call her that, at least not to her face. Talk to you later."

He disconnected and I was still smiling.

I sat in my empty penthouse and stared at my phone. That was probably the coolest conversation I'd had with my brother in years—even before our fallout.

This new venture with the Charlotte Crew was developing so many new and interesting twists to it.

I shifted the phone in my hand.

The team was such a small sliver of my portfolio of responsibilities

—in the grand scheme of things, it was a mere distraction. My father even chastised me for it the other night.

I grabbed my beer and stood, leaving the den and walking to the palladium windows overlooking Chicago.

My other hand still held my cell. I found myself thinking of Harper way too much. Business and personal never meshed well.

Harper. Harper had trouble written all over her.

Yet. Yet…

I finished my beer.

I sent a text.

Cal: Caught the interview. Entertaining as always, Boss Lady.

Harper: Bite Me, McBane. I'm not in the mood.

I laughed again. She had a habit of making me do that.

And I had to admit that I really liked it.

The next evening, my mom met me as I walked in the marble foyer of my parents' home,

greeting me with a smile and a hug. "Cal, honey—you're a wonderful sight."

I leaned down and wrapped my arms around her thinning frame. I didn't like how much weight she seemed to have lost. The strain of the bad blood between my brother, father, and myself was hard on her.

What I didn't like seeing was that now, even though things were patched up between me and Grady, there were still dark circles under her eyes.

Dammit.

"Cal, why are you scowling at me?" She stepped back from me, but still held me by the arms.

"Mom, are you feeling okay?" I cupped her cheek, guilt starting to plague me for how little I've paid attention to her lately.

She stepped back farther, patting my hand and giving me a placating smile. "I'm fine darling. Just having trouble sleeping lately.

You know how I am—touch of insomnia. I'll go see the doctor about it next week. No worries." She turned and led me to the family den.

Yeah. No. I wasn't leaving it at that.

"Where's Dad?"

"He'll be out in a moment. Want something to drink before dinner? How about a beer or a scotch?"

"No, I'm good. I have some work to catch up on later, and it's been a long day already," I said, taking off my coat.

My mom took the coat from me and hurried down the back hallway. "Okay, well...Let me check on dinner."

I glanced around the dark, wood-paneled room, the fireplace on the opposite wall with the ornately carved mantel, the leather furniture—it was rich, but it was warm. This was the room our family spent most of our time in. The rest of the house was for company—for my father— for his image. This room was solely our family's.

God, I was tired. My hands rubbed over my face and through my hair. I needed a shower and a bed—but I wasn't lying when I told my mom I had work to catch up on when I got home. Undoubtedly, my father would also bring that up tonight.

Speak of the devil—my father came walking in then, my mother following—both of them a bit dour, but simultaneously tilted up their heads when they spotted me.

I stood to approach my father and held out my hand. Yes, my father insisted on shaking hands when I greeted him.

"Cal," my father said. "Glad to have you back. Thought we may not see you again until Thanksgiving."

I let it go.

"How's our latest investment doing?"

"Fine—so is your other son, by the way."

He sat in his leather armchair closest to the fire without further comment about Grady. Although Grady and I had mended things, he and our father hadn't had their come-to-Jesus moment yet.

My father crossed his legs and smoothed the leg of his pants, contemplating something.

"How is Grady? And CJ?" My mother sat in her chair between the sofa and my father's chair.

"They're fine. CJ's busy with the new team, and Grady is busy with CJ," I joked.

"Can't believe we spent all that money investing in a team he's not even involved with."

"We had the capital from selling the Indy team. You won't even miss it. Besides, I think you'll be pretty impressed once this group gets up and running."

"He should be focused on his own career, not following her around like a lovesick—"

"He's happy and he's doing well," I said, sitting at the end of the sofa across from him. "Honestly, I've never seen him so focused, or taking his life so serious."

"How's his recovery?"

I nodded for reassurance. "He's better."

"Idiot move he made," my father grumbled. "Putting CJ before his own career. He could've been blackballed from another series because he wrecked that driver—just so CJ could win that race. Look what it got him." My father flung out his hand.

"It was chivalrous and honorable. That driver was targeting her, and Grady had her back. Besides, he had no hope of winning that race—"

He waved it off with annoyance.

"Did you have time to check out Fast Lane Automotive while you were there?

I nodded. "It may be a good prospect. I talked it over with Trey, and he worked on a proposal to present them." Trey Walker was one of my executive vice presidents, a good friend, and my right hand when I was out of the office.

"Good, I looked it over and it may work—"

"Enough—this wasn't why we asked him here." My mom turned back to me; unease swept over her face. "Um, well…"

Here it goes…time to discuss *my* life. "Your father and I asked you here because we have something important to discuss with you. Something your father actually has to tell you." My mom was pulling at the button at the bottom of her cardigan sweater. Twisting it for all it was worth and glancing down as if to check on its progress.

There was a pause. My father? Surely my mother wasn't going to condone another lecture about my commitment to the company?

"We're sorry we didn't tell you sooner, but, um, we waited to find out more information...and then there was one thing after another with your brother, and it never seemed like the right time to bring it up..." Her hands were shaking.

I shot a look to my father for a quicker answer, and he stared at a spot on the rug, his lips tight.

"What the hell is going on?" I moved to the edge of the sofa.

"...and then your brother's accident..."

"Mom." I grabbed her hand to save that poor button that was hanging on by a thread, much like I was at the moment. Her eyes shot up and dual tears overflowed and raced down her cheeks as if they'd been held in for months and were set free—finally.

But it was my father's voice accompanying my mother's heart-break. "I have a brain tumor."

My head snapped around to my dad, his legs crossed, elbow perched on the armrest, his hand stoically framing his chin, while he observed my mom and me.

My mom's hand squeezed mine.

The mantel clock ticked. So loud.

My mom sniffed.

I blinked and looked between my mother and father. This was what was happening last year. This was the reason for my father's mood swings. Why he took off so much work. His excuses...

"How long have you known this? This has been going on for at least a year, hasn't it? This was what all the secrecy was about last year?" I glared at my father, furious that I was kept out of the loop. That my mother had to carry this burden herself. "How bad is it?"

My father tilted his head, the picture of calm, and folded his arms over his lap.

"I started having headaches a year and a half ago. It's near the pineal gland. They don't think its cancerous, but can't tell for sure. It's difficult to operate on, and therefore also difficult to biopsy, so we decided to manage with medication and wait and see."

My mom grabbed my arm again. "It's why we kept it quiet and decided not to tell you or Grady."

"Did you get a second opinion?"

"Second, third, fourth, fifth...your mother has had me flying all over the United States. It's why I'm out of the office so damn much." His voice started to rise. "It's why you're needed at the office and not gallivanting around—"

"Michael." My mom's voice was terse.

My dad's mouth shut. She was the only one who could do that—it didn't happen often, but by the tone of her voice, my mom's patience with whatever was going on was at its breaking point.

He took a deep breath and quietly started again. "The consensus is they could operate, but it may be more dangerous than just leaving it alone. They wanted to treat my symptoms and see what happened."

I clasped my hands, elbows to my knees, and hung my head. Taking it in. It all made sense now. My father's even more extreme mood swings. My mother's stress and evading whenever I tried to discuss her appearance.

"You lied to me—told us they were migraines. Told us not to worry. It was the reason you gave for drawing away from the office. Son of a bitch! I knew there was something going on..." I turned my attention to my mother, who wouldn't meet my eye.

"Don't blame her." My father's tone was firm. "I didn't want anyone to know. It was my choice not to tell you."

I stood, walked to the fireplace, and put my back to both of them, sifting through my emotions. All this time, I'd feared it was my mom —my small, gentle mother, who seemed to be weathering some great storm.

The storm was the weight of this secret my father had her bear —alone.

"I don't blame her." I glared at him, at that moment not caring he had something in his head. I was...I don't know what I was...hurt, angry...confused...at the deception.

"I had a right to know, as the person you expect to take over the operation of this company...as a son—I had a right to know what was going on," I yelled.

"It was my health...my decision to tell you—"

"Fuck that!"

My mother jumped.

My father stared me down, his face turning red.

"You wanted a few weeks, a few months to figure out your options —fine, I get that. But a goddamn year and a half? What the hell—you could've died in that amount of time. Jesus Christ! Have you had any treatment? Radiation? Chemo?"

"Cal..." Still seated, my mother reached for me.

"You told me it was nothing—I told Grady you were fine!"

He continued to glare at me, his mouth pursed. Defiant. Like a child.

"Have you considered the burden this has been on your wife? On my mother—to carry this secret—to not have anyone to talk to about it? Have you thought about anyone else, but yourself—"

"Cal, please..."

"Have you seen what this has done to her? Because we have. Grady and I—we've seen

the worry etched in her face. The sadness in her eyes." Everything over the past year started clicking—conversations, events, memories. "Jesus, I've carried guilt that the stress on her has been because of us."

My father finally stood, anger causing him to jump out of his chair. "It hasn't helped with you two behaving like children without any—"

"STOP!" My mother jumped out of her own seat and roared, her arms outstretched, and her eyes shut, unwilling to look at either of us.

"I can't...I can't do this anymore." Her voice hitched. "We're a family. We're going to stay a family."

She breathed. "Your father has a brain tumor. He decided to wait to see what would happen. I respected his decision. I handled it the best I could; it wasn't his fault. It wasn't an easy eighteen months for any of us."

She gave him a pointed stare. "Fear, uncertainty, and regret can make people behave in ways they otherwise wouldn't." She shifted, her energy ebbing.

I put my hands on my hips. "Are you going to tell Grady? Why tell me now?"

"We are going to tell Grady when he comes home for Thanksgiving." My mom sagged

back into her chair.

My father stood tall. "They decided to operate—to get a biopsy and try to take out some of the tumor."

"Why? I thought you said that was dangerous."

My mom's voice was quiet. "It is."

"I've been having...episodes."

"Episodes? What do you—"

I turned on her and then glanced back to him. His head was tilted up as if that would defy any weakness.

"Seizures." My mom spit out. "He's having seizures."

8

CHICAGO, IL

Cal

My parents' home was only a fifteen-minute walk from my high-rise, so I normally walked there. But it was Chicago, and it was November, so it was wet, and it was cold. And like an idiot, I now regretted my lack of forethought. I hadn't bothered calling an Uber because I just wanted to leave. My mind was reeling, and at the same time I couldn't form a coherent statement. I excused myself from dinner—gave an excuse about having work waiting for me, kissed my mom, and left.

As I walked, a block from my parents, my phone rang. "Mom—I'm sorry, I just can't—"

"Cal? It's Harper...I've got some fantastic news."

I pulled the phone away from my ear, checked the display.

"Cal? Are you there? I'm sorry to call...are you out? Oh, God. Is this a bad time?"

Shaking my head until I could shift gears, I replied, "No. It's fine. I thought you were someone else..."

"I'm just so excited and I called CJ and Grady and Sadie and everyone else and I wanted to tell you..."

I stopped at a crosswalk. I absently glanced up at the night sky, as I had when at Grady's lake house, and realized the lights of the city blocked out the stars. "So, I'm the last on the list and you still had energy left."

She stuttered, "Uh, no. But..."

I dropped my gaze to the light, waiting for the signal to walk. "CJ and Sadie told you to call me."

"Well, yes..."

"And Grady told you he wouldn't do it for you." I smiled a bit.

"Well, um, yes..."

"Okay, now that we have it cleared up where I fit on the phone tree, let me hear it." The light changed and I continued walking home, weaving around a crowd of people.

"Where are you?"

"Chicago."

"I know that...I meant you're outside." A horn blared while driving by.

"Yes...I live in a city."

"Why did you answer if you aren't at home?"

"Because my phone rang. Harper, did you call to tell me something?"

She gave me a sound of annoyance.

"Remember, last on the call tree..." I said quietly.

"So, what I wanted to tell you is even though the interview with Tyler didn't go as planned—"

"Even though you walked off in the middle of the interview..."

"He was being a prick."

"Yes, he was."

"The last thirty seconds of the interview went viral and got a lot of attention. Amara Chopra—my PR person—is fielding calls from other interview requests. It seems my dangling carrot at the end sparked more interest—people want to know more about the women who put Tyler in his place. This exposure could help us land more sponsors."

"That's great, Harper," I said, but even I heard my tone was flat.

"Wait, hold up. Did you just pay me a compliment?"

"Sure." And now my tone turned flippant.

She was quiet for a beat and I played back our conversations so far. I was being an ass.

"Um, well. We can talk about it tomorrow or whenever you're up for it. I didn't mean to disturb your evening. I wanted to let you know we didn't completely blow it today."

I reached the door to my building and would lose her in the elevator. "Okay, let me call you later about it." A group of people came in behind me and it was hard to hear her.

"Alright, sorry to bother you," she said. "Goodnight."

She hung up.

To avoid the large group still congregating in the lobby, I jumped in an elevator and hit the button for my floor, slipping my phone in my back pocket.

I fell against the back panel and dug the heel of my palms into my eye sockets, wishing this day would end.

The conversation with Harper played back through my head.

Son of a bitch.

I was short and completely disconnected from what she was saying. But I'd just left a very heavy situation and wasn't exactly on my A game. Yet that wasn't her fault.

The elevator let me off and I practically jogged to the end of the hall that led to my apartment. I simultaneously kicked off my shoes, threw down my keys, grabbed my phone out of my back pocket and hit her number while walking into my kitchen. I refused to end the day like this.

9

CHARLOTTE, NC

Harper

I poured a glass of pinot noir. It should be merlot to celebrate the occasion, but I went with the old favorite.

Was I celebrating? Was I relieving some stress? Or was I hiding from that awkward call with Cal?

The verdict—all three.

Screw it. I threw up a toast to myself as I walked back into my living room and curled up on my sectional in my favorite yoga pants and oversized t-shirt, my hair in a high ponytail. Crossing my legs, grabbing my Sherpa blanket and the remote control, I was now ready to check out and binge watch for a bit before my brain turned off for the night. I needed to get my mind disconnected from the mistake I made in calling Cal.

Grady and CJ can kiss my butt. "Call him," they said. "He's a partner and should hear what's going on."

I took a healthy sip of my wine. Yum.

Sadie gave me a lecture about how I should update him whenever there's a major development like the one we had today. Yeah, well, next time she can call him late in the evening and catch him out on a date. Because clearly with the way he was responding to me, that was obviously what was going on. I mean, the only reason he answered his phone was because he thought it was his mom.

Another sip.

And who answers their phone when they are on a date—even when it's their mother? Is that the sign of a good son or a bad date?

Sip.

Nonetheless, it was awkward as hell for me—but why? Not my fault he answered. He could've said, "Hey, Harper, not a good time. Can I call you tomorrow?"

I feel sorry for his poor date—that's who it would've been awkward for.

Sip.

I was mindlessly flipping through my channels, finding nothing. Old *Friends* episodes—not in the mood for Rachel and Ross tonight. *Pride and Prejudice* was on—I love me some Mr. Darcy—but didn't think I could handle a pretentious, arrogant hero tonight. Even if it was Colin Firth's strong, silent type and not the smirking, condescending, type.

Or the way he stared into Elizabeth's eyes—the way Cal did in my apartment. I played back that moment a thousand times. I must have imagined it. I must have—it's the only thing that makes sense.

Big gulp.

Maybe I'll settle on nerds this evening—*The Big Bang Theory*. That might work. I snuggled in and sighed.

But I was interrupted in committing to anything as my phone rang —of course it did. I considered letting it go for a brief second, but with the state of things going on my life right now, I needed to be available.

"Ugh!"

I stomped over to the counter, grabbed the phone, and then the opened bottle of wine, and brought both back to my nest on the sectional.

"Yes?" I answered, figuring it had to be someone I knew to be calling me after ten. I grabbed my glass, bringing it to my mouth for a sip, preparing for whatever was on the other end of this call.

"Hey, Harper. It's Cal."

Cough. Cough.

"Are you okay?"

Cough. Cough. "Yes, I'm fine." I was just choking. "Just a moment." I put the phone aside and cleared my throat. Choking on wine sucked. I wasn't going to die from it—at least not physically, maybe just from embarrassment. I went for a drink of water. A minute later, my face red from coughing and relief he didn't witness the mortification that his voice could do that to me, I came back to the phone.

"Hey." All casual and cool. Yep. That's me. "Sorry about that."

"Are you okay—did I catch you at a bad time?"

"Nope. I'm good." I grabbed my remote as Sheldon started shouting "Bazinga!" and

turned down the television—I had such an exciting social life.

"I was just calling to apologize for being so abrupt earlier. I was walking home, and it was noisy on the street. I had—"

A life—he had a life. Unlike me.

I held up a hand as if he could see it. "No need to apologize. I shouldn't have called so late. It could've waited until tomorrow. It's just that Grady and CJ and even Sadie were giving me a hard time about calling you and keeping you in the loop and all this other crap, and I wouldn't have called if I knew you were in the middle of...if you were...um...out." I shut my eyes painfully tight, putting my hand over them to hide from what a dork I sounded like.

"Well, I'm home now. Why didn't you want to call me?"

"Because Cal, I was angry at myself for letting Tyler get the best of me and was afraid you were going to chastise me for the same thing. That I made us look amateur."

"Harper, I'm not your enemy. The guy was being a dick. He deserved what you served him." He let out a long, weary breath. "Now, I'm going to bed in a few minutes. I'm glad things worked out. Was there anything else?"

Oh, Jesus. Did that mean he had someone there, or that he already ended the date?

"Harper, please. I'm exhausted."

What the hell? I wasn't responsible for his lack of manners, and besides, he called me back. I went to finish off my wine and found only a drop.

"Well, like I mentioned, CJ and I caught some attention by walking off Tyler's show. It actually worked to our advantage. The anticipation of what we have to say has built. My friend Amara Chopra pulled some strings and Gwen Friday is going have us on her evening talk show. The premise will be to discuss our interview with Tyler—and then reveal what we had come to discuss originally with him."

"Gwen Friday—Harper, that's a major network and great exposure. Great job."

"That was definitely a compliment." I smiled and made sure it came across in the tone of my voice. "We were going to have Sadie come with us—show the three of us as a team. Is that good with you?" In other words, are you still good with the "silent" part of the partnership?

"Yes, I think that's a good move. When is this going to happen?"

"Wednesday. We're going back to New York on Wednesday."

"Good." He sighed as if he were sitting down, lying back. "This made my evening so much better. I'm glad I called you back." His voice lacked its usual strength and spark.

I grabbed the bottle and poured myself another celebratory glass. I impressed him. A small glow lit inside me, and I don't think it was from the wine.

He was quiet. There'd been no banter. He didn't criticize. He hadn't inserted any advice or instruction. Something wasn't right.

"Well, regardless, I'm sorry I disturbed your evening. I hope you weren't eating—"

"No, I was walking home from my parents." His voice was not the Cal I was familiar with. It was filled with weariness and his tone was soft. "You...were unlucky to have caught me when I had a lot on my mind."

"Your parents live near you?"

"Close enough...maybe too close," he deadpanned. "Maybe why I travel so much. Seriously, though, thank you for calling tonight. It was a great diversion."

"Honestly, I was goaded into it." I leaned back on the sectional.

"Goaded, huh?"

"Yeah...Grady told me I had a responsibility as a business partner to keep you informed. He was the one who put it in my head that you'd be disappointed that I let Tyler get to me."

"Was he now..." Cal said.

"Yeah, he told me he spoke to you, and you didn't sound too happy with how it went. And after CJ tore into him, she set her sights on me. Eventually, she double-dog-dared me to call you."

He chuckled. It was half-hearted, but I was proud to have gotten that much out of him. "Double-dog-dared you?"

"Yes. And in our world, you can't go back on that challenge."

His voice dropped to a sexier, deeper tone, "Am I so scary that I was worth a double-dog-dare?" And there he was—the cocky-yet-charming Cal—peeking out of whatever slump he'd been in. I pictured the tilt of his lips, almost wishing I could see it.

I took a long sip and took my time responding because I had no response.

"Now that loaded silence from Harper Merrick—well, that just made my night a whole lot brighter."

"Well..." I struggled to find my words, "I'm glad I did. Before I do something to ruin it, I'll let you get some sleep. Goodnight, Cal."

"Sweet dreams, Harper."

I ended the call with a smile as big as the sun. With no one there to witness it, I let it consume me.

10

CHARLOTTE, NC

Harper

I was in my office, spinning back and forth in my executive chair, remembering the times when I was little, sitting in my daddy's big chair while I was visiting his office. My legs were too short to touch the ground, so I'd kick off his large mahogany desk to gain leverage. Spinning back and forth, while he would be down at the garage. I'd pick up the phone at his desk, pretending I was the boss. Not for the first time, I wondered how my father would've handled this situation.

Dewey fucking Dupree. I try not to use the "f-word" as freely as CJ. But when it came to Dewey, most people used the word somewhere around his name. The same man Grady saved CJ from before he could wreck her at Talladega last year, who'd been harassing and bullying her since her teenage boyfriend, Dewey's brother, had died several years ago, had his sights set on ruining us now, it seemed.

Someone else for me to focus my ire on popped up on my screen, when my computer alerted me that Cal was calling.

I punched the keyboard as I opted to answer the call and sat back and waited for my nerves to hit as I tried to pull off calm and cool.

Michael Callahan "Cal" McBane, the epitome of corporate power and an excellent male specimen, leaned back in his throne with the visage of the Chicago skyline behind him.

After our late night call this weekend, I didn't know what kind of vibe we'd have. Were we corporate partners, were we bantering buddies, flirting friends, or reluctant allies?

"Good morning, Ms. Merrick."

I glared at the screen.

"What can I do for you, Mr. McBane?"

"Did someone have decaf this morning?"

I glared.

He sat straight up, palms out and said, "Alright, alright. I can see you aren't in a teasing mood this morning."

I reached for the keyboard to disconnect the feed.

He quietly chuckled. "Tell your ol' buddy Cal whose reputation you are plotting to shred before their tortuous death?"

I paused. He sat still, and then with more sincerity said, "What happened? Seriously, Harper…who pissed you off?"

"I had a phone call with Jameson Jones this morning."

He looked perplexed. "Jameson Jones with Snap Tight Tools?"

I gave a sharp nod. "He's been with Butler for years. He was supposed to be with us. He jumped ship. Said he felt more comfortable with Dupree—said they were more with Snap Tight's image."

I didn't look at the screen. Finding the random sheets on my desk more interesting, even though I had no idea what they were. Then I realized how cowardly it was, closed my eyes, took a deep breath, and stared at the screen. "Screw 'em."

The side of Cal's mouth tilted up.

"I know Jameson and other people at Snap Tight. We almost had a deal with them three years ago. It didn't work out, but I know them well enough to make a call—"

"No. No." I shook my head and waved my hand. "Don't." And then something snapped in me and I let the truth fly. "Jameson said having a woman who was supposed to be representing our team, but who felt entitled to mouth off to a respected member of the race community on a televised show—" I bit my tongue. "It wasn't the wholesome, family image they want to project or support."

I reeled in anger under control. "If they don't want to do business with me—with us—I don't want to do business with them. Their loss. Not mine. They'll be back. Just give me a full season and they'll be back. This was 100 percent Dewey, whispering in their ears, poisoning the waters. I was expecting this." I stood and walked behind my chair, leaning over the back and still making eye contact with Cal on the screen.

"You know it's so abhorrent that a grown man with a personal vendetta against CJ, who publicly targeted her on the racetrack, is still allowed to race a team in the series he was blackballed from as a driver. How does he get away with this shit?" I pushed my chair into my desk, rocking my monitor.

He was leaning back in his chair again. A pen held between his hands, a pensive expression hiding all other emotion behind his calculating, hazel eyes.

Ugh. He had gorgeous eyes. I shook my head with more vehemence.

I clasped my hands and looked at them.

Then I gathered myself and gave Cal my sunny-side-up smile. "I got this. You'll see. Dewey Dupree is no match for us."

"No doubt…" Cal's half smile returned with a slight nod, I tried to believe wasn't mocking.

I tilted my chin a bit higher.

"On the brighter side of things, the rest of the staffing is coming together." That was a slight exaggeration.

"Glad to hear it." He muttered, making note of something. "I have to get to a meeting, but I'll be back out that way later this week. We're working on a deal with a chain of auto parts stores that happen to be located in Charlotte."

"Well, isn't that convenient," I deadpanned.

"Quite. Maybe we can all meet. I'll have Dean try arranging something with Amy."

"Great. That sounds…great." Truthfully, it didn't sound great. I had a ton of things to do and no time to keep reporting every movement, every decision to him. Plus, he was becoming a distraction—not that I would admit it to anyone.

At the last second, I remembered to hide my reaction.

The twitch of his lip as he studied me, questioning whether or not I was successful.

"I'll see you later this week, Ms. Merrick."

"Talk to you soon, Mr. McBane."

11

CHICAGO, IL

Cal

Trey strolled in as I hung up with Harper. His taller-than-average, athletic build making him a standout in crowds, even in a sea of business suits. My mind was still on what she said about Jameson and the strong front she put up over his defection. Of course, she knew not everything was going to go smoothly. People were going to balk at the change in ownership and all the other changes she made over there. Losing Snap Tight as a sponsor wasn't the first and wouldn't be the last —nor would it be the biggest account they'd lose.

"You ready for the presentation in the conference room? They're all set up and waiting for you," Trey said, popping his head in my office.

"What? Oh. Yeah." I stood abruptly, and rolled down my sleeves, stepping around the desk. "Hey, remember Jameson over at Snap Tight Tools?"

Trey looked up from his phone quick enough to glance at me. "Yeah, what about him?"

"Could you find out what's going on over there? What's the latest on that company? Any new information? Maybe get me their contact information."

He glanced up, this time staring at me longer. "O-kay? I thought you weren't interested in them."

She wasn't going to be happy about this. But I was just gathering information. "I'm not. Just curious about something." I waved it away. "No rush. Whenever you get a chance."

"They're getting some stiff competition right now—I remember reading about that." Trey typed something into his phone as I grabbed my jacket, and we left the office.

"Give me a minute." Trey continued to type away on his phone and then looked up. "Here it is. Hewitt Hardware is ruffling Jameson's feathers."

"Really?"

"Yeah, Hewitt's the younger brand appealing to the DIY crowd and hobbyists. Snap Tight is your father's toolbelt tools."

I smiled. "Perfect. That's exactly what I was looking for. Do we know anyone at Hewitt?"

"I could get to know someone…" Trey suggested.

"Get me a name," I said, grabbing what I needed to move on to the conference. I'd text her later. Hewitt would be the company to approach.

It would fit more with Harper's brand, and it would also burn the hell out of Jameson. Two birds, one stone.

Mission accomplished.

12

LAKE NORMAN, NC

Cal

I flew into Charlotte later that week and, this time, decided to take Grady and CJ up on their offer to stay with them. I had meetings set up for during the day and they'd already planned on having people over for dinner that evening, so it made sense and gave me a chance to talk with Harper and Sadie there.

I let myself in and walked through the house and out onto the back patio where everyone congregated. Sadie, Harper, CJ, Grady, and even Gus all turned when I joined them.

I'd expected a celebratory mood, given the excellent way the ladies handled their interview on Gwen Friday's show—the complete opposite of what happened the last time they were interviewed.

I hadn't expected all the serious faces.

"What's going on?"

Grady came over and clapped me on the shoulder. "Okay, Master Problem-Solver. Just in time. You're up. Have a seat."

Harper sat back, her face flush, arms crossed on her chest, and looking everywhere but at me.

CJ sat forward and hissed. "Standard Stock Racing canceled their contract with us. They'd been providing support to Butler for over ten years—the car manufacturer provides smaller teams like ours with the engines and data and technical assistance. But smaller teams also rely on alliances with larger teams for chassis support, access to technology, and simulators and other services. When you all bought the charter from Butler, it was with the contract with Standard Stock Racing. They've found a way out of their contract."

"Okay—"

"It will be almost impossible to find another one—especially at this point," Harper said, quietly. "No one wants to—"

"No one is going to want to work with us," CJ finished, with venom in her voice.

Sadie softly said, "That's not entirely true—"

Harper shot a glance at her, coldness shooting at her aunt. "I won't ask him."

"You don't have to—" she waved her off. "I—"

Harper practically jumped out of her chair. "You won't ask him."

Sadie's voice was steel. "If it means getting this team on the track, yes. I will talk to your father. Your pride isn't more important than our purpose."

CJ stood and held out her hands. "Let's discuss this."

Gus, as the representative present for Merrick Motorsports, stepped up. "We have the facilities, and we don't have an alliance with any other team, so we could do it."

"My brother would never allow it." Harper tilted her head as if striking a point.

"Your brother doesn't own the team—not yet," Gus said.

"My father is still angry at me." She leaned back, crossing her arms.

"Your father won't want to see you fail—"

"Yes, because it's a reflection of him—I would fail as soon as I stepped out from under his shadow. How would that look?" She threw her hands in the air.

I jumped into the fray. "This is business—it's not about you."

Everyone stilled. She swung around at me, her eyes blazing.

"Oh, shit." Grady muttered.

"If you have no other options, and we need a team we can trust, one that will support us out of the gate...well, your aunt is right. Your pride, darling...your pride will have to be the cost."

Harper stood suddenly, pushing back her chair. "You don't know—"

I held up both my hands in subjugation. "You're right. I don't. I don't need to know. What I do know is that tens of millions of dollars were already poured into this company. People's jobs are at stake. Take a moment for some perspective and I know you will come to the same conclusion." I stepped around the table we were all sitting at, but noticed Grady and CJ eye each other.

"I've met your father, he's a good man. He knows a good business decision. He believed in you and CJ enough to have you work for him. I don't think he's a vengeful man, I don't think he'd want to see you fail, or would take pleasure in having you ask for help. What I can tell is this isn't something you can control—so...go ask."

She held my eyes and bit out, "Fine. I'll call him."

"No need. He's on his way over," Sadie casually shared as she put down her phone. "I texted him. No Junior, just Everett. Let's get this settled so we can move on."

I nodded at her. "Woman of action—I like it."

She winked up at me. "I'm all about action, darling."

CJ, Grady, and Gus groaned, but Harper walked off.

Everyone dispersed, getting out some food, talking among themselves, but mostly leaving Harper alone.

She stared at the lake, not giving me a glance.

"Listen, I'm sorry if what I said was blunt—"

"No, you're right." She glanced over her shoulder at me briefly, but her expression was cold. "I was being selfish and emotional. I'm accused of both, often. I really want to do this on my own—it just shows how naïve I'm being."

When she went to walk by me, I gently grabbed her arm. "Harper, wait. Listen. I can talk to him—"

She threw off my arm. "God, no." Her voice held contempt—for me, for herself? "I don't want to be a coward also." She slipped by me, her back ramrod straight as she marched into the house.

This was going to be interesting.

13

LAKE NORMAN, NC

Harper

I sat at Grady's kitchen table when my father came in, wearing a UNC-Charlotte sweatshirt, jeans, and a baseball cap. My father still entered a room with authority, as if he were in the office or walking through his team's garage. He was congenial, giving his hellos to everyone as if nothing monumental had ever happened between any of us. Even giving Sadie a kiss hello on her cheek. I guess after decades of sibling feuds, they had the routine down.

Without a word, his tall figure lumbered to the fridge with familiarity, grabbed a beer, twisted the top, and said, "Let's go..." walking past me and out the back door. I took a deep breath and followed him to the dock.

It was a gray, overcast day, but mild for November. I wrapped my sweater tighter around me—but not from the breeze—more to contain my jumbled emotions.

My father lowered himself into the Adirondack chair at the end of the dock, groaning slightly when he finally settled. I settled in next to him.

He took a sip of the bottle and placed the bottle on the armrest of the chair.

"Grady picked a nice place."

"Yes, he did."

"I'm happy for them. He's good for her—CJ seems settled."

"They're good for each other." I stared out over the lake searching for my words.

"So, Sadie thinks you and I need to talk."

I nodded. "Yeah."

"I think so, too." He took another pull on his beer.

Silence.

I picked at my nails. "Are you still mad?"

My father gave me his patented side-eye that, when I was younger, would have me running for either my room or behind my mother's legs. Now, I stood my ground and gritted my teeth.

I stood out of the chair, standing in front of him and essentially blocking the view of the lake so he had no other choice but to look at me. "I'm sorry. I'm sorry about the way I told you—not sorry about the way that I did it."

I held his gaze and took a good look at my father. I didn't see anger behind those irises. I saw age.

The spark that was in my father for the last year was replaced with a small bit of weariness, some obstinacy, a dash of regret.

"Daddy," I whispered. "I'm sorry if I hurt you. I'm sorry if what I did was a betrayal. But I didn't feel like I had any other options left."

"I don't get that." He turned in his chair to look at me. "How did you not have any options?" His voice was raised. "You didn't need options. I've always taken care of both of you. Neither of you were ever without what you needed." He threw out a hand. "I could've easily just hired Grady. His name, his reputation would've been enough to bring in investors, and he's proven to have adapted to stock car quickly. I didn't have to put money and time behind CJ."

"So, you were patronizing us?"

"That's not what I meant. I told you both why I brought Grady on —I couldn't just put CJ in the car. Everyone would've thought I did it for you—or because I favored her. By pitting her against Grady, she showed her mettle—"

"She's been racing all her life. With her record in the other series, why did she have to beat Grady McBane to prove she deserved that contract?" My voice was raised to my father like it rarely ever was.

"So you felt like you had to storm off like a spoiled child denied your way?"

I knew my father loved me. But at that moment, it stabbed at my heart. He was the first man to hold my heart, and while he wasn't the first one to break it, he certainly was doing a good job now.

My father's face fell as soon as the words left his mouth, realizing he went too far. Tears rolled down my face faster than I could wipe them away.

He stepped back and took in a deep breath, staring up at the sky, and we both were silent.

"Harper, I don't want to fight about this."

He knelt down in front and reached for me, gathering me in his arms.

And I let him. Because when all was said and done—he was my dad.

"I gave up a lot to stay in Charlotte, to stay with Merrick—you know I did. But no matter what I did, I don't think you saw me as anything more than your little girl."

"I love you, sweetheart." He cupped my face. "More than anything else, I am so damn proud of you." He swiped his thumb over my cheek to wipe away my tears like he used to when I was little.

"And you might be right...I know you think I favored your brother, but the reason I took more time with Junior was because I knew you didn't need my encouragement as much." He reached out and held my hand, squeezing it a bit. "Besides, you and CJ were a dominant duo—sometimes I felt sorry for the guy." He smirked.

I let out a small laugh, breaking the tension.

He sat back next to me, and after some companionable silence, he started asking questions about how things were coming along. I told him about the situation with Standard Stock.

He sat back in the Adirondack chair and was quiet, staring at the lake, playing with his now-empty bottle of beer.

He placed the bottle on the dock and steepled his hands. "I could offer you an agreement with Merrick—that would be the easiest thing to do. But I don't think it would be the smartest."

My heart sank.

"Two reasons. First, deep down you don't want it. Second, I think it would be difficult to separate you from Merrick—and me from you. So, no, I don't think it would be a good idea."

I dropped my head.

"I will stand behind you publicly and shout from the rooftops how proud I am and how much you have my support. But you know, with CJ, I thought I was helping her by keeping her close—keeping her under Merrick's wing and protecting her. If anything, I think it isolated her and did more damage than good. She should've gone and raced for other teams, made other alliances.

If you wanted to do this, go fight for it. You aren't alone. You have a whole gaggle of people up there." He pointed at the house. "And Lord knows, you know just about everyone in racing and have charmed more than half of them. Go work your magic."

He stood. Bent to pick up his beer bottle and held out his hand, pulling me to my feet to face him. He squeezed my hand. "You—you are my daughter. Whether you are part of Merrick Motorsports or with —what's the name of the team?" He tilted his head.

"Not telling you yet."

"Well, regardless, you're one of the smartest people I know and you're a Merrick...don't you forget it. You'll have people lining up at your door by next season. For now, you need to go pound the pavement." He pulled me to the house.

I gave him a sad smile. I heard what he was saying. It was going to mean more work, but I heard every word.

"Now, let's go see if I can get out of the house without my sister cussing me out."

A few more of our friends came over later that afternoon to enjoy the unseasonably warm temperatures, and even though we put on some music and grilled outside, dinner that evening was subdued. I tried not to let my father's decision—to let us learn through trial by fire—ruin the mood. But there was no way I could relax, and I never was a good actress anyway.

Once the sun went down, everyone had gone, and it was just the four of us sitting around the firepit on the patio. Music played in the background and we all had spiced cider warming our hands. CJ and Grady were curled up together on a chaise with a blanket. I was on a chaise with my own blanket, and Cal sat in a chair across from me, more relaxed than I think I'd ever seen him, in jeans and a well-worn sweatshirt.

I couldn't help but stare at him—at how different he seemed. It was like seeing an animal out of their natural habitat. He had a bit of stubble on his cheeks, his hair was windswept, and his expression was softer, more relaxed—maybe from the beer and cider he'd consumed—maybe from the atmosphere.

"What?" He tilted his head, peering at me from the side of his eye.

"Nothing." I shook my head slightly. "You just look so different. Less—I don't know…"

"Less likely to have a stick up his ass?" Grady offered.

CJ smacked him.

Cal ignored him. "This is a nice place…it's relaxing."

I nodded. "I practically grew up on this lake. My parents have had a house here all my life."

"You're lucky your father took the time…to enjoy a place like this," he said, and there was a hint of regret in his voice, maybe bitterness.

"Yeah," Grady piped in, "Our mom usually was the one who took us places. But we went on some cool trips with her. Dad always said he was too busy to get away." He smiled down at CJ, who hadn't noticed, since she was in his lap with his arms around her from behind. "I won't be that way with my kids."

To my surprise, Cal, who was staring into the fire, said, "Same."

We sat in companionable silence, listening to the fire crackle.

CJ changed the subject. "Harper, don't worry about your Standard. We'll get on it bright and early tomorrow. We'll call the—"

"I'm not," I lied, and put on a brave face. "I'm not going to let it get to me."

"The important thing is you and Merrick worked things out and the tension with the two of you is gone." CJ added.

"I know. That's true. Silver lining."

"Who are our options for affiliations? Who do you have as high potentials?" Cal asked.

I waved him off. "I don't want to do this now."

Cal sat forward. "We might as well, you can't get it off your mind. Let's hash it out. There can't be that many."

CJ started counting them off on her fingers. "Standard Stock, Bradford Racing, Erikson Motorsports—"

"What about Rodderick Racing?" CJ offered. "You know Rick— maybe we can work something out with him?"

I shrugged. "Maybe." I'd been thinking about Rick—I knew him, not well though.

"I don't know the guy, which could a be a good thing," CJ added.

Cal had his leg across his knee, palming his chin. "Is that company connected to Rodderick Shipping?"

"Yes, it's their parent company. Why?"

He nodded slightly, his elbow perched on the arm of the chair, his chin resting in his hand. "No reason, saw their name mentioned recently."

Grady said, "I think they are worth approaching. Why don't you at least ask your father's opinion—

"I'll check on Rodderick Shipping—" Cal pulled out his phone.

"No, that won't be necessary—I'll handle it," I said.

"That's fine...you can handle it, but I'm going to see what I can find out." He reached in his pocket and pulled out a small piece of paper, handing it to me. "Before I forget, I meant to give this to you."

As he sat back down, he explained, "It's the name and phone number of a contact at Hewitt Tools, Snap Tight's competitor and

Jameson's biggest rival. You call him and tell him Jameson used to have a deal with you, but left because the all-women team you're putting together wasn't the image for his brand, and they'll definitely bite."

He stood up and smirked at me. "You're welcome."

Condescending ass.

He strode past me and to the door leading to the kitchen.

But damn if I didn't appreciate his condescending ass right now.

14

CHARLOTTE, NC

Harper

And the condescending ass was right.

Sam Hewitt was more than happy to set up a partial-season deal with us for two reasons—first, he bought into my idea of appealing to a younger, hipper audience (his words) and second, to piss off old-man Jameson (also his words).

It was a win to put in our column. But as far as accomplishments, it felt like Cal gave me the answers to a test. I only passed because I cheated.

But I had other news I was preening like a peacock to tell him about, so the admission about Hewitt was a little easier to report.

"I have a message that you called." Cal's face appeared on the computer screen in front of me as I sat in my torn-apart office. He glanced around me. "How are the renovations going?"

I glanced around the office that resembled the "before" photos from an HGTV show and tried to imagine the work that would be done over the Thanksgiving holiday while I worked from home. "Eh, it's getting there."

"So, what else is going on?"

I sat up straight, glad to finally have good news to report—news that was a result of a deal that I closed.

"I locked up an alliance with Rodderick Racing. Turns out they were more than accommodating with our needs, and happy to sign a contract with us for next season." I was jumping out of my skin to tell him. I mean, I had more pride in this deal than in telling my father when I got into Wharton Business School.

This win was mine.

"Wow. That's fantastic, Harper." He sat back in his seat, picked up a pen and started sliding it back and forth between his hands. "What a relief it must be to have that taken care of before the holidays. Are they going to send out an announcement?"

"Yes, as soon as we finalize on the contract. We expect to send out a joint press release before this weekend."

"Congratulations." He tipped his head to me. "You seem happy with the deal."

"Very relieved to have that off my plate." I nodded. "Another piece of news is Hewitt is signing a partial-season contract."

He pushed that pen back and forth some more, but his smile grew larger.

"I could have Amy send you a copy of the contract to review if you're interested, since you were instrumental in arranging it," I offered.

He held up a hand, "No need. It was your deal. All I did was supply you with the contact information."

I rubbed my forehead. I should be grateful. I should appreciate this. But him staring at me this way, with that adorable half-smile—as if he were proud, but not in a condescending way—it was confusing me.

"Cal, about Hewitt, I thought I asked you not to go out of your way…"

"I didn't." He put the pen down and sat forward. "I asked someone for the details, and asked someone to make a call, and I forwarded the information to you to close the deal—what's the problem?"

"No problem. Thanks." I sagged.

"I appreciate you looking out for us. I know how busy you must be. It helps to have someone to hash things out with, let alone all the assistance you offer. It just...I don't know. I don't want to feel like you have to swoop in and save me—I mean, us—all the time. I feel like a pet project to you, when this is my life."

He clasped his hands in front of him on his desk and got closer to the monitor. "Listen, I enjoy our talks, Harper. It helps break up the monotony of my day. It gets—well, it's a nice change of pace from everything."

We paused.

And I couldn't help it. My tone was small, soft as I said, "Is everything okay?"

He held up his hand. "No. I'm fine." He seemed to reach out to the screen. "Sweet of you to ask. It's nothing. Just a lot going on." He gave a small, forced smile, different from the genuine half one he wore before. This one didn't meet his eyes and failed to hide the fatigue that was etched on his face.

We both grew silent.

"I'm sure your family will be happy to have Grady and CJ home for Thanksgiving."

He didn't answer, just nodded a bit and looked up at me.

Taking a deep breath in through his nose as if doing a cleansing breathing exercise, he said, "Have a wonderful Thanksgiving, Harper. Please give my best to your family." He leaned into the screen and winked. "Especially your father and brother. Make sure to tell them about Rodderick—I know your Dad will be proud of you."

I gave a small laugh at his gesture and it made him smile.

"Actually, text me with the play-by-play at your Thanksgiving dinner. I'm dying to know how CJ handles meeting the parents and all," I said.

He rubbed his hand over his five o'clock shadow that, from what I could tell, was a permanent fixture on his face. "Yeah. Well, at least I won't have to worry about keeping my ex-girlfriend, Vanessa, and Grady in separate corners."

"I remember Grady mentioning something about her. They really don't like each other." This was very telling. "I just can't imagine Grady like that."

"Yeah, well. I can only imagine what he said. It all surrounds the same thing—Grady's past and him leaving. Vanessa was very judgmental."

Deciding to drop it, I added, "Well, it would've been amusing seeing CJ take Vanessa on if that's true. CJ is a bulldog to those she loves, so it's a good thing Vanessa won't be around. As you may have guessed, she doesn't pull any punches."

"Then I would've insisted you would've come along to referee for me," he said off-hand and raised his brows.

"Me, your ex-girlfriend, and CJ..." I laughed.

He leaned his head back in his chair and laughed also. "Yeah...just that image makes me want to run for my life."

"Well, you'll have to let me know how CJ does with your parents. You have my number if you need me to talk her down." I reassured him. "Or if you need to be talked down." And I winked.

I winked at him. What the hell was I doing?

He looked off in the distance before a sly look crossed his face and he stared back at the screen and said, "May take you up on that."

I nodded, needing to divert this obvious flirtation. "Besides, I doubt dinner with my family will be peaceful. It will be my brother and my father at one end, and at the other Sadie, me, and alcohol."

He leaned back in his executive chair and smirked. "That sounds more amusing. Want to switch dinners?"

"Gladly, but I need to face the music with my own family."

"Harper."

I turned back to the screen. "Yeah?"

"The phone works both ways. Call me if you need to be talked down. Deal?"

I smiled back. "Deal."

"Talk to you soon."

"Bye." I stared at the screen after he clicked off and was proud of the fact that he left with a true smile on his face...and that I had put it there.

15

CHICAGO, IL

Cal

I love my mother. But right now, I'd like to throttle her and her soft heart.

That's because when my ex-girlfriend gave her a sob story about not having anywhere to go for dinner, my mother invited her to ours.

Yes.

Thanks, Mom.

After what had to be the most arduous Thanksgiving dinner in my memory, Vanessa cornered me in the kitchen. "Cal, I've been meaning to ask—"

Grady, thank God, saw the maneuver, "Hey, bro—we could use some more wine in here." He stepped in the room, purposely breaking up what was sure to be the unveiling for Vanessa's true reason for being here.

"I'll get some." I walked over to where my mom had a few bottles on the counter and grabbed one, along with the opener. When I turned to walk back into the dining room, Vanessa stopped me with a hand on my chest. "We need to talk."

"Uh, why?"

"Because..." she pouted. "I miss you and—"

CJ came bounding in the kitchen door from outside. "Hey." She was carrying her cell phone, her cheeks were rosy, and a chill was running through her.

"Do you mind..." Vanessa seethed.

CJ ignored her, but I caught the grimace as she walked by me.

I grabbed the wine. "Now isn't a good time for this..." I said over my shoulder to Vanessa and followed CJ as she headed back to the table.

"Where were you?" I asked CJ.

"Outside talking with Harper." Everyone turned when we came back in and we all sat back down. "Harper says, 'Hi' to everyone. Cal, by the way, she wants you to give her a call when you have a chance." She shot a glance at Vanessa and smirked.

Oh, CJ. That was going to cause me so much drama with Vanessa when it was essentially no longer her business.

"We have several rooms in this house...you could've gone in one of those. You didn't need to go outside and freeze," my mom said.

"That's okay. I needed some fresh air." Again, she pointedly stared at Vanessa, who happened to be glaring at me and missed the obvious dig.

CJ turned to my mother as she walked in. "You haven't meet Harper yet, have you, Mrs. McBane?"

My mother smiled at CJ and said, "No, I haven't had the pleasure. And I told you, CJ—it's Meredith," my mother softly chided. "But I'm looking forward to it. I'm curious about the young woman who is defying tradition and is strong enough to be *your* best friend.

Grady piped in, "She holds her own...and she's drop-dead gorgeous." Under his breath, he added, "And very single."

Vanessa threw down her napkin and stalked off.

Well, and now starts the drama portion of our evening. I glared daggers at my brother and breathed through my nose.

My father looked over at me and said, "Do you want to go deal

85

with that?" He looked exhausted...and were those dark circles under his eyes? Where'd those come from?

I shook my head. "Not now. Let's go talk. That..." I vaguely nodded at Vanessa's retreat. "Is something that can wait and could've been avoided if Mom wasn't such a pushover."

My mom shrugged apologetically. "What should I have done? She showed up yesterday in tears about missing you, and our family, and not having anywhere to go for Thanksgiving. Her parents aren't around..."

"Oh, please." Grady sneered.

"Mom, you have a soft heart, and you got played," I said as I kissed the top of her head. "She really shouldn't be here for this...maybe I should take her home first."

She patted my hand and then squeezed it. We were going to go break the news to Grady about my father's condition. Vanessa had no business being here now. "Go talk with your father so he can go lie down."

My father nodded slowly. He blinked, tried opening his mouth, ready to say something, but nothing came out. He stared at me. His face was blank. I reached out to him.

"Dad?"

He was halfway between sitting and standing, and it was as if he was frozen in place.

"Dad?"

No expression. No response. He stared at me and I waited for him to say something.

I put my hand on his shoulder. "Dad, sit back down. Are you okay?" He stared up at me—a perfect stranger to him. He didn't know who I was or what I was doing touching him.

"Mom—Mom—come here. Something's wrong!" The urgency in Grady's voice as he ran into the kitchen didn't panic me. It was my father's lack of response to it that had me panicked.

He was supposed to say, "Son, shut the hell up." "Sit back down. I'm fine." "Too much turkey." "Too much wine." "Don't freak your mother out."

Instead, I was looking into the vacant eyes of someone who couldn't respond.

Where had my father gone, and how was I going to get him back? "Dad! Dad?"

My mom came rushing in from the kitchen, Vanessa from the back of the house. My mom said with a firmly controlled voice of authority, "Cal, lie him on the floor. Now." She went to pull out the chair from under him. "Hurry."

I grabbed my father, but it was too late. His face had gone red, his eyes had rolled up. His body bowed out stiff as a board. Then came the trembling. The seizing. Before he could fall out of the chair, Grady and I caught him, and we fell to our knees to cradle him as his body was thrashing.

My mother and CJ moved all the furniture away from us.

"Mom, his face. His face!" Grady was panicking, with good reason. My father's face was distorted as if in pain, morphing from deep crimson red to a dark shade of purple. "Oh, God, someone call 911. Why isn't anyone calling 911?"

My mother kneeled by my father, guiding us to lie him flat. "He's fine. Let's give it a minute. It will last a few more seconds and then it will stop."

"Mom, he's not breathing. His teeth, he's clinching them so hard—"

"Leave him be. Turn him on his side, and stay out of his way, honey. His body will stop soon, and he will start breathing. It's all normal." Mom was trying to maintain a reassuring tone as she would when we were children, but I saw her hands shaking. "Vanessa, grab my purse, would you, please. I have some emergency medicine in there in case we need it."

"Normal? How the hell is any of this normal? Since when did this become normal, Mom?" Grady all but shouted at her.

My mom's lips thinned as she stroked my father's hair. She soothed my dad with shushing sounds he probably couldn't hear. "Shhh...it'll be okay, just a little bit longer," she said to him, to us—to herself.

"Mom, what the hell is going on?" Grady demanded.

My brother was used to pushing the edge of control. But in all my years, I'd never seen him afraid.

I reached over and got his attention. I made eye contact with him and said, "Not now. I'll tell you later."

He ran his hands through his hair. "We need to call an ambulance." He jumped up, realizing no one was doing it.

"It's fine, honey. I have this under control." My mom, with one hand on my father, reached for my little brother—who seemed to shrink to a small boy in her eyes, judging by the tone in her voice. Her eyes darted to me, the older brother, tasking me with the responsibility to handle Grady.

"Grady, Dad will be fine. Mom has it handled." I put my hand on his shoulder.

"He doesn't need an ambulance..." She stroked his hair. "He's already coming out of it." The violence of the seizing was decreasing, and his body was relaxing. My brother dropped to the other side of my father. Tears welled up in his eyes as he looked up at me, his big brother, to do something.

Vanessa stood behind me and touched my arm. I tried not to shrug her off, but I hated that she was witnessing this.

My mom drew in a breath. "Your father was going to tell you about it tonight. He's going to be so angry this happened in front of everyone. He was trying to avoid it." She shook her head and put her hand over Grady's. "Let's just wait until he wakes up and discuss it with him, okay? Let's give him that opportunity. He'll be okay, believe me." She patted my father's hand. "See? His breathing is already getting better."

She forced a smile for our benefit. We all stared down at my father, whose color returned and who seemed to be in a deep sleep now, his mouth relaxed and partially open.

"Come on, man, let's lift him and take him to his room." The only thing I could think to do for him was give him some dignity and get him off the floor before he woke up.

"Good idea," my mom said, and she preceded us toward their bedroom, and my brother and I helped get him settled, leaving CJ and Vanessa alone downstairs.

We returned to find CJ, stone-faced and cleaning the kitchen, and Vanessa typing on her phone. Vanessa's face lit up with expectation when she turned to see me. "How's your father?"

"Resting."

"Good, I'm glad he's okay." She looked over to Meredith. "It didn't seem to be as bad this time."

My brother saw red. "She knew…she knew, and I didn't."

Vanessa preened. "I've been around, you weren't."

He turned on me. "How long have you known—how long have you kept this from me?"

"I just found out about two weeks ago. I swear." I said, "Dad, wanted to tell you himself when you came home."

My mom put her hand on my brother to settle him. "It's true. Vanessa was at the office one day when he had one. It's how she knew." She glared at Vanessa for the dig at Grady.

I rubbed my hand over my face. "Vanessa, I think it's time for you to leave."

She stepped up to me. "I took a car service over here. Can you drive me home?"

"I think it's better I stay here," I said. Jesus, my father just had a seizure. I can't be a taxi right now.

"I was hoping we could talk," she whispered and gave me her best sad eyes. "I'd like to be here for you."

I threw up my hands—unable to find the words.

CJ walked from the kitchen with her phone in her hand. "Vanessa, it's time for you to leave—"

Vanessa turned on her with such disdain and haughtiness in her expression, I wondered how I ever thought she was attractive. "I don't recall you ever being invited into this conversation."

Then, Vanessa turned on me. "The prodigal brother returns, and all is forgiven? He brings home a classless tomboy and all is good? I'm the one who gets tossed aside. I've had more loyalty to this family than he ever did—"

"Vanessa…" My mom's face blanches at seeing the real her for the first time.

Grady stepped forward. "I've had enough…"

CJ stepped in front of him, blocking him, and de-escalating things. Without emotion, she held up her phone and said, "Vanessa, I mean you need to leave. Your Uber is here. This family has had enough to deal with for one day. Please, leave."

"Fuck you," Vanessa growled.

I stepped in front of CJ to open the door. "Just go, Vanessa."

"You all can go to hell," she screeched and walked out, slamming the front door.

We sat in silence as I dropped to the chair in the foyer and ran my hands over my face and then through my hair. "Goddammit!" I growled. I wanted to throw something out of frustration, but it was my parents' house. "I'm sorry, Mom. You didn't have to deal with that tonight."

"No, it's on me. I knew it wasn't a good idea, but I let her talk me into it." My mom came over and put her arm around my waist.

Grady turned to CJ. "Good call on the Uber. I'm not sure what impressed me more—the fact that you didn't knock her on her ass, or that you had the presence of mind to order one."

CJ touched a few buttons on her phone and then glanced up at us. "Oh, as soon as you took your father upstairs, she got on the phone and was talking about how she was going to rope you into giving her a ride home. While she was distracted, I dug into her purse, got her address, and ordered her an Uber." A small smile crossed her face. "I knew that if she was bleeding, the Uber driver wouldn't take her away, and my patience with her was running thin."

Grady threw his head back and laughed. "That's my girl."

I'll admit a snicker may have escaped me too.

Then, my mom and I pulled them both into a cathartic McBane hug.

And all I thought was, I can't wait to tell Harper about this.

16

CHICAGO, IL

Cal

I paced the wall of windows in my penthouse that overlooked the Chicago skyline.

I took a healthy drink of the scotch, letting it burn the hell out of my throat and enjoying the warmth hitting my stomach.

I sat down and tossed my phone on the sofa next to me.

Dad woke with a hell of a migraine, and Grady and CJ offered to spend the night in case Mom needed them. They agreed to discuss things in the morning when Dad would feel up to it.

Vanessa. How did I ever get into a relationship with someone so self-involved? How had it lasted as long as it had? I didn't love her. Hell, we hadn't even been that sexually intimate near the end. It was more like she was socially convenient—she'd infiltrated the family, the business, my life. Apathy. Plain and simple. I'd become so busy, and maybe a bit dependent on her to pick up the slack. She was satisfied because of what I had and who I was.

Jesus. How did I let my life become no longer mine?

I picked up the phone and decided to check my email for distraction. Scrolling through—one after another that could wait—I came upon one that caught my eye.

Date and time stamp indicated it was sent an hour prior.

Harper was working.

She'd asked for my opinion on a proposed contract with a company I was familiar with.

She didn't ask for my opinion often. I opened it up and took a look at it, and replied with suggested changes.

A text quickly shot back to me.

Harper: Cal, what are you doing working at this hour? I didn't expect you to reply this evening.

Cal: Not a big deal. Why are you working?

The dots danced and I found my mood lifting.

Harper: Well, it's better than drinking at this point.

Cal: That good of a night, huh? How was your dinner?

Harper: I'm sober and I'm working, so there's that.

There was a pause before the dots danced again.

Harper: CJ told me about your father. I'm so sorry. How's he feeling? I know Grady was shocked, but how are you dealing with all of it?

That was the first time someone asked me.

Cal: I'm fine. I've known for a few weeks now. We were supposed to tell Grady this evening, but it turned out to be a shitshow. I had to fill him in a bit. My father's going to talk to him tomorrow. I'm lucky he is still speaking to me—again. And then there was my ex...

Harper: I heard about that too...maybe talking about her the other day was jinxing you?

Cal: Ha.

Cal: And did CJ tell you about the finale of the evening?

Dots danced and there was a pause.

My phone rang.

"I'm sorry, but I was tired of typing and was trying to figure out whether

to say no, she hadn't told me or tell the truth. But yes...she did. She told me what happened. One thing you have to understand about CJ and me is we basically tell each other everything. Grady is learning that on the fly."

"Poor guy," I muttered. I didn't mind. I preferred hearing her voice anyway.

"First of all, I warned you about CJ. But I'm sorry, I would've had CJ's back on the thing about Vanessa and would've dragged her out of there myself if Uber hadn't taken her. You all didn't deserve that."

"I have a hard time imagining you throwing down."

"Are you kidding me? Don't let the dresses and Manolos fool you. I grew up among all boys at the track. I know how to take care of myself. CJ may be a scrapper, but I have a longer reach than her. You'd be surprised what I'm capable of..."

"No doubt." My mood was already lightening, the weight of my chest lifting.

"But seriously. Are you okay?"

"I'm fine." I paused. That seemed like a canned answer and something told me I could—I should—say more. "I think I'm just disappointed in myself for not seeing what Vanessa was all about sooner. She was really toxic, and I never noticed. I feel like I should give Grady an apology for subjecting him to her."

"I get that, but Grady's a big boy, and for God's sake, he's dating CJ. You can't get much more abrasive that." We both chuckled. "If it's any consolation, my family hated my ex also. In fact, I think in hindsight, it was one thing CJ and Junior could now probably agree on."

"Well, now that sounds like a juicy story."

"Yeah, maybe for another time. I think we've all had enough emotional turmoil for one day."

I let it go.

"I'm really sorry about your father, Cal."

"You know what really bothers me is he kept it from us for over a year." I stood and looked out my palladium windows, putting my free hand in my pants pocket. "That still bothers me more than the brain tumor. I feel selfish in admitting that."

"Why?"

"Why does it bother me or why do I feel selfish?"

"It's the way you feel, Cal. There is nothing selfish about it," she said softly. And at that point, in the dark, with only the lights of Chicago in front of me, she eased me.

"It bothers me because he let my mother carry that burden alone. He didn't trust me enough to tell me."

"Did you ask him why he didn't tell you?"

"No—it's just…he makes these decisions to keep stuff from us, to make decisions for us as if we are still children—as if he's in control of everything still. It pisses me off."

"Well, give him some time to get settled, and you and Grady can sit down and talk it out. I'm sure he has a reason for his actions."

"That sounds like something my mother would say."

I could hear the smile come across the line. "She sounds like a smart woman."

"She likes CJ, thinks she's adorable, so I'm starting to question her sanity."

She let out a small giggle as she said, "CJ—adorable. That wouldn't be an adjective I would use in her presence."

The side of my mouth lifted at hearing Harper's giggle. I went back to sitting on the sofa, finishing my scotch. The sound of her amusement had my thoughts not quite as dark and tangled.

I slumped back and laid my head on the back of the sofa. I closed my eyes and let out a frustrated noise. "What a shitty day."

Harper's voice became soft, reassuring. "Cal, your father hasn't been himself, your family fell apart, you had to pick up the slack at work, you took on me and all the craziness of Merlo. You've been a little preoccupied. Cut yourself some slack."

"I think running to Charlotte was an excuse," I confessed low, quietly. "I think I was running from Chicago. I think I still am…"

"New Year's is around the corner. It's a time for a fresh start for all of us," she said, trying to lighten the mood.

"Thank you, Harper."

"For?"

"This. For getting my mind off things."

"You're welcome." She said it with a tinge of sweetness I didn't feel I deserved. "What are friends for?"

17

CHARLOTTE, NC

Harper

December was a flurry of putting out fires and maybe lighting a few of my own. It was long days and exhausting nights, and when studying my list of things I still needed to do, not quite feeling like I was accomplishing much.

Our interview and subsequent announcement of the team curried a lot of curiosity. We had requests for other interviews and appearances. Amara and our team were very selective in who we met with—careful not to oversaturate the public with our story—leaving them wanting more of us.

We gave them enough that the sponsors were curious too.

If we weren't doing interviews, December was taken up with filling positions vacated by Butler's employees who weren't on board with the changes "these women were making" and trying to come up with a cohesive team.

CJ—well, CJ was trying to see eye to eye with her crew chief, and it wasn't going well. They had two months to get it together.

I hadn't seen Cal since before Thanksgiving. I spoke to him occasionally to update him on changes being made, new prospects in sponsorships, financial updates. But he had his hands full, and I tried not to burden him.

He'd mentioned he was busy juggling the company and trying to force his way into his father's doctor's appointments. His mom had gotten their father to work from home more often—holding over him the fear of seizing in the middle of a meeting as a reason, even though it was a cruel method of getting him to slow down.

When I did teleconference with him, the stress showed, and I'd wished I could do something to help him. He had this line on his forehead between his eyebrows that I would use to gauge his stress. It had been deepening and I wanted to run my finger over it to relax it. It was such a weird thought to have. But I was becoming somewhat obsessed with that line and had to stop myself from reaching for the screen sometimes.

Tonight was New Year's Eve, and in Charlotte there was a regular charity event held on this evening every year. Industry big-wigs, automotive executives, and even top industry sponsors were all in attendance, as well as some local celebrities, and other assorted, invited guests.

And here I was stuck in the middle of my old social circle of women where I was normally positioned every year. The difference was, I had work to do—I had networking and socializing I needed to get to, and even managed to keep CJ close at hand and out of Grady's clutches.

Tracy Silvers had been talking my ear off for what felt like hours about her upcoming wedding.

"It's my wedding." With the tone only a bride-to-be could pull off. "I should be allowed to choose the colors I want. I've always loved the color yellow. It's cheery and it's a spring wedding, so it fits.

Here I was, standing in a room full of some of the top executives in the southern states, and I was forced to hear about her choices in bridesmaids' dress colors and how her cousin refuses to wear chartreuse. Her cousin was about the same coloring as I was, and of course she'd refuse—she'd look ghastly.

That was the point.

Tracy wanted her to wear the color because Tracy was petty and didn't want her cousin to steal her limelight. Her cousin was also dating the man Tracy had been crushing on for two decades, so that was the crux of it.

CJ was about to fall over with boredom. "What are we discussing?"

"The color of Tracy's bridesmaids' dresses."

CJ mouthed to me, *Why?*

"CJ, what do you think about chartreuse for the bridesmaids' dresses, wouldn't that be perfect for a spring wedding?"

"Tracy, if I binged on Mountain Dew after an all-night bender and then puked—that would be the color of chartreuse. No one wants to see that, let alone wear it."

That mental image saved Tracy's cousin from any further argument.

"Excuse us. Harper, didn't you want to introduce me that Severs guy?" She yanked on my arm, but it didn't take much for me to follow her willingly.

"Whew. You owe me for those last ten minutes of my life," she said.

I stared around her. "Add it to the tally. Where is Rich Severs?"

CJ shrugged. "No idea. I just mentioned you wanted to introduce me to him—didn't say I
saw him."

I gave her a small shove. "Well, let's go mingle anyway. I know how much you hate it, but it's the nature of the beast."

"I feel like one of the marionettes you drag out at these things to smile and shake hands."

"A glorified one, that I dress up and cart around—it's pretty close to accurate. Unfortunately, I can't pull a string and control what comes out of your mouth, though."

"Why are you sugar sweet to everyone but me?"

"Because you like me just the way I am." I winked at her. "And you hate that crap."

"Yes, I do." She linked her arm through mine, smiled up at me, and said, "Let's go dazzle the pants off some peeps."

Later, after CJ managed to ditch me, I'd made it to a bar-height table with three men I'd been trying to wrangle throughout the cocktail hour. Ben Miller, Todd Easton, and Joe Glass—all executives for companies that had sponsored other cars in the past, and I'd hoped would be interested in getting back into the game.

"CJ is a breath of fresh air into the sport, you can't deny that—" I said to them.

"She's also a Tasmanian devil of controversy and a wild card," Todd declared, lifting his drink.

"She garners too much of the wrong type of press," Joe Glass interjected.

"How so? And what is the wrong type of press? Isn't all press good press?" I tried to lighten the mood.

"Not for my customer base," Joe declared. "Our restaurants are family establishments—having your woman driver throwing punches at a man after a race isn't exactly wholesome."

I tried not to visibly grit my teeth. "Joe, Dewey Dupree had just tried to wreck her—"

"Allegedly—" the man stood back and folded his hands over his chest.

"And threatened her numerous times—"

"Unsubstantiated—" He tilted his head up, digging in on his stance.

"He just wrecked the man she loved—"

"Uh, no." He slouched in his stance and rolled his eyes at me. Rolled his eyes. At me. "If you look at the playback, Grady wrecked him—"

I lowered my head slightly but didn't break eye contact. "Be that your opinion, if she were any other driver, would what happened have been a problem?"

Joe was turning, opening his mouth to respond when Todd elbowed him, and all three glanced at me and then behind me.

But my ire was riled. "There are usually rivalries and hot tempers at many races throughout the season. You have been known to sponsor hot-tempered driver's before—Dewey Dupree's disdain for CJ is well documented—"

All three men's faces fell as their backs straightened.

Wow, was that all it took to get them to lay off?

"Drivers like Dewey Dupree are one of the reasons we have started Merlo racing. We

are developing a mentorship development program also—"

The men continued to glance between me and then over my shoulder.

What the hell?

I turned in a snit and flew into the chest of a what seemed like a perturbed Cal McBane.

"Cal? What are you doing here?"

He quietly stared at the three men who appeared...smaller...just less than...

He bit down on his bottom lip before saying, "Just listening..." He shifted to glimpse at me and then did a doubletake. "You look gorgeous this evening."

His double-take made his comment seem all the more sincere, and my hand involuntarily flew to my cheek to feel the color that rushed there.

Jesus Christ. I was supposed to be this hard-edged business-woman, and the man swooped in, backed me out of my corner these nimrods had me in, and then made me blush with only a few words.

"Who do we have here?" Cal tipped his head up, his hands behind his back as if studying less-important subjects.

I stood in wonder at how he commanded the group, when I knew for a fact he was younger than all three of them.

Ben Miller stepped forward. "I'm Ben Miller with MCG Electronics, Todd Easton with Eastway Insurance, and this is Joe Glass with Glasshouse Restaurants."

They showered Cal with compliments about McBane's different divisions, and even commented about his college football days.

Wait—what?

Cal held out his hand, firmly shaking each of theirs. "Good to meet you all."

"You played college football?" I stared at him. Just as I thought I was getting to

understand that man.

Todd interjected, "Star defensive back—"

"Why didn't you ever go pro, anyway?" Ben asked, the last to shake Cal's hand and

wincing a bit. I glanced at Cal's tensing expression and figured he wasn't pleased with the direction of the conversation.

He waved it off. "Old injury...same old story. Anyway, what business are we discussing?"

I took the hint and helped him redirect. "None it seems, the three of them don't agree with CJ's method of dealing with bullies."

Cal's brows exaggeratedly flew to his hairline. "Is that so?"

"That was Joe's comment, not ours." Todd motioned to Ben and himself. "We don't have any issue with CJ or how she ran last season."

Joe glared at Todd. Cal eyed Joe like shit on the bottom of his shoe before angling his body away from Joe so he didn't have him in his vision any longer.

"So, then you'd be interested in speaking with Harper about possible sponsorship deals?" Cal pressed.

"Cal?" I said.

Todd and Ben stared at each other.

"MCG Electronics, you're based in Atlanta, right?"

"Marietta, actually. Yes."

"Hm..." He turned to Todd. "And Eastway Insurance...didn't you sponsor an Indy driver a few years back?"

"Yes." Todd's face brightened at the fact that Cal remembered them. "Yes, our guy ran against your brother. Lost, of course." The man gave a nervous laugh.

Cal clapped both men on the shoulders as if they were now in his club. "Why don't we get a drink and talk with Harper some more about potentially sponsoring CJ with Merlo. You know she's running now against my brother—it's quite a complication." He smirked. "Nothing like keeping a man on his toes, to have your woman trying to run you off the road." The three of them laughed with newfound camaraderie. "Wait until you meet them."

And I was stuck behind with the fuming Joe Glass. We stared at each other as if to say, "What the hell just happened?"

Well, I know what just happened. Cal McBane just happened.

By the end of their drinks, I had two new sponsors. And I was inexplicably ticked off.

18

CHARLOTTE, NC

Cal

Granted, I hadn't known Harper that long, but I'd never imagined she could ever turn this shade of angry. "What the hell was that about?"

Her face was pinched as if her shoes were too tight, even as she stood up to me. "What?

"I don't need you to keep rescuing me. I can close my own deals."

"I locked down two sponsors for the season? And all it cost was a free glass of scotch?" I held her shoulders and stared at her. "What is this all about? It wasn't a big deal."

"It was to me. They were my targets. I was working on them. I wanted to land them."

"You did land them—"

"No, you landed them...I was inconsequential. I had it covered, and you swept in and took over."

"They were talking about how bad a bet CJ was—they were talking about her unwholesome image and you were drowning."

"No." She growled, before reeling it in. "I wasn't." She softened.

"Joe was going off on a superiority tangent. I was getting ready to turn it around when you approached and blindsided me."

"Blindsided you? You were having a problem with those three pricks. Do you want to know why? The other two were following the asshole's lead. You needed to separate them—and I did. So instead of battling an asshole—who was never going to change his stance—and his two minions who followed his lead. I locked down two who were easily influenced."

She paused for a moment, and for a brief second, I saw her relent— I showed her something she hadn't thought of.

"Jesus Christ. You have enough on your plate without having to run after idiots like Twiddle Dumb and Twiddle Dumber. That took me all of fifteen minutes and you didn't have to pull your hair out. Accept the assistance and move on to bigger and tougher situations. Or...maybe enjoy yourself for the rest of the evening."

She finished her glass of wine, slamming it down on a table so hard I was surprised it didn't break. "Go get back on your horse and ride back to your castle, dear knight. Go rescue another damsel. This one doesn't want you." She turned and stormed off.

Ouch. That didn't go the way I expected.

At all.

Later, I was still quite prickly about my run-in with Harper and trying to figure out how to handle it. Why should I handle it? I still don't understand what I did wrong. She was offended because I stepped in to help. That's ridiculous. She was being ridiculous and naïve. You take the hand that's offered when trying to get shit done.

She's got two months before the season starts, and a new team to whip into shape. She didn't have time to chase assholes around begging for money.

What the hell?

This woman was infuriating. I rocked back on my heels, my glass of scotch up to my lips, and pretended to survey the subdued crowd, but found myself scanning the area for the beautiful she-devil. Because no matter how infuriating she was being, I'd been looking forward to seeing her for weeks, and she was the balm to soothe me. This wasn't how I'd planned tonight to go. Honestly, I didn't really have a plan except I really wanted to see her. And that dress...with her hair...and when she turned around and flashed those amazing blue eyes at me...I was, well...I was glad to be here, let's leave it at that.

Grady came up behind me, clapping me on the back. "You need to loosen up, brother. It's a party, for God's sake. Not a board meeting or a wake."

While I enjoyed hanging around with him again, I didn't appreciate him calling me out on my moroseness.

"Doesn't seem like your kind of party."

"That's why we need to shake things up. Gotta make it my kind of party." His smile surveyed the crowd.

I shook my head.

CJ threaded her arm around his, and staring up at him said, "I'm all the excitement you need for this evening." Her black cocktail dress complimented her petite frame and gave her a feminine softness she usually tried to hide.

My brother's demeanor softened as he took her into his arms, lifting and swinging her around, catching the attention of many people in the vicinity. She squealed—which is about as odd as hearing a country singer busting out a rap—before he set her on her feet. She held onto his arms trying to steady herself and then hitting him.

"Grady McBane, behave. This is not the time or the place. I'm supposed to be acting sophisticated and grown-up. Harper will kill me if I make a scene and become another PR nightmare for her again. Where is Harper anyway?"

"Far away from me, you can bet," I mumbled, staring down at my glass
at them.

It was enough for CJ to hear. "What did you do?"

"I'm sure you'll hear all about it later."

CJ's brows drew down. She began surveying the room, getting up on her toes—as if it

would help her see over the crowd, given her short stature. "Can you guys see—"

She froze as something toward the front of the hall caught her attention. She stepped two steps away from us. She grabbed Grady's hand, and by evidence of his grimace, she was squeezing it. "Son of a bitch..." she whispered. Grady and I instinctively drew closer to her, staring in the same direction she was.

Her fists clenched; her lips thinned. "Son of a—" Her voice raised as she began to repeat herself, and people turned—so much for not making a scene. She moved toward the door of the ballroom and we both utilized our long legs to catch up to her and whatever hell she was about to rain down. Grady caught her from behind and swung her around and to the side of the room.

"If you value your manly bits, you will put me down now," she gritted out.

"We both value my manly bits, but you need to tell me what's wrong."

"That's Harper's ex, Spencer Pruitt, making a beeline toward her with her old college roommate hanging on him like a cheap suit." CJ threw herself out of Grady's arms, not getting far before he caught her again. The last thing we needed was CJ causing a scene, and with the redness on her face, and the way she was pushing up the sleeves of her cocktail dress, she planned on doing exactly that.

We were all staying at the same hotel next to the venue where the party was being held and had come in together before Harper was lost to the crowd and my failed attempt at being helpful. I knew she was dressed in an amazing black, formfitting dress that allowed one of her long legs to peek out when she walked. Yes, I enjoyed watching her walk, even when she sashayed away from me earlier. Sue me.

Regardless, I could easily zero in on her beautiful blonde hair wherever she was in the room like it was a tractor beam, and my attention was easily snagged like most warm-blooded males.

No matter how frustrated I was with the woman, I wasn't going to let her be blindsided by this Spencer guy. It must be the ex she said CJ hated. And if CJ disliked him so fiercely, I doubted I was going have a good opinion.

Besides, he was her ex. That already had me hating the man, and I refused to analyze what that meant.

I pushed my way through the crowd without giving an explanation or any reassurance to CJ. I wouldn't reach Harper before she had to deal with the couple, but at least I would have her back, and I sure as hell wasn't going to let them ruin her evening.

19

CHARLOTTE, NC

Harper

The nicest thing to say about the evening so far is I liked my dress. It was a shallow thing to say, but it was New Year's Eve, and instead of spending it with someone special, or even with my friends, I was wound up after snapping at Cal, and was now standing in front of a bunch of stodgy old men, forced to nod my head and smile.

I'd approached the group to strengthen relations since they still only knew me as Merrick's daughter and were quite entrenched in the industry. Now, I was caught in a conversation about golf and country clubs.

"Doesn't your daddy belong to Quail Valley?"

I nodded. "Yes, he does." I put my wine to my lips, knowing what was coming next and needing a moment to formulate a polite response.

"Well, maybe you could get me an introduction to your father...I'd do anything to play on that course."

I was in mid-swallow when a voice from my past somewhere behind me caused me to almost choke on a perfectly chilled chardonnay. "Oh, it will take a recommendation from God to get you an invitation to play with Everett Merrick."

Chardonnay was going to be the death of me. The burn stuck in my throat, I turned slightly and closed my eyes and focused on swallowing.

No. Not him. Not now.

Nails on a chalkboard followed in reply. "Oh, Spencer. That's a perfectly wretched thing to say about Harper's daddy. He's a wonderful man." Okay, now I wished I would've spit it out—at her.

Spencer and Susannah.

I purposely held my wine glass with both hands to stop from dropping it, my hands were shaking so badly.

No. No. I won't be that cliché—the poor woman confronted with her ex-boyfriend and his new girlfriend—the one whom I used to call friend. The one who wants to rub my nose in her new status as his new girlfriend.

I glanced over my shoulder with the best smile a Southern girl could plaster on. The one that said, "Oh, what a wonderful surprise." I was so tempted to add a "Well, bless your heart." Because, even if it was only for my own satisfaction, I wanted to use my private phrase when I wanted to call someone an asshole.

"Susannah. Spencer." I grappled with every piece of etiquette drilled into me, every piece of indifference I could muster to step forward toward them. I leaned forward and gave her a half-hug and fake kiss meant to maintain my lipstick and her perfectly highlighted and bronzed foundation.

Stepping back to take them in, I garnered strength from the bemused expression on their faces. It worked. They were the ones surprised, not me.

Of course, I knew there was a possibility they'd show up. Susannah was nothing if not predictable.

Like now, she was dressed in a five-thousand-dollar, sleeveless, square-neck, black gown that was very body conscious and accentuated her very slim, petite build. She had diamonds at her ears and neck

—classic, not gaudy. On his arm, she was the picture of modern elegance and wealth—the perfect accessory for an ambitious man.

Exactly what Spencer always wanted.

Susannah's family was from Charleston; her family owned Outdoor Sports, with stores all over the southeastern states. A perfect pedigree for a wife of a man wanting to social climb.

Last I heard, Spencer moved to Atlanta after Susannah's father introduced him to executives at one of the PR/marketing firms in the city. Susannah followed shortly after, establishing a small interior design business until she could become Mrs. Spencer Pruitt. From what I heard, it wasn't going as quickly as she would like, though.

Being in Atlanta, they were close enough that Susannah wouldn't miss an opportunity to flaunt Spencer in my face. I had hoped Spencer, being aware of our rivalry and her intentions, wouldn't have gone along with it.

I straightened and stared right at him. My knees were far from stable, but my dress was floor length with a side slit and was perfectly good at camouflaging my shaking legs.

I tightened my thigh muscles to gain stability and my smile grew to something more genuine when I noted the way she surveyed me and unconsciously pulled closer to him—afraid I'd try to snatch her toy from her hands—similar to how I held my wine glass.

The difference was my wine wasn't going to break my heart.

Spencer leaned forward as if to greet me, pulling away from Susannah. I cut off the movement by hastily moving my wine glass between us, gesturing at the two of them. "How wonderful it is to see you both tonight. What brings you up here?"

I took a sip from my glass, peering at them over the rim and promising myself I would not choke this time.

Spencer dropped his head slightly, and I darted my eyes between the two of them and the nearest exit.

"Well," Susannah gathered her bravado. "*We*"—she emphasized the word so much it was embarrassing— "heard about your new business venture and just had to come down and see what you were up to now." The tone in her voice hinted at how "cute" she thought my new hobby must be. I would've expected her to wave her hand at me, but she was afraid to let go of Spencer's arm.

My smile stiffened at the condescending air she gave the comment.

Spencer jumped in, "My firm has clients attending. But we also came to congratulate you, Harper, and wanted to wish you luck. It must be so rewarding to have a team of your own—and to have CJ be a part of it."

Susannah held back her eyeroll, but it was there. "Yes, of course. And to find out how you managed to pull that off?" She pretended to lower her voice conspiratorially. "Your father must be furious."

As if I'd ever confide in her.

"Oh, I'd say her father is probably pretty proud of her." A deep voice demanded our attention as a strong bicep snaked around my waist, and a large body came up and enveloped me from behind.

Cal.

The electricity of his touch awakened my senses to the scent of cedar and sandalwood that immediately fortified me and refocused my attention to every inch of my back—molding to every inch of his.

His breath caressed my neck as he whispered, "I got you." My knees weakened a bit more, but his arm held me as he straightened and addressed the group. "After all, she's taking the industry by storm and rocking it to its foundation—" Holding onto his arm wrapped around my waist, I turned to look up at him. He smiled down at me. "Kind of like what her smile does to me."

And then he winked at me. Winked.

The knight—as tempting as the devil—had come to rescue me...again.

And this time, I couldn't say a damn thing, because I needed the rescue, and he knew it.

He leaned forward a bit, holding out his hand. "I'm afraid we haven't met. Cal McBane, and you are?"

Susannah's gaze was fixed on Cal, her mouth parted. I followed her gaze, once again staring up at Cal, but this time studying him and the unusually congenial expression on his face. Cal wasn't much taller than Spencer, maybe bulkier in his shoulders and chest. Now that I heard about his football days, I saw the reason for them.

His hair was a bit longer, less coiffed than Spencer's, his eyes were hazel to Spencer's deep brown, and his skin a bit more sun-kissed to Spencer's paler tone. But when face to face, Cal just appeared to be "more."

Not that I had any business comparing the two.

Nope, not at all.

Spencer held out his hand by habit, "Spencer Pruitt." He studied Cal, and I wondered if they were doing the squeeze-the-hand thing.

With the upturn on one side of Cal's mouth, I would guess Spencer was.

The silence between the four of us went for a second of awkwardness too long until Susannah was done being forgotten. "Susannah." She held out her hand directly between the two men. "Susannah Smythe."

Cal graciously took it, making eye contact with her and adorning her with such a warm smile, I hid my smirk.

"And how do you know my Harper?" Cal asked them.

The "my" wasn't missed by any of us. Spencer stiffened; Susannah was actually at a loss for words.

"Um, well, Harper and I went to college together," she sputtered, while motioning between us. She made her tone lighter, sweeter. "Plus, our daddies are old friends."

He leaned back. "Oh, wonderful. Well, then, it's great to meet you." He nodded, but then his brow furrowed a bit, staring at the perplexed couple and then bending down toward me. "I'm sorry to break up the reunion, but there are some acquaintances of mine here who were asking to meet you." He glanced up at Spencer and Susannah. "Do you mind?"

"Oh, no. Not at all." Susannah looked a little too pleased to end this chat. "We can catch up later." She attempted to smile at me, but it was strained. The smile I returned, gracious and confident, because their ambush had failed, and it showed.

20

CHARLOTTE, NC

Cal

As we walked away from the lovely couple, Harper's ex's eyes were throwing daggers at me as if I were encroaching on something that belonged to him.

It was all I could do not to look back at him and smirk. *You idiot.*

I tightened my arm around her waist, leading her as far away from that toxic duo as I could.

"Are you getting better at figuring out when I do actually need rescuing, or did someone tip you off about this?" Harper murmured as we stepped away.

"CJ nailed him as soon as he walked in." I guided her around a crowd of people. "You can thank Grady for running interference before she reached you. I volunteered to give the rescuing gig another try and see if you were more receptive this time."

She gave me a half-hearted glare. "Yeah, well. Thanks...that one was appreciated."

"Besides, I wasn't sure which one CJ was going to take out first."

Harper finished off her wine and paused, tilting her head. "Yeah,

I'm not sure who would've gotten top honors either." She squinted up at me and I was curious about the story behind everything. "She strongly dislikes Spencer, because he's my ex and, well, your best friends are supposed to hate your ex when the breakup didn't end well. But she never warmed to Susannah—they were oil and water. Plus, CJ is loyal to a fault and she believes—"

"You don't poach on your friend's man?"

"Something like that. Susannah made everything with us a competition. It seemed to be the basis of our friendship somehow. It was exhausting. This is a pathetic example, but also a painful one. She knew how painful our breakup was. I knew she coveted my relationship with him, but this was just too far."

"Well, he had a choice," I said, finishing my drink.

"Yes, he did. And he knew how I felt about her. He knew what she was like. But he also knew what her trust fund and her daddy's company is worth."

"Is he that shallow? Is she that oblivious?"

She shrugged.

"Then they are better off together—and so are you without them."

"I know." She studied her empty glass. "But he was my first love." She closed her eyes before tilting her head back up. "And he broke my heart."

I stared at my wounded warrior. I'd known she had a softer side— I'd seen glimpses of it. But now I saw shades of how low he must have brought her, and I wanted to ruin them both.

I didn't care if she thought I was a chest-thumping, overbearing caveman. I wanted to repay each tear he must have caused her.

She glanced down at her glass, caressing the edges, and I wished I could feel it on my skin. "I'm sorry about before. About going off on you the way I did. I—it just infuriates me...how easily you succeed at what takes me so much effort to fail at. I'm not familiar with failing— especially with people—and it's very humbling."

I didn't want her feeling this way. I wanted to see her smile. I wanted to feel her sunshine and her warmth.

"Enough of that." I grabbed her glass. "It's New Year's. You are officially my date now, and I have a reputation to uphold. So, let's get you a glass of wine and let's see if I can summon up some of the McBane charm my brother seems to possess in spades."

She smiled. "Don't strain yourself—"

I placed my hand on her back again, liking the way it felt there, enjoying the familiarity—as if we belonged together. We fell into sync as we walked in unity toward the bar through the sea of people.

What the hell is going on with me?

She stopped so suddenly, I almost knocked her over. "Oh! There is Duane Gooding. I wanted to talk to him about meeting up next week—"

"No." My voice was firm. "No more work." Work would ruin this…whatever it was. "This is a party." My hand traveled down her arm and grasped her hand, she followed the progress until our fingers were locked, her gaze traveling up my suit coat until she met my stare.

We both froze.

I meant to pull her along to the bar to get our drinks filled. Instead, I didn't move, I pulled her to me, until she was flush to my body, our gazes still locked.

A flurry of activity around us increased…but our focus only ventured to each other's mouths and then back to the eyes—helplessly paralyzed in the moment.

A chorus of voices raised around us. "5-4-3-2-1—Happy New Year's!"

What was happening?

I was going to kiss her.

I leaned over. Paused.

Her eyes flickered between questioning, wanting, daring.

Weren't you supposed to kiss the person you were with when the clock struck midnight?

Wasn't that a rule—like mistletoe?

Lips or cheek? Lips or cheek?

I leaned in slowly. Giving her a chance. Not breaking eye contact. What would she do?

Her lips parted slightly.

I moved my hand to the small of her back.

She let out a small, wine-scented gasp, and she clung to the lapel of my jacket. Our intent fixed as I leaned in and kissed her. It was a fairly innocent kiss—soft, sweet but so damn enticing. My entire world was centered on it.

I wanted to part her lips and dive into her. She tugged on my jacket and I pulled her closer, my lips shifting over hers, ready to take more.

Someone bumped into the back of me, and I was so off-kilter, it actually moved us apart—taking us out of our orbit above the world and slamming us back into the noise-filled room of confetti and balloons dropping.

She bent her head down and away from me, but I needed her eyes again.

My finger tilted her chin up. "Happy New Year, Harper."

She gave a small, sweet-as-hell smile. The strobe lights illuminated the slight blush on her cheeks. My girl was blushing. Just a while ago she was ready to tear my balls off, and now she was blushing.

I caught myself—my girl. Really?

Flirty came back to her as she laid her hand on my chest, smoothing out the lapel she'd been grasping, and leaned in close to me. "Happy New Year, Cal."

I cupped her face, studying her lips, and let out a long-beleaguered sigh. "Something tells me this is going to be one hell of a year."

21

CHARLOTTE, NC

Harper

Oh my God, he kissed me—we kissed—or did I kiss him? No, it was definitely a "we-kiss."

It's New Year's—everyone kisses on New Year's. It doesn't mean anything. Except, it could've been a cheek kiss or a peck. And it didn't feel like a peck. He shifted, and I think he was definitely going to go for more if we hadn't been interrupted. Hell, I wanted him to go for more.

I excused myself to the ladies' room to gather my wits, as Cal tasked himself with going

to get us some much-needed fresh drinks. I found myself touching my lips on my way back to the ballroom—mindlessly trying to replay the memory. A hand reached out and touched my back—the same spot Cal had claimed earlier, and I wondered if I had willed the action. But this touch seemed foreign.

"Harper…"

My stomach did a flop and then sank. It wasn't Cal.

I didn't want to do this again. I forced a smile and turned.

"Spencer."

"Hey, glad I caught you." What he didn't say but seemed to imply by the soft, knowing look he flashed me, was he was glad he caught me alone.

Dammit.

I shifted, uneasy on my feet. Spencer and I hadn't even spoken since we'd broken up.

He stepped closer. I instinctively stepped back. Hurt flashed across his face as his hands kept moving as if to reach out for mine.

"I'm glad I got to see you this evening. You look...great," he said, gently.

"Thank you." What was I supposed to say to that? "Is Susannah's family up with you all?"

"No. Just me and her." He didn't make eye contact. "I...we... wanted to come see everyone and get out of Atlanta for a bit." He refocused on me. "I was excited to hear you made a move out from under your father, Harper. Really. I'm proud of—well, I guess that sounds condescending. But I'm happy for you."

This was a sore subject because one of the reasons we broke up was because of my father and Merrick Motorsports.

"What made you decide to finally make the move?"

I wasn't going to get into it with him. Nope. He left when I didn't fit the mold he wanted in a girlfriend—in a wife. But honestly, if he hadn't left, who would I be now? Nonetheless, I didn't feel like having that conversation right now.

"An opportunity presented itself...seemed like the right thing to do."

"I think you're right—I saw everything going on with CJ and you last year. I wanted to reach out and see if I could offer any assistance. But, figured you may not want that."

Awkward silence settled as I looked down at my hands and then up to survey the area and see if anyone was around to rescue me.

This man had once been my world. We'd made plans together— How many babies we wanted; what their names were going to be; what kind of house we'd live in—the only problem was where that house would be and what say I had in my future.

"Anyway, I caught the Tyler Wilson show and…well…" He rubbed his hand over his face. "I couldn't *not* do something. I hope you don't mind that I helped Amara get that interview with Gwen Friday?"

"You what?" The jolt of the surprise had me take a physical step back. "She didn't tell you—"

"Spencer Pruitt, as I live and breathe, what rock did you crawl out from under…" Gus walked toward us with a predator's smile focused on Spencer.

My friends had tolerated Spencer when we were together, but none of them were all that disappointed when we broke up. What they were angry about was how and why he left me.

From Gus's expression and CJ's reaction earlier, they weren't all that crazy about him reappearing, either.

"Hey, Gus. I hadn't seen you earlier." I took a step toward one of my closest friends, a man who had been like an older brother to me as we grew up.

We'd never been anything more than friends, but since he'd worked for my father for years and was always around, people speculated—including Spencer.

"Hello, Gus." Spencer didn't make an effort to step forward with a welcoming hand to shake, and neither did Gus.

"Got here a little late. Hadn't planned on it, until I heard there was a possibility of old friends showing," Gus said. "Then I knew I had to make an appearance. See what's going on."

Spencer dropped his head slightly and shifted; he maintained a plastic smile, but his eyes went cold. "Just catching up a bit. Congratulating Harper and wishing her success. Brave thing she did…leaving and going on her own." He crossed his arm, put his finger to his chin in contemplation. "You're still with Merrick, aren't you?" With the inflection of his voice, he'd implied Gus was either not brave enough or loyal enough to follow me.

Gus stood, no response. No reaction except his charming half smirk that lit up the hormones of most women and was basically his resting face. "It was nice to see you again, Spencer. I'm sure it will be a while before you're back up this way again."

Spencer walked by him. "Oh, I'm not sure about that. Turns out we have clients up here now and may be up quite a lot in the coming months. Plus, I want to be there for Harper and see what I can do to be supportive. I'm an executive at one of the top PR marketing firms in Atlanta now. I could be a great resource, Harper. We should really talk."

Spencer proceeded to walk in measured strides to me and leaned in, and before I could figure out a way to politely deflect his intention, he gave me a kiss on the cheek, and whispered, "We can keep the thing about Gwen Friday between us and Amara. It was wonderful to see you, Harper."

He ignored Gus and turned away from me as he said, "I'll give you a call and we can have lunch." He walked back into the ballroom before I had a chance to respond.

"Harper?" Cal came over, drinks in hand. "Is everything okay?"

Cal studied Gus and me as we stared at each other and the door Spencer walked through. "Hey, um…people are looking for you." He held out my glass of wine.

"What did I miss? How did you manage to find trouble on the way to the bathroom?"

I took the glass from him and took a healthy sip because I had no response.

I couldn't hide from trouble these days if you camouflaged me.

22

CHARLOTTE, NC

Harper

"Well, last night was...interesting," Sadie said with a dramatic flair as she took a sip of her Bellini. We were having a "Ladies' Brunch" the next morning that Aunt Sadie arranged, solely to run down the events of the night before and to gossip.

CJ smirked behind her orange juice. "Spencer and Susannah were a precious couple..."

"Stop." I sharpened my tone. "I appreciate that you both kept your distance from them, though. I didn't need any more attention drawn to me."

"I was on my best behavior. I even managed to stay in my heels all evening," she pointed out as if she deserved a sticker.

"I still can't believe the nerve of that girl. Showing up with him. Just trying to get a rise out of you..."

I took a long sip of my own Bellini. "It's the past..."

Sadie waved me off. "She's always been jealous of everything you had, did, said, etc. Let her have your cast-offs and sloppy seconds."

I covered my expression with my glass, about ready to catch the waiter's attention for another one, even knowing that it would only encourage Sadie.

CJ leaned toward me, her elbow on the table, her head in her hand, and batted her lashes. "I'd say Harper's upgrading..." She awaited my reaction.

"Oh yes, let's get to the good stuff." Sadie leaned forward on the table; her tone was laced with gossipy sass. "A little birdy told me about a kiss Cal landed on you at midnight—hm?"

"What?" was in stereo.

I went bright red before hushing them. "It was an obligatory midnight kiss."

Oh, geez. I surveyed the table...who saw us?

I got a circle of "Uh-huh..." and speculative "Yeah, sure."

"Well, at least Cal came to your rescue from Shit-for-Brains and Buffy-the-Bitch." CJ gave a side-eye innocent expression, and when I glared, she shrugged as if to say, I changed the topic, didn't I?

That topic didn't sit much better. I still had to process the fact that my ex-boyfriend arranged the interview with Gwen Friday.

Sadie put her drink up in a toast to CJ. "I do love your way with words, darling."

My mom ignored them and focused on what really interested her— me with a man. "Oh! I missed that part." My mother sat forward in her seat waiting for manna to fall from heaven. "Did he rescue my darling daughter from the dastardly duo?"

"Mom, this isn't a silent movie...you give Spencer and Susannah too much influence over my life." I waved her off and then I waved for the waiter.

My not-so-smooth-at-gossiping best friend kicked back in her chair, settling in to lay out the details. "As soon as I pointed out who he was and what he was to Harper, Cal flew into action. Wrapped his arm around her waist as if he were her shield, protecting her and letting Spencer know, in no uncertain terms, that Harper had upgraded." CJ raised her eyebrows.

"Oh! I love it." My mother clapped her hands. "God, I wish I saw it. Your father had me stuck with his old cronies. I was bored all evening. Sadie, where were you?"

"I blew that pop-stand early, I had my own celebration...don't you worry about me. Aunt Sadie is right as rain this morning." She waggled her sunglasses.

I smiled knowingly at my vivacious aunt, who glanced above me and whose own smile grew before winking at me.

"Well, this looks like a lively bunch of lovelies..." a deep voice drawled. A warm hand was on my shoulder before I had a chance to look up to see him. Cal. I wasn't startled to see him, but butterflies fluttered, and multiple magnets activated inside me before I even turned and saw his face. Like a lust-struck idiot, I immediately stared at his lips. I wanted to kiss him again.

God help me, I regretted not dragging him back to my room last night. If Spencer hadn't caught up to me and told me about his intervention with the Gwen Friday interview, I probably would've pulled Cal into a dark corner to finish that kiss—and who knows where that would've led.

Ex-boyfriends reappearing can mess up a girl's libido.

"Hello, ladies."

"Hi, Cal, won't you please join us?" my mother invited.

"I'd love to, but I can't. I have to catch a plane in a bit. I wanted to speak to Harper, if I may?"

My mother practically tipped over her seat in an effort to push me out of mine.

"Yes, please—go!"

Okay, that's not embarrassing. It was as if a boy asked me to dance and my mother was shoving me out onto the dance floor.

I cringed internally.

Cal held out his hand, helping me up, and then guiding me through the tables with his hand on my lower back. The contact was better than a shot of caffeine. He'd touched me that way last night, but in the light of day, it still affected me—seemed more real.

Oh, this was bad.

This was so bad.

It was probably the whole white knight thing—him coming to my rescue last night. Me confronting Spencer and him sweeping me away. I had to squash this.

I turned as we made it outside to the sidewalk, and he smiled down at me as if he knew the effect he was having. Was he thinking about that kiss? Was that what was behind the crinkle of amusement in his narrowed gaze? Or did he know I was thinking about the kiss?

"So, what's up?" I said, trying so hard to be casual. Just two acquaintances—okay, maybe friends. We were friends.

Friends who had kissed.

Grow up. It was New Year's—it's a free night on New Year's.

He stood back and put his hands in his jeans pockets. His casual collared, untucked shirt defined his biceps and chest as if it were just a tad too small for him. Maybe it was because I was used to seeing him in business attire. The dark blue of it did wonderful things to brighten his eyes. *And* he was wearing jeans—well-worn jeans.

Stop. Just stop.

I was falling real deep into this fairy tale bull crap.

I searched the street around us for something else that was mesmerizing enough to stare at.

"Just playing my part in saying goodbye to my girl," he drawled out.

My head whipped around, and shock must have lit up my face before I could hide it, because he let out a laugh. "Relax, Harper, I was joking. Geez, is even pretending to be my girl so scary?"

His girl.

Those two words ran through me like an unidentifiable wave.

Uh, yeah. It scared the crap out of me.

"Don't be ridiculous, I know I'm not your girl."

I crossed my arms over my chest.

He studied me as if deciding what to say next. He opened his mouth to say something but stopped. And I so desperately wanted to know what it was that I almost blurted out, "Tell me," and even had a hand ready to grab him.

"Anyway..." He rubbed a hand across the back of his neck. "Last night was fun. Let me know if you need my sub-boyfriend duties again."

"I'm sure we'll be fine. Spencer and Susannah live in Atlanta, so I doubt we will have a chance to run into them again..." Then I remembered Spencer mentioning he would be spending time in Charlotte and cringed a bit. Well, that didn't involve Cal—he'd be in Chicago anyway. "Besides, it's probably best if people don't think we're a couple. I don't want to give the impression that you are propping me up in Merlo. I need people to know that I'm doing this on my own. That it's just me, Sadie, and CJ.

"If we broadcast that we're a couple—or, um, let people think we're a...couple...they'll assume you're behind everything and it will hurt my credibility, and the credibility for all of us as women in the industry."

He stared at me. "I don't think that's true, but I don't want to start that debate again,

so—" He pulled me in, wrapping me in a warm but friendly embrace that I could've lingered in for a long while.

I imagined taking him home and covering him like a human blanket while we lounged a lazy day away, never having to stop touching him...ever. Exploring him...all of him.

Jesus. I was clinging to his back.

Stop it, Harper! Get ahold of yourself.

Wait, did he just smell me? Maybe he was just breathing.

I couldn't expect him not to breathe while he hugged me.

He kissed the top of my head.

I was probably crushing him in my death grip of a hug. Heat flooded my cheeks. It had been a while since a man held me, let alone anything else.

Ugh.

I pushed back and forced a smile—even though as anxious as I was, it probably resembled someone who was going to puke their brunch up. I certainly couldn't make eye contact. "Well, I guess I'll talk with you later this week?"

"Yes. Actually, I'd like to set up a routine time—if that's possible.

Have Amy get in touch with Dean and work something out. I think with both of our schedules getting crazy, it would be best to slice out a permanent time in our calendar."

I nodded. "Probably a good plan…"

"I mean…you could call whenever you needed me. But this would be our time—I mean, uh…a scheduled time," he added.

"Okay. I'll talk with Amy."

He took a step back. "Alright. I'll talk to you later, then."

He hesitated. And in that moment, with our stares locked on each other, it was if that kiss hung there between us—replaying in bright HD color without sound—waiting for subtitles or the background dialogue explaining what it all meant.

I broke the stare, fidgeted with my hands to my sides. "Okay."

"I know seeing your ex last night was probably the last thing you wanted to deal with, but I had a good time playing your wingman." He reached out as if to stroke my face and brushed my shoulder, instead.

I smiled. "Me too."

He glanced over my shoulder at something and nodded before stepping into a car with a driver waiting for him at the curb, and my heart sank a little as the car pulled away.

"Don't tell me it's nothing."

I jumped. I'd been so caught up in my own world of denying my growing attraction to Cal that I didn't hear the attack approach.

My best friend sauntered up behind me—her arms crossed and her trademark smirk laced with a mixture of suspicion and amusement. "Because that was about the silliest, cutest, most awkward goodbye I ever saw. For Christ's sake, I need a shot of insulin for all that sweetness I just witnessed."

I smacked her shoulder. "Shut up."

23

CHARLOTTE, NC

Harper

I stared out my floor-to-ceiling office window at the naked maples and birch trees interspersed with evergreens on the cold and rainy morning. The chill went through me as if I were standing under their branches and not in the warmth of my office—as did the bleakness.

We were a little over a month away from the opening of the season, and we weren't even close to being ready.

I was truly too young for an ulcer.

The migraine punching at my temple had me reaching for the ibuprofen in my drawer again—probably exacerbating the ulcer. I pulled out the TUMS as a chaser.

My office door opened, and I knew without looking up it was Sadie —she was the only one who entered without notice. She purposefully closed the door behind her.

Her good mood died when I looked up, concern laced her face as she pretended to draw a line on her forehead. "At least I know I will be getting you a Botox gift certificate for your birthday this year."

"I have a headache."

She lifted an eyebrow and her mouth tilted up with a smug expression. "Well, darling, if it's over a man, I'll pull up a chair and you can tell me all about it. If it's about our crew chief and our driver, well...I don't know what to tell you."

"I should've replaced him." I walked around my desk toward her, grabbing some folders off my desk. Cal was right about one thing—well, one thing I would admit to—I stretched myself too thin. I should've been more focused on the crew and personnel and accepted his help, maybe hired someone more skilled with the business relations staff to handle the sponsorships.

I should've gone with my gut and replaced him instead of keeping him on from Butler's team."

"Probably."

"I guess I'm just naïve and am used to the crew from Merrick like Wild Bill and Gus—I always watched them do their thing. Never considered what went into their jobs." I rubbed my forehead again.

"But we're a month before Daytona. Jeff has a decent record—albeit not recently, but there were more problems with Butler's program that could have attributed to their record besides Jeff's leadership." We both headed out of my office and down the hall toward the conference room. I hated my excuses even as they left my mouth.

"What does CJ say?"

"She thinks the guy's an ass—but she thinks everyone except Bill and Gus are asses. It's because she never really worked with anyone else, and even though she would never admit it, she finds the fault to be in her inability to adapt. Truthfully, I'm not sure it isn't part of the problem."

"Well, let's get both of them in the room together and see if we can try to smooth all of this out. Do you have one of your 'enthusiastic, let's work together' speeches you can pull out of your hat?"

I tossed the folders on the conference room table and walked around it, almost pacing. "I'm going to have to—it's too late to find someone now."

Amy came in with sandwiches on a platter.

In the distance, from somewhere down the hall, came the raised voices of Jeff and CJ—the two guests of honor.

"What a waste of time—we got things to work on," Jeff grumbled.

"Give it a rest. Jesus, every damn day. You can make a woman want to scratch her ears out," CJ retorted.

"Yeah, well, if you would do something about that mouth of yours, we'd all benefit."

"Jackass."

Amy gave me a sympathetic grimace as she set up the conference table. "I think it's safe to say that your next meeting has arrived."

"Wonderful."

She nodded and walked out the door.

Jeff Brooks, Butler's crew chief for the past six years, came in, smoothing out his hair and glaring daggers at CJ.

Jeff was probably in his early fifties. His muddy brown hair was close-clipped and laced with gray. He had a full, but slightly outdated, mustache that still worked for him, and glacial blue eyes.

I crossed my arms and cocked out a hip, with my stare letting them know I wasn't going to tolerate the name-calling playground crap.

"Can we sit and discuss how to make this team more cohesive and have a somewhat pleasant lunch?"

Sadie stood behind them and remained quiet, letting me deal with smoothing the bad attitudes.

Jeff had won races and even a championship in his younger years. But it had been a while, and his record with Butler was less than stellar. He chose to stay on when Butler sold to me, but I suspected it was because he knew his prospects of being hired elsewhere were slim. His qualifications were as outdated as were many others of his generation.

Crew chiefs were more like Gus nowadays—college graduates, most with engineering and computer degrees. It wasn't just about mechanics anymore. It was about fuel consumption calculations, simulators, aeronautics. Computer nerds and engineers were more the norm, not former drivers turned mechanics.

Jeff stayed. But he wanted things to stay the same, also.

And they weren't.

He held out a hand for me to shake.

"I'd like to try to figure out a way to smooth things out in the pit so we can work together and be strong for Daytona."

I leaned on the conference table and put steel in my voice. "We don't have to like each other, but we have to respect each other. We need to come out of the pit with a strong team and knowing we can win. If you two can't get past the bickering and show leadership out there," I gestured to the garage, "we might as well not show up and waste money on gas and tires."

"Sure thing, Boss Lady." As I contemplated if the moniker was given as a tease—as Cal had done before—or as a snarky insult, he walked over to stand on the other side of the conference table. Out of his mouth, the term "boss lady" seemed condescending, as if a substitute for "bitch," but he couldn't be accused of insulting me directly.

CJ and Jeff stared at each other and each took a seat.

Lord, grant me patience.

I rolled my shoulders, straightened my back, and whispered to Sadie, "Remind me why we decided to do this?"

She nodded her head, gesturing to him and grumbled, "Because of people like him."

24

CHICAGO, IL

Cal

Trey caught up to me as I was getting off the elevator on my office floor. "What does the rest of your day look like—want to grab a drink later?"

"Busy. But thanks."

"Your reaction to Fitz at the meeting…I was afraid you were going to get up and leave."

"The man is beyond dull and drones on and on. I have little patience or time for it these days," I grumbled.

"Yeah. You made that quite clear. I think you need to get out and relax. Let's go to the Hickory Room for a drink—blow off some steam."

I immediately began to shake my head. "Nah, I have a ton of work to do—"

"Man, you haven't been out since before the holidays. Your breakup with Vanessa, back and forth trips to Charlotte, and the situation with your father...the company…you're wound tighter than a two-dollar watch."

I waved him off as we walked past my assistant and into my office. Trey began to close my door, indicating he was just warming up to this lecture, when Dean popped his head in—"You have Harper's call in ten minutes, should I get her?"

"Yes, Dean, that's fine. Trey's lecture shouldn't take that long." I eyed my friend as I shifted the new folders that had been laid on my desk in my absence.

"Harper, huh? From Charlotte?"

I glanced up. "Yes. We have a call every Friday afternoon so she can update me on what is going on with the race team."

Trey leaned a hip on my desk and crossed his arms. "Do you, now?"

I aimed my eyeroll at him. "Yes."

"I'm sure that's something you could delegate to lighten your load." He leaned on my desk, in no hurry to leave. "I'd be happy to handle that for you."

He was fishing.

"It's fine. I'll handle her—I mean, I have it handled."

I could hear his chuckle before I looked up to see his shoulders shaking. I slapped some folders against his chest. "Here, you want to lighten my load—take these."

That made him laugh louder. "And when will you be heading down to Charlotte again to see Ms. Merrick? Her last name is Merrick?"

I ignored him—he damn well knew her name. He did the research for Hewitt Hardware and knew why I wanted it.

"But you didn't answer my question...when will you see Ms. Merrick in person? Are you traveling to Charlotte anytime soon?"

"I'll be heading down soon to check on the acquisition of the Fast Lane stores." I sat in my chair, crossed my legs, and folded my hands in my lap. "Do I need to give you a copy of my itinerary?"

Trey's hands went up, palms out. "No, you do you. I won't push. I think it's great you're spending time outside of Chicago."

My phone buzzed, saving me from Trey's form of tactful prying. "Harper is on telechat."

"Oh, maybe I can meet her now. I heard she's gorgeous—"

"Go." I pointed at the door.

"You ruin all my fun." Trey smiled. "I'll catch up with her later in person. That way she can catch the full experience of meeting me." He stood and pretended to dust himself off.

"Are you done?

"Tell her I can't wait to meet her."

I waited until he closed the door before I turned on the monitor and there she was, too busy to even look at the screen.

"Hello, Ms. Merrick."

"Hey—how's it going in the windy city?"

I ran my hand through my hair. Is it sticking up now? Why was I worried about my hair?

"Things here are fine." I glared at Trey. "How about with you all? Is bail money needed

yet?"

She finally stopped whatever she was working on and leaned back in her tall-back, leather executive chair. "I told CJ it wasn't in the budget. Some days I wonder if it's the only thing stopping her from killing Jeff." She was tired. It showed all over her face—her vivacity was missing. The spark was dulled.

"You look amazing today." And she did. She'd gotten her blonde locks cut shoulder length and was dressed in a dark navy blouse which made the color of her eyes even more enchanting.

That got her attention and she stared at the screen. "Um, thanks."

"I like what you did with your hair."

She ran her hand down the shortened hair, and I swore I saw color touch her cheeks. "Yeah, um. I wanted to try something more—well, just wanted to try something new." She straightened and dropped her hand, "Anyway, Jeff…"

"Why don't you replace him—"

"Because Daytona is literally next week—replacing him would cause major upheaval with the entire crew, and it's shaky around here as it is." She folded her arms across her chest and her shields were going up. "We simply don't have time—"

"Then you need to have a talk with CJ. This bad blood between them—someone has to step up and be the bigger person. A leader."

"It's not that simple." Her tone was edgy, her volume was rising. "He baits her. And he's the crew chief. He's supposed to be leading—not baiting—the driver. Why is it her burden to make things civil?"

"I understand. It's not about fault, it's about getting things to work. But you should watch your bias—" I warned. It went downhill from there, with us talking over each other.

"Seriously, I don't need this from you—" she bit out.

I held up my hand. "Okay. I'm sorry—"

"You don't know what you're talking about—"

"Harper." My voice was firm, not placating. It was enough to interrupt her. "You are in charge. If you want the truth—the burden is on you to show them what you will and won't tolerate. You aren't just another employee who has to put up with crap from co-workers. Start thinking like the person who signs the paychecks."

She glared at me. I struck a nerve.

"Jeff knows damn well he has you in a tight spot—it's why he's an ass. Would your father or any other owner put up with this crap no matter where they were in the season?"

She stared off camera, her lips were thinned, and her face was flushed. I wasn't sure if in anger, embarrassment, or what other emotion was being held back.

The man in me told me I should back off.

The partner in me told me she needed to hear this.

"You're the one in charge. Act like it. Be willing to put in an engineer temporarily to cut out the cancer. If it's something that's hurting your company, eliminate it. Don't agonize over how to fix it—move on —because he's not going to change." I debated on how to say the next bit without being any more condescending, but she needed to hear it. "He's taking advantage of you. Being in charge means being decisive."

"I know that," she grumbled.

"Line something else up. Cut him loose," I repeated. "Soon. Or others are going to see what they're allowed to get away with."

"Are we done with our pep talk for the day?" She glared.

I nodded. "I'll probably be in Charlotte in the next few weeks. I'll swing by and see you then."

"Something to look forward to," she muttered, her tone laced with sarcasm.

"Alright, well—" I started, leaning forward to disconnect. Fine. She thought I was being an overbearing ass. But this was what happened when you became interested in someone you worked with, but I wasn't doing her any favors by placating her. She needed to hear it. If she were any other business partner or employee I already would've intervened.

"Wait..." She shot up in her chair, her face washed of annoyance, the past disagreement pushed aside. "Cal...how's your dad?"

A weight lifted off my shoulders as she gave me a stay of execution, and settled in my gut thinking of my father's health. "He's okay— the new medication seems to help with the seizures, but it makes him tired. So he's not in the office often. It doesn't mean he's taking it easy and not working though."

It means he's driving me crazy.

She sat back. "Well, I hope things improve."

"Listen, I know it's lonely at the top. And I know you are still figuring things out. I don't mean to come off as your self-appointed instructor. I'm just trying to teach you things I had to learn the hard way."

She gave me a quick, small nod.

"People walked over me all the time. Especially because I was the owner's son. They try to see what you're made of. It's human nature. People are going to treat you the way you let them."

She leaned forward on her elbows; my monitor was so consumed by her soft face and her beautiful, modest cleavage, that I used every ounce of restraint not to stare at.

She ran her hand over her hair and turned her head to hide the expression blanketing her face. "I...I feel like I'm making a million wrong decisions," she whispered.

And I wasn't helping by pointing them out and shining a light on them.

I studied her. "You probably have, and you probably will. But the thing is, Harper— basing your decisions on what others may think, or overthinking them, that'll always lead to regret. But if you gather as much information as you can, take it in, ask the right questions and go with your gut, you won't second-guess yourself as much."

She considered me and then smirked. "Maybe I should have that put on a t-shirt or something."

I let out a laugh and said, "I'll look into it."

It was times like right now when being in Chicago really, really sucked, because all I wanted to do was wrap my arms around her and give her a hug. The miles between us were pretty damn inconvenient.

25

DAYTONA, FL

Cal

Daytona 500.

The opening of the season. I pulled up to the track just in time.

Being February in Florida, the weather was mild and a far cry from Chicago's blustery winds.

I breathed in the scents of gasoline, rubber, and asphalt, and the pressures of Chicago were left behind, along with my other persona.

"Mr. McBane—Cal! Over here!" Amy, Harper's assistant, flagged me down outside the back of their pit box.

I nodded my head and headed over, scanning the area, and waving at a few familiar faces before leaning down to the petite brunette and lowering my voice to her. "How are our ladies doing today?"

She pushed her aviators up on her head before tilting her head up and smiling with amusement. "Well, they haven't killed each other yet —or anyone else—so I'd say the day is still young."

"That good, huh?"

She nodded, replaced her glasses, and continued to weave through the crowd. "Harper's with the crew right now."

I slowed down as we approached their pit area so I could study the area for the blonde bombshell. The crowd seemed to part around her—the conservative blouse and slacks stood out from the polo shirt and jeans among the executives, let alone the t-shirts and shorts of the other attendees. Even with her new, more professional haircut—I could still pick her out of a crowd. And not because of the crew chief, who was waving his hands wildly as other members gave them a wide berth.

She straightened, laid a hand on a cocked hip, and her chest heaved as she took in a deep breath. Jeff was about to find out that his time for bitching was up.

"He's been trying both of their patience all day." Amy came up behind me. "Harper has a mess on her hands. Trying to keep CJ calm, and both of them in their respective corners while trying to figure out how they are going to get two hundred laps accomplished with the driver and crew chief unable to talk without cussing each other out." She shook her head.

"That bad, huh?"

"Harper is lucky if they don't kill each other before the race is over."

I didn't like the sound of that and started toward them. Amy grabbed my arm. "Don't. She doesn't like anyone interfering. Gus tried to step in and she turned on him. Poor guy slunk back to his pit area with five or six reporters trailing him—drumming up new drama about team rivalry between Merrick and Merlo for her to have to address after the race."

Jeff's face was turning a bright shade of red, but he'd lowered his voice so only he and Harper could hear. Harper dropped her head. I hated how much stress was etched on Harper's face and restrained myself.

"Uh-oh," Amy said, "She's giving him her 'sweet-as-pie' smile." She glanced at me and explained. "It's the one that basically says, 'Don't fuck with me' in a polite manner in case anyone overheard the words that actually left her mouth. Harper pointed at Jeff, and even from this distance I saw her hand tremor. She turned and walked toward us.

This man was fucking with them. Whether she thought I was being a caveman or a knight in shining armor—she was my friend, and that asshole was making her hands shake.

"McBane."

"So, I'm McBane now?"

"Cal."

"That's better. Want to tell me what that's about?" I motioned to the pit.

"Jeff's threatening to walk out of the pit box moments before the green flag."

"I thought you were going to take care of him."

"It's not like you can call up the local temp agency and request a new crew chief," she gritted out. "I'm working on it. But obviously it takes some time."

I took a step, loosening my arms, my intentions clear. "Fine. I'll have a word."

"Cal, don't. Last thing I need right now is another testosterone-fueled temper in the ring, or for it to look like I need a man to step in for me." There was more than annoyance in her voice. It was weariness —and the race hadn't even started. "It's not even about needing a new crew chief, it's about how much of a media shitstorm it will turn out to be if anything goes down."

"The man's being an asshole—" My voice was one notch away from yelling.

She glared at me and I knew she was holding on by a thread at turning her exasperation on me. I took a step back and breathed before starting again.

"Is there anything I can do?"

She shook her head, shrugging me off. "Go see Grady. He had an excellent time at the Duals and will have great positioning for the start of the race."

I didn't move.

"Anyway, I have a race to oversee and a driver and crew chief to referee. If you're not going to see Grady, go find somewhere to sit."

I stopped her with a hand to her elbow, pulled her aside out of the crowd to a shaded corner to the side of some stands. "Harper."

She refused to look at me, fidgeting with the bag I noticed she had slung over her shoulder.

"Harper?" I tilted her head up to me with a finger under her chin until I had her full attention. I became fixated on her lips when they parted slightly, and I was stuck in an orbit around her. A current flowed around us, between us. I put my hand gently on her hip, afraid she would bolt, but not wanting her to feel trapped.

The revving engines, the milling crowd, the smells of rubber, gasoline, and people, the slight breeze that pulled a piece of her hair across her forehead, and the sun that we hid in the shadows from... all were background scenery. Her lips were all I saw. I hadn't come here to kiss her. Although, I hadn't gone a day, alright, maybe an hour without thinking of finding another opportunity to kiss her, and then spent more time castigating myself for it.

But now, her hands were on my chest and I was leaning closer— my forehead inches from hers.

I moved the finger from beneath her chin to caress down her cheek, watching its progress and enjoying the sensation of touching her. Her eyelids fluttered and she let out a shaky breath—I almost gave in. I was inches from her mouth—

"Harper." Her name escaped me as if asking for permission.

She pulled back...shaking her head a bit and taking in her surroundings, then stepping out of my arms.

"Good luck." I stepped farther back to give us both some space—I needed space or I'd

take her in my arms right here among the crowd.

Her head dropped and her hands went to her hips. "Thanks." Suddenly, she straightened, and her head snapped up. "Go get a seat."

The spell was broken. My moment lost.

But damn—it *was* a moment. New Year's Eve wasn't a fluke. There was something there. I held back the dumbass smile that struggled to break across my face.

Who was I fooling...I couldn't hold it back if I tried. I was definitely going to find her when this was done, and we were going to pick this up—but more privately. I wasn't waiting any longer. She walked backwards, briefly stumbling in her heels, as she watched me stare at her mouth. My smile grew.

I winked at her. "Go kick some ass, Sunshine."

26

DAYTONA, FL

Harper

Sunshine? Sunshine? What the hell, calling me some cutesy name like Sunshine? I...I...I didn't know how to respond to that.

I walked away. Like an idiot. I walked fast so he didn't see my face burning...it wasn't a blush. It was indignation. Yep, that's what I was telling myself.

I could only deal with one man at a time, and right now it was Jeff. It wasn't because Cal threw me off my game by calling me "Sunshine."

No, this feeling in my stomach...the wobbly knees...they weren't because he almost kissed me again—or because he kept looking at my lips. No. It was because he keeps coming close to crossing the damn line.

I didn't need this—not now. Why is he messing with me?

I ran my hand over my hair.

"Harper!" Damn, I walked right by our pit box. I was walking so fast, so determined, Amy caught up with me and turned me around. "Where the hell are you going?"

Straightening, I shook myself. "Nowhere. Nothing. Where's CJ?"

"I convinced Gus to release Grady for a quick moment to calm her down before putting her in a quarter-of-a-million-dollar race car."

"Smart idea, and Jeff?"

"Up in the box, nursing a snit." She pointed above us to the box overlooking our pit area.

We walked around the back, weaving through the crew, a few sponsor representatives, and other onlookers with pit passes. I was caught by a person or two, wishing us luck. I gave a polite smile but continued to the stairs of the pit box. Enough time went by that when I reached the top of the stairs, Cal was shaking the hand of a more visibly relaxed Jeff.

"Good luck today, Jeff. We'll talk soon," he said, clapping the man on the shoulder as if they were old friends.

"Thanks, Mr. McBane..." He shifted, and even gave a half smile. "Cal."

"Have a good race."

What the hell? Cal turned from Jeff, walking back down the steps. "Harper, I came by to wish Jeff and the team good luck on their first race."

"Did you, now?"

Yeah. My smile would've given CJ's Ice Queen title a run for her money.

My toes were aching from being stomped on. Yeah, it was petty, and the fact that it seemed to have a positive effect pissed me off even more.

"I think Grady's pit is a few stalls over, Mr. McBane. Shouldn't you be wishing your brother good luck?" I thumbed in the direction of Merrick's pit and glared my meaning at him—leave.

He drew up short but stood so close we were almost chest to chest. I didn't blink and my face remained cold. His smile fell slightly as he took in my expression.

"Well, let me get out of your hair, then." Lowering his voice to a volume only I could hear, he said, "I thought an outsider could diffuse the situation by diverting his attention and keeping him distracted and away from CJ before she got in the car. That's all."

I took in a deep breath through my nose and caught his scent of cedar and sandalwood even over the smells of a racetrack and became very aware of his hand lightly touching my arm.

"We're good?"

I blinked and broke eye contact but gave no indication we were "good."

There was an increase in volume coming from the stands to signal movement in the pit area. "The drivers must be coming on the track. You should find your seat before they get started. It's going to get very loud around here very soon." I leaned forward, grabbing my headphones. "Amy has a set of these for you at your seat. You won't be connected to the team, but you will hear the race and it will protect your ears." I stepped around him. "I've got to go check on CJ and wish her luck."

"Okay, I'll see you after—"

I didn't wait for him to finish…I was already gone.

It was just about the worst race I'd ever seen CJ run. It was more like a demolition derby than a stock car race. I stood in the back of the box the entire time, arms crossed, unable to sit the entire race. I could've been mistaken for a statue.

She spun out into the wall in the last stage, even after avoiding a major pile up that wiped out half the field earlier in the race. It didn't make sense why suddenly she wrecked. Danny Fuller had been drafting her closely; all he did was bump her slightly. CJ should've been able to recover.

When the mesh cover came down, it was a hellcat that burst out. Her helmet flew off, balaclava tossed to the ground, and she climbed into the emergency vehicle to come back to the infield.

She and Jeff argued the entire race about the state of the car. I don't think either one thought about the other people who were listening in on the track scanners with the profanity that was flying between them. By the point when she spun into the wall, she was stone quiet—which for CJ was the eye of the storm.

The rest of the race, I stewed.

After checking on the rest of the crew, I climbed up to see Jeff the most relaxed he'd appeared all day. His driver was out of the race and on the way to the infield hospital center to be evaluated, and here he was, right as rain—kicked back, his hands linked behind his head as if his work for the day was done.

"It's her own damned fault. If she'd listened to me…" He shrugged to the member sitting next to him. "She's not used to people telling her she's wrong—that time's over." He rubbed his stomach, satisfied with his righteousness. "I told her not to go to the outside."

I wanted to kick him.

"Jeff, what the hell just happened?" It took extreme restraint to hold the tone in my voice to a professional level.

He casually looked over his shoulder, not lowering his chair. "What happened is your prima donna of a driver had her ass handed to her because she doesn't listen."

"Something tells me there is more to it than that." I glared at him. "If I didn't know better, I'd say you wanted it to work out this way." I walked back down under the box's canopy, not trusting myself to have this conversation among the crew or the reporters who were coming toward us. I had to get a better handle on my temper, so I made my way through the crowd toward the garage to where our destroyed car was being towed, with a front end resembling an accordion.

Almost an hour later, CJ walked toward the garage with a trail of fans and media tailing her, the mask of fury firmly in place.

"Damn," I whispered as I tried to head off my friend. I was going to need reinforcements. "Amy!"

Already a step ahead of what I needed, she shouted back, "I'm on my way." She ran for Grady, who was the only person besides me who could probably stop her from getting arrested. With his Top 10 finish, however, he was going to have to get through his interviews and sponsorship photos first.

Jeff must have spotted her gunning for him because he came out of the garage ready for the confrontation. I turned on him, throwing up my hand. "Don't—don't do it, don't even think about it," I yelled at him.

He turned his scorn on me. "Don't do what?" He threw his hand out, yelling as if wanting everyone in the area to turn and witness the show. "I'm not afraid of the brat."

As if on cue, CJ emerged from the throng that had held her back. "You motherfucker." It was a growl from deep inside. My friend wasn't just pissed. She was enraged.

She shoved Jeff from behind.

Crew members held her back—at five-foot-three inches and a hundred-and-fifteen pounds with her flame-retardant race suit on, it would seem it wouldn't take much to hold her back. But CJ was feisty, and these guys didn't have as much experience restraining her as our old crew did. She elbowed one guy in the stomach and jammed her foot on the toes of the other.

"You mother—" she bellowed. "I told you what was wrong...I told you to fix the fucking car—"

She fought them, and this time I caught her as a last line of defense. Her momentum swung me around until we were both facing Jeff, who was being blocked by crew members from other teams.

"CJ, it's okay. I'll handle him. Don't ruin your career over this ass," I said into her ear.

"Let me go, Harper." She gritted low, just between us as she wrestled to get free.

I was a good half-foot taller than my best friend and had my arms wrapped around her. She didn't say anything to me, but she turned her fury on me with a glare. She blamed me for this. Something bad could've happened to her because of this cocky bastard. Even if I couldn't prove it, he wanted to see her lose. And I let it happen.

"I'm sorry. I'll make it right," I whispered to her.

CJ didn't say a word and she wouldn't look at me. I knew my friend. She was silent because she was afraid of what she'd say to me.

But it was probably along the lines of, "I told you so..." with a few colorful words thrown in.

CJ threw her weight into her shoulders and broke my hold, but I readjusted and grabbed a hold of her again before she could move far. She tilted her chin at me, her lips tightly thinned, and her face flushed with anger. Years of friendship—of sisterhood—were called upon in that moment. "Don't." My voice was demanding now. "You will not let him bait you further. I swear to God, I will handle it."

"Harper?" Cal entered the fray.

"I got this," I shouted. My attention was caught by the media that had weaseled their way through. Cameras and microphones were hovering over the crowd that had gathered.

Shit. I wasn't one to cuss like CJ. But if there was a time and a place, this was it.

Two of Jeff's guys stood at his back as he approached and puffed out his chest. "Listen here. I've been running stock cars since before you were a swimmer in your daddy's nut sack."

Oh, shit.

CJ had a gleam in her eye that didn't bode well. Her face calmed as a new challenge had been presented.

Not the reaction Jeff was expecting.

No one got into a battle of words with CJ Lomax. A small thing like her, learned early where she could wield the most power.

Her voice leveled off, hands on her hips, she said loud enough for everyone to hear, "If you shot some of your own off once in a while, maybe you'd manage to loosen the stick out of your ass."

Cal's laughter led a gallery of others as Jeff turned an ugly shade of purple.

"CJ." Those two letters were filled with mixed emotions of a boss and a friend. The friend was laughing inside and wanted her to gut him. The boss was eyeing all the phones out recording this and cringing at all the viral videos.

Now, she stared at me, not the least bit penitent. "I lost control because that car was a mess. Then he had the audacity to yell at me for wrecking it."

She was absolutely right—both the friend and boss in me realized it —and this was what Cal was talking about. It went this far because I allowed it to.

Why was I acting like a bystander? Because of him, we wrecked our car. This was *my* team they were representing. No way my father, Cal, Gus, or any other man I respected, would let it get this far. Hell, no way any women would either—they would've had Jeff's balls in a vise grip the moment the race was over—just like CJ wanted to weeks ago.

Why was I just standing here?

"I don't need this shit—not from a bunch of fucking women—you don't know what the hell you were talking about. The car was fine. All this bitching and moaning...Murray never had trouble with the way I ran things. He listened to me."

"Yes, by all means, tell me, Jeff, how many races did Murry win last year—hell, how many did you all fail to finish?" I spoke loud and clear. If he wanted to do this publicly than he was going down that way. "Were they all Murray's fault? Or did you tell Murray the car was 'just fine'?"

There was a collective mumbling from around the crowd as if it were a high school

parking lot, and she just laid out a scathing come back.

"Because CJ's record indicates she didn't have as much of a problem with another crew chief."

"You uppity little bitch!" He lunged and the men behind him grabbed him. "Think you're the shit. But you don't know dick."

CJ stepped beside me, widening her stance, clenching her fists— sisters defying the bully on the school grounds. "I know enough to look at the records from last year—"

"Gus Quinlan carried you last year. You ain't shit without him now. No daddy to carry Harper. No Gus to carry your sorry ass. You don't have anyone to shout your praises or capitalize on the novelty of your tits and ass being in a race suit." Then he turned his hatred on me. "And you, Princess Barbie...you think the world owes you...daddy's girl playing big Boss Lady…how many times did you have to spread your legs to—"

Someone pushed past me, past a struggling CJ. The swing at Jeff was fast and furious and then he was flying backwards, the crowd absorbing him and his friends behind him. Gus and Grady suddenly appeared from nowhere. Gus and another Merrick crew member began pulling Cal away from Jeff. Grady was lifting CJ back from the rest of the crowd before she landed a punch and got suspended.

"Whoa, man," Gus said as two men grabbed Cal by the arms and Gus got in front of him, breaking off his line of sight to Jeff. "It's all good. You got him. It's fine."

Jeff struggled to stand, pushing off his friends and the crowd he had fallen against. He held the side of his face, dazed, warily searching for whoever landed the punch.

"Come on!" Cal bellowed at him. "You cowardly piece of shit." Gus and the other men were struggling with a now pissed-off Cal, pulling him back as the crowd grew and was closing in.

Grady tightened his grip on CJ, stopping her from jumping into the fray. He swung her around. "Not today, darlin'. Cal's got this." He scooped her up, glaring the promise of death at Jeff, and nodding to me and Cal.

"Amy," I yelled, "—go with them." I ran over to help Gus, and jumped in front of Cal.

"Cut it out! You're going to get yourself arrested. He's down. It's over."

Cal was a red-faced beast being held back by two men, trying to get a lock on Jeff again.

"CAL!" I yelled at him. "Stop! It's over. You ended it. Now calm the hell down."

I put my hands on his chest and he stilled, staring down at me as he slowly straightened.

"Please, stop. Things are fine. I'm fine. CJ's fine."

Behind me, I heard Jeff mouth off about suing as he was carted off by a group of unsympathetic members of other garages. Gus yelled back, "I suggest you get the hell out of here."

"Fuck you, Gus."

I turned, leaned my back into Cal and said deadpan, but with as much volume as I could find inside me, "By the way, Jeff—you're fired." I added as much Carolina twang as I could muster. "And as God is my witness, you'll be lucky to work amusement park go-karts when I'm done with you."

2 7

DAYTONA, FL

Cal

Harper held onto me, and without further words we plowed through the media circus shouting questions and hovering with their cameras and lights around us. When a few became overzealous, I held out my arm to block them—my adrenaline still running high, my expression still hard—and they quickly realized I wasn't going to tolerate being stopped. Security finally arrived, running interference as we sought refuge in a sea of motorhomes.

We were safely in her motorhome when I realized she was trembling and pacing the aisle. Her arms alternated between crossing over her chest and then fisting by her sides.

She refused to look at me and when I stepped into her path, she held up a hand but said nothing.

That's when I saw it.

The lip quiver.

"You shouldn't have done that. Dammit, Cal. Now this became an even bigger issue." She turned on me, but it wasn't just anger—it was the crash of adrenaline and a mixture of other emotions that battled for dominance and that had her shaking.

"You better call your lawyer because he's going to come after you —he's going to come after me—after us—"

Harper began moving around in the small space. Flitting from one area to the other, unsure what to do with herself.

"Goddammit! She could've been hurt, or worse," Harper said, the slightest hitch in her voice.

That was it.

"I should've been the one to deck him," she gritted.

"Then you would've been the one with the swollen knuckles and in trouble with those in charge. That wouldn't have helped the team. And nothing personal, but I pack a meaner punch." I gently tugged her into my arms. It didn't take much effort. She buried her face in my chest.

"She could've been hurt. I shouldn't have let him near our pit box today. We would've been better off with me as crew chief than that disaster."

I kissed the top of her head. "You had no way of knowing it would've gone that bad."

Cool wetness seeped through my shirt and reached the skin of my chest. Tears. She was giving me her tears. Trusting me with them. I caressed her hair. Kissed the top of her head. "Hey, now. It's over."

She settled after a few moments and was quiet, resting her head against my chest. "She's my sister, you know. Besides Grady, I'm all she has. I've been taking care of

her—I've had her back for so long. And I failed her. I let her down. You should've seen the expression on her face..." She pushed back. "I'm going to rip him to pieces. By the time I'm done with him, he won't be able to find a job changing oil at the local Quick Lube."

"You made that clear, don't worry. He has a long list of people who will make sure of that."

After taking a moment to appreciate the fervor in her tone and the commitment in her statement, I lifted her chin with my finger and leaned down until she made eye contact.

"Enough." I kissed her forehead. "We should go find my brother and CJ before they either find Jeff and tear him to shreds, or put on a full make-out session for the media."

"My money is on the make-out session." Her eyes were bright with tears as she wiped her fingers under each of them.

"They do have a problem keeping their hands off each other."

"Well, you McBane boys are irresistible." She placed her hands on my chest, not to push away, but as if to steady herself. I'm not sure who was more surprised at her comment, but I know my smile was bigger than hers.

"Are we now?" My voice was low, my eyebrows teased, and even I will admit there was not a small amount of seduction in it.

"Cal?"

"You seem pretty good at resisting me."

"Not really..."

We gravitated toward each other. "Lord knows I'm having a hell of a time resisting you..."

She was silent and stared at my chest. "You know just talking this way is a very bad idea."

"Why?" I ran a hand along her cheek, tucking a piece of hair behind her ear. I didn't miss the way she leaned slightly into my hand.

"It just is—"

So I went for it—cutting off her words, cradling her face and kissing the velvety sweetness I always knew her lips would be— plump, soft, and a bit salty from her tears.

Not being able to stay sweet, one of my hands went into her hair, tugging it gently.

My other hand splayed across the small of her back.

Closer.

She responded instantly, tilting her head, opening her mouth so I could tease my tongue inside. She gripped my shirt tightly before traveling up my back, pulling me closer to where she wanted me.

My hand glided down her beautifully rounded ass—fitting perfectly over the globe, before pulling her closer and squeezing it gently. I wedged my leg between hers, rubbing it against her core and almost losing it when she wrapped herself around me—good God, this woman was everywhere, and I still wanted more.

I kissed her neck down to her collarbone.

"Cal."

Hell, yeah. Moan my name. But I wanted more.

Harper was taller than most women, and closer to my mouth, but it didn't stop her from yanking me down to where she wanted me. I loved how strong she handled me. Nothing demure or shy. So contradicting from the sweet, sunny image she gave everyone else.

Our kiss was a dance of lips and tongues, quickly finding a rhythm, while we glided over each other's bodies, the rest of us falling into step. Our frantic movements backed her against the counter, just as a sudden jolt brought us to a stop.

Our heavy breathing caused us to break apart, and I stared at open, swollen lips and then her breasts. I couldn't stop touching and exploring her curves. "I've been full-on obsessed with you since New Year's Eve, just so you know."

She leaned into me, her breasts rubbing against my chest, causing my cock to want to return the action. "Obsessed. I like the idea of you being obsessed with me."

I lifted her onto the counter, cupped her face, aware that her breasts were now closer to eye level, but stopped myself from diving right into them.

I kissed her again—her lips, her jaw, her ear, and down her neck.

She moaned and it was my undoing.

My cock was rock hard, and I swear the rumble came from down there and up to my vocal cords as a release of sexual tension. I growled —yes, like a fucking caveman.

I know...cliché. But it was completely instinctual.

I moved my hand from her back to around her front, just below and in position to cup one of those glorious breasts that have been taunting me—

Bang. Bang.

"Harper, are you—"

Fuck...

154

"Harper, it's…it's Dad."

Double fuck.

Harper flew off the counter, out of my arms, and straightened in front of me—thankfully blocking the bulge in my pants.

"Just a minute, Daddy." She shoved me into the back bedroom whispering frantically, "You can't be here!"

"Why?"

"Because I don't want him to get the wrong idea about us."

"Is there a wrong idea about us?"

Her eyes got impossibly wide with a mixture of frustration and exasperation, and she forced me backwards into the bedroom. "Shut up and go, hurry!"

I turned. "Jesus Christ, it's like I'm in high school getting caught by someone's parents."

"You *are* getting caught. Shut up and go."

I closed the door, laid my back against it, and tried to mentally convince my cock to die down. I'd have thought hearing Mr. Merrick's voice would've cured it already.

"Hi, Daddy…why are you here?" I heard a muffled Harper say as the door slammed shut.

They walked farther inside. "I saw what was going on with CJ and couldn't find her. Then Gus told me about what happened later at the garage. Wanted to check if you two were okay."

"Yes, we're fine. CJ is cooling her heels with Grady, and Jeff managed to slither out of here with his male anatomy still attached, though it was a close call." The captain's chairs squeaked. "If Grady and Cal hadn't shown up, I wasn't sure I was willing to stop her."

Merrick chuckled. "Well, Jeff is an ass, so he probably would've deserved it. Heard Cal got a piece of him. Don't know why you kept him anyway…"

Silence.

"Not like there are many qualified people lining up for us to choose from, let alone a decent crew chief."

"You should've known better. The man's always been a chauvinist. But it's water under the bridge. That's how you learn, I suppose."

Well, that was condescending as hell. Did I sound that way when I talked to her?

They were both quiet, then, and I wondered what Harper was thinking.

"What are you going to do now?" Her father's voice was flat.

"Don't know. Working on it—but nothing that will resolve quickly. Guess I'll have Bobby come down from spotting if I have to—"

"Don't be ridiculous. Bobby isn't a chief. You need a backup plan. Don't you have a backup plan? Anyone in the wings? What about Clive?"

"Yes, he's a technician, but he threatened to walk when I asked him to step in." Harper's voice was chafing from her father's insertion.

The captain's chair made a noise as I heard him get up. "Fine. I'll make a few calls." His tone held a hint of exasperation as his footsteps led to the door. "I'll get a few guys over tomorrow to your office to talk with you. Scooter or Toby from Energy Blast could come over for the season. I can afford to loan them to you until we find someone else to take—"

"No!" Harper's footsteps followed her father toward the door. "I don't need you to step in and solve this for me—"

"Don't be ridiculous, Harper. You can't race in Cup without a competent crew chief—your team should've started off smaller in the Energy Blast series and worked this shit out before taking on the grand scale of the Cup and looking so foolish."

"I thought you said you weren't going to interfere with Merlo." Her voice was low, but there was a slight shakiness in the tone.

"I wasn't going to, but you're up shit's creek. Jeff screwed you." Her father's voice was that of an exasperated father. "With how this is going to be perceived, he got the last word. It's all over social media—not only is it going to hurt your image, it didn't do you any favors in convincing someone to come work for you. CJ already had a reputation, and now you look difficult to work with—you accused a veteran crew chief of endangering a young, rebellious driver with negligence. Who do you think other chiefs are going to believe, darling?"

"I don't care if I have to go out and change the damn tires on CJ's car myself—"

I was inches away from going out there and backing her, but I knew she'd never forgive me.

"—you told me to go and figure this out myself. That's what I'm doing."

"Fine." His voice was resigned. "I'm just trying to help. But you need to get a grip on your team."

And with that the door slammed.

2 8

DAYTONA, FL

Cal

I gave her a moment before I opened the bedroom door.

"Sunshine…"

"Just don't…" She walked past me to the door to her room. "You need to leave."

I tried to drag her back into my arms.

She pulled back from me. "I have to go find CJ and see if she's okay."

"She's a grown woman and more than likely in my brother's motorhome. I doubt she wants to be bothered right now." I tried to put some levity in my tone as I let her go. "Harper, everything will be fine."

She stared at me with the weight of the world crashing down.

She was wallowing in failure, a feeling she wasn't familiar with this evening. She wrapped her arms around herself. "It wasn't enough to have failed my best friend, probably torpedoed my team, humiliated by an asshole in front of an entire industry, and be castigated by my father, I had to do it in front of the first man I've ever wanted to impress." She grabbed her hair in her hand. "Please leave so I don't humiliate myself further this evening by breaking down again in front of you. At least give me that."

"I can't."

Her entire body deflated in front of me.

"I can't because I care for you too much to leave you alone right now. You need someone to lean on, and I need to be that someone. I gathered her in my arms and pressed her to my chest. She was limp for a moment, and my heart picked up speed, afraid I had made a mistake. "I can leave—" and suddenly her arms wrapped around my waist and she held on—tight.

She buried her face in my shirt as if it would quiet the sobs, and I stayed still and quiet. "Let it go, you'll be stronger for it on the other side."

I stroked her hair and kissed the top of her head.

After a few moments, her body began to relax and her breathing and crying slowed. I moved her to the couch and sat her across my lap, wrapping my arms around her.

"I know your father didn't present the idea in a positive light, but why not just borrow someone from Merrick? You can do a better search, give CJ time to gather a few good races under her belt—"

She held up her hand to stop me and said, "Don't." Standing suddenly, she broke the embrace and continued, "Please, don't. I'm tired of people trying to manage me. Is there something about me that screams I need rescuing?"

I bristled. "That's not what I'm saying at all. If you would just stop and think of the big picture—"

"Put yourself in my shoes, Cal. How would you feel if your father tried to manage every move you made in your life? Made every decision? What college you went to? What you majored in? Hell, who you dated? And didn't even consider what your aspirations were."

A hole in the Earth opened and my demons escaped, surrounding both of us.

They danced and taunted as her words struck me.

159

Then her words found my own open wounds—the weight, the moroseness, the apathy I'd been carrying was defined.

I did know what that was like—to lead a life on someone else's leash, with expectations and goals, under a predestined plan you never consented to follow.

The difference was, she was rebelling against it. I was drowning deeper into it. And possibly, I was doing the same to her.

"My father is frustrated, not because I took CJ and left." She spoke to the universe around us, not to me. "I'm not a piece on his chessboard he can move or predict..." She flung out her hand, walking past me, "Or a crowning achievement he can line up on his shelf with his trophies—" She turned to face me. "And to make it worse..." She paused, her lips thinned as she locked them tight to stop them from quivering as she tried to gain control before speaking. "I'm failing and he will think that's a reflection on him."

Her body was trembling with the effort it took to contain her emotions. She turned her back on me.

I'd never felt so incompetent—so utterly incapable of caring for someone. I had no words of wisdom because, hell, she was doing a better job trying to lead her own life than I was, at the moment.

I stood and slowly stepped close so she could sense me approaching her. I put both hands on her shoulders from behind, leaning down to whisper in her ear, "I understand more than you know." Wrapping my arms around her, I buried my face in her hair, breathing in deeply. "And I truly think you are one of the gutsiest people..." Tears fell onto my arms. She was crying again.

I was screwing this up.

"Shh..."

"I hate crying. I really do." She eased up and pulled back just enough to wipe her tears. "If I'm not laughing, I'm crying. I swear. Any negative energy enters my body, and it flows out in tears." She looked down, using both hands to wipe her dampened face.

"Dammit," she whispered to herself. "I'm sorry. I'm such a freaking mess." She turned to look at me. "Thank you for being here for me tonight. Thank you for stepping in with Jeff and..." She looked away. "I'm sorry if I seemed to attack you earlier."

"Attack me anytime you feel the need..." My words had a deep inflection, and it earned a blush and a smile. "It was a joint assault, let's say."

"I don't think it is a good time for us to continue this—" She motioned between us.

"I'm a mess, this situation is a mess. And I don't want to complicate things further. I hope you understand. I don't have the head space for—"

I cupped her face and gave her a reassuring smile. "We're fine, honey." I nodded. "I may continue to want to see you naked, but I value the friendship and partnership...almost as much as I desire you," I teased.

She pulled back with another point to make. "Plus, there's Grady and CJ..." she added.

"Yes. Who knows how the children would react..." I said with a serious, deadpan face. "They may act out."

That earned a bigger smile to negate her bloodshot eyes.

She was still beautiful, maybe more so because I saw more of her now.

"Goodnight, Cal."

I tilted my head in acknowledgement before leaning in to kiss her cheek and taking in one last deep breath of her scent. Even after a day at the racetrack, my girl still smelled like wildflowers in the sun. I stepped back.

"Goodnight, Harper." I snuck one more peck. But as I walked down the stairs and turned to close the door behind me, I saw my girl close her eyes and gently touch the cheek I kissed. No, we weren't just friends—not at all.

29

CHARLOTTE, NC

Harper

Aunt Sadie flew into my office clad in a rainbow of color and with her white, large-frame sunglasses perched on her head. "Hello, dear niece, I came to take you to lunch."

"I'm sorry, but I'm slammed." I surveyed my desk and gestured to the piles. "I have a conference call later to prepare for, a boatload of reports to review from marketing, and a proposal from Amara, and the pesky job of finding a new crew chief."

One thing I took away from my conversation with my father was that I begged one of our engineers to fill in temporarily as crew chief until I could secure someone else. As casual as I was acting, it was keeping me up at night.

Sadie flung herself into a guest chair in front of my desk and moped. "I hardly ever see you anymore. At least when you worked for Merrick, we'd have lunch together."

"First of all, it's your fault I'm in this position. Trust me, I'm reminded of that more than once a day. Second, you have an office here, Sadie. If you came and worked *with* me, we could have lunch every day while we work."

"Darlin', you know I don't do well behind walls." She batted her lashes at me. "Besides, do you really want me around people all day? I'd be a major distraction." She patted her perfectly coiffed hair.

She had a good point, and I shrugged my shoulders as a knock sounded, catching both of our attention.

"Harper, Spencer Pruitt is here to see you." Amy's eyes widened, asking *what should I do?*

Spencer stood behind her, making it impossible to make an excuse not to see him without being impolite.

I briefly glanced at Sadie, whose eyebrows reached her hairline and who crossed her legs, settling back into the chair, making it clear she wasn't going anywhere.

Great.

I pointed at her and whispered low enough for her to hear, "Not a word, and don't you dare go chasing down CJ. Let me see what he wants."

She tilted her head in acknowledgement but didn't promise anything.

"Sadie," I growled. "You can leave."

"Fine. I won't tell CJ...right now."

"—or Gus..."

"He's not even here," she mumbled.

I shook my head, praying for divine patience. "Come on in, Spencer."

I checked my wall clock and motioned to my aunt. "Don't you have somewhere to go? Surely someone of your notable social status has something they could be doing...or someone they could be annoying besides me—why don't you see if Dad wants to have lunch?"

"No, I'm good." She tucked her hair behind her ear and straightened. "I believe this situation has my full attention."

Spencer walked in with confidence, swagger, and a smile that used to melt my heart. He was collegiately handsome with a swimmer's build, perfectly styled hair, wearing a tailored navy suit, baby blue shirt, and an expensive tie.

But my heart was now filled with mixed emotions and a dash of wariness.

I walked from behind my desk, but not reaching out for a welcoming hug. "Hello, Spencer, what a pleasant surprise." I wasn't sure if I meant it, but it was a reflexive response.

I plastered on my most gracious smile that disguised all my thoughts, and extended my hand for him to shake. He stared at it in confusion, then glancing over his shoulder and noticing Sadie, he took the hint. I wouldn't be offering a hug or any greeting of a physical nature.

His expression was warm and reassuring. "Harper, so glad you had time for an unexpected visit."

Not like he gave me much choice. "Please, sit. What are you doing in Charlotte?"

Spencer acknowledged Sadie as he sat, nodding at her. "Hello, Ms. Sadie."

"Spencer," Sadie said, his name drawn out and through narrow side-eyes as if he were there to steal company secrets—or my heart, again.

My aunt was an adorable chihuahua with the bite of a pit bull—she appeared harmless, but those who knew better knew not to piss her off, and went after her family at their own peril.

"Ms. Sadie, you look lovely. I've heard so much about the company you and Harper have started. Congratulations."

My aunt pursed her lips and made a non-committal, "Hm." She wasn't impressed with his ass-kissing attempt. "I bet you have," was said under her breath, but loud enough for me to hear.

"I'm sorry?"

"Nothing, I heard you were engaged, Spencer. Congratulations." She perked up, ready to increase the level of discomfort in the room.

And she did—Spencer shifted. "We aren't engaged." His glance shifted swiftly at me and back to Sadie.

"Oh, that seems to be what Susannah is telling everyone." Sadie's false confusion was blatantly obvious. She wasn't exactly in line for any acting rewards.

I cut in— "You mentioned you had business in Charlotte?"

He was happy to be rescued out of Sadie's web, and turned his energy to the smile he gifted me, inching up in his seat, toward my desk. "Well, I was in town on business and decided to stay for the evening and see if an old friend would be free for dinner?"

"Okay, but why are you here seeing Harper?" Sadie's voice had an edge of impatience now.

I narrowed my eyes at her to cool it.

She waved me off. "Pfft."

Spencer caught the exchange but continued, "I was hoping Harper would be the old friend who would have dinner."

"Old friend—" Sadie'd had enough. She stood abruptly and Spencer jumped out of his seat, putting the chair between the two of them. "Old friend...are you kidding me with this sh—"

"Sadie!" I barked, while keeping my teeth clinched.

If I wasn't so concerned for bloodshed in my own office, I would've laughed at my five-foot-nothing, middle-aged aunt intimidating a full-grown man. But men often don't know how to handle Sadie because she really didn't have a filter and was a bit of a wild card.

"That man," she stepped up to my desk, pointed an accusing finger at Spencer. "Breaks your heart, gets together with one of your so-called friends because her family has a net worth almost as big as yours—" She starts walking toward him, and he inches back from her. "Then shows back up here when you get your shit back together—" She walked away, glaring at him and shaking her finger. "No. Nope. Nopity-nope-nope."

"Ms. Sadie, that's not the case. I swear. I'm here on business."

"What possible business could you have with our Harper?"

"I heard rumors that her sponsors are spooked, and that Dupree is causing trouble. I came to see what I could do to help." His hands flew up in a show of surrender, and then down over his groin as she got closer. "I swear, I mean no ill will toward her or your company."

"Of course, Dewey the Devil's Spawn is causing trouble—he always causes trouble—this isn't news." Her hands were on her hips and she leaned toward him menacingly, which was awkward since she only came up to his chest.

"First of all, your former crew chief ran straight to Dewey the moment the showdown at Daytona ended—"

"How do you know?" Sadie was cross-examining him on the stand.

"I was there."

"Why were you with Dewey?"

"Dewey hired our company to handle the PR and marketing for their team. I was invited down to the race." That got my attention.

"It wasn't my idea—" He held up his hand. "However, Dewey asked for me specifically.

I'm not an idiot. I knew it had to do with you." He shifted. "I sat with them during the race. Dewey poked around asking about the end of our relationship—if we still talked, etc., and I told him we hadn't talked in years until New Year's Eve when Susannah and I saw you."

He walked over to the office windows. "There was a lot of boasting and blustering about how they were going to crush you all, now that you didn't have Merrick to stand behind or Gus to bolster you. But then Dewey kept hinting about someone giving things a nudge here and there, and that you would self-implode, and it was going to be satisfying to watch."

A shadow fell between us as he looked at me, and anger flashed over his face and his hand went to his necktie, smoothing it down. "I wanted to wring his neck, Harper. I did. But I just smiled and played along. I did it to see what else they would confide in me."

Spencer was a good-looking man—I'd be lying if I said he didn't still affect me. I used to love laying on his chest, listening to his heartbeat as he played with my hair—I felt cherished, special. Until I no longer was.

Sadie stepped forward—I'd forgotten she was even there—and began to clap. "Good job—'A' for effort." She leaned in front of my desk and crossed her arms over her chest. "Now what are you really up to?"

Oh Lord. "Sadie—" My aunt's audacity was reaching new highs.

Spencer's tone was clipped. "Nothing. I'm genuinely trying to help." He turned to me. "What I'm trying to get to is Jeff ran straight to Dewey, holding the side of his face, swearing down the heavens on you, Cal, and the lot of you all. Talking about suing you—arresting Cal." He held his head up high with his nugget of information. "I'm pretty sure it was a setup. Dewey's chest was puffed out like a peacock. He embraced Jeff like a man coming home from battle and walked off with him, smiling."

Sadie wasn't changing her stance. She wasn't moved by anything he said.

"Think about it, Harper—I'll bet you, you won't hear from a lawyer. Cal won't hear from the police." He threw his arms out wide. "Because Dewey won't want an investigation. He got what he wanted —your reputation is damaged, you're down a crew chief as soon as the season opens, and it all went viral. The only thing he was disappointed about probably is CJ didn't throw the punch and get suspended."

"Harper, I'm here because I want to help. I want to show my support." His tone seemed so earnest, like the ones I remembered when we were young college kids. They flooded me with memories of high, fanciful emotions, and reminded me of times when I thought my future with him was so bright and laid out before me.

It was sweet to catch a glimpse of the memories of the bright colors I used to think my future with Spencer was painted in, even if it was just for a moment. Then reality threw the tears this man cost me on that watercolor image, and it bled straight through the pages.

As if he read my face, he reached for my hand "Harper..."

Sadie cleared her throat. "Thanks for the info. We got it from here, Spencer."

His back was to her, so she missed the flash of frustration that was quickly masked as he straightened, while being reminded that she was still in the room. He drew in a breath as he turned, ready to explain himself.

"And how will Susannah feel about you being here—offering Harper your support?" My aunt wasn't letting it go.

"She won't want Harper being hurt by a vindictive asshole."

"She's a vindictive—"

"Sadie, please. Stop." I practically barked at her, begging for deliverance. "Spencer, I appreciate the offer. We're okay, really. It's a rough patch—all new teams have them, and we are finding our way. But I promise you we're getting back on our feet."

"Nonetheless, I would like to discuss how I can help. Besides consulting for you on promotional and marketing opportunities, I could also introduce you to potential sponsors. Surely no team wants to turn down a sponsorship offer that knocks on their door."

"Who wouldn't want to talk sponsorship?" a masculine voice drawled, seizing all of our attention, all three of us turning to see Cal, his arm leaning on the doorjamb, his hand in his pocket, the picture of understated dominance. A smile lit his eyes at his perfect timing as they scanned Sadie, Spencer, and landed on me.

He straightened and strolled in. "I know Ms. Merrick would take advantage of every opportunity offered to Merlo." He leaned down to kiss my cheek, and whispered in my ear, his breath sending shivers over me, "Hello, Sunshine, reporting for white knight services."

"I didn't know you were in town?" I whispered to him and attempted to control the enthusiasm of my smile. "I didn't know you had the ability to flash at a moment's notice?"

"Only when unwanted ex-boyfriends are sniffing around." He winked before drawing back and taking in Spencer and Sadie.

He extended his hand to Spencer. "Spencer, right? Good to see you." He shook Spencer's hand, giving him a cursory glance before turning back to me. "Didn't mean to interrupt the business meeting. Just wanted to surprise my girl." He reached for my hand, pulling me to his side. I played into it, placing my hand on his chest and gazing at him briefly—not masking my genuine happiness in seeing him.

I dared to glance at Sadie, who was doing a poor job at disguising her amusement and elation at Cal's timing.

"Good to see you again, McBane," Spencer said through a forced smile and trying not to track my hand as it ran from Cal's chest, down his arm and to lace with his hand. "Yes, I'm afraid I had the same idea

—trying to steal her away from her office and take her to an early dinner in a little while."

The predatory focus in Cal's gaze locked with mine as he brought my hand to his lips and kissed it. I hadn't realized I was biting my lip until someone cleared their throat.

Cal blinked as if remembering Spencer was there. He turned, tucked my hand into the crook of his arm as a gentleman would, escorting me out of the room. "I thought you were located in Atlanta?"

"Yes—" Spencer began.

"Is your wife with you?"

"Girlfriend, and no, not this trip—it was strictly business."

"Ah. I see." Cal walked me back to my desk, and away from Spencer. "I overheard some of what you were telling Harper. You have a sponsorship deal for her?" He leaned against the side of my desk and crossed his arms as I sat in my chair.

"I'm a vice president at Anderson, Wickam and Associates."

Cal sat blank-faced, waiting for Spencer to explain what that was supposed to mean to him.

Spencer continued, a bit of tension in his tone. "It's one of the top marketing and PR firms in the southeast."

Cal nodded. "And how do you think you could help Merlo?"

Sadie stepped between them. "They're working with Dupree." She scowled at Spencer.

Spencer stepped closer to my desk. "Yes, but I'm here to explain why and to give you information that could probably cost me my career."

Sadie waved her hand at him.

"Well," Cal turned me, and leaning over my chair, kissed me on my forehead. "I tell you what." His voice was deep, intimate, but loud enough anyone could hear. "Honey, why don't you finish your meeting with Spencer. I have some business a few blocks from here. When you're done, I'll take you out for drinks and dinner—okay?" He used his thumb and forefinger to tilt my chin to him. "Text me when you're ready." Then he gave me a quick peck on the lips. I wasn't prepared. I didn't see it coming.

It was so quick—too quick. But it scrambled my brain like nothing ever had.

He stared at my mouth as he pulled back and turned to walk toward the door, and I had to grip the armrests of my chair to stop myself from leaping after him.

Was this for Spencer's benefit? Was he messing with me? Did he have to kiss me, or did he want to kiss me?

Dammit—I hated that gleam he had in his expression because it confused me even more. Now he was smirking because he saw the effect he was having on me.

Cocky bastard.

I stood, walking over to him and touching his shoulder, letting my hand trail down his lapel.

"Okay," I breathed in a tone I saved for sexier moments, and Cal's eyes flared a tad wider as his hand rested over mine.

Two can play at that game, buddy.

He grabbed my hand, squeezed it, and stepped back.

Oh shit...Spencer and Sadie—yeah. Totally forgot my ex and my gossipy aunt were watching this exchange.

Oops.

Cal leaned over to Sadie. "Aunt Sadie, it was wonderful seeing you— I'd invite you out with us, but I'd like to have Harper to myself tonight."

Sadie's smile was blinding as she waved him off. "Not a problem, darling."

Spencer maintained a sour smile. "McBane, nice to see you again."

"Likewise." Cal smirked. He walked back and took my hand, pulling me close again as he wrapped his arm around my waist, and he touched his forehead to mine. "I'll make reservations, Sunshine. Finish quickly, I missed you." Then, he whispered in my ear, "I'm serious, call me when this clown is gone. I want you to myself."

And I'll be damned. I didn't know if it was still an act, if he was teasing, or if he'd really missed me—I didn't know if I wanted to know the truth. I just know that those words had my heart racing faster than any car CJ had ever driven.

He slipped his hands in his pockets and didn't bother closing my office door as he walked out, as if he'd known I'd take pleasure in watching him walk down the hall.

Sadie snuck up behind me and whispered, "Well, I'd say that's a much better offer."

Satisfied that Cal had things under control, even though he left the building, Sadie decided she no longer needed to chaperone, and left without even a backward glance at Spencer.

Spencer and I sat at the small conference table in my office and discussed the team and what he may be able to offer.

He discussed everything from cross-promotion with other women sports organizations, to some of his clients who may be interested in sponsorship deals.

"So, how long have you and McBane been an item?" he casually asked, as I went to my desk to retrieve some marketing reports.

I shrugged and reached for my intercom. "Amy, could you ask Pete to join us? I think he may have some ideas to add to what we're discussing."

That helped us steer the conversation back on course.

Predictably, as soon as I pulled in other employees, Spencer discovered he had to get going and suggested maybe we could talk later that week.

When I reached out to shake his hand, he held it close in both of his. "Maybe we can catch up at the next race. Dewey invited me to join him again."

"Maybe, but I'm usually pretty busy those weekends. Tell Susannah I said hi," I said, as I pulled my hand out. A breeze of pain flew across his face.

Yeah, well, seeing you isn't a barrel of monkeys either, buddy, I thought, as I forced a smile.

As he walked out the door, he gave one last glanced over his shoulder, almost as if to say something, but then thought better of it and kept walking.

I went back to my desk, ready to finish my day and pack up. I grabbed my cell to text Cal, but slumped back in my chair for a moment, pinching the bridge of my nose and closing my eyes.

Why did Spencer show up—now—out of the blue?

Nope. I shook my head and took a deep breath. Him being here brought up memories of me at a time in my life when I felt very lost and uncertain—when what he wanted and what I wanted out of life seemed to be blurred.

My door flew open, and CJ burst in as if she had a battalion behind her. "Is he here?"

My unbidden cavalry had arrived. Sadie had been busy.

Her mouth opened and her face was hardened. She walked into the office and slowly closed the door. "You okay?"

I folded my hands in my lap and tilted my head, realizing, "Actually, I am."

She crossed her arms and kicked out her hip. "Where's the asshat?"

CJ didn't always hate Spencer. She didn't like him—but she didn't hate him. For CJ there was a big distinction. But she couldn't forgive disloyalty.

I cleared my throat, shrugged my shoulders, and rolled my neck, ready to get back to work. My vision was now clear, and a path was rolling out before me.

"Don't know. I'm not concerning myself with him." I pulled out my cell and texted Cal. "*I'm done*". I considered typing "*Come and get me*" but figured that was a bit too obvious.

She straightened and scrutinized me some more.

"I'm fine, CJ—honestly. You can call off the troops. There won't be any ass-kicking needed today."

She tilted her head. Disappointment crossed her face as she pulled out her phone and tapped a button and put the phone to her ear.

"Hey. Yes, she's fine." She paused, listening. "No. He's not here." More listening. "Yeah."

Pause.

"Don't know." She studied my expression as if waiting for me to break.

I let out an exaggerated huff and threw out my hands. "For heaven's sake, I'm not going to fall apart. Now you are insulting me."

Pause.

Still watching, she said, "Alright. Tell Gus I have it handled." She turned her body away from me slightly.

"Yeah, yeah..." Then she whispered, "Love you too."

She sheepishly looked up, motioning to her phone. "Grady."

"Well, I'd hope so or you'd have some explaining to do..." I smirked.

CJ slipped her phone in her back pocket and casually dropped in the chair in front of my desk. "So, I hear Cal is in town."

I closed out the files on my computer. "He is."

She nodded, studying her nails. "Grady wanted to call him and tell him Spencer was here."

I studied my agenda for the next day. "He already knows."

"How's that?"

"He came by and asked to take me to dinner...in front of Spencer."

She stilled, glanced at me, her legs crossed, a half-smile and brow crooked, waiting for more information. "And..."

"Nothing—I need to call him back so he can take me to dinner, I guess."

"You guess?" She barked at me. "Come on—you're my best friend." I expected her to stomp her foot in frustration. "You're supposed to tell me what's going on. I can't figure you two out, and Grady refuses to gossip with me." Her voice took on a petulant tone. "It's frustrating."

"It's nothing. We're friends." ...who have kissed. "He's letting Spencer think it's more." I smirked. "But it's not." *Or maybe it is. Maybe it could be?*

She folded her hands in her lap and tilted her head. "Not buying it. You two have scheduled weekly calls. Whenever he comes to town or a race, he comes to see you first—not Grady. He finds a lot of excuses to spend time in Charlotte. You both have grown very cutesy, and bicker like a married couple."

Cal's grown cutesy? I shrugged. "He invested several million dollars in the company, CJ."

"Grady says he never showed that much interest in their Indy team when he was the driver—and they were located in Chicago." She pointed at me. "Face it. You're more than a financial investment." She leaned forward, her elbows on her knees, "And when are you going to admit that he's more than a pain-in-the ass investor?"

"I really don't have time to figure it out right now." I shuffled more papers around. "But I'm having dinner with him—"

"Yes, you are. You have a date." She teased with the word "date." The lilt in her tone was bothersome.

"Don't start. Remember, we're partners—"

"Is Sadie invited?"

"No."

"Am I invited? No. Is Grady coming—no. Sounds like a date to me."

"He caught me stuck with Spencer. He invited me out tonight in front of him—"

"Screw Spencer."

I held up my hand. "Really, CJ. I don't have time for anything right now. Even if there was something between Cal and —I couldn't think of a worse idea."

She threw her hands in the air and leaned back in the chair, letting out a groan of frustration.

"I kind of have a lot on my plate—"

"Then make room on the plate—because, girlfriend, you need to indulge a bit. And from the way Cal looks at you, he wants to feast," CJ said.

And now I was hungry—but it wasn't for food.

30

CHARLOTTE, NC

Cal

I lied—just a little white lie—but from the looks of it, the lie was well-placed. I didn't have a meeting down the street from Harper. Truthfully, it was outside of Charlotte and was earlier this morning. I'd planned on stopping by and seeing her at the office—until I saw Spencer standing in her office.

Spencer—what a pretty-boy name. Spencer Pruitt. While I sat at the coffee shop down the street, I texted Dean, and after asking him to change my flight to tomorrow morning, I instructed him to do some digging.

I didn't like seeing him in Harper's office today. Not at all.

It was a split-second decision to stay for the evening and fly out tomorrow. Yes, I know it sounds territorial. But I was giving him no reason to linger.

At least I didn't pull up a seat in her office and insist on sitting in on whatever fake excuse for a meeting he planned to have.

I was pretty proud of myself for leaving the office with him still in it.

Besides, she didn't seem unreceptive to my ruse—so I'd assume she was accepting of it all.

I arrived at her favorite restaurant, ordered a bottle of merlot for us to share, and waited.

How should I read this dinner? I told her I missed her—I had. I missed her face, even though I'd seen it on our teleconference calls. I missed touching her—even if earlier it was part of a role I was playing. I told her I was serious about taking her to dinner.

I had told her I wanted her to myself.

Hmm. That may have been giving too much away?

Screw it.

I took a deep sip of the merlot. "Well, something must be weighing heavy on your mind. I hope everything's okay?" With just the sound of her voice, I knew telling her I wanted her to myself was an understatement.

"It is now." The warmth of her smile was enough to lighten my week.

I stood and pulled out her chair as she took off her jacket, laid it next to her purse, and sat.

"I hope you weren't waiting long—CJ ambushed me before I could leave," she said, arranging herself and not quite meeting my eyes yet. There was a beautiful shade of pink on her cheeks, and I wondered if she'd been rushing or if it was a blush.

"About?"

"Spencer being in the building." She placed the napkin on her lap, regal as always. I poured her a glass of wine and handed it to her. "And wanting to know why you showed up. Thank you for ordering the wine."

I tilted my glass to her. "You're welcome. Figured you'd need it." I took a sip. "Did you tell her I have Harper radar? Especially when you need stand-ins to fend off dastardly ex-boyfriends." I put the wine down and waited for her reaction.

"Oh, don't worry, she's definitely Team Cal."

"Yeah, I've gotten that impression," I said. "So, how did the meeting go?"

She shrugged. "Fine. I guess. It was just weird. Before New Year's Eve, I hadn't seen him since we broke up a few years ago. Plus, I think he was more interested in finding out about you, anyway."

The waiter brought us our menus and told us the specials.

I leaned forward on the table. "Should I be flattered by Spencer's interest in me?" I smirked.

"I think you left an impression."

"I think he doesn't like the idea of you moving on."

She shrugged, staring at her wine before taking another sip. "He moved on."

The words were soft, slightly bitter and a bit sad. But as she lowered her wine glass, the emotion was gone. "If he wants to throw some business my way, I'm open to it. But he doesn't have a right to anything else."

I sat back, studying her.

"Don't look at me like that. With the way everyone acts in regard to him—you've already figured out he broke my heart."

"And he's a fool."

"So was I." She shrugged. "I was young, ready to change my whole life for him. Become a Stepford wife and everything—"

"Seriously? I can't picture that."

"Can't you? Small career until I had children and then it would be country clubs, social standing, and charity committees—whatever was necessary to help my husband's career," she said straight-faced. "Looking back now, I cringe at the path I was going down."

It was a gut punch. I wanted to rip his—I clenched my teeth, remaining silent.

She paused, took another sip, and stared at the stem of the wine glass.

"We were together all through business school. We'd been talking about getting engaged even and had come home to visit my family." She played with her silverware and I was gripping my knife. "I think he was planning on talking to my father—to ask permission." She took a sip of her wine.

"The problem was he'd expected me to conform to his path—his

177

plan for our future. My friends and family didn't agree with that idea and made it clear. It was a mess. It got intense. It became a 'me' or 'them' situation."

She played with the stem of her glass and then stopped and took in a deep breath. "He was interviewing in Atlanta and a few other cities at the time. He gave the ultimatum that either I left Charlotte with him or we broke up. When I wavered, he left a note saying I didn't have enough of a commitment to our relationship that he would need from someone he'd plan to share his life with. And that was the last I heard from him."

"Jesus, how could any man walk away from you?" And I don't know who was more stunned at that admission—her or me.

Her shock quickly dissolved into a sad smile to mask her still-lingering hurt. "That's why CJ wants to neuter him, and Sadie offered an alibi."

"I'd hold him down for her." I joked, but there was little levity in my tone. I finished my glass, waving off the waiter as he approached and refilled our glasses myself. "I regret being so nice to him."

"Trust me, your civility was digging deeper than any insult you could've laid down. It was as if he didn't signify being a threat—and that would hit him hard."

"Let's talk about how wonderful I am and how excited you were to see me today." I held up my wine glass in a toast.

She smiled—a true, beautiful, the sun-is-shining-down-on-me smile, and even a small giggle snuck out.

And my world aligned—because I put that smile there. It was one of the best gifts I ever received, and my sweet girl didn't even notice the value of what she just gave me.

We talked the entire evening about everything and nothing—nothing about Merlo, Grady,

CJ, or my family, or Chicago, or McBane. In fact, we were so busy talking about classic rock versus millennial rock music, that I parked and walked Harper up to her penthouse without discussing it.

When we reached her door, there was a brief pause as we both realized what it may imply and stared at each other. She fished out her key.

"Would you like to come in—"

"Well, it was a fun evening—"

What?

We both smiled awkwardly.

"It wouldn't mean that we—" her face flushed a brilliant pink. She unlocked and opened her door.

I held up a hand. "I wouldn't presume anything." I tilted my head in jest. "Although, I'm not opposed to anything. But seriously, I wouldn't jeopardize what we have by pressing you. I really enjoy spending time with you, Harper."

"Me too," she said, so softly I almost didn't hear it. But then she gestured me inside.

"You act like enjoying my company surprises you. Should I be insulted by that?" She'd put her purse down on the back of a sofa, kicked off her heels, and walked into the kitchen.

I followed her, leaning against a counter just inside the kitchen doorway.

"It's just—" I shrugged as she opened a cabinet and reached above her head for something. Yes, I noticed her skirt lift, exposing more of her legs. And I'm not sorry about noticing.

"Well, I don't feel comfortable around many people—" I softened my tone. "Not completely comfortable."

"And you do with me?"

I crossed my arms and gave a stiff nod. I blinked and my face warmed from my admission. "Yeah, I do."

She froze. Coming down off her toes with two glasses in her hand and the sweetest surprised expression on her face. "Why?"

"Why, what?"

She carefully placed the glasses on the counter, and she searched my face for the explanation. "Why do you feel comfortable with me?"

I straightened and stalked toward her. Stalked. I realized I was cornering her in her kitchen. It was natural, being with her.

There was the cliché about being a moth to her flame.

That wasn't it. I knew the fire that drew me to her, could burn me. But like a phoenix, it would be what I needed to rise and be renewed.

Because that is what she did to me—she set me on fire.

She held her ground, flicking her gaze down to my lips, and that was all the invitation I needed. I cradled her head in both my hands wanting to erase how any man ever made her feel less than precious.

I lowered myself and tasted her lips, her arms gently settled on my forearms, furthering the connection. The chemistry between us hadn't given me a moment's rest. I grazed my tongue across the bottom of her lip; a shiver went through both of us as she moved her hand to my waist and then tightened.

This. This was more. I pulled back, daring to look at her and caught by the blue of her eyes as they widened a fraction, springing the trap.

Jesus. What…what has happening.

I traveled my hand up her neck and she leaned into my touch as my thumb caressed her cheek.

Her eyes fluttered shut.

"Sunshine…" I whispered on a breath.

She kissed the inside of my palm as if I were special to her and I was engulfed. My hands dove into her hair, my tongue dove into her mouth and I savored her. She ran one hand through my hair and the other over my back—she wanted me.

I kissed her cheek, then over to her ear. I gently pulled open the neckline of her blouse, allowing my kisses to travel from her ear to her collarbone. Her breathing grew heavier and when my hand brushed breast, a moan escaped. It made me feral, instinctively cupping her breast and swiping across the peak, just to hear more.

"Oh…" Her lips fell on mine again and I went for the buttons on her blouse. So intent on getting to her breasts, I was caught off guard when she started to kiss my neck and Jesus Christ—she was so delicate, licking and teasing behind my ear, it gave my cock ideas.

Oh, hell, I had so many ideas.

The immediate one involved lying her on that big sectional sofa in the other room, just a few mere feet from us and me on my knees—

Whoa.

I pulled back. I was breathing hard with the effort it took to stop. But if I didn't, we weren't going to—and I sure as hell wasn't going to have her regret this tomorrow.

Her breathing was just as heavy, but she knew what I was doing without explanation. Slowly, she covered the back of my hands and pulled them away, stepping back.

The connection was cut and something vital was lost.

"Wow. Um..." her voice hitched. She sucked in a quick breath.

"Yeah, that's what I was afraid of." My voice was ragged, and I ran a hand over my face, trying to bring myself back to reality. I tried to pull her close to me, to hold her. But she stepped back farther, holding up a hand.

"I know we—I know I was...um." She put her hand to her forehead.

Fuck.

"Please, Harper. Don't—"

"No, I...I was right there with you. I just don't think we should do this." She waved between us. "Thank you for slowing—stopping us."

Fuck.

"I didn't want to spook you and I think I already fucked that up. Harper, trust me—stopping took every ounce of willpower—"

She held up a hand to me. "I know. Clearly," she emphasized the word, "I didn't have any. It's probably better if you leave." She began walking to her door. "I...we can't do this. I...it's not a good...idea."

I stood tall and had to take a minute to gather my emotions, level my head, and put my heart back in my chest. My head dropped so she couldn't witness the struggle as I drew in a deep breath.

What to say...I didn't regret it, so I'd be damned if I apologized. "I'm not sorry, Harper. I won't apologize for kissing you—for wanting more. But I sure as hell don't want you to regret me." I leaned over, kissed her cheek, I dragged my hand through my hair, said, "Good-night, Sunshine," and walked out.

What happened was a promise of something more than chemistry.

She wanted to be stubborn.

Fine. I was patient.

I had to make sure I kept reminding her of what we could be—if she'd only try.

31

CHARLOTTE, NC

Harper

After my evening with Cal ended so abruptly, I spent the weekend contemplating if I'd made a mistake shutting things down with us. It had been the first glimpse of excitement and wonder that I'd felt in...I don't know how long.

He made me feel alive—and not just at that moment—whenever we talked. Yes, he could be arrogant, but he was sharp. When I stopped being prideful, I'd learned from him.

But I think the most important thing I'd received from him— besides toe-curling desire—was that need for more.

More.

I wanted this team to be more. More than just a bunch of women proving men wrong—that wasn't our purpose. It was about empowering and fulfilling our own goals.

I began doing what I set out to do—I began to think past my own expectations and outside the box.

Go big or go home—it's one thing my father drilled into me. But I think even he would be shocked at what I proposed to do.

Cal's nickname for me stirred in my memory—Sunshine. Lately, I'd been sliding into rain clouds—giving up the bright colors for drab navy pants suits and cutting my hair to a more professional length.

What was going on with me?

I crossed my arms under my chest and vaguely heard CJ repeat my name. "Harper, are you okay?" She and Sadie strolled in the room to meet with me.

I turned and faced two of the most important people in my life. Glancing between them, I decided to speak the truth. "Yes. I am now. This," I motioned to the entire building, "wasn't what we set out to do." My voice laced with frustration.

"What do you mean?" Sadie asked.

"This…this daily damage control…waiting for someone to sweep in and help us, trying to figure out what our next move is before it's too late to make it." It was my own ineptness that I was lashing at.

I stood behind my desk and braced my hands over it. I straightened and smiled at my red skirt and favorite red Louboutin heels, I usually saved for special occasions. I wanted to feel the power today.

"We said we were going to march to the beat of our own drum. We weren't going to necessarily do things the way the old guard did —remember?"

"Yes, but we haven't gotten to the position where we can even operate soundly yet," Sadie reminded me.

"Screw that," I said.

Both my aunt's and CJ's brows shot up.

I walked around to the front of my desk and leaned against it.

"The old guard doesn't necessarily want us to play—so, let's shake things up—starting with the crew chief. Wait until you hear who I have in mind. It's time to show these boys how unpredictable we really are."

We called Wild Bill, an employee of my father's, and CJ's old mentor, to get the number of a man my father had a fallout with years ago.

Daddy would be fit-to-be-tied if he knew I was even contemplating talking to him—let alone if I hired him.

Bill was on speaker while we told him our intentions. "You know he's been courted by almost every team out there, even some European ones. He always says no—insists he's retired."

"Doesn't hurt to ask a question," I said.

CJ studied me—and I allowed my determination to show in my stature and tone. Bill blew out a breath. "I'll make the call. See if he'll meet with you. But, Harper, I thought you and your Daddy made up—this won't go over well. He may see this—"

"My father told me to do whatever was necessary to make this team successful. If he was in this position, I don't think he'd do any less."

"Alright. I'll call you." He hung up and my blood hummed with the possibility already set in motion.

"Okay, I want to brainstorm new sponsorship opportunities and what we need to do to go after them? Think outside the industry. Think outside the box. I don't want to reinvent the wheel, but I'm tired of competing for the same big pieces of cheese and scrounging for scraps. Let's get the team together and discuss it."

A few minutes later, my phone rang.

"Hey, Harper." It was Bill. "He wants to meet with CJ alone. Can she come out to my house—"

CJ jumped out of her seat as if her butt was on fire.

Her head snapped up to me with the excitement of a child who just caught Santa at her house; she stared at me expectantly.

"Go!" I waved her out the door.

Bristling with a jolt of energy, she ran out the door.

My smile was so wide my cheeks hurt. Just knowing we had motion—we were onto something new—something fresh that could shake things up, it was invigorating.

Now, if we could just keep it going.

Jackson Groves was the epitome of someone's grandfather. With a balding head he hid under his trademark ballcap, he was of short stature, had gray stubble, and a pot belly he earned from years of beer and the past few years of retirement, yelling at the races from the solitude of his recliner.

He hobbled into the garage the next afternoon with CJ walking a respectful half step behind him, her hands fidgeting and her face expectant.

I strolled over to greet him, "Mr. Groves, it's great to meet you."

He surveyed me up and down. Not salaciously, but just taking my measure. "So, you're Everett's girl?" he drawled. Most people would walk right by him at his favorite Cracker Barrel restaurant, but any race fan worth their weight knew he was racing royalty. His easy-going gait, Carolina accent, and always-present baseball or trucker hat—he was someone who would fade into a crowd on a track.

I stood tall and said, "Yes, sir. I'm Harper Merrick." Disliking that I wasn't being identified as my own person but humoring the older gentleman.

He tilted his head toward me. "Your daddy and I go way back, he tell you that?"

"Yes, sir. I remember hearing."

A small smile snuck out on his face. "You know we don't talk anymore?"

"Yes, sir. I do."

"You know why?"

"I don't believe anyone knows except the two of you."

He gave a quick nod.

"Does he know you're talking to me? That you're thinking of hiring me?" He peered at me from under his bushy eyebrows.

"I haven't made it his business, no."

He studied me some more. "Hm." He walked around me, taking in the garage. I glanced

to CJ, who shrugged a bit. The men were gone for the day, and the garage was quiet. Jackson walked over and ran his hand over the backup car we had parked across from the car currently being worked on for this week's race.

He motioned to CJ. "Whose idea was it to come see me—you or her?"

"It was mine, sir. I'm sure you heard about what is going on with our personnel issues."

A small grin showed before giving me a sharp nod. "Oh, yeah…I think everyone saw that recap." A small hoarse chuckle rose out of him. "Jeff's an ass. Not right for the girl either."

I glanced at CJ who, surprisingly, didn't take offense and remained quiet.

He continued to stroll around the garage. He disappeared under the hood of the car.

"Mr. Groves. We need—"

He leaned a hand on the car. "And how do you think it would go over once it comes out that you hired me? Your daddy would think it's like inviting a fox into the hen house."

"Mr. Groves, my last name may be Merrick, but trust me when I tell you I am my own person. I do not answer to my father…or any man."

He nodded his head once in acknowledgement, continuing to walk around, inspecting but not saying much.

I walked up behind the older man, leaned behind him, and said, "To be clear, Mr. Groves—that includes you."

He stepped back, raised his eyebrows, and for a split second I feared I may have insulted him. Then he straightened, and laughter spilled out of him so fast I thought his stomach would make a sudden appearance as well.

"Oh, Harper, we're going to get on just fine. And call me Jacks." He patted me on the back and reached up to leave it on my shoulder as he turned me back to CJ. "Don't you worry. This ol' man isn't here to ruffle any feathers." Then he smiled a mischievous smile. " 'Cept maybe your daddy's. Because he's going to have a conniption when he finds out what you just did hiring me." There was a distinct twinkle in his eye.

CJ's face lit up like Christmas morning. "So, you'll do it!"

"Mr. Groves, um, Jacks? Are you willing to come out of retirement—"

He stopped and all seriousness washed over his face as he took turns staring both of us in the eye. "I will give you one season and that's it." He pointed at us. "I spoke with Bill and CJ, and I'm intrigued enough to give you a season and watch what you make of it. I have a few conditions and want to bring on some of my own people, including a young driver I want to CJ to mentor."

I nodded like a bobblehead. "We can discuss it."

"I've been enjoying my retirement and frankly, I'm too old for the pace and stress this job demands." He placed his hands on his hips. "I'll help you find a more permanent chief for next season and I will get CJ through this one."

Then he grabbed CJ by the shoulders, braced his legs and with a calm, but serious tone said, "Darlin', you are a very talented and determined driver, and that's one of the reasons I'm agreeing to this—along with the fact that Bill is one of my best friends and he thinks of you as a daughter." He held up a finger and pointed at her. "CJ, I respect you." He turned and pointed at himself. "You respect me. We are going to get in a few tussles. However, don't even think of catching one of your *legendary* attitudes with me. Because I have no problem throwing it back at you. And I'm not as nice as Bill. Disrespect me one too many times and you'll end up with someone like Jeff or find yourself off the track. Got it?"

CJ cleared her throat and muttered respectfully, "Yes, sir."

Well, damn.

"Alright, Jacks. Let's go discuss things in my office."

"Sounds good. I'm going to take a look around, and I'd like to talk with the crew tomorrow."

He started to walk off and turned back to us as a thought occurred. "Also, Harper—I want a clause about CJ mentoring my driver. If she goes, I go."

Uh-oh.

CJ said, "It's not a big deal. I can handle her."

He winked at me and walked off.

I whispered to CJ, "I think he could ask for my kidney at this point, and I'd give it to him."

"You have two of them—you could spare one."

"My father *is* going to have a conniption, but I can't pass up the opportunity to have him help us out. Because this is a major feather in our cap—the publicity alone—"

"I know." CJ was as giddy as a girl on her first day of school. Excited, nervous, and wanting acceptance.

We fell silent.

"CJ, this has to work—"

"I know. I promise you—it will. I respect the hell out of Jackson Groves. I would never do anything to jeopardize him being here. I would never want him to think poorly of me."

"Did he agree to the salary amount? I hadn't even asked about that."

She waved it off. "He wasn't concerned about it. Actually, his only request was that I mentor a girl who was working in the lower circuits. He said he was going to discuss it with you, but he really wants me to take her under my wing like Bill did with me."

"You good with that?"

"Yep. Haven't met her yet but shouldn't be an issue."

I crossed my arms over my chest, feeling the checkmark on the box of my mental list of obstacles to overcome. I clapped my hands together.

"Okay, I'll meet with Jacks and then put out a press release announcing our new crew chief. When this news hits—this is going to help with everything—the sponsorships, our reputation. Having him with us is a huge deal. Now you need to kick some ass on the track."

"Uh, a call to your dad may be a good idea too."

"Eventually, I will." Nothing was going to deter my mood today. Not even another disappointment from my father.

32

CHARLOTTE, NC

Harper

The next morning, I called my dad at home, hoping any reaction he had to me hiring Jacks wouldn't be office fodder. My father took the news surprisingly well. "You do what you have to do. Pretty impressive that you got him off his ass, I guess." It was pretty mild for Everett Merrick. "At least you got a crew chief now." It was a short conversation that ended with him handing the phone to my mother, and I took it as a compliment.

I shook my head, trying to lower my pulse rate from the anticipation of breaking the news that I hired his nemesis in what turned out to be a very anti-climactic confrontation, when Amy came over the intercom.

"Spencer Pruitt is on line one for you..."

And there went my pulse rate...

Why? Why was he calling? And why was the world landing him back in my path now when my life was already complicated?

"Hello?"

"Hey, Harper! I'm glad I caught you." His voice was coming in over a speaker, as if he were in a car.

"Hi, Spencer. What could I do for you?"

There was a slight hesitation. "How is everything going?"

"Busy. Lots going on." I stood, restless. Because that wasn't a lie, and this was not something I had time to unravel.

"Right. Well, I was on my way to the office and wanted to see if you had to time to meet this week? I'll be in town for the race, of course."

"As Dupree's guest…yes, I know." Damn, that sounded petty. I didn't want him to think I was jealous. I just wanted to get off the phone.

"Yes, well, business is business. But I wanted to float some names and ideas by you. So I thought we could—"

"Spencer—"

It must have been in my tone because he said, "Listen, I've seen what you are up against—"

"Spencer, we're fine. Things are going to settle. We have a new crew chief who will have them eating their insults." Shut up, Harper.

"Yes, I heard. Wasn't Jackson Groves one of you father's rivals? How'd that go over?"

"Not as bad as I would've thought," I said. "But he's been unpredictable these days."

"Huh. It's no secret your father and I didn't get along—still don't know what I did to get on his bad side. Maybe he's softening in his old age. Maybe I can get into his good graces now that I'm not an immediate threat. Let McBane take on that role."

I didn't respond—come to think of it, my father didn't have issue with Cal.

Interesting.

Spencer switched topics. "Did you get a call from the people at Brownsmith

Food Services?

"Yes, it was actually a very lucrative deal." Reminding me why going through all of this potential headache with him would be worthwhile. "Thank you for introducing us. Between that deal, and adding Jacks to our team, things are starting to look up around here."

"Harper. Hold on."

The phone was quiet for a moment and then he returned, this time without as much noise in the background. "Okay, I had to pull over for this conversation."

"What conversation is that?"

He let out a sigh. "Harper, what happened between us—" Oh hell. I didn't have time for ex-boyfriends. I barely had time for my current— no, he wasn't a boyfriend. I don't know what Cal was—but if I didn't have time for Cal kisses, his hands, and everything that could come along with them…I certainly didn't have time for Spencer's trip down the memory lane of regret.

"What happened is in the past." There was no disguising my impatience. "There's no point digging it back up. I'm sure Susannah can't be thrilled about you hanging around Charlotte."

"What happened *is* in the past. And just as I told Susannah…we were all friends. You're starting a new risky venture. If any of our friends were starting a new business, we'd be there supporting each other. When Amara started her firm, didn't we refer people to her— send her first clients to her? When Jason started his investment group, didn't we all support him? I remember hearing about you pulling some strings for Jason's girlfriend to get an interview at that news station, and you didn't even like her. How are you any different?"

I closed my eyes and pinched the bridge of my nose.

"I can't work on the cars for you, I don't have millions of dollars to invest, but I can at least help where I can," he said, and his tone went from calming and persuasive to annoyed. "Christ, Harper. I've always wanted you to succeed—to be happy. Why the hell do you think I even left—" He abruptly stopped talking.

Softer, he continued, "Just because things didn't work out with us, doesn't mean I stopped caring about you. I'd like to at least be friends. I'm not going to stand by when others are trying to tear you down. I can't."

I took a moment to process what he said.

"I appreciate it." I was confused over how it made me feel but as he pointed out, I did need people in my corner.

"I'm happy to help. Now, listen I have a few other contacts I'm working on—including Tri-State. Maybe we can meet with them and you can dazzle them?" He teased.

"That sounds good. We could arrange a dinner for when you and Susannah are in town," I said, making my point. "I'd like to see her." If this was going to work, I needed to include Susannah in on this, even though the thought of spending time with her made me cringe.

There was a slight pause before he replied, "Sure. I'll see what I can arrange. I better get to work now. Maybe I'll catch you at the track this weekend."

"Okay, sure."

"If I don't—good luck this weekend, Harper."

"Thanks."

And I hung up as another weight settled on my shoulders.

33

CHARLOTTE, NC

Harper

There were a few moments in life where time comes to a crawl, keeping emotions on edge to further solidify and define the memory of the life-changing event.

This was one of those moments.

Charlotte—our hometown track. No better place for magic to happen. Jacks and CJ worked out some kinks over the first few races together and now the team was running like a well-oiled machine Jacks had created and wielded.

"That-a-girl...you got this," I whispered low as if I were sitting next to CJ, and not in an owner's suite above pit road.

This was the precipice of a fulfilled goal; a dream being met for both of us.

It was the edge of glory.

"Lomax and Griffin are pulling away from the pack..."

I listened with one ear on a special headset giving me the play-by-play as Jacks spoke to CJ in what would be a defining moment in our team's history.

My professionally manicured nails dug into my palms, and my jaw hurt from clenching it, as I shifted back and forth in my designer heels and prayed silently for my best friend as she flew by on the final lap.

And all I could do was stand still and wait for time to crawl by—or in this case, drive by. She was so close. The team would survive if CJ lost, but if she won...

I'd done my part—this team may be held together by figurative duct tape and a prayer, but it was racing. Now, it was in the hands of fate, and my driver.

CJ did what she did best—she raced.

She drove like the hounds of hell were on her bumper, and the wings of Aries were on her tires.

CJ was battling at the front of a field of forty-two race cars going 160 mph.

All I could do was sit and wait. Without hearing her voice or seeing her face, I knew...I could picture my best friend's mouth slowly tilt up and the gleam in her eye...

She had this.

"Harper..." Someone was trying to get my attention. Was that Spencer? I waved him off.

CJ edged up past Griffin on the back straightaway, going into turn three, ready to take it like a slingshot.

"Last lap, battle between CJ Lomax and Anthony Griffin going into turn three..."

The announcer's voice faded out. I didn't need the commentary to see they were tagging the hell out of each other.

CJ's grit was being tested. At these speeds for over three hours of racing, a simple brush of metal could end the race for either of them, and a quarter-of-a million-dollar car could end up as scrap metal.

I focused on CJ's car, my muscles tensed and my lips barely moving with a mixture of prayers and concealed curses. My best friend was fierce, but the other driver was good. They barreled down the stretch to the checkered flag, and it was the moment of truth—would Jacks's hard work, CJ's talent, and a blessing of luck be enough for us today?

I blinked and the suite erupted. But my mind didn't register the noise.

That was it. Over. Done.

It took me a moment to catch up to reality and realize…

We'd won.

CJ pulled it out and we won by a nose.

Not until a set of arms were around me, shaking me, did I realize— we did it. We won. Our first win as a newly formed team.

"Congratulations, Harper!" Spencer had me in a bear hug, practically picking me up off the ground. "Merlo's first win! Hell, yes!"

Another set of hands wrapped around me. Sadie pulled me out of Spencer's arms with a quick glare, and hugged me, then another set wrapped around us…and another…

Instinctively I swept the area around me. I knew he wasn't here. He was in Chicago. For a fraction of a second, I'd wished…well, it didn't matter.

CJ finished coming around the track and headed to the finish line. My best friend was burning out her tires doing her victory donut, smoking up the track. The noise in the suite and beyond was a muffled crescendo that seemed to be growing and deafening. I pulled away from the celebrating group and grabbed the headset from the chair as I turned toward the door and walked out, down the stairs. I held onto the railing as my legs wobbled.

I pushed the button on the headset and spoke to my driver, "CJ— darlin', I think you've done the impossible…"

"What's that?" she said.

"You've left me speechless."

"You have until I get to Victory Lane to think of all the different ways to describe how incredible I am. I kicked ass tonight!"

"I'll see you there. Congratulations." Amy caught up to me and we made the quick walk toward Victory Lane, dodging well-wishers and reporters.

Months of bolstering, clawing, and inflated self-assurance—it was all worth the expression on CJ's face as she got out of her car, stood on the door, and thrust her arm in the air. She pointed at me, and our silent communication of appreciation was exchanged before the crew doused her with champagne and grabbed her off the car.

My cheeks hurt from smiling so hard.

A vibration rang in my pocket—my heart knew who it was, and it gave me a bolster of energy. I pulled out my phone, ignoring the pandemonium around me.

Cal: Congratulations, Boss Lady.

Those stupid words made the back of my eyes burn. He knew I hated that moniker, which is why he did it. It was reassuring. It was arrogance, teasing, and flirting. It was condescending, focusing, and complimentary.

It was what I needed—and like all things involving me and Cal McBane, it was complicated.

3 4

CHICAGO, IL

Cal

Merlo Racing.

"Hell, yes!" I pumped my fist.

Alone at home in my den, I'd like to say I was relaxing, kicked back in a sectional, jean-clad legs propped up on my coffee table with a beer in hand.

But I wasn't. I'd been pacing round the room, my hair a mess with my hand running through it—and when CJ passed that fucker Griffin, I almost lost my mind.

How had Grady handled it? Last year, watching from the sidelines and while CJ raced, how had he watched other men go after her on the track and not want to tear their heads off afterwards?

"Serves you right, fucker!" I yelled at the screen before grabbing my phone. So excited for Harper, and so pissed off I wasn't there. It figured, the one race I missed was the one they win.

Son of a bitch.

Dad's treatment was starting soon in preparation for the surgery, and I'd been working almost seven days a week so he would feel I was ready to take over everything.

But I wasn't going to think about that—not tonight.

This was Merlo's first win.

And I was in fucking Chicago.

I was smiling too hard for my girl to think of anything else and focused on sending her a text—grinning like a fool.

Jesus, were my hands shaking?

The cameras focused on CJ as the team celebrated, and she waved around the champagne bottle and laughed. I was happy for her and waiting for what was sure to be a sickening-sweet display of pride and affection as soon as my brother got out of his race car and sprinted over there.

Grady may be driving for a competitor, but when out of the car—hell, even when he was in the car—he was first and foremost in love with CJ Lomax.

Whipped, was what he was—and he didn't give a damn who thought it.

It filled me with a strange sense of pride and even more annoyance that I wasn't there to experience it firsthand. I zeroed in on the blond bombshell in the background as she stopped smiling and dodging the champagne as she slipped her phone out of her pants pocket. Her celebratory smile turned into a smirk—she'd read my text.

She glanced up and seemed to be putting the phone back in her pocket when she suddenly pulled it back out. Even from a distance, the camera picked up the tilt of an eyebrow as she typed out something before slipping it back and turned back to the celebration.

Harper was cut out of the camera shot as Grady arrived to sweep CJ off her feet, twirling her around and practically throwing her in the air.

Wait! Pan back to her.

Damn anticipation—waiting for that data to fly through cyberspace and arrive on my phone was killing me.

The camera panned out capturing more of the team, Harper included. Gus had come up and given her a massive hug from behind

—lifting her up and spinning her around as if it were his first win, and more of the Merrick team swarmed them.

Spencer Pruitt—the little shit—came up behind her, talking with her, touching her, and smiling down at her. He and I were going to have to have words.

My phone dinged with the texted I had been anticipating.

Harper: Thanks, Asshat.

It would've made me laugh, but the asshat was the one standing way too close to her in Victory Lane, as if he had a right to be there. As if he were part of the goddamn team. And I was cooling my heels in fucking Chicago—alone.

I tried not to take out my aggression on the piece of technology in my hand as I typed out my reply. Trying to stay light, flirty, and fun.

Cal: Wow. That's the thanks I get? Let's try again...maybe something along the lines of "Mr. McBane, I could never have done it without your guidance, wise advice and encouragement."

Fortunately, the trackside reporter wiggled between the asshat and Harper to get to CJ. I couldn't see Harper's reaction to my text but would've sold a large holding of McBane stock to have caught it.

I didn't, however, have to wait for her reply.

Harper: Bite me.

Oh, so we're going to play—I can do that, and I smirked as if she were there for me to tease.

Cal: Whoa. That's not how a nice southern young lady should be talking to her mentor. Do you kiss your mom with that mouth?

I checked the television screen. She was still there in the background—but no Spencer.

Good.

My phone dinged and I grabbed it.

Harper: Bless your heart for worrying about my mouth. Trust me, my mamma is fully aware of what it is capable of saying. I've got to go wrangle CJ and your brother before they start 'celebrating' in front of the paparazzi and I have to pull out the hose.

I chuckled as I typed back.

Cal: Good luck with that.

I paused, debating what to say next. Because I couldn't let her go without saying it.

Cal: I am proud of you. Even if it sounds condescending as hell, surely it's something you can bear hearing.

I was on a roll of being a grade A ass. And now for the finale...

Cal: Wish I was there to celebrate with you all. Have fun—but not too much fun.

I should've let it go. Damn, why did I say that?

There was radio silence and I thought she signed off. Then she did one worse with the next volley she sent—she firmly put me in my place.

Harper: Thanks for the congratulations. And thank you for the guidance, advice, and friendship.

Friendship?

What the hell, friendship?

Friends don't do the things we did with our tongues. But I didn't say anything—not yet. That was a conversation we were going to have in person, when I can remind her of the difference between friends and more than friends.

35

TALLADEGA, FL

Cal

Harper Merrick was a queen as she stood in the team's Talladega pit box overlooking her subjects below, observing the practice runs. I drew up short and caught my breath. She was so stoic and alone, I was thrown at what a breathtaking island she'd become.

With my father's increasing absence at the office, it was harder to get away and find an excuse to fly to wherever the race was that given weekend. My father finished his treatment, and there was a waiting period before he could have surgery, so my parents decided to travel to Talladega and see Grady race in person. It was a lifesaver since it gave me an excuse to see her.

I needed to see her.

We talked almost daily—either by phone or video conference. Seeing her on a screen just wasn't the same. I needed the opportunity to hold her again.

There was just enough breeze to catch a rebellious strand of her hair before she pulled it behind her ear. From behind her mirrored aviator sunglasses, she scanned the area, taking in everyone below her, but giving away nothing. I knew when her gaze zeroed in on me, when she softened her features and shifted her stance, even though we stood with an ocean of asphalt and people between us.

My God, just a few feet above me and she seemed so unattainable. It had only been a few weeks since we were together. But now, I raised my hand slightly, a young man unsure of his approach.

A side of her mouth lifted before she shied away, but I caught the blush stealing up her neck even from this distance.

I quickened my pace, dodging fans, and other onlookers, until I reached the steps of the box. A man stood below and stopped me. "Sorry, authorized personnel only."

"Oh, I'm authorized." I was annoyed at times like these when people didn't readily know who I was or my relationship to Harper or the team.

"It's okay, Henry." Harper motioned me up.

"Hey," I said, trying to remain casual and calm when all I wanted to do was touch her. "Everything good?"

"It's getting there." She wore a blush on her cheeks, and it seeped down her neck into the collar of her shirt. I desperately wanted to see how far down under the collar it went but tried to quickly advert my eyes.

She raised her sunglasses and cocked an eyebrow at me—guess I hadn't averted them fast enough. She glanced around us. "To what do I owe the pleasure, Mr. McBane?"

"While I like the submissive tone, I prefer hearing you say 'Cal' with it. When you say 'Mr. McBane,' I keep looking for my father, and that kind of weirds me out."

She tilted her head; annoyance laced her tone. "Do I really come across as someone who would be submissive?"

"Under the right circumstances…"

She held up her palm and turned to dismiss me.

"I'm kidding, Harper. I'm kidding." I grabbed her hand and held it a bit too long, wanting to pull her to me, to hold her. Our conversations lately had always started off professional, but eventually turned flirty or laced with innuendos, and it wasn't always me who turned them that way.

"Please, don't." Her tone was tense as she searched the area for someone to jump out and yell, "*Gotcha!*"

I was annoyed, but I caught myself. "Alright, but just for the record...I really, really want find out how far down you blush."

"Cal...please..."

I lowered my voice so only she could hear me. "Change the inflection on that line and we could be on to something..."

"Harper—" Amy called from below. "The executives from Winston Hotels have arrived. They are at Merlo's courtesy tent waiting for you."

"Got to go."

She was down the stairs of the pit box so fast I had to raise my voice. "Are you going to your parents' barbeque after the race?"

"Wouldn't miss it," she yelled back without turning around.

I turned on the petite brunette who stared at me, sheepishly.

I walked down the stairs and over to Amy, slipping my hands in the pockets of my khaki shorts. "Amy, we have to have a discussion about your timing."

"Sorry." She teasingly smiled.

"Hm." I switched gears, scanning the area. "Is everything set for the other event?"

Amy's face beamed. "Yes, I coordinated everything with—"

"Shh..." I stopped her with a hand on her arm. "Yes, so we're on the same page and can get everything and everyone where they need to be?"

"Yes. I can't believe it's happening. What a remarkable night it will be—what a memorable weekend."

"That's the plan. One that no one in either family will forget anytime soon."

3 6

TALLADEGA, FL

Harper

My parents outdid themselves. Again. They made sure their motorhome and the McBane's were parked next to each other. Motorhomes were luxury suites on wheels and offered more privacy and better accommodations than most five-star resorts. It was literally a piece of home you took with you. Mine was parked several spaces away. No need to be that close to your parents—ever.

Laid out on the table was a feast for an army.

My eyes immediately found Cal, and he was talking with my father. I steeled my back as I was about to approach them.

"Harper, come get your skinny butt over here," CJ yelled from a chair sitting next to a couple I assumed was Meredith and Michael McBane.

"Come, let's meet my parents," Cal came up behind me and whispered.

His parents were seated in chairs talking with Grady and CJ, so at least that was a good buffer. Cal and I weren't anything—not really. So why was I nervous about meeting his parents? Hell, even CJ didn't know what was going on.

Hell, I wasn't even sure what was going on.

Because there wasn't anything to know. I had to keep reminding myself of that. If he'd just stop touching me, it would help…immensely.

CJ's voice carried. "Harper, it's about time you got here."

I glared at CJ, while Cal retrieved a chair for me and placed it between Meredith and CJ. I glared at him before turning to his mother. Gracious Harper in place.

Meredith stood and I said, "Hi, I'm Harper Merrick."

Meredith leaned in and hugged me. "Yes, darling, I know. And you're more gorgeous in person. Wow, and tall." She looked up at me from her diminutive height, similar to my mom's. "Violet, what did you feed this child? She could easily be a model, she's beautiful."

"And smart as a whip," Cal added.

"Yeah, yeah. She's wonderful. Cal, get the woman a drink," CJ said.

"Just a water, please," I said.

Michael McBane was quiet, studying me with a faraway look on his face. I walked over and held out my hand. "Hello, Mr. McBane. It's good to finally meet you. I've heard so much about you."

"Oh, well, great. That starts us off on a bad note already." He produced a dry tone that was hard to discern. "Please, sit with us, Harper. I've wanted to meet you ever since we met CJ. I hear you two are kind of a package deal."

"They're hellions," my mother joined in. "From the day CJ's mother and I put them on the same blanket together. They were thick as thieves." My mother put her hands on her hips. "You couldn't find two girls who were such opposites but so closely connected."

Cal brought me a bottle of cold water. When he handed me the bottle and his fingers brushed mine, a shiver ran up my body. I glanced up and by tilt of his lips, I'm pretty sure he caught it.

"Well, then, starting Merlo makes perfect sense," Michael said. "Although, I have to say, it was incredibly brave and maybe even a bit ballsy for three women to go out and do that." He sat back, tilted his head, and studied me. "Risky investment for my son to make without a horse in the race—so to speak," he said in a low tone.

Sadie appeared out of nowhere, leaned into the group, and piped in, "Oh, he definitely has a horse in that race." She tilted her head, contemplating. "I'm trying to think of a veiled reference to a 'stud out to pasture' but I think I need a few more cocktails before I can get that creative."

Then Cal tipped his bottle to Sadie and said, "Well, thank God for small favors, then."

Michael let out a laughed and his sons stared at him in confusion.

I detoured the conversation back on track to reassure Michael, "Yeah, well, we were raised around the track, so risks are part of life for us." I nodded toward Cal. "And I'd like to think Cal was part of the team, not just an investor."

"Indeed," Michael replied, and for the life of me, I couldn't decipher his meaning.

Cal and Grady spent the entire dinner checking their phones and whispering in corners whenever they thought no one was looking.

It was dusk, and the infield was still going with parties and people milling around, anticipating the next day's qualifying and the lower series' race. After dessert, Amy pulled up in a golf cart with Grady's buddy, Cooper, following her in another one.

Grady got up from his chair, his mouth twitching, and he rubbed his hands down his legs. "Mom, Dad, Cooper's going to take you on a tour of the track."

"Now?" Meredith said.

"Come on, Mom, I'll go with you guys." Cal motioned them to the cart, not giving them time to argue.

"Amy, what are you doing here?" I asked.

"Oh, Jacks wanted to see you and CJ—he said it was urgent."

"Crap. I hope there isn't anything wrong with the car. I don't want to go to the backup, not after the decent qualifying we had," I said.

"Come on, Harper. Jacks wants you too," Amy yelled over to me.

I paused briefly to see what Cal was doing. I'd been hoping to find time alone to talk with him. So much for that idea. I shook my head before climbing in the golf cart.

As Amy pulled away, I checked over my shoulder and saw Cal talking with my parents. I wasn't able to see what he said, but my mother's hands flew to her face, and my father's smile was warm as he wrapped his arm around her. What the hell?

When we reached the garage, Jacks had some senseless conversation with CJ about the next day, and I texted Cal to ask what he said to my parents.

He didn't reply.

Amy, however, was about as antsy as a long-tailed cat in a room of rocking chairs. Not much rattled my assistant, which was what made her a fantastic assistant. "Is everything okay? You don't seem like yourself tonight."

"What?" she looked up from her phone after checking it again. "No, I'm fine. I'm just in a hurry."

CJ finished with Jacks and joined us in the golf cart. "That was a complete waste of time. I don't know why you even had to come." She shook her head. "I want to get back and grab some pie from your mom before Grady finishes it."

"Hey, where are we? I thought we were going back to the motorhome?"

I studied our location. We'd just passed the north tunnel and were rounding an area of RVs close to the track. As we came to an entrance to the track, Amy stopped her golf cart and leaned her arms over the wheel.

Talladega was a 2.66-mile superspeedway. With average speeds of 210 miles per hour, the track had banked turns that caused the cars to slingshot through to the straightaways. Dega wasn't set up for night races and, because of its size, didn't have lights. However, this evening, there was a spotlight in the middle of the thirty-degree bank at turn four with a man sitting on the track, his legs pulled up as if waiting for something—or someone.

I sucked in the air, remembering what took place at that exact spot last year. It was the turn Grady sacrificed himself, saving CJ from being wrecked and allowing her to win the race. It was also where CJ declared to the world that she was his.

And now, I stared at my friend as she slowly got out of the golf cart. CJ, wordlessly, dumbfounded, stared at Grady.

People were gathered around the barrier that cut them off from the track, watching and wondering what was going on. A security guard, recognizing CJ, let her through without comment. CJ's gaze never deviated from the man on the track.

Once she hit the asphalt, she broke into a run. His golden hair was a halo around his head, but it was his smile that lit up the night.

Amy and I walked over to the security man who also let us through. We joined my family and the McBanes along with Cooper, Gus, some crew members, and Cal, just in time to see CJ jump into Grady's arms as she had months earlier. He stumbled back just as he had then.

Grady gently put CJ down, whispering words to her, cupping her chin, and kissing her forehead. She nodded and whispered back. He held up his finger as if to tell her to wait.

A laugh escaped me, and my hands flew to my face, trying to hold in all the emotions I was feeling.

She was being impatient. My guess is she was shouting yes before he asked.

Tears of joy and amazement for my friend ran down my face, and there was a brush of a hand across my back.

Cal.

His presence had me wishing for the familiarity, the intimacy, where he could wrap his arms around me and still the energy rushing through me.

Cal's warm hand moved forward and engulfed mine and I didn't pull away. I squeezed it. Wanting to share the joy with someone.

Grady pulled out a ring box, and the small crowd around us erupted as if they were a stadium of 175,000 fans, and not an infield of RV campers and motorhomes.

The glory of happiness on both of their faces lit up the night as Grady got down on one knee, trying to balance on the steep angle. There was a slight chuckle as CJ had to help him gain his balance.

His mouth moved, the question was asked, she nodded, and he slipped on the ring and then kissed her thoroughly as horns erupted from all over the infield to celebrate the event.

There wasn't a dry eye among us.

I glanced over my shoulder to Cal. He stared down at me, his eyes warm. Two people we loved were blissfully happy with each other. He readjusted his arm around me, engulfing me in a one arm hug, as an endearing friend, and leaned over to kiss the top of my head.

No words were spoken as I put my arm around his waist, as if he were Gus and we were sharing a companionable moment.

But my body never responded to Gus this way. Every part of me wanted to stay here. I didn't want to let him go. I caught a moment of bliss—was it carried over from Grady's and CJ's happiness?

Or was it my own?

That made new tears fall. I dropped my head and discreetly wiped them away.

Cal caught my movement.

"Harper," he whispered, and glanced down at me, beneath his arm. I let out a small, delusional laugh. I wasn't sure if I was sad, happy, coming, or going. I knew I was extremely confused and tempted.

Those around us were too caught up in the excitement to notice as we were having our own moment. My breathing was unsteady as our gazes caught and he leaned down slightly until his forehead touched mine, as his hand possessively cupped my jaw.

"Please," he whispered again. "Please don't look at me that way if you don't want me."

I licked my lips, not even realizing I did it.

"Jesus." The movement broke our gaze as his attention went to my lips. "Please don't do that either."

I didn't have a response because I wanted him so badly, it took all my control not to jump up and kiss him, duplicating CJ's very move from earlier. I didn't want to be duplicating anyone. I also didn't want this to be an emotional response to watching my best friend getting engaged.

I closed my eyes, stepped back away from him, and turned my head—breaking the spell.

He let go of me.

When I opened them again, he was gone.

37

TALLADEGA, FL

Harper

I tried to shake off what happened with Cal and me to focus on the impromptu celebration for CJ and Grady. My best friend was engaged! I fawned over her ring and the surprise they pulled off. CJ hugged Cal. I hugged Grady. Cal avoided all eye contact with me but maintained a celebratory smile for them.

After we all managed to wrangle the joyous couple from the crowd of well-wishers, we went back to the motorhomes for some champagne.

Cal still avoided me. I didn't blame him. I was a basket of mixed signals.

"Cal, get the lady some more champagne." Michael stepped forward, motioning to the bottle.

Cal pushed himself off the side of the motorhome where he'd been standing and picked up the bottle, bringing it to me, not making eye contact.

His face blank. I didn't like it.

As he filled my glass, the group continued talking, and I whispered, "We need to talk."

His face didn't change.

"Cal?" I stared up at him, pleading for him to look at me. God, I didn't know what to do—but at that moment, I knew I hated what was between us.

He nodded and went back to refill other glasses.

I drank the champagne, listening to everyone discuss CJ's and Grady's crazy courtship until they snuck off to be alone. "Don't forget you both still have a job to do this weekend. And technically, you're sleeping with the enemy."

"Yes, yes." CJ waved dismissively at me, as we all went our separate ways.

Back at my own motorhome, I texted Cal, asking if he was going to come by. No response.

I needed to talk to him.

I just didn't want to go to sleep like this.

I didn't think I could go to sleep like this. Energy was coursing through my veins. The way I felt when I saw him today after weeks of not seeing him. Images of each time he touched me today, each look, each word, each implied thought.

I went to the bedroom and changed into a pair of yoga pants and a t-shirt.

I'd give him a few more moments. Then what? Go look for him? I didn't even know where he was staying.

Memories of when we last kissed and how I pushed him away flooded my mind.

Our conversations before that, how easy they were. Our time together, how right and natural it felt.

Whenever Spencer brought up my relationship with Cal, I didn't deny it. I responded in my heart as if we were together—not just pretending.

I thought about him all the time. He was the one who calmed me, challenged me, propped me up, made me feel like I could take on the world. The one I knew was in my corner but would lay it out for me even when I didn't want to hear it. He was who I wanted to talk to first thing in the morning, and the last thing at night.

What was my problem?

Fear.

Fear that people would think I got to where I was because I went from my father's office to Cal's bed.

Fear that I'd hand over my heart to him and he'd want to change me, or leave me utterly destroyed.

Knock. Knock.

And just like that—butterflies.

Knees weak.

I had to hold onto the banister as I walked down the stairs to open the door.

And there he was, the moonlight behind him in a sea of motorhomes and RVs. Not exactly the most romantic setting but—my God, with this man in front of me—the way he looked at me, the way I burned for him, I could be in one of Dante's rings of hell and it would be Eden to me.

His beautiful hair had been mussed, as if he'd been running his hand through it. His hazel eyes glinted as he let them roam over me and bit his bottom lip, taking in a deep breath.

He stepped forward, without invitation, and slowly walked in, commanding the entrance, and causing me to step backwards until we were standing in the living area.

"Hey," I said, and I even raised a hand in greeting.

What the hell was wrong with me? Where were my words?

His lips thinned as if he were holding back what he wanted to say. He dropped his head, ran his hand behind his neck, and with a breath that surged out of him, said, "Goddammit, I don't know what is going on in that beautiful head of yours, but I can't stop—"

And I didn't care what was going to come out next and like a wild cat, I leapt on him.

I was not a petite woman, but with him I wanted to be enveloped and consumed.

He instantly wrapped his arms around me and took a step back, bumping into the back of a chair before bracing himself.

I latched onto him—my arms around his neck, my hands in his hair. I fused my lips to his, taking in his next breath.

"Thank fuck...Harper—" he breathed out before I cut him off, licking his lip and wanting more of his mouth.

His hands traveled down—one settling on my ass, and one on the back of my thigh. He squeezed them both as I shifted, wanting more of him.

I'd denied the connection with him for weeks—and like anything a body craves but has been denied—now I was fixated. I wanted to feast.

I wanted him to feel what I was feeling—the need.

The perk of long legs was I was able to wrap them completely around him, locking myself into place. I wasn't going anywhere.

It was glorious.

He lifted me higher, my core framed his arousal and when he moved me, we both moaned—we were definitely on the same page, and I was thankful for the thinness of yoga pants.

He broke the kiss and surveyed the area.

He walked over and put me on the counter, his arms now free to wander over my body. We were both breathing heavily as we pulled off our shirts.

I was first, tugging on his. "Off," I commanded.

He nodded with a half-grin of satisfaction as he reached behind his head with one hand,

giving me the move all women loved, and the one that seemed to seductively accentuate the muscles in his arms, chest, and abs.

Yum.

Good God, both my hands fell to his pecs, and I bit my lip to stop from drooling. It had been a while since I'd laid my hands on a naked chest—and his was worth it. I'm not ashamed to say I may have whimpered.

His full smirk was panty-dropping. Of course, that was already a given.

He cupped my face and tilted my head before consuming my

mouth in a blazing kiss. I held on to his strong biceps, making note to inspect them later. My legs wrapped again around him, drawing him in closer to me.

"Uh-uh," he said, his tone teasing. He grabbed my shirt, tugging. "Your turn."

Thankful for the soft light, with lust and the boldness I tried to channel, I pulled my shirt over my head and tried not to imagine how red my face must be. My lacy bra was a see-through tease, but still a barrier to total nakedness.

He studied me, his jaw slack. His tongue traced his bottom lip as he stepped up to me, our mouths apart just enough to catch our breaths as he exhaled, "Gorgeous."

His hand climbed from my thigh to my stomach and cupped my breast with such reverence, I was regretting leaving the bra on. But when he swiped his thumb over my nipple and the silk of the bra accentuated the feel, teasing it even more, I didn't mind the slower pace.

Cal watched his hands as they stroked both breasts, watching me squirm on the counter, and listening to the cacophony of pleasure-filled sounds I made.

The devil himself couldn't have been more seductive with the flames he stoked in me. I thought he was going to kiss me, and I parted my lips, but he dove into my neck and down my chest.

Slow licks and kisses, his hand still caressing the silken-wrapped breasts. I was about to tear that bra off myself. His mouth teased under the material, as he played with the strap of the bra...

Yes, take it off—take it off...

If I wasn't so dizzy with need, I would've chanted it.

He looked up again.

"You have no idea how much I'm enjoying watching you. I could do this for hours."

I stopped squirming and grabbed him by his hair. "Cal McBane, don't you dare." I

growled.

He chuckled as he pulled down one of the straps, lowering the cup, and finding my nipple through the material, clamping his mouth down on it, forcing a gasp out of me.

"Oh...fuck." I gasped as he latched on and he moaned, with my nipple still between his lips, the vibration adding to the pleasure. He distracted me with a swipe at the other breast before that hand traveled down my stomach, going lower.

Thank God. I was about to push his hand down there myself.

"Cal, please."

"Yes, that is what I like to hear."

Cocky bastard.

But instead of going between my legs where I wanted it, his hand detoured to around my back, unlatching my bra in one motion and tearing it from me like it was offensive to him.

He pulled back, both hands cupping me, and he held my breasts in his hands, stroking with his thumbs. I was mesmerized by the look of his hands on me. His skin was so much tanner than mine, there was no resemblance, but they fit.

I couldn't wait. I grabbed the back of Cal's head and brought it down to my chest. Letting him know I was done with the teasing.

He chuckled as he licked and then sucked my nipple into his mouth —hard. Pleasure to the point of pain. I inched myself closer to him, wanting—needing—friction between my legs.

Cal saw my hips unable to stay still and pulled them to the edge of the counter. His hand on the crease of my thigh, next to my apex, moved over my sensitive mound, the yoga pants were almost a non-existent barrier.

I arched my back, Cal still attached to my breast. "Oh, fuck. I may die before we go any further," I bit out.

He hummed, the sensation taking everything to another level. He moved both hands to my thighs, both thumbs were stroking me through my yoga pants.

"Oh, God, Cal. Seriously it isn't going to take much."

Abruptly, he stopped everything and lifted me, straddling him again as he walked swiftly through to the back where the bedroom was. "Hell, we need a bed."

I giggled as I pressed myself up to his chest, showering his neck with kisses and running my hands through his mussed-up hair. "Damn right we do."

3 8

TALLADEGA, FL

Cal

I needed a bed. Now.

The lights were dim in the bedroom of her motorhome, but light enough that I'd be able to study Harper's body with all my senses.

I laid her on the bed with my arm cushioning her as she laid back. Her blush intensified at my visual perusal, and I wanted to explore how far it would go down her body.

Pink sheer panties to match the pink and white sheer bra I'd just removed greeted me as I removed her pants. Her blush went all the way down her stomach. Or maybe it was arousal.

I laid down beside her, my finger roamed over the panties lightly, teasing. "I have a mind to tear these off of you."

In response, she writhed and parted her legs slightly. "I never took you for a tease, Mr. McBane."

Lord, give me strength, she was glorious, and I didn't know if I was going to survive. I adjusted myself discreetly.

"I wouldn't call it teasing, Ms. Merrick. Just drawing out the pleasure."

I focused as my hand wandered her body, and how she responded to me. I traced her breasts, brushed a nipple, down her stomach and teasing the skin between her thighs before pressing the spot between her legs with the panties still in place.

She'd watch the progress of my hand—her eyelids heavy, her mouth panting, her chest rosy and her nipples erect. She'd moan, try to direct me, and I brushed her off with a kiss to her hand and a lick of a nipple.

She was swearing my name between cries of denied pleasure.

My erection was straining against my boxer briefs. At this rate I was going to go before her.

I slipped my hand into her panties and found her most sensitive spot, rubbing it with a determined circle until her back bowed off the bed and she released the most glorious cry of pleasure. I had to stop watching her expression for fear of exploding without her even touching me.

She kept her hand on mine until she was done riding the wave, sitting up in an endorphin haze, and grabbed me by the face, kissing me deeply, dragging me back down on top of her.

"I need you on top of me." She kissed my lips.

"I need to feel your weight…" She kissed my cheek.

"I need your warmth…" She kissed my other cheek.

"I need your kisses…" She found the button of my shorts and then it was a mad struggle to get us both naked. "I need you inside me…" She rolled me over onto my back and astride me.

Lord, give me strength. Part of me wanted time to stand still long enough so I could memorize everything about this moment—

"Condom?"

Shit. I leaned over the side of the bed and went for my shorts. I wasn't stupid. I'd been carrying it for weeks, hoping.

She impatiently tried to grab the condom from me. "I need…you." She stroked me as I tried to focus on taking out the condom. I stilled her hand, because, Jesus Jones, I was going to embarrass myself.

I took in several deep breaths, even tried reciting this year's college draft statistics as I put on the condom. I cupped the back of her neck and kissed her deeply as I rolled us over, wedging between her legs.

I slid my body over hers, maximum contact—never losing her eyes. I leaned over, cupped her face, and gave her the sweetest kiss I could manage. Because this wasn't me fucking her. This wasn't sex. This was…more.

I didn't just want her body. I wanted all of her. She may not be ready to hear that, but maybe she could feel it.

I hesitated, trying to find the right words. But she answered the unasked question. "Cal, I'm sure." She nodded. "I want this…so badly."

"So badly," I repeated, echoing her, unable to formulate my own words as I slid inside. She gasped.

Oh, God, she was tight. The heat, the—oh, God. I squeezed my eyes shut. Focusing on the pleasure and trying to remain slow. It was taking all my control to do it slowly and not slam into her, even as she squeezed my ass and dug her feet into me, urging me on. "Please, Cal. More."

Now how the hell is a man supposed to focus with those breathy words?

"Killing me, honey."

"Want more." She tilted her hips up as I seated myself completely and kissed her, so she'd stop with the verbal aphrodisiac—because I didn't need any more encouragement.

I struggled to keep a slow pace, determined to make this first time special.

She pushed at my chest and got my attention.

"Harper?"

"Take off the gloves, I know you want to…" She smirked. She wasn't happy with slow, she wanted the frenzy.

My sunshine—she wanted to burn.

"You're tight, darling. I don't want to hurt you, but I can give you more. We'll take the gloves off next time." Because there sure as hell will be a next time.

I pulled back and came up on my knees. I hitched one of her legs up over my arm, giving me a better angle. When I drove into her again, the thrust moved her entire body away from me and I had to pull her back. She yelped and then laughed with delight. "Yes!"

I gave her long, deep strokes, taking pauses in between to hold myself back. I laid a palm over her flat lower belly to hold her in place, and moved a thumb down to her pleasure point, caressing it as I drove into her.

That did it. Her moans turned into muffled screams. "Oh... son-of-a—"

I captured her mouth as she crested, her cries of pleasure drowning in my kiss—both because I wanted it, and to remind us both we were surrounded by RVs. It only slightly tamped down her cries until her next orgasm hit, this one taking me with her—adding my deeper groan to the cacophony of sounds emanating from her mobile home.

She was going to break me—one way or another. But it was going to be a beautiful death.

"Come to Chicago over Easter. Come stay with me." I pulled her down and kissed her, not wanting her to get out of bed yet.

She collapsed back down, giving up the fight and letting out a half-hearted groan. "I wish I could—"

"And why couldn't you?"

She propped her head in her hand. "Because what reason would I have for being in Chicago, Cal?"

"To see me, of course?"

She traced the tattoo on my bicep with a fingertip. The caress was soothing even as her words were stinging. "What's the story with the tattoo? I never would've imagined straightlaced Cal McBane hid a tattoo under those suits."

"I got it in college. It was a rebellious act against my father." I pulled her hand away and kissed her fingertips. "Come to Chicago and I'll tell you all about it."

"Cal, people can't realize we are seeing each other. I don't want to flaunt it. Not now. If they know we are together, they will assume you are funding Merlo."

"I am partially funding Merlo."

"Don't be obtuse." She frowned and pushed away slightly. "Don't make me explain this again."

I leaned over and began kissing her ear, her neck.

She ran her hand down my hair and over my cheek. "We'll see." She was quiet for a moment before contemplating. "You really are hard to resist."

"Good to know. I was worried my powers of persuasion were failing on you."

She gave a half-hearted smirk. "No. But they're a challenge." She nudged me. "You need to sneak out of here, though. No sleepovers."

I fell back. "Come on, please."

"As adorable as that plea is, I can't have you doing the walk of shame among a campground full of RVs, and I need to get my beauty sleep for tomorrow. I have a full morning of meet-and-greets before the race." She pulled me up, and when I complied, she kissed my nose. I grabbed her around the waist, turning her over and back under me. She giggled and wrapped her arms around as I pushed open her thighs and nuzzled her neck again.

"I need to work on your resistance a bit first."

39

TALLADEGA, FL

Cal

The day after the best night of my life, I sat in a pit box suite, dazed from a massive, lingering sex high. I was undoubtedly wearing the goofiest look and barely paying attention to what was happening with the race.

Both Grady and CJ were doing well, considering they weren't the only ones to have a life-altering event the night before. In fact, the way the two of them were dancing around before the race, I could only imagine the smiles as they continued to pass one another. Both my mom and Violet Merrick were wearing scanner headphones, listening to the communication going on between the Merrick and Merlo teams and laughing.

My father came over and sat with me in the back, knocking me out of the daydreams I was having of Harper, and the plans I was making for this evening. How soon could I lure her back to her motorhome? Could I convince her to join me at a hotel? It would be safer that way? I didn't have an issue with RV sex, but maybe then she'd let me hold her while she slept.

I wanted that.

"I can see the appeal…" my father said.

I sat up. "Hm?"

"The appeal of stock car racing. I see why your brother is drawn to it—not just because of the beguiling CJ either." He leaned back, crossing his ankle over his knee, resting his arms on the arm rest. He was a man relaxed and contemplating his surroundings.

"Your brother is engaged." He shook his head. "Didn't see it coming. Knew he loved her. Knew she was different and that she was settling him. But didn't see that coming." He glanced at me. "Thought it would be you who'd fall first."

I side-eyed him with a "Yeah, sure" expression.

He chuckled. "Didn't see it being Vanessa, though. Would've been easier if it had been. She would've made a good wife for you. She was sophisticated and desired to see you succeed—"

"Dad, please." I held up my hand, my good-mood buzz fading.

"I figured when you started traveling so much without her it wasn't going to last. I also figured it was probably more than brotherly love that brought you down here." He crossed his arms over his chest.

Here we go…

"She's lovely, by the way. I see the reason for wanting to be involved with Merlo, now—"

"It wasn't the only reason—"

My father held up a hand to silence me. "I hope you're right. I'd hate to see this be a multi-million-dollar gesture to get in her—.""

"Don't finish that sentence." I growled. "Don't insult her or me with that line of thinking."

I shifted, trying to calm my indignation. What the hell?

I bit out, "We had the money from the sale of Grady's Indy team. It wasn't something that was missed. It solved a lot of problems—"

"How did it solve the problem of getting your brother back to Chicago? It did quite the opposite. Now he's going to stay down here."

"Dad, that ship had already sailed. He wasn't coming back." And that was on him—but I didn't add that.

My father crossed his arms over his chest as he tried to rein in a sore topic. "Regardless…I hope you thought with your head and not with your—"

"You had to go and ruin it, didn't you?" I shook my head. "I'm having a fantastic morning and you…" I held up my hand. "Don't start with me—not here. Not today. I really don't think any of us wants history repeating itself." At the mention of the fallout between my father and Grady that lead to Grady leaving the family, my father quieted. My mother would never forgive him if he pulled another stunt like that, brain tumor or not. And he knew it.

"We aren't pieces on your gameboard for you to place where you want us to go." I leaned toward him. "I've been dancing to your music for years. Don't…don't push me…not on this."

My father refused to look at me, he just stared out at the track. He subtly held up a hand. "Fine."

He was feeling vulnerable. His mortality was staring at him and he didn't like the lack of control. I felt the leash being tugged on more frequently at home, but here…on a day where I'd woken up happier than I'd been in years. No, he wasn't going to piss all over it, and I wasn't going to respond to him yanking on my leash.

"You know, I'm not dead, yet," he said, turning to me, and his glare blazed with determination. "I do still have a say in what happens with the company."

I put my hands in my pockets. "Yes, and you won't die—not yet, because you are a tough SOB, and I know you hate sitting there and watching me run your company—making deals, buying auto parts chains, and stock car teams. So, get that damn tumor out and take it back from me so I can get on with my life."

He shrugged, as if it were no big deal I just called him an SOB. "Fair enough."

He began to poke. "People respect her father and Merrick Motorsports. Why isn't he backing her more?"

"Both she and her father thought it would be best if she was seen as doing this on her own."

He pursed his lips. "It's a bit naïve. I hope it doesn't work against her. Seems like she could use some allies—from what I hear."

I had this overwhelming need to defend her. But my father was repeating what I've always thought.

"She's getting there." There was more pride than defense in my tone.

"I admire what she is setting out to do—she's a woman following her dreams and seems very focused." He aimed his attention on me to drive home the point. "It will be hard to have a relationship with your schedule and hers—unless, of course, she chooses to move to Chicago. Maybe you can convince her to relocate the team to Chicago."

I began to shake my head, vehemently.

"There are teams that aren't located in North Carolina—it's not in the bylaws of racing." His tone held a trace of mockery.

I kept shaking my head. "She won't move."

"I'm sorry, son." He patted me on the shoulder. As if he could already see an inevitable end. As if I didn't have a choice—as if I were heir apparent and it was a title I was born into and never given an option.

I ignored what he was implying—that my relationship with Harper didn't have a future. "Dad, you aren't going anywhere, and we have plenty of time—"

My mom walked over, trying to dispel the tension with levity. "Enough male bonding over there, CJ's about to dust your son, don't you want to see this?" She gave a flourish to the track. "I'm torn between cheering on my soon-to-be daughter-in-law, who is quickly becoming my hero, or rooting for the child I spent twenty-one hours in labor with…"

"I'll leave you to ponder where your loyalties lie…I'm going to go stretch my legs," I said. I couldn't breathe in my father's presence at that moment.

"I know where to find you if I need you," my father mumbled with a smirk.

"You always do."

40

TALLADEGA, FL

Harper

CJ was running mid-pack. More importantly, she and Jacks were on fire. Jacks finally relented and let me sit in the back of the pit box quietly as he stood overlooking the pit like a lord overlooking his land. With my headset on I could hear the CJ, Jacks, and the spotter, Aaron, who with Gus and my father's blessing, I was able to convince to come over from Merrick. Having Aaron up above the track watching everything that was happening and having his familiar voice in CJ's ear—someone she trusted and understood—also helped settle her on the track. Things were moderately calm with the exception of—

"Number 51 on your back," Aaron relayed.

"Son of a bitch—" CJ yelled as a car bumped her from behind. "That's not on my back that's up my ass. Fuckin'—"

"CJ—" I warned. My friend still had trouble with remembering what 'live mic' meant—and that there were many, many others who listened besides me and Jacks.

A loud growl was picked up by the audio. A Dupree driver was intentionally bumping her. It wasn't a friendly attempt at bump drafting

—trying to decrease air resistance and increase the speed of both cars —no, this guy was out to cause problems. But it was subtle, and without knowing what was going on in the pits, not everyone would be able to tell the difference.

"Aaron, tell that son-of-a-bitch's team, I don't want to dance with him."

Jacks came on. "Relax, CJ. Just hang tight and let's see if it happens again. Maybe it was a mistake."

"Mistake, my ass…" she mumbled.

I checked on Grady and was both pleased for him and a bit competitive that he'd pulled up front, battling for sixth position.

It was taking some getting used to, but CJ was trying desperately not to think about Grady and his positioning in the race, so we didn't mention it. It was a challenge, though.

Two more laps until she pitted. If she asked, I'd give her a brief update.

The Dega race was 188 laps of a 2.6-mile track, or 500 miles. They had about 54 laps to go. It was time for CJ to make some moves.

But they hadn't had "The Big One"—the wreck every spectator at Talladega waited for; so big it could take out half the field of cars. Superspeedways like Dega were famous for them. Cars tight together, bump drafting at over 200 mph, late in the race, especially when drivers are tired, wheels are worn, and they have to become more aggressive to make moves on the pack—it's when "racing hard" takes on new meaning.

It was also what ended with Grady in a tangled mess the year before when he saved CJ. This year with Grady up front, it was a chance for redemption.

Nonetheless, I knew CJ. As much as she loved her man, and wanted to see him finish big, she didn't want to be so far behind.

She flew into her pit and the crew went to work.

Five crew members go over the wall, change four tires and fill the gas tank and get clear of the car in about 15 seconds—less time than it takes you to wash your hands.

I stood to see her as she said through the comms, "How's he doing?"

I smiled. "He's in fifth. He's got to pit soon. Car looks fast."

" 'Kay."

Second tires were on, the car fell off the jack and she jetted out as soon as the team was clear.

I stepped forward to Jacks and mimicked his stance—arms crossed, legs braced, head high, contemplative.

"She looks good."

"Eh, she's okay. For now. We can do better," he said, biting his bottom lip and watching the monitor as he watched our girl on the backstretch.

I nodded, figuring that was as much of high praise as he was going to give her. If he thought he could make her even better, we were on the right track.

"Okay, I'm going to step out for a moment."

His nod was so slight, I wasn't sure if I was even acknowledged.

Stepping down, I turned and ran into Cal. He touched my arm and in his deep voice said, "Hey, I was just coming to see you. How is everything shaping out?" It made me lose my train of thought for a moment, remembering the other phrases that deep voice had murmured to me last night.

I shook my head, trying—and failing—to hold back the heat traveling to my cheeks. "Good, your brother is having a fantastic day. CJ is running okay. Not her best. But she and Jacks are still gelling, so I can't ask for more than that."

His smile was small, but warmth lit his hazel eyes—making the green in them shine.

"I want to kiss you so bad right now."

Yep, my cheeks were blazing hot. Anyone watching would know it wasn't the heat from the day or the pavement. It was from the sexy man in front of me. He had scruff on his face—probably from not having time to shave this morning. And dammit—I had to stop my hand from reaching out to touch it.

"You're biting your lip and it's giving me ideas. Please stop. These shorts don't conceal much."

I dropped my head, not realizing I even did that.

"Will I see you later?"

I peeked at him up beneath my lashes. "We'll see. I guess it depends on how this all ends. When are your parents—"

BOOM! BANG! SCRREEECHH!

Massive noise vibrated the air like a sonic boom. All other sounds were cut off in the immediate area. The sounds of engines and wheels, and metal on metal, hit after hit with split- second pauses in between, was painful because everyone knew what it was before they even looked.

It was The Big One and it was fairly close.

I was on the steps to the pit box before the crashing even stopped, Cal behind me.

"Jacks!" my voice, panicked.

Jacks had out binoculars and was scanning the area and studying the monitor. "It's not our girl. She made it through." He turned, noticing Cal with me. Jacks's face dropped at seeing Cal. "It's Grady."

I grabbed the binoculars from Jacks as Cal stood in front of the monitor.

It was a bad one.

"Aaron—Aaron!" It was CJ.

There were at least fifteen to eighteen cars strewn around turn one in various levels of destruction.

"Are you sure one was Grady?" I asked Jacks.

"Yes, hon. He went airborne, before hitting the barrier wall."

I grabbed the headset. "Hey, girl. It's me."

"Was it—"

"CJ, switch channels."

We both switched to a private channel on the headsets. "Grady was in it—I'm waiting to see what is going on. Head in the game. You're under white flag. You need to stick with it." I was firm and hard with my instruction.

Turning the mic off, I yelled at both Cal and Jacks. "Find out what the hell is going on." Cal was bent over staring at the monitor.

"Harper, I just passed them and I didn't see him. There are too many cars…too much smoke. Where the fuck is he?" She was trying to cover her panic with anger, and it wasn't working.

Memories of last year were racing through my head. His car being slammed against a barrier wall. The long minutes before we knew he was okay. I couldn't even imagine what it was doing to her.

"Focus, CJ. You can't drive that car if you aren't in control. Let's just find out what's going on. Let me get ahold of someone."

Jacks yelled at a team member who took off down pit row for answers and barked at Aaron for the same.

Last time, he walked away with just a slight concussion, scrapes, and bruises, and generally pissed off. All par for the course with drivers. *This won't be any different*, I told myself.

Cal motioned to me to look at the monitor.

"Tell her his net is down, and he's waved. The car is banged up but there is movement."

"CJ, Cal says his net is down," I relayed. "He's waving."

That wasn't enough for her. "But he's not out. Why isn't he out?"

I didn't have an answer.

Cal grabbed the headset. "Hey, CJ, It's Cal. He's probably having a full-blown meltdown, pissed off and sitting in there cussing up a blue streak." He handed it back to me.

She was quiet for a moment. "That's probably true. Can I talk to him?"

"No. You need to focus, or you could end up the same. He's fine. He'd be pissed if he found out you lost a chance to capitalize on this. It took out fifteen cars, most from the front of the pack."

"He's out and being taken to the infield center," Cal said, and I conveyed it. While CJ knew that was standard procedure in any crash, we both shared a concerned look before silently agreeing not to share that it took two people holding him steady to get him to the ambulance that would take him there.

"I'm going to go check on my parents and reassure them. You got her?" Cal whispered.

I nodded and motioned to Jacks to jump back in.

If he started barking orders at her, it would put her mind back where it needed to be. I didn't need my best friend freaked out about her boyfriend—fiancé—while driving 200 mph with other assholes trying to run her down.

"Go win this thing. Two in a row—girl—go get them and show them what you're made of."

"Okay...but Harper—"

"You focus on what is going on inside your car—I'm going now. Trust me to handle this. Go finish your job so you can give him an earful when you're done for scaring you."

"Damn straight I'm going to yell at him. I may require a provision in our marriage contract that he's never allowed to race at Talladega."

"Go get 'em girl."

I took off the headset and almost ran down the steps, yelling for Amy to find me a golf cart to the infield medical center.

Dammit.

41

CHICAGO, IL

Cal

My brother has nine lives, I swear it. Another concussion. The doctors were starting to get concerned about the repetitive concussions. If he kept it up, there may be lasting damage. It was too horrible of a thought for any of us to make a joke out of it.

Otherwise, Grady was fine. However, he had a fiancée who swore he'd never set foot on Talladega's track again. Being grounded for two weeks, getting that kind of prognosis, and convalescing at home—had him in a rare, foul mood.

"It wasn't my fault!" he kept repeating like a mantra. "Zalbaski got loose, took out Owens who ran up behind me, I never even saw it coming!"

CJ wasn't having it. She'd just walk away, shaking her head. "Nope." It was the most she'd give him when he started to argue with her. Then she'd walk over, stare at him, push up on tip toes, and kiss him.

CJ ended up finishing third in the race, which, given the situation, was pretty damn admirable. She almost drove her car directly from the finish line to the infield hospital. The weekend was pretty shot after that. My mom was a mess, my father brooded, and we all flew back to Chicago with Harper and me struggling to figure out when we could see each other again.

Eventually, I wore her down and she came to Chicago.

I stared at her on my veranda as I unceremoniously uncorked a bottle of wine and poured two glasses, taking my focus off her silhouette long enough to make sure I didn't spill any of it. As giddy as a teen on his first date, it was almost as if two of my worlds had collided— no, not collided but finally connected.

I picked up both glasses and joined her outside.

"Cal, it is beautiful out here."

"Isn't it a bit cold for your Southern blood?" I handed her the glass.

She wrapped her sweater around her tightly before accepting it, smiling at me before saying, "We aren't complete wimps, give us some credit. It's what, in the fifties? That's still kind of cold for spring."

"It's a bit unseasonable at sixty-five degrees," I teased.

"Yes, but we are, like thirty stories high, the lake is right over there, and there's a breeze." She pointed, trying to defend the reason for her warm blood.

My smile grew. Damn, she's adorable. "I'm so glad you're here. I can't even explain how much you brightened my week when you said you'd stop here on your way to this week's race.

"I'm glad I was able to swing it. It's a nice break for me too." A piece of hair blew across her face and I gently tucked it behind her ear. Her expression warmed, even if her nose was a bit pink, belying the truth of her being a bit cold.

"We can go in, honey. You shouldn't stay out here if you're cold."

She turned back to the banister, overlooking the city below. She took a sip from the wine before saying, "Don't be ridiculous, your city is beautiful in the twilight. I want to watch it."

I wanted to wrap myself around her but wasn't sure we were to that point of intimacy yet, so I settled for standing close to her side, hoping my warmth would help shield her from the direction of the wind. "So, you like Chicago? Haven't you been here before?"

"Yes and yes. I'd been to Chicago, but never saw it like this. Not from this angle, not at this time of day, and definitely not through your eyes." She turned her head and glanced up at me. "Your city makes my little ol' city look like a small town."

"Well, until two decades or so ago, your city was just shy of being a small town." I faced her as she leaned on the balustrade and took in the skyline. The lights in the penthouse were dimmed, and with the sun setting, only the light from the moon and the city illuminated our evening.

"Yeah, I guess you're probably right." Lost in the view, she sipped her wine. "It really is a gorgeous view."

Fascinated by pieces of her hair dancing with the breeze, I said, "Yes, it really is."

Her face angled enough for her to see I was staring. She gifted me with a smile that ran through me. Damn, I wanted to kiss her.

She was here in my home. She was smiling at me.

I took my hand and slowly, tentatively, traveled a finger down the outline of her face and over her cheek, following its progress with my gaze and watching for her reaction.

She parted her lips as I leaned in and kissed her. Softly, at first. She grabbed onto my shoulders and leaned into me. I deepened the kiss just enough to taste her, wanting to take her in my arms.

Wine glasses.

I stopped long enough to place both glasses on the table next to her.

Turning to her, I cupped her face in my hands and she fell against my chest, her hands holding onto my arms. "God, I missed you."

She smiled as I fell on her mouth. "I haven't been gone that long. We just saw each other—"

Her arms flew around my neck, her fingers threaded through my hair, giving it a slight tug. I loved that.

As I pulled her against me, I cupped her backside, squeezing it, possessively.

"Honey, we need to take this inside or we're going to give the city of Chicago a show."

"Then, let's go inside..." The seduction in her voice was enthralling as she dragged me in my own home. The woman could drag me through the gates of hell, and I'd follow her on our way to heaven.

42

CHICAGO, IL

Harper

I wasn't here for even an hour and already I was climbing this man. What was wrong with me?

I'll tell you what was wrong with me.

No sex for…well, a few years. A very, very long dry spell.

And then BOOM.

Cal McBane—a man who had challenged me, taunted me, tempted me, teased me, and distracted me since the moment I met him. And now he looked at me like he wanted to devour me. And I wanted him to.

Lord, give me strength—I definitely wanted him to.

As we made it to his bedroom, and I'd congratulated myself for allowing Aunt Sadie to take me lingerie shopping the other day and was thankful for CJ running interference on some of her selections.

I was frantic to get Cal's shirt unbuttoned but paused halfway as Cal undressed me. I wanted to watch his reaction as he undid my wrap-around dress.

He pulled on the ties slowly, unwrapping me like a present and building the anticipation.

It was empowering to watch the heat grow in his eyes, to watch his mouth fall open just a bit more as he took in the sheer lace of my red bra. We both stood completely still, my smile and the bulge in his pants grew as he traced his finger around the outline of the bra, down my cleavage and then my stomach, reaching the lace of the thong. Both hands landed on my hips, gripping them softly. He lowered to his knees, peeling the dress off as he turned me around to see the back.

"Oh, Sunshine," he growled deeply. "This ass…" He palmed both my ass cheeks and kissed them, nipping one of them, causing me to yelp playfully.

"Cal!"

He stood suddenly, taking me into his arms and lowering me to the bed before practically tearing his shirt off and toeing off his shoes. His pants were gone, and he slid his body over mine, parting my legs.

"I don't think I could ever stop looking at you—" He kissed me before finishing his thought. He palmed my breast through the material of the bra, flicking his fingers over my nipple before pinching it with two of his fingers and I gasped. "I almost don't want to remove this." He pulled down the cup of the other breast and bent down to lick the nipple. "But I love what they cover too much not to taste them."

I threaded my hands through his hair. "Please, continue. I have others…"

Suddenly, to surprise him, I wrapped a leg around his back, launching myself up and rolling us over, him on his back. He let out a laugh of surprised amusement as I stared down at him, straddling his groin.

"A woman in control, huh?"

My hands were propped on his chest, but my gaze trailed down, studying the slightly tanned skin, dusting of hair around his pectoral muscles, and trailing down his abs into his boxer briefs. I caressed the tattoo on his arm, skimmed a finger around a nipple, letting my nails skim and follow the same path.

He let out a groan, knifing up and as he cupped the back of my neck, claiming my attention for a kiss.

After kissing him thoroughly, but before surrendering control to him, I pulled back. Our other time together hadn't allowed me any opportunity to explore or study him. As much as I wanted him, I also wanted to look. I wanted to savor. I pushed him back down.

"I want to play…"

I teased my hand down his abdomen. His gaze dropped to watch my progress as I moved slightly off him in order to slip my hands under the band of his boxers and explore more thoroughly. I found him, wrapped my hand around him—

"Harper…fuck."

Cal dropped his hands and closed his eyes in supplication. He bowed his head back and pleasure spread over his face as my name escaped his lips like a prayer, again and again.

God, he was a beautiful man.

Right there, in that moment, as I wrapped my hand around him, I'd never felt so desired or so powerful.

Encouraged, I pulled the barrier of his boxers and pants down and worked on improving my goal of bringing him pleasure with my hands and mouth in numerous methods—studying what he enjoyed the most.

Without warning, one hand halted me, the other grabbed me around the waist, and attempted to roll me over to my back.

"Uh-uh." I pushed him back down on his back, taking off my panties and my bra and then straddling his legs, smiling as I resumed stroking him. We'd had the safe sex talk and were ready to go without the condom. Hallelujah.

I held his eyes as I slowly inched my body up until I hovered over him. He leaned forward to lick my nipple, trying to trap it in his mouth.

"I told you, uh-uh." I shoved him back down.

"Oh, Jesus." He moaned. "If there was one image, I could capture for the rest of my life…"

I didn't wait for him to finish. I positioned myself over him, and slid him inside me, throwing my hair back, thrusting my breasts out as I moaned.

My gaze was hazy as I adjusted to the feel of him, so deep inside. But our eyes communicated when our voices were lost. *"Move."*

I smirked.

His breathing was heavy, but his patience was thin. He gripped my hips and began to move me himself—trying to take control from me.

I leaned over and kissed him, grinding down on him and regaining it. He cupped both breasts as consolation, and I was more than happy with that.

"This. This is the image I burned in my brain." He looked down to where we were joined. "Fuck, Harper—"

"I know," I moaned. "I'll take care of you…God, you feel good."

His response was incoherent.

I moved, trying to take it slow. Wanting to tease him like he teases me. But I'd been craving this, and I couldn't just do slow. We could do slow and teasing next time. I stepped up the rhythm, grinding down on him.

"Damn, you're good at that." He cupped my neck, pulling me down into a desperate kiss. When I sat back up, his hand flew down my abdomen and to the apex where his thumb just barely grazed me, and I was gone.

My hands to his chest for balance as we both rode into oblivion.

We took a break to order some take-out and cuddle up on the couch to watch some television—mostly *Friends* (me) and *The Big Bang Theory* (him) re-runs.

I was lying on his chest, as he stroked my hair, and it was all so comfortable. Too comfortable. Without thinking too much about it, I leaned up and kissed him gently. His eyes danced between mine, as if searching for something.

I ran a fingernail over the tattoo—"So…tell me about this…"

He lifted his head, peering at his arm. "I played football in college—"

"That's right, I forgot you mentioned that before."

"Yeah—Division 1—defensive back. My father calls it my rebellious years. I wanted to try for the draft. He wanted me to go to business school. Guess who won?"

He shrugged, but I knew it meant more than a shrug. "One night some friends went to a tattoo parlor; I decided to go with them. I was pissed at my father—" He rolled his arm so I could get a better look at the beautiful gothic rose on his bicep almost camouflaging a skull. "I still enjoy the expression on his face whenever he sees it."

I traced it with my finger and kissed it lightly.

Then, he slowly tilted my head and deepened the kiss, pulling me over him so he could rub his hands up and down my back and sides, as if memorizing every curve of me. We just kissed and fondled for a deliciously long time until I was too hot to be satisfied with just that, and began to stroke him through his cotton pajama bottoms and pulled off his t-shirt.

He broke the kiss, forehead to mine, and breathed, "You have me as on the edge as if I were a teenager, woman."

That did amazing things to my ego and my libido.

"I like that." I giggled.

"I'm sure you do," he smiled. "My turn."

I liked the sound of that, too.

He turned off the television, and with only the lights of Chicago from his full-length windows, we took turns on our knees, playing and discovering each other.

We exhausted our physical energy. The mood was peaceful and quiet. I couldn't find words. He carried me to his room, gently laid me down, straightened the blankets to cover us in his now-disheveled bed, and lulled me with the steady breathing of a man well-sated.

And as I laid wrapped in him, my mind warred with itself—what was this?

This wasn't a fling. This didn't feel like casual.

I stared at this man. He was fiercely loyal to his family, to those he loved, and to his company. He stole my breath and was exactly *not* what I needed in my life right now. This was not casual, and it was making things really, really complicated. This was dangerous—and I knew this because I was behaving like I didn't care how complicated it was becoming.

43

CHICAGO, IL

Cal

"Spencer calling..."

Wasn't exactly what I wanted to see pop up on my woman's cell phone the morning after the mind-altering night we'd just had.

It took everything in me not to answer it and tell him she was in the shower—my shower, and I was about to join her. But instead, I pushed the button that would send him straight to voicemail and congratulated myself on my restraint.

She came out of the bathroom, a goddess—one towel wrapped around her gorgeous body and drying her hair with another.

I leaned back, playing it cool. My hands behind my head, leaning back in repose. I'm good. I'm calm. God, she's sexy. She's mine. I want to hold her, caress her, lick her, devour her—

"Why is Spencer calling?" popped right out my mouth. There went all my cool. *Real smooth, McBane...*

Even I heard "jealous boyfriend" in that tone.

She halted, shaking out her hair, and stared at me. Her attention darted to the phone on the end table beside me.

"Did you answer my phone?" she said, missing the point but looking almost as annoyed as I was.

"No, but his name came up on the display." I sat up straight in the bed. Trying hard to soften my words and not sounding like a goddamn asshole.

She sat down on the edge of the bed next to me and let out a long, labored sigh. "He's setting up a meeting for me and the head of Telestaff Services for a sponsorship deal. He plays golf with the guy."

"Does he know you're here?" My anger was simmering.

"I don't know, Cal. I don't remember giving him my schedule." She tried to make her voice light—but it fell flat. "I'll call him back later."

She got up and went to her bag, pulling out some items and heading back to the bathroom.

I was quiet—brooding. Because that shit-for-brains was really starting to piss me off.

She came back in the room dressed in a soft, white robe. Seductively sweet, she sat next to me.

Nope, not letting it go—because I'm an ass. "Why the sudden interest in helping you?"

She shook her head. "He's aware of the challenges we've had with sponsorships jumping and was trying to be helpful." She put her hand on my thigh.

Sure, he is…

"There isn't anything left between me and Spencer. Being with him seems a lifetime ago."

She moved her hand to my chest. "Spencer wanted me to be someone I wasn't. He knows it, I know it. Susannah is the type of woman he wanted to be with—someone willing to mold around his career and who has similar goals. It wasn't me. You have nothing to be worried about."

I tried to ignore what she didn't say in that sentence—that she didn't love him anymore.

She traced circles on my chest. "He was never supportive of my own goals and dreams."

"And then there was this cocky, know-it-all guy who challenged me at every turn, and no matter what I do, I can't seem to stay away from him." She gave me a quick peck, and it went straight to my heart.

All I could say was, "You're damn right." I grabbed her, pulling her on the bed with me, and as she giggled, I wondered if I'd ever be able to let her go…and silently prayed she never asked me to.

4 4

CHICAGO, IL

Harper

I was running on endorphins and living in the clouds. But tomorrow I was due to catch up with the team for the race this weekend, and Cal was bracing for his father's surgery in a few weeks. He'd been quiet all evening, and I wondered if the stress was building up already.

I linked fingers with his after we were seated at a posh steak house complete with round booths that offered privacy. "I'll try to fly back with Grady and CJ for the surgery," I whispered, stroking his hand.

He squeezed my hand and brought it to his lips as the waiter came over for our drink order and discussed specials.

The waiter returned and had just poured our wine when Cal's expression soured.

"What's wrong? Don't like the wine?" I asked.

"No, the wine is just fine. But I may have just lost my appetite."

I followed his gaze and saw a beautiful brunette walk in with a few gentlemen.

"What is it?" I focused back on him and placed my hand on his arm to capture his attention. "We've had such a wonderful time together—I don't want to let anyone ruin it."

He captured my heart with his stare as he studied me with such intensity. He threaded our fingers together before kissing my hand again. "It won't."

"Hello, Cal."

Cal's eyes closed as he bit out, "Fuck my luck."

Her voice would probably have been sultry, if she wasn't trying to mask how pissed-off she was.

Cal opened his eyes and directed them at the woman. "Hello, Vanessa."

She stood before us—long, flowing, dark hair. Not quite as tall as me, but with curves most men probably found desirable. She dressed to accentuate her body without being obvious, yet still elegant. Her green dress caught mahogany highlights and brought out a beautiful tan undertone in her skin. She was model-worthy beautiful.

But the way she stared at our joined fingers, the way her perfectly reddened lips thinned in disgust and the hatred growing in her glare, she was going to be a royal bitch.

Cal leaned back, the picture of complete disinterest, bordering on annoyance. But he still held my hand on the table for her to witness. She tilted up her chin, crossed her arms, plumping up her perfectly round breasts and cocked out a hip—waiting, wanting acknowledgement.

So, I gave it to her.

My smile was slammed into place like a piece of armor. My well-practiced charm and decorum was wielded like a weapon. "Cal, where are your manners?" I playfully swiped at his arm before launching my graceful assault on her. "Vanessa, nice to meet you. I'm Harper Merrick." I held out my hand for her to shake.

She stared at my hand as if I'd offered her a viper on a platter and glanced to Cal. "Is she for real?"

Cal's visage broke just slightly with the tilt of one side of his mouth. "It's called having manners, Vanessa," he drawled, letting go of my hand in order to stretch his arm over the back of the booth behind me. "She's trying to be polite. What can we do for you?"

She straightened, regathering her haughtiness. "Nothing. I was just having dinner with some of my new associates at Prince, and thought I'd come by and say 'hi.' Ask how your parents were doing. Wanted to check on your father. I called your mother the other day but haven't heard back from her."

"I'm sure it was an oversight on her part," he deadpanned.

I doubted it.

"Yes, I'm sure. She's had so much going on and without me there now. I've been so busy I haven't had a chance to see her. Dermott has me working on so many projects—"

I snapped my fingers as if a lightbulb turned on in my head and interjected, "Oh, you're a friend of Meredith's." She was thrown by my blatant interruption. I was purposely being obtuse about their relationship as if it wasn't important enough in Cal's life for me to know about it. Vanessa was purposely trying to rile me up with their past, but it wasn't a factor in our future—or Cal's family. They'd scraped her off and she needed to learn that. "She's fine. We just had lunch with them this afternoon. She's just the sweetest. But I'll let her know you were asking about her."

Cal's tilted mouth turned into a full-blown smirk and he lowered his head slightly, side-eyeing me.

"What?" I was the face of innocence.

I glanced at Vanessa and she was the face of indignation.

"Harper, honey. This is Vanessa VanDusen. Remember, I told you she used to work for my father—"

"And the woman Cal spent the last two years fucking." Vanessa lost her cool.

"Classy, Vanessa," Cal muttered.

"Ohhh...Now I remember. I looked over at Cal. *That* Vanessa." I turned back to her and with all innocence and apology said, "I'm so sorry. Yes. Grady and CJ told me about you." I gave Cal an exaggerated grimace that I pretended only he could see.

She glared at Cal, "This—" She pointed her sharply manicured nails at me. "This is the best you can do? Really? Have fun slumming it." She turned and—no kidding—in true diva fashion, she flicked her hair behind her.

I cupped my chin in my hand and rested my elbow on the table, reaching for my wine and lifting it up to him in a cheers motion.

Cal hid his laughter behind his napkin, but I saw his shoulders shaking.

I caught her glaring at us as she weaved through some tables and I winked at her, unconcerned, before turning to Cal, unable to hide my amusement. "Well, she's charming."

"Sorry about that." He rubbed his face.

I grabbed his bicep and kissed his cheek. "Don't worry about it."

"I've never seen Vanessa handled so well."

I waved her off. "Cal, darling. I may look like a sweet, Southern belle—I may even sometimes sound like one. But I grew up surrounded by grease, cars, and mechanics. I was a tomboy before I was a debutante. I learned how to hide it behind manners and genteel-ness—how to take someone out with my words and a smile on my face. Spiteful girls like her don't scare me. You forget who my best friend is."

I took a sip of my wine. "I'm all about supporting a fellow woman, and not making a sister an enemy over a man, but sometimes a bitch was just a bitch."

45

CHICAGO, IL

Cal

I tried to climb out of my slump of Harper leaving the next morning by stopping by my parents' house on the way to work. I don't know where that dumbass logic came from. I guess the impending surgery was beginning to worry me.

Dad was sitting at the breakfast table reading on his tablet when I walked in. The sun was haloing him from behind, but the soft light didn't soften the dark circles and weariness the whole ordeal was having on his body. Even though his hair was perfectly coiffed, he was dressed in sweatpants and a hoodie—not my father's regular wardrobe, even for a weekend. It was taking some time to get used to seeing him this way.

"Hey Dad. You're up early."

"Cal. I thought that was my line?"

"Got work to do but thought I'd swing by and check on you. Any word on Grady?"

"CJ said he's 'angrier than a hornet in a Coke can' because the doctors still won't clear him for this week's race. Said he doesn't have all his faculties back or something."

"Yeah, I heard."

Concern laced my father's features and his voice lowered. "Supposedly, your brother's taken too many hits to the head. It's a concern."

He stared me down. "Don't you dare make a joke and don't mention it to your mother—she has enough to worry about with me."

I didn't like keeping this from her, but he was right for the time being. I nodded.

"Anyway, onto more pleasant thoughts. Did you have a good visit with Harper?" He scrolled through the tablet, skimming headlines, peering at me over his reading glasses.

"Yes. We did."

"Did you manage to leave your home? Venture out and show her what Chicago had to offer besides you?"

I gave him a side-eye glare. "Yes, I took her to dinner last night. She had to fly back this morning."

"Where did you take her?"

"Smiths and McCorkles."

"Good choice. I can't wait until I can venture back out without needing a nap between courses," he mumbled.

I nodded. "We ran into Vanessa."

"How'd that go? Can't imagine Vanessa was gracious."

I chuckled reliving the moment Harper managed Vanessa so thoroughly. "Vanessa wasn't even a match for her."

"Hmm," he said, before he put his tablet aside and stood. "Everything good with Fast Lane's new distribution and shipping? How are things working out with the Rodderick Shipping contract?"

Fuck.

My father poured himself another cup of coffee.

"Yeah, I put two and two together and got Merlo." My father said, pulling out the sugar and spooning into his coffee. "So does Harper know you gave Rodderick a lucrative shipping contract in exchange for their alliance with Merlo?"

I dropped my head. "It's not how it happened and if she did, you wouldn't be asking me this question." I glared at my father. He never said anything without a reason, "What's your point?"

"Don't you think that's something she's going to figure out? She's a bright girl, after all."

He shrugged, walking back to the table and sitting down, as if he hadn't tossed out a piece of information that, if handled poorly, could wreck everything.

If she heard I bought the alliance with Rodderick Racing by signing a contract with their parent company to do shipping for the chain of stores McBane had just purchased—I closed my eyes to the thought. She would think it was me interfering—worse because months have gone by and I never told her.

I meant to tell her—I'd planned on telling her. But things had been dicey between us during that time. She was defensive—so resistant to anything I tried to contribute. When she called me so excited about getting the alliance with Rodderick, I didn't have it in me to tell her about how it happened.

"Fast Lane needed a new shipping company." Did I call them because Standard Stock broke their contract with Merlo before the season started? Yes. "By entering into a contract with Rodderick, I got a reputable shipping company for our new chain of stores and was able to solve a problem for Harper—for the team." She needed the confidence boost. When Rick asked if I wanted Harper to know about our conversation, I didn't think much about it—I just told him no. I figured, I'd tell her...eventually. Then it never seemed to be the right time. There was the problem with Jeff, bringing on Jacks...In hindsight, keeping it a secret wasn't my smartest move. But she was so defiant, and I was—well, I was being arrogant and impatient.

I leaned back in my chair, wondering what this was going to cost me. What would my father do with this knowledge?

He took a sip of his coffee and stared out the window.

"What?" I said, unable to deal with the suspense of what he was going to drop on me next.

All innocence, he replied, "Nothing. Was just wondering what you were going to do about it, that's all. "

He lifted himself from the table. "Don't let this distract you, Cal. Harper may have to stumble and fall before she learns to ask for help. You need to focus on the bigger picture. As the acting head of McBane, you need to delegate and move on."

"Come on, let's go into my study and go over a few things before you leave for the office."

I tried not to thin my lips in frustration. I did not appreciate being micromanaged.

"Dad, I have a meeting in an hour."

"Then I won't keep you long. I want to give you my thoughts on a few things that'll come up while I'm recovering."

46

CHICAGO, IL

Cal

It had been one of the longest days of my life.

Dad was out of surgery and resting as comfortably as possible in intensive care.

"We believe we got all of it," the surgeon told my mother. "Let's wait to get the lab results back to determine the next course of action. For now, he's resting, and you may go see him briefly. He's going to have a hell of a headache, and terrible vertigo. We will try to make him as comfortable as possible."

I stepped forward, "Doctor, what about…side effects?" What about permanent damage? Those were the words I wanted to ask but didn't dare in front of my mother.

The doctor put a hand on my shoulder. "Let's see how he does over the next two weeks and go from there. Each person is different, and the placement of your father's tumor was pretty rare."

The doctor and I had previously talked about possibilities with my father at a visit my mother didn't attend two weeks ago. We knew the risks. Right now, I was the only one conscious, besides the medical team, who knew the risks he now faced.

And even though the family was together, I felt alone.

Arms came up behind me, wrapping around my middle, and Harper's head laid against my back, enveloping me in her warmth and comfort. I knew she felt me tremble because she tightened her grip, drew me in closer. I laid my hand over hers and squeezed gently. "I'm okay."

But I wasn't. I needed to be strong for my mom. Hell, even for Grady.

I turned, kissed Harper on her forehead before walking to my mom, who stood on wobbly legs even as her chin tilted up in determination. "Let's go see your father, boys."

She didn't want to go alone.

Grady and I flanked our mom and held her hand tight as we walked down the hallway. I hit the button to open the wing doors leading us to the recovery room.

We stayed at the hospital the rest of the day and until visiting hours ended; convincing my mother to leave was no easy feat. But we finally explained to her that while he was at the hospital, he was surrounded by nurses. When he got home, he needed her to be well-rested to care for him there. Of course, I didn't mention that I already arranged for a night nurse to come in and sit with him once he was home, and a chef to cook meals for them while my father was laid up. They would both argue—but I'd cross that bridge when I got there.

For tonight, Harper and CJ took a car and picked up some dinner on their way home.

I knew what Harper's schedule was like—and how hard it was for her to get to Chicago even for two days. I really hadn't expected her to make it. But God, I was so glad she was here. To have her walk into my arms when I got to my parents' house this evening—it wasn't joy, it wasn't relief, it was putting air back into my lungs and warmth over my skin. It was giving me something beautiful to focus on, to draw strength from.

With her arms around me, I whispered, "You being here—you don't know how much this means to me."

She squeezed tighter. "You'd do it for me."

"I'd move Heaven and Earth for you." I buried my head in her almond-scented hair and I meant it. I kissed her softly on the cheek.

She pulled back, and her eyes glistened. "Don't make me cry—not now, it will upset your mom."

I framed her face with my hands and kissed her on the mouth.

Right there—I wanted to say it.

But I knew it wasn't the time. It wouldn't have the right meaning. But I wanted to say those words.

I stared at her beautiful face, the one that gave me such peace, and gave her another small peck. "Okay. Let's go eat." The words would wait. The feelings were already there.

4 7

WATKINS GLEN, NY

Harper

It had been almost three weeks since Cal's father's surgery, and I hadn't been able to get away to see him. Between interoffice issues with staffing, our tight race schedule, and getting the newly developed Driven Women mentoring program off the ground, it was getting increasingly difficult to find time in our schedules.

The team was at Watkins Glen in New York; a roughly three-and-a-half-mile road course with eleven different turns, instead of the standard oval. Not exactly CJ's favorite, but for a former Indy Champ like Grady, it was more like home.

There was a bit of bantering going on between them that morning that was amusing and provided a distraction from my disappointment of not having Cal there.

"So, where is my favorite, soon-to-be brother-in-law," CJ asked, while getting into her fire-retardant suit.

I leaned in the doorway as she got ready.

"His father needed him to stay in Chicago so he could prepare him for a meeting he has Monday."

"He's got Cal on a bit of a short leash," CJ said.

"Yes, and it's chafing."

"Cal isn't exactly straight out of business school."

I sighed. "Everyone seems to recognize that except his father." I shrugged. "But the man just had brain surgery. It's hard to argue with that."

I studied my feet as I said, "He suggested he may look into relocating part of McBane down south when his father is back on his feet."

CJ finished zipping up the suit and stared at me. "Did he?" Her eyebrows lifted.

"Yes." I crossed my arms and studied the more sensible, designer pumps I decided to start wearing on race day after finally admitting my stilettos and sandals weren't practical.

CJ put her hands on her small hips and asked, "And how did you react to this?"

I shrugged. "He caught me off-guard, and I may not have been as excited as I probably should have." I looked up at her and saw her face fall with empathy. "I don't think he read my nonresponse correctly, and now I don't know how to handle it."

"Do you want him here? Do you want full access to him 100 percent of the time—or is he safer in Chicago?"

I stood from the doorway and straightened. "What does that mean?"

She sat down and grabbed her special fire-retardant race shoes. "It means, what do you want with him?"

"I don't think now is the right time to start breaking down my relationship with Cal."

She shrugged while putting on her shoes. "At least you're admitting it's a relationship."

"CJ—"

"Don't forget who you are talking to. You have Spencer sniffing around here as if he's waiting for his moment to weasel his way in."

"Don't be ridiculous." I threw my arms up. "Spencer has a girlfriend—"

She held her hand up to me. "Don't deny it. No man is that

involved in an ex-girlfriend's career without an ulterior motive. You may convince yourself that he's there with good intentions, and because you need what he's delivering—and maybe you also get a small amount of pleasure from his attention—"

"That's not true and very unfair—" That stung and shocked me that CJ would say that to me.

"But you know damn well, a man like Cal isn't going to tolerate it much longer. Would you?"

I pictured curvy, catty Vanessa circling Cal and it made me queasy and I gritted my teeth.

"Yeah, that's what I thought."

"What possible future could we have, CJ? I'm not going to leave Charlotte. He can't leave Chicago—"

"Says who?"

"He's running McBane. McBane is in Chicago, along with his mom and dad."

She stood up with her gear all assembled. "He's in Chicago, but it doesn't mean he wants to be—doesn't have to be. Hell, he's just told you he's considering a move down this way." She stepped up to me. "Grady told me his mother is painting his father's recovery in a totally different picture than what Cal is reporting to you. She says his father's recovery is going remarkably. She thinks he may be completely recovered soon."

"Huh…"

"Yeah. You better decide what you want from that man. Because I know he wants everything from you. That boy is head over heels."

"Don't. Just stop. You have a race to get ready for—focus on that and not on psychoanalyzing me." My tone was clipped and no-nonsense. "This isn't the time to discuss this—" I turned to walk out of the hauler.

CJ and I argued occasionally—our friendship wasn't perfect. We fought like sisters because we loved each other like sisters, and when we fought, it was usually because we thought the other one was sticking their nose in where it didn't belong, or because the other had their head in the sand.

Like now.

"You're being an idiot and you know I'm right." She yelled at me as I took long strides out the door. "Come see me when you're ready to fix the shit-storm you're stirring.

I thought about it a bit more later as I went to find Amy and check on the after-race schedule. Maybe I could get away for just one night and fly straight to Chicago after this to see Cal? Being away from each other, and with both of us under such immense stress—it left so much room for uncertainty.

I pulled out my cell to text Amy and find out her location.

"Harper! Hey—Harper—"

"Oh…Spencer." Not exactly the man I wanted calling out my name. CJ's accusations about how I enjoyed the attention he gave me were on repeat in my head.

He came jogging up to me. "Hey, I thought that was you. You look great, by the way.

Where are you off to?"

"Just trying to locate my assistant. What's going on?"

He motioned to the stands behind pit row. "I've got Emerson and some of his friends here—they are going to meet Jacks in the garage, and then when CJ's ready, your people were going to lead them over to do some photo ops." He tilted his head. "Is everything okay?"

"Ah…" I nodded, and stared back at my phone, pretending there was a response. "Yes, fine. She should be out soon."

"Harper, wait." He grabbed my arm but let go quickly when I stared down at where he was touching me. "Please. I'm glad I ran into you, actually."

I stood with my feet together, crossed my arms and tilted my head. I was cold, rude, but CJ's words were haunting me. "Why is that?"

"I wanted to see how you were doing—how things were going for you?"

"I'm fine, Spencer, but I am really busy. I'll find you and Emerson when the race starts.

Thank you for bringing him. I'm sorry, but I really must get going —I have to go…check on a few things."

I wound my way around him just as a crowd of spectators walked between us, offering me an escape. "I'll catch up with you later."

In the end, CJ finished in the top ten, which was one of her best finishes at a road race. Of course, Grady won it. There'd be no living with him, so even though she pissed me off earlier, and I was still fuming, we had an image to maintain and we both put on our best smiles.

"He's going to be a pain in the ass about this..." she grumbled.

"Yep," I said, and inwardly took some enjoyment in that prospect, because I was still ticked at her.

CJ did a few interviews, did the round of photos and autographs while I spoke with Jacks and Amy about our schedule. We all began to walk back toward the garage where Grady was waiting for us, still in his race suit and fans all around him—mostly women, of course.

CJ stood with her hip cocked out and arms crossed, a smirk on her face. "Well, as long as he's swarmed, he can't give me shit, I suppose."

I had to admire her reasoning.

"Harper!" Spencer's voice penetrated the myriad of fans and crew people walking around.

CJ looked over her shoulder. "And here we go..."

I put my hand on her shoulder. "Don't. There is a lot of press and cameras around—I don't want anyone trying to figure out why my driver started verbally eviscerating a man right in front of her fiancé. There will be talk and we don't need it."

She glared at him, then cocked an eyebrow at me, "I'm not a bully, Harper. You want him here—fine, he's your problem." She turned and walked away from us.

I dropped my head and pinched the bridge of my nose.

"What's wrong with you and CJ? I didn't think she did bad today?" I cringed at his backhanded compliment. Then his tone became stern. "Is she taking it out on you?"

I shook my head. "No...You were looking for me?"

"Hey, I'm getting ready to leave, taking Emerson and his group out for dinner, but I needed to tell you something—" He pulled me aside, trying to find a place nearby that wasn't as crowded.

"I'm not going off into a dark corner with you, Spencer."

He shook his head impatiently. "Listen, I don't have time—Just listen. Dewey's been relentlessly pursuing me for dirt on you. I think he's even tried paying off some people in your garage—"

"What the hell? What could he possibly be looking for? We haven't done anything wrong!" I practically yelled.

Spencer glanced over my shoulder and around us. "Keep your voice down. People are staring at us." He pulled me over to an area between two trailers, where it was more private and darker. "I didn't tell you because I knew you already had enough on your plate. I thought I could handle it and tried to find out what was going on…"

"I thought he was just going to try to steal some sponsors, maybe some employees…but it's more than that. He really, really hates you guys."

"And…" I rolled my hand, motioning him to tell me what I didn't already know.

He stepped closer, and my back was almost against the trailer. "He's been pressing me for information about you—about CJ—about Merrick. Anything." He leaned closer and whispered, "He's asked personal stuff about you and me."

He held me by both my arms. "He's digging to find out anything he can from anyone. And I have a feeling if he doesn't find anything soon, he's going to start making shit up."

Out of the throng of people came, "Harper Merrick—as I live and breathe. Oh—don't the two of you look so cozy." He greeted us as if meeting old friends through a crowd of people.

He was followed with the flashes of cell phones. I held back a curse as I realized with Spencer's back turned toward them, at this angle, our position appeared compromising.

Fucking Dewey Dupree.

Spencer thinned his lips in anger before he turned, blocking me with his body from their view as if we were doing something that required him to defend my honor. Jesus Christ. That made it worse.

"Spencer, we were looking for you—thought we'd grab some

drinks on the way back to the hotel. I didn't know you already had your hands full." Dewey's voice was louder than it needed to be.

I pushed Spencer out of the way and strutted out from between the trailers, toward Dewey and his buddies. "What do you want, Dewey, except to spout innuendos and be overall slimy?"

A gauntlet had been thrown down and the crowd drew closer.

"Don't start with him, Harper. He's baiting you." Spencer walked up behind me, lowering his voice.

"Aw, how cute. The lovebirds are even whispering sweet words to each other. No doubt there is a reconciliation in the works—I'm sure your family will be thrilled to hear it. Maybe a certain investor would be equally interested…"

"Dewey, enough with your theatrics—just leave." I walked by him. Spencer followed, putting himself between me and Dewey and his buddies.

"Won't Cal be a bit put out that you seem to be putting out while he's away?"

A general silence fell, but the lights on the cell phones were blazing.

I was well aware of the cameras, and of how less than fifteen yards away, Jacks was holding CJ back in the garage—her stream of curse words were drowned out by the growing crowd's buzz. If CJ came after Dewey, it would make his year. If she knocked him out again, she could get suspended or even kicked out of the season—same with Grady. Cooper and Grady moved over in CJ's direction. Gus stared at me over the crowd, the tilt of his head asking if I wanted help.

No, I got this. I shook my head slightly. Still, being my pseudo-big brother, he began walking over slowly, as private reassurance.

But I'd had it with Dewey. He'd been a thorn in our side for as long as I could remember.

I turned to meet Dewey face-to-face. With all the exasperation I could muster, I crossed my arms, jutted out my chin and said, "What do you want, Dewey? This whole villain scheme thing you have going on is getting so old." I overemphasized my annoyance.

He blinked.

I flicked out a wrist. "I mean you are kind of wearing it out a bit. Don't you have any new material? Don't you have anything else going on in your life besides the relentless need to destroy little old CJ and me? I mean, I'll speak for CJ when I say we're flattered that you think so highly of our importance that you've set your life's goal as destroying our lives." I shrugged.

"Personally, I guess I don't know how to handle the fact that we mean that much to you."

His taunting expression was gone, replaced by the ugly fury that was the true Dewey Dupree.

"But I'm beginning to feel like a rerun of Bugs Bunny, and you're Elmer Fudd." I turned to Spencer and tapped my finger against my chin. "Or maybe I'm the Road Runner and he's the Coyote?

"You do have those gorgeous long legs?" Spencer said, playing along with a sly smile.

I turned back to Dewey, who was now turning purple, and walked a bit closer. "Either way...I think you need therapy—maybe a life coach and a new set of goals, because I'm seriously thinking you need to rethink your purpose—"

Dewey's fury turned maniacal, and he lunged at me.

Spencer encircled me in a bear hug, yanking me back and turning me, putting himself between me and Dewey.

Dewey broke from his friends and swung, connecting with Spencer's back, hitting him blindly in the side of the head and throwing Spencer to the ground.

Dewey managed to straighten just in time for me to kick him in the balls. After all, I did have my gorgeous long legs. There wasn't any reason to hurt my hand with a fist to his smarmy face.

Besides, I just got my nails done and even if my shoes were more sensible than my normal stilettos—they were still pointed-toed. They still got the job done without me risking a twisted ankle.

Once Dewey soundlessly dropped to the ground, I glared at his friends.

Gus came sauntering over, hands in his pockets. He leaned down and pulled Dewey up by his collar, practically throwing him at the gang of sycophants he walked over with. "Take this idiot and get him out of here before these fine people get more footage of him getting his ass handed to him by our Boss Lady."

Gus stood next to me, watching Dewey limp away, throwing a murderous glare over his shoulder before a guy turned him around and pulled him along. I asked, "How does an idiot like Dewey even have friends?"

"They aren't friends, they're sycophants."

I wrapped my arm around his neck and kissed his cheek. "You're my friend," I said.

He pushed me back playfully. "You just dropped five levels on the bad-ass meter. Stop being such a girl." He moved his hand to put it on my head.

I blocked him with one hand and pointed with the other. "You ruffle my hair, and you'll suffer Dewey's fate."

He chuckled before we both turned to see Spencer on his knees, shaking his head.

"Oh, right," I said, bending down to help Spencer up.

"Spencer—are you okay?" I dropped to the ground to check on Spencer, placing my hands on his face and chest to check him out.

"I'm okay..." He tried to get up and I propped him with my arm and helped him to a seated position.

CJ and Grady joined us just as security sorted everyone out.

Spencer rubbed the side of his head, above his ear, near his temple. "I got my bell rung, that's all. He caught me from behind—just a cheap shot."

"You should go to medical and get checked out," I said, searching the area for a cart.

"Don't be ridiculous." He waved me off. "I took worse blows to the head in college fraternity brawls."

"No. I saw it—where he hit you—you should go." I motioned to Amy who had a cart. "Come on, I'll take you and we'll get you checked out."

CJ grabbed my arm and turned me to her. "Are you okay?"

I nodded and put my hand to my forehead, trying to get my bearings. "I'm just so tired of him looming over us."

"Well, I don't think you kicking him the balls was going to be the way to make him stop." CJ had her hands on her hips, and I almost laughed at the change in roles we were having. It felt a bit liberating.

"Yeah, well. I'll tell you what...not sure I care, because it felt great doing it."

4 8

CHICAGO, IL

Cal

Fucking Dewey Dupree. Something in my hand went sailing across the room and smashed against the wall.

Great. It was the remote for my television. The sound it made smashing against the wall wasn't even that loud to be satisfying.

Fucking Spencer.

Fucking Chicago.

Fucking McBane Industries.

I should've been there. I should've stopped that shit.

I paced my den. It wasn't enough. I walked throughout my home like a caged tiger. I wanted to pick up my phone and call Harper, but I needed to calm down. I didn't trust my voice. I wasn't sure exactly what I was going to say either.

I was just so pissed off at everyone.

I was pissed at Dewey the dickhead and I wanted to rip his dick of and shove it down his throat.

I was pissed at Spencer for being there and defending her when I couldn't—for being her hero.

I was pissed at myself for being so selfish as to hate Spencer for defending her—if he wasn't there, she could've been hurt.

I was also pissed at her for mouthing off to a sociopath like that. He had a hard-on for ruining those girls. He was a masochistic, incredibly unstable, and insecure man who won't rest until he can satisfy some unmeasurable need to destroy them. And she taunts him? Was she insane? She told him he's foolish and needs therapy; compared him to Elmer Fudd and Wile E Coyote—alright that was kind of funny and creative.

What the hell was she thinking?

I went to my side bar and pulled out my scotch and poured a generous glass—promising myself not to throw it. I drank deep.

I took another deep swallow.

And what the hell was she doing with Spencer anyway? Why was she off in a dark corner of the garage area with her ex-boyfriend? What situation allowed him to imply she was cheating on me with him?

What the hell was going on when I wasn't there?

I decided to call my brother first. Maybe warming up on him will help calm me down before talking with Harper.

"Hello, bro," he said with a casual tone.

"Is she alright?"

"She's fine. Never laid a hand on her."

"Where is she?"

"She's at medical with Spencer making sure he's okay. He got blindsided on the side of his head. Was a bit slow to get up."

"Pussy."

My brother guffawed. "You'd think so."

"Why was he there anyway?"

"No idea. But probably not the right time to start the third degree."

"I know," I said sharply, and anger was creeping in my tone. Deep breath.

"Rein in the macho man. There's nothing you can do about it."

"You'd be the same way if there was livestream footage of your woman caught in a dark corner with her ex-asshole, and she mouthed off to a crazy man who swung at her, only to be saved by the ex-asshole, and because your ass is stuck in another city."

"I know. But you know Harper would never go behind your back. Dewey was determined to get his pound of flesh from her, so she gave as good as she got. He couldn't handle the comeback—he never can. I think that's why he has a hard-on for our girls. They don't back down —and they humiliate him each time they're pushed against the wall."

"It's probably why we love them," I admitted, running my hand over my face, absently.

My brother was silent, "Damn, bro."

"What?" I said, annoyed, and ready to be done with brotherly bonding.

"You love her?"

"Shut the hell up."

"You know I'm going to pick the most inopportune time to announce that, right?"

"Don't you fucking dare."

49

WATKINS GLEN, NY

Harper

I was in the medical center with Spencer when I finally had a moment to look at my phone. There were numerous missed calls and texts — several from Cal.

Cal: Are you okay?

Cal: Harper, are you okay?

Cal: I will send Grady to find you and put a phone in your hand if you don't call me.

I texted him back.

Harper: I'm fine. Everything is fine. I'll call you in a few minutes. I can't talk right now.

"Hey, Harper!" It was Grady who caught up with Amy and me on the way back to my trailer. "For the love of God, could you call my brother back? He's driving us nuts."

"I know, I'm heading back to my trailer now to call him." I went over a few things with Amy about calling our media people and also our lawyer. The confrontation was viral, and even network news picked it up—with audio. Great.

I was within sight of my trailer when I dialed his number and Cal picked up on the first ring.

"Are you alright?" Cal immediately said, but terse.

"Yes, I'm fine. I'm on my way back to my trailer. I was surrounded by people for the last few hours and didn't want to call. But I wasn't even touched. Dewey was being a douche—as usual—"

"Then why not just walk away?"

"Because I couldn't," I bit out, because I didn't think I should have to explain that.

I walked in my trailer, locking the door behind me and tossing my bag on the captain's chair.

"You shouldn't have engaged him—"

I halted in the middle of the trailer, unable to see anything but red. "Again, I didn't start it—I had nothing to do with him being there. And are you seriously scolding me—as if we were children in a play yard?"

"You were acting like it!" he yelled. "You took on a bully and gave him exactly what he wanted—a spotlight."

"I hit back. That's all I did—"

"Without any thought to your own safety or how others would perceive you?" His tone turned condescending. I could challenge yelling, but I would not tolerate condescension.

I knew he'd be concerned, maybe even upset about the fact that I was with Spencer. But I was speechless at this reaction.

"Why was Spencer even there?"

"He wanted to warn me about Dewey...and he was there when Dewey caught up with us." I was brisk.

"Isn't that convenient."

"What are you saying?"

"Don't be naïve. Spencer dragged you into a dark area to *talk* with you, and Dewey happened to find you alone with him as a dozen people recorded it. We may not be flaunting our relationship, but Spencer knows, which means I'm sure so does Dewey."

"And with Dewey's comment today, about you being put out..." I didn't finish the quote. "Everyone else will know we're together."

"You're not seriously focusing on that as being your biggest problem, are you?" His tone was cutting. "Your team, once again, looks volatile, emotional, non-professional, and drama-laden. Exactly what you've been fighting back from."

It was a kick in the stomach.

"So you're saying, because I defended myself... because Spencer came to warn me about a bully who'd been trying to sabotage our team, because that bully publicly attacked my reputation, and he even took a swing at me—I'm the one who looks volatile, emotional, unprofessional, and what was the other one? Oh, drama-laden?" My eyes were burning, my hands were shaking, and I fisted the cushion of a chair from the spike of adrenaline coursing through me.

"Harper..." his tone impatient. "Wait..."

I held up my hand as if he stood there in front of me. I couldn't believe this was happening. "Because I defended myself, because I had the balls to stand up and say, 'Fuck you'...it makes me look unstable? Makes me appear unprofessional?"

"Harper, that's not what I—"

"What the hell was I supposed to do, Cal? Let him publicly humiliate me? Wring my hands? You weren't there...you didn't see the smugness on his face—"

"I know I wasn't there!" he roared. "That's my point!"

I held my phone away from my ear. I was done.

DONE.

I put the phone back up to my ear but remained quiet. But my breath was heavy enough for him to hear.

"Harper..." His tone was more conciliatory, as if unleashing his anger and frustration allowed him to think more rationally now—lucky him. Now he successfully transferred it to me, the weight of his anger, his disappointment, his frustration all on my chest now.

"Harper, I didn't mean—"

"Shut up." It was clipped and loud and full of resentment. "You listen to me. I know you're used to controlling situations and influencing decisions and how people behave, but I've dealt with that my whole life."

"Sunshine—"

My voice was steady and hard. "Don't be so fucking condescending right now and think calling me an endearing nickname is going to calm me. Your ability to cloud my head with memories of kisses and warmth I've never felt is not going to let you have any semblance of control over me."

"Harper—" his voice was raised again, but the tone was different— more anxious and impatient. "Wait. Listen. I didn't mean it that way. I'm just—I'm just upset. I was angry—"

"Yeah. Well, congratulations on unloading it on me. With all the battles I was in today—this one..." I paused because I knew if I spoke without drawing a breath, my voice would crack, and I didn't want to give him that. "I thought you knew me. I thought you liked me and the person I was trying to become." I took a deep breath to stop a hitch in my voice. "I certainly don't need another self-righteous man dictating the way I behave or who I'm supposed to be. It's what I've been fighting to get away from all along. Goodbye, Cal."

And then I dropped the phone, fell into the chair, and was filled with so many mixed emotions...for once, I couldn't even cry.

"Have you talked with him?" CJ asked as we walked into Rodderick's main offices later that week. She was scheduled for time in their simulator to go over some calibrations with the car for that weekend's race.

"No, but you already know that, don't you?" I walked by her.

"Well, obviously not from you since you wouldn't return my calls."

"I don't want to talk about it," I grumbled, because if I talked about it, especially to CJ, I'd start to cry again. The moratorium on my tears only lasted for five or ten minutes. Once the adrenaline calmed down, the tears ran free.

"He knows he fucked up," she said, trying to keep pace with my long strides as we went down the hall.

"I don't want to talk about it." And goddamn the hitch in my voice. Damn my emotions.

She grabbed my arm. "Harper." And damn the concern in her tone.

"Not here. Not now." I held up my shaky hand to stop her from saying more.

From behind us came another set of footsteps. "Harper—oh, nice to see you. CJ, glad you're here." It was Rick Rodderick, and his welcoming voice was an intrusion into our tense standoff.

I turned around with the well-practiced smile plastered on my face, blinking quickly as I silently prayed the wetness in my eyes would dry up quickly. "Hi, Rick." I took in a deep breath, hoping to camouflage my small sniffle. "How are you today?" I straightened my back and approached him with my hand out to shake.

"Well. I'm doing well." He took mine in a light, quick shake—because, you know, I'm a girl, and it would be unseemly to actually give me a real handshake.

I might break.

Yeah, I was in a bitchy mood.

Then he stepped back and clapped his hands together. "CJ—Moe is inside ready to start. I believe Jacks is in there looking rather lost. He brought Mel along with him and she's a pistol." He chuckled. "If she can drive as well as she throws attitude, she'll be a force to reckon with.

I'd met Melody Ferguson, "Mel"—CJ's new protégé, and the driver Jacks had told us about a few weeks ago. She was a dynamic driver and a wild card. She was young, cocky, and very rebellious. But the one thing that kept her in line was she loved driving, and she wanted to be like CJ—even if it was the last thing she'd ever admit.

"Yeah, somehow Jacks is under the misconception that like-calls-to-like and thinks I'm the one who can focus her." She chuckled as she pointed to herself with her eyebrows raised. "Me? Focus someone. Who would've had that crazy notion?" she said, lightening the mood. "As if I'm grown up or something and they're looking to replace me with the next pain-in-the-ass."

CJ walked off, leaving Rick and me in companionable laughter. "God, help us all—another CJ. I'm not sure the series could take one more," Rick said, but it was in jest.

Ever since we signed our agreement with Rodderick, Rick had been firmly on Team Merlo—it was very refreshing to have an actual ally whom I wasn't related to.

"Hey, let's go outside and enjoy the weather while they do their thing. I'll get us some drinks and we can sit on the patio," Rick said.

"Just water for me, please."

"Got it. I'll be right back. Maybe you can give me the dirt on what happened with Dupree last weekend." He walked off and I strolled through the back of the building to the veranda, finding a seat at a table and chairs off to the side and under a flowering tree. Here we go. I don't think I can handle being polite if he gets condescending and judgmental.

Rick came out and sat across from me. We exchanged some updates that we'd heard about other teams and their drivers. We'd talked about upcoming tracks and race predictions, and I'd been enjoying talking with a fellow owner in a companionable way that wasn't rife with friction.

"I have to say, it's been a real joy working with Merlo and watching your team come up." He took a sip of his water. "Everything y'all are doing with the new developmental program also, I'd like to be part of that next year."

"That would be great," I said, leaning back in my chair and beginning to relax. "We have Mel for now but have other candidates we're interviewing."

"Cal mentioned you were going to bring on some engineering students too—maybe possible crew members. That'll be exciting. I actually have an automotive engineering degree from Clemson. I'd love to get involved with that." He pointed his water bottle at me and smiled with enthusiasm that was contagious.

Wait. Cal?

I coughed a bit while it registered what he said. "Cal?"

"Yeah, when I spoke to Cal last week, he mentioned you were interviewing college engineering students for an intern program. I told him I'd be interested, and he said he would discuss it with you and get back to me when he was down here."

I covered because that's what you did when you didn't know what the hell was going on—you covered and pretended you did. "Sure, we could do that." I took a sip, trying not to let my face fall. "When were you planning on talking with him again? Maybe I could set something up before then?"

"I'd have to check my schedule. He's supposed to come out to check on Fast Lane's new executives and was going to swing by and see how things were running with the distribution—make sure things are working to everyone's satisfaction."

"Oh. I see." I tilted my head, trying to remain casual. "I wasn't aware you shipped for Fast Lane."

He shifted in his seat. "We didn't until McBane bought them last winter." He checked his phone. "Looks like I'm needed upstairs. I enjoyed our visit, Harper. I hope things work out for CJ in the simulator today, and good luck this weekend." Rick began to walk to the door of the building that led back inside.

I nodded. Not sure if I wanted to ask this question but needed to get the answer from him.

I turned in my chair. "Rick, one more thing, when did you sign a deal with McBane—for Fast Lane's shipping?"

He held the door open. His face fell, probably realizing I may not have known about the deal Cal had made with them. "I was already considering your offer, Harper, when he called me—but getting McBane's contract sweetened the deal."

My hands shook.

Cal sat there and listened to me gush about landing Rodderick's alliance. How proud I was of getting that agreement on my own after my own father turned me down. What a fool I was.

I ran my hand through my hair and stood on shaky legs. He bought that alliance. Did his father know? Who else knew—who else knew I was duped to believe that I was a success all on my own?

At least now I was definitely too angry to cry over the ass. Forget being hurt by him—I was furious.

50

CHICAGO, IL

Cal

The rain the next morning would've gone unnoticed if I hadn't stepped in a puddle outside my parents' house, further darkening my mood.

The very last thing I wanted was to be called to my father's study to have "a word" before I went to the office this morning. I hadn't told anyone of my problems with Harper, except laying into Grady about it when he called me after I'd had a glass—or three—of scotch.

I was on my parents' front step with a soaking wet shoe, equally wet leg of my trousers, was late for the office, and on my very last shred of patience, when my mother met me at the door.

"Oh, look at you—you poor thing?" She grabbed my soaked umbrella and jacket. "Take off your shoes and socks and let me see if I can get them dry while you go speak with your father."

"Mom, I'm fine—"

She pushed me down on the chair in the foyer as if I were six, and bent over, pulling off my shoes.

"Mom—" I tried to fight her for my shoes, but the woman wasn't having it.

"I can't have you traipsing around my house with wet shoes and socks." She pulled off my socks. "I'll throw these in the dryer and get you a pair of your father's." She turned to walk off, then stopped. Eyeing my pants.

"Absolutely not." I pointed at her. "You're not taking my pants." I emphasized by stretching to my full height, which was a foot above her. "You may have caught me off guard before, but you won't take me down again." I edged out of the foyer in the direction of my father's office in my bare feet on the cold marble—feeling a new level of low.

My father stood at the doorway of his office with a knowing smile on his face as I dragged my ass down the hallway—exhausted, in a wet and very expensive suit, barefoot, and missing my jacket.

"Well, you look like hell..."

"Isn't that my line?" He actually looked good. Not as bad as he did in previous visits.

"It's the morning, so I always have the most energy in the morning, which is why I wanted to catch you on the way to the office."

We went in and he motioned for me to take a seat at the chair in front of his desk, as he often did when I was younger and he wanted to have a "serious talk" about my future, or some transgression I had made.

"How did your doctor's appointment go yesterday? What did they say about your recovery?" I asked as I put my computer bag down in the chair next to me. "Mom seems in a good mood, so it must have gone well."

He waved me off. "You know your mom—ever the optimist."

"What's going on, Dad?"

He situated himself in his chair and sighed. "Grady told your mother that you and

Harper have hit a bit of a rough patch."

Grady and I were going to have words, because I didn't need him running to our mother about my love life—or what was probably the end of it.

Another gut punch hit me. I needed to talk to Harper.

"Grady has better things to do than gossip about me," I grumbled.

279

He leaned back. "Did she find out you bought the contract with Rodderick?"

"I didn't buy the contract—"

He waved me off. "Whatever, semantics. Did she hear about your deal with them? Is that what this is about?"

I ran my hand down my face. "No. I was just being a jealous ass. I said things I shouldn't have, and now she's not taking my calls. I'm hoping to fly down there tomorrow and try to clear things up."

He propped his elbows on the armchair and steepled his hands. "I see."

"What?" I didn't have the patience for this.

"Son, you can't run down there every time you two get in a disagreement. You have commitments here." My father stared at me with the same expression he used when he laid down his expectations for me. When he told me what my grades were expected to be, when he explained the colleges I was to apply to, and when he told me to give up football because it was too much of a distraction. "You have the meeting with the Kensington people on Friday and—"

Drowning him out, I took a breath in through my nose and held it before releasing it—trying hard not to lose my temper on a man who recently had brain surgery—because, really, how low could I go?

He prattled on with what were essentially my commitments for the next week, explaining what I should be focusing on instead of my actual life.

My father stood to walk from behind his desk, as if his home office was his new corporate location. "Also, Trey gave me the numbers on last quarter's—"

I rubbed both hands over my face and through my wet hair. "Father, when did the doctor say you can return to work?"

He froze and glanced up at me from under his reading glasses. "I'm sorry—what?"

"Clearly, you're working, just from this location. If you can check on my schedule, manipulate those around me, and prioritize my life, I think you are well enough to start taking back this goddamn company."

"I have a right to watch what is happening at my own company. I'm not dead, yet."

"Clearly. And stop playing that card with me. Was this supposed to be a test? A trial run for when you do kick the bucket? Maybe test my loyalty—my dedication?" I squinted, possibly seeing things for the first time. "Or do you simply not trust me to become you? Because I won't...I won't become you. Not for any money in the world."

I began to pace. "Is that why you've been micromanaging all the work coming across my desk and secretly directing staff people from here—because, yes, I've picked up on that, too."

He still didn't blink.

I stared at him. "I'm right." Indignation swept through me as I began to raise my voice.

"You've been distracted—"

"Damn right, I'm distracted." Years of pent-up anger and frustration were boiling up. "I'm trying to have a life outside the walls of that building. Outside of your directives and prospects. It's my life."

"Don't be so dramatic." He waved me off. "It's not like that—"

"You either trust me to handle the company in your absence my way, or get your ass back in the office, because I'm not thrilled about dancing on the end of your strings."

He ignored me and walked around his desk to the table by the window, shuffling through some folders. "You should've told her about Rodderick," he repeated, and sat in his chair as if the conversation was over.

"Jesus, what is it with you and the Rodderick deal? I'll tell her—give it a rest." I ran my hand over my face. I tried to control it—tried to control my tone. "Right now isn't exactly the right time."

He didn't look up as he walked back to his desk, studying the sheets in his hand. With a deadpan tone, he dropped the next bomb to shatter my day. "It's too late. She already knows."

"What?" My mouth went dry. No. "What the *hell* did you do?" I yelled.

My mother stepped in the room, her mouth agape and her face

turning red as she approached my father's desk. "My goodness, Cal... what's going on?"

I couldn't even look at my mother with the anger I was failing at controlling. I was a beast in a cage that had been poked too many times and was unhinging the lock.

"What did you do?" My voice boomed and I stepped up to my father's desk.

My father's resolve turned on me. He stood and raised his voice. "You had no business buying that damn team—none." He threw a hand out at me. "It's been nothing but a distraction to you. The last thing we need is another son being sucked up into that nonsense—"

"Michael!" My mother moved forward, slapping a pair of shoes and socks on his desk.

"What? He had his twenties to get the rebellion out of him—he had his football years. It's time for him to settle down and act serious, for Christ's sake. Have we not learned anything the last few months? What happens when I'm no longer around? What happens to the company?"

"Does your ego demand the complete sacrifice of my future and any happiness to McBane as a loving memorial?" I leaned over his desk. "I'm not you—it's not my mission in life, and it sure as hell is not my dream, to be Michael McBane 2.0." I stepped back, but my father's only movement was the tick in his jaw as he clenched his teeth.

I stared down my father, who was unsettled by the level of push-back he was getting from me. His facial features were twitching, and it was the most emotion I'd seen in him since Grady's scandal broke.

"You hand over millions of dollars to a pretty face and a nice set of legs—a girl who barely knows what she's doing—"

"Don't—" I spat out, held up my hand, then growled, "You don't get to be so damn condescending. That *girl* had the courage to go after what she's wanted and the guts to break away from her father's yoke and expectations. Something I clearly need to learn from."

"Yes, well, now that girl knows that you've been the man behind the scenes pulling all the strings and making her little team work. Maybe we can at least cash out and not lose all our money on this—"

My ears were ringing, my pulse was racing, and I couldn't do this anymore.

"Find someone who will fit into your shoes…or become immortal." My voice was unusually dead. "Those are your options. I stepped in to help because you're my father." I stared at my father—the man whom I was supposed to model myself after—and saw nothing I wanted to be. "I'm stepping back now because you're not acting like one."

I grabbed my bag off the chair; I reached inside and pulled out a notepad and a pen. I scribbled on it, tore off the sheet, went over and slammed it on my father's desk. "Find a different marionette—I'm off to find my own life."

I turned to leave when my mom grabbed me. Her glare was solely focused on my father, but she squeezed my arm to offer support and understanding. A tear appeared as I kissed her cheek, patted her hand, and gently pulled away. I wasn't sticking around to see how that played out; he was on his own. I leaned over and took the shoes and socks, then walked out of my father's study without another word.

On the desk in big, bold scribbled letters were two words, "I quit."

I barely got my socks and shoes back on before stalking out of my parents' house and into the rain—no job, no woman, and no clue what I was going to do next.

5 1

CHARLOTTE, IL

Harper

After driving back from Rodderick, I sat in my car in the Merlo parking lot. CJ went into the garage and I told her I needed a minute— but all I was doing was staring at my phone. I knew I shouldn't have done it, not while my hands were still shaking. But something in me needed to speak to him—maybe needed the confirmation that he kept this from me. Surely, I misunderstood something somewhere. He wouldn't let me look so foolish in thinking I did it all myself, only to have masterminded the whole thing.

He picked up on the first ring. "Harper?" There was muffled street noise coming through the phone as he spoke, his tone a bit rough. "Is everything okay?"

I paused.

"Harper?" he repeated, worry seeped into his voice.

"I just left my meeting at Rodderick."

"Shit," he bit out. "I was just getting ready to call you—"

"Why would you need to call me about Rodderick, Cal? What would you need to talk to me about?" Even I could hear the snippiness in my voice, and that wasn't the attitude I wanted to portray. Screw it.

"Dammit Cal—did you bribe them with a shipping contract to work with us?"

"No—not exactly. It wasn't a bribe—"

"Why am I just hearing about this? What did you do?"

"Harper, I didn't do anything. I just helped you find—"

"You made me think I got that agreement locked up by myself. God, I'm such a fool!" I practically yelled it from inside my car.

"It's not a big deal. They wanted to work with you anyway. Rick just told me the other day they're planning on renewing for next season —" he said.

"Great. Glad you heard about that. He just told me today. Glad you heard it first since you clearly are the one in charge." I sounded like such a bitch. I sounded petty. I hated it—it was making me feel worse.

"Harper...I was just trying to help. You were being hit from all sides earlier in the season."

"Jesus, when are you going to get it—the difference between help and interference? Help is when someone asks. Interference is when you're stepping in unwanted."

Cal's voice boomed. "I help those I love—it's who I fucking am! I can't apologize for that. I may be an ass in how I go about doing it— but dammit, Harper, everything I've ever done was to lighten your burden, not add to it."

The only thing I could hear after that was his heavy breathing and the city background noise.

"Listen, things here just took a major turn for me. I'm flying down to Charlotte. I'll talk to you about it when I get there. Okay?"

I didn't know what to say. There were too many negative emotions inside me—and I didn't trust any of them to form coherent words.

"I need to go." It was all I could manage, and I hung up. I continued to stare at the building. Merlo's building.

Merlo was up and running and doing damn well. We had good part-nerships, good team members, and a good start. I looked down at my phone. Did it really matter, how we got there? I palmed my phone as I got out of my car—then it hit me. *"I help those I love—it's who I fucking am!"*

Those I love.

Well, damn. I closed my eyes so tight, it almost hurt.

What was I supposed to do with that?

NEW YORK CITY, NY

Harper

Amara Chopra, our PR media consultant, was circling me. "Are you sure you're up for this?" she asked. "This interview was booked weeks ago, before the fiasco at the Glen, and to be honest, you're not exactly yourself."

I strode forward. "No, I'm good." Amara had set up a series of interviews to promote our new Driven Women non-profit group. It was developed to mentor and promote women in racing—on the track, behind the wall, in the shop, and behind the desks, and it was ready to be unveiled.

We brought Melody "Mel" Ferguson along as our first participant, and I prayed it was a good decision. She agreed to join CJ and me on stage with Tyler Wilson—the sports commentator I verbally sparred with a few months back and created an uproar when we walked off his set before announcing Merlo's inception—effectively withholding the scoop we promised because he was being a jackass.

When Amara first approached me about this possibility, I asked her to find a different news outlet. Tyler himself called me, apologized for our original squabble and his behavior, and asked us to come.

"I know we didn't get off on the right foot this winter, but I really do admire the work y'all have been doing. Hell, you got Jackson Grove to come out of retirement. Plus, you managed to find a way to give back by forming this group. Come on the show, bury the hatchet and let's talk about it."

I agreed to it, only because Amara had lined up other interviews with online magazines and even a morning talk show, and we'd already be in New York, so it made sense. After all, any publicity was good publicity, and the second appearance would generate a lot of buzz, both for Tyler and for us.

Cal had tried calling several times. But with everything going on, I just ignored his calls. I didn't know how to deal with everything. I didn't have the time, and if I were honest, I was afraid if I did talk with him, we'd end things in the way we couldn't find a way back from. I wasn't ready for that either.

I help those I love—it's who I fucking am!

Cal hadn't ever given me the impression he was trying to mold me into someone else or trying to convince me to be someone different. If anything, he'd told me to stick up for myself more often—not to let employees get away with things. Which is why his reaction to Spencer and Dewey didn't really make sense.

We were situated on the dais and Tyler came on while talking to someone on his cellphone, smiling before saying, "Okay, great. Got it. Yep. That'll work. I'll remember that. I've got to go…" He hung up and greeted us all with a smile. A very unsettling smile.

He introduced himself to Mel, who was unusually reserved as she shrank back a bit behind CJ, to whom Tyler just nodded. I still found it amusing how much she scared him. He was practically twice her size; his beefy hand enveloped mine when we shook.

"I'm so glad you agreed to come on," he said, while the sound guy was hooking him up and people were still milling around.

"Thank you for inviting us." I sat in a tall chair next to him, in a blue pants suit, and crossed my legs, brandishing my new cherry-red stilettos—my new power shoes. CJ and Mel flanked my right side, with CJ wearing her wine-colored Merlo team shirt, as was Mel, to show the team's brand. Sitting next to each other, even though their appearances were different— their confidence and petite, trim frames unified them as athletes. Also, they were both fidgeting, shifting in their seats, and obviously not comfortable having to sit still. "I must admit after our last visit, I thought we'd be persona non grata." I gave him my most charming smile, wrapping my clasped hands around my crossed legs.

He waved me off. "Bygones. It's television. It's racing. No problems." The crew got in place and the director counted back, giving Tyler the sign.

"Hello Race Fans—" His voice faded out while I scanned the set. I shifted in my seat, with a smile plastered on my face as I focused on Tyler, promising I wouldn't allow myself or CJ to be goaded.

Nonetheless, the vibe felt off.

"Even after having a rocky start with Jeff Brooks' surprising departure, Merlo Racing has quickly found their footing with CJ Lomax cranking in one win and a few top fifteen races."

He turned to me. "Not bad for a debut season—"

"It's not over yet," I said. "We admit it was a rough start, but with Jackson Groves joining us, the hard work put in by CJ and our entire organization, and some amazing sponsors like Eastman Insurance and Hewitt Tools, we're getting to where we want to be."

"Yes, getting Jacks was an amazing coup—"

"It's how we found Mel Ferguson." I gestured at Mel and smiled. "Jacks brought her to our attention, and she's one of our first recruits to 'Driven Women'—the program we've started to support women in STEM careers and in racing."

"Yes, very admirable. Jacks has long been known for championing the underdog. It's one of the things people admired him for—even your father. Speaking of your father, how did he take the news?"

Ugh. I wasn't going to avoid talking about Dad. "He thought it was great. It's no secret he and Jacks had a falling out years ago, but he knows what a valuable asset Jacks is to any organization—"

"Especially one just starting out—one a bit young and green, so to speak." Tyler's smile wasn't kind—it was a cat about to pounce.

"Anyone would be lucky to have Jacks, yes." I didn't know where he was going with that, but luckily, he moved on.

"And your sponsors...I heard it was tough." He gave a disingenuous, concerned face, his brows lowered, his smile gone. "Some jumped ship after the sale, and even more after CJ and Jeff's scene after Daytona. It seemed CJ's antics weren't what they signed up for..."

CJ subtly nudged my foot. She felt it too, we were being set up. She sat forward in her seat and I brushed the side of her arm. "We're proud of the relationships we have with our sponsors now and are looking forward to a continuing partnership with lots of wins." I smiled at the camera.

"Yes, of course. It was a good thing you have friends in high places with strong financial backing and good connections, huh?" He winked at me.

"We came back stronger—as we always do," CJ quipped. I squeezed her arm and glanced over at her and Mel, who was still sitting there with her arms crossed, now glaring daggers at Tyler.

He focused on CJ, daring her with a predatory smile, and back at me. "After Standard broke their agreement with you—did you ever find out what was behind that, by the way?" He didn't wait for us to answer. "You were lucky to have your boyfriend, Cal McBane with McBane Industries, strong-arm Rodderick into an alliance with you. Is that how McBane operates? Can't race a car without an engine and supplies, can you?"

BOOM! One bomb dropped.

"And having McBane behind the sponsorships with Hewitt and even Eastman...did he bully them into sponsoring you also? Maybe 'McBane' should be on the side of the car."

BOOM! Another one.

"Is it possible that McBane positioned himself to buy a team for his brother, Grady McBane?" He pointed at CJ. "He's your fiancé, correct? Keeping it in the family at least. It's not easy for an outsider to buy a team in this series. This way he could use your connections and those of your father to get the best lineup of people for the team he wanted. The last time you were here, you made a point to say how the Merricks only hire the best." He pointed at CJ. "Plus, he gets all the attention and publicity from *your* antics. So, when he swoops down to save the team with a champion like Grady, they'd be set?"

"Don't be ridiculous..." I gritted.

Tyler snapped back, "He owns more than half of the team, doesn't he?"

"He's an investor—"

"And how much does he have invested, Ms. Merrick? Enough to replace who he wants, when he wants? Or at least his father probably could...ever think of that?"

BOOM. That one hit a target.

My whole body went cold. Because I hadn't. What happened to Merlo if Cal's father didn't want it anymore? Or what if he wanted someone else to run it or—

"And then there's Jackson Groves—"

No way Cal had anything to do with Jacks—he didn't even know the man.

"Turns out your father and Jacks aren't as much on the outs as everyone believes. My sources tell me your father went and begged Jacks to come out of retirement and," he glanced down at his notes, "'take you in hand' I believe were the words I heard."

"We approached Jacks—it wasn't like that. We asked *him*..." CJ jumped in, because I was practically shutting down. "You get him on here, you two-faced rat, and ask him."

"Tyler wouldn't do that," I said, low, but loud enough to be heard. "It doesn't feed into this drama he's perpetuating."

"For being a self-proclaimed, independent woman...a 'Boss Lady,' as some around the garage like to call you..." He chuckled with clear disdain. "Are you sure you aren't more of a front man—or woman, I guess—maybe even a socialite with a clipboard. Should we have Cal McBane here to do the interview instead?"

I sat back, crossed my arms with a blank expression.

He tilted his head, furrowed his brow farther and sat a bit forward as if readying for my secrets. "So tell me Ms. Merrick," his voice was chilling, "Exactly what did you do yourself that contributed to the team's success? Except get a new haircut, and smile pretty for the cameras?"

I wasn't smiling now.

I was speechless. I was on television and had just been torn to shreds—my biggest fears and insecurities proven. But I wasn't going to give him the pleasure of seeing it. He'd get nothing from me.

Screw him.

"Are you finished?" I said.

"So, where is Mr. Cal McBane today?" He pretended to look around the studio. He pretended to listen to his earpiece. "Is the worst-kept secret in the series about you two already over? Is that why he's not around anymore?"

He shuffled his notecards around, pretending they interested him as he muttered, "Guess he already got what he wanted..."

Out of nowhere, Mel flew past CJ and me, to Tyler, who was reveling in his shots and insults. With both hands on his barrel chest, she threw her weight behind her and shoved him hard, sending him toppling back off the dais.

She straightened, wiped her hands on her pants as if he had cooties, and then turned to us as if she'd just smacked a fly.

CJ and I glanced and each other and then back at her, trying desperately to hold in our laugh and look parentally disapproving. But her actions snapped both of us out of our stupor.

"What?" She shrugged, then gestured at Tyler who was flopping around like a turtle stuck on his back. "He was being an ass."

CJ muttered and stood still trying not to laugh, "Girl...we got to do something about your impulse control." Then, pushing Mel out of the way, she strode over to Tyler who was still struggling to get up. "Just as soon as I castrate this mother f—"

I cut them both off. "Ladies…" I motioned to the cameras that were still live. I stepped forward, my cherry-red stilettos inches away from Tyler's fingers. "I got this." I smoothed down my pants and cocked out a hip, waiting for Tyler to get vertical again.

Tyler finally stood. Realizing he'd been tipped over like a cow in a pasture by a girl a third of his size…his face was almost as red as my shoes.

He pointed at Mel. "You need to control that hellion—I don't know where you find these bitches—" the word was spat out like a bad seed. "But you're lucky you're a girl, otherwise, I'd—"

I cocked an eyebrow at him as he tried to turn his chair to the upright position. Seeing the expression on my face, he put the chair between us. I shoved it out of the way and, being mindful of the camera angle, I got up close to him so everyone could see our expressions and hear every word.

"I really don't know why you seem to have a need to degrade us— to spread lies just to score a few points—"

His machismo returned, slightly. "Oh sweetheart, they aren't lies. I have sources who can back up everything I just said. I think you're the one who has been spreading lies—misrepresenting who you are and what your group is all about."

CJ came to stand behind me and I knew if the cameras weren't rolling, Tyler would be picking up his balls out in the parking lot trash can. It was a testament to how much she'd grown that she was not only restraining herself, but clamping her hand on Mel to keep her in check as well.

"What we are about is trying to get past petty little men like you, who spend Monday Morning quarterbacking because they couldn't hack it in the racing industry themselves or tearing other people down better than them because they're jealous. It's juvenile."

I turned back to the producers. "I thought this was supposed to be a legit show about racing…not a gossip rag."

Tyler pretended to laugh. "You've got no come back, so it must all be true."

I turned back to Tyler. "If it were true, where are your sources? They're hiding, because they're scared of us. Just. Like.You."

Two crew members came to stand between us as he began to get closer to me. I didn't flinch.

"I'm sorry if you felt the need to invite us on here, have us come here in good faith, just to try to tear us down, because the last time we were here, a girl bested you—called you out for being condescending and dismissive."

He picked up the chair and threw it. "You are all a bunch of entitled bitches—"

I pointed at him, ignoring his outbursts, because I'm sure they just cost him his job.

"We're done here." I stepped far enough away so he couldn't reach for me, but right in front of the cameras, I turned toward him, braced my legs apart, hands on my hips, and made sure all could hear me.

I finally stopped and tilted my head. "I'm sure your 'sources,'" I used exaggerated air quotes. "Will appreciate this drama, especially at your expense, because you won't get out of this unscathed. But you see..." I turned to the camera, "If they'd concentrate on staying in their own lane, they may have had a chance at beating CJ once in a while, instead of wasting their energy trying to tear us down."

"No, they wouldn't..." CJ added in.

"Like hell they would..." CJ's mini-me, Mel, chimed in.

"Making a point, ladies."

"Fuck off." He glared at me with menace.

I took in a deep breath, clapped my hands together, and flipped off my bad ass switch. "Okay, then." I started to walk off stage. "Well, I can't say this was particularly productive." I straightened my jacket and looked over at my girls. "But how about we go get some dinner?" I looked over at Amara. "Italian or Indian before heading home?" I walked past the cameras, CJ and Mel following, as we handed off our microphones to befuddled crew members.

Tyler was yelling in the background, while producers were trying to talk to him in hushed voices.

CJ came next to me, confusion and not a small bit of suppressed violence in her tone. "That's it?"

"His cheap shots aren't worth dignifying. We know the truth. We'll let our success speak for itself." But my best friend knew me and could see the rage in my eyes as I clenched my hands to stop them from shaking. I was calling on every minute piece of patience and ounce of respect I had to hold my shit together.

53

CHARLOTTE, NC

Harper

The next day, we drove Mel to Jacks' house to drop her off. Jacks met us outside and motioned me to the front porch and outdoor seating area he had there.

He leaned forward, elbows to his knees and without greeting or preamble, he started, "When Bill called me and said you and CJ wanted to talk with me, I knew why. I'd been watching you two and knew y'all were mischief. I was also struggling with trying to figure out what to do with Mel. I called your daddy before CJ came to see me. I didn't want to disrespect him and go behind his back. Even though we had bad blood years ago, it was over our stupid pride, and I wouldn't get between a father and daughter. That's not how I do things."

I nodded. "Yes, I get that. I understand—" I leaned back, crossing my arms.

"Your father didn't have to convince me of anything, Harper. I'd been watching CJ all last season. I saw what she was doing—I wanted to figure out how to whip Mel into shape. I'd never even considered coming out of retirement or that a young team like yours—with your technology and new way of doing things—would want an old dog like me."

"But why—"

"Your father didn't want you to think he had any sway over my decision, so he thought it was better we didn't tell you we spoke."

"Win or lose, hiring me was your decision—and mine, I guess." He smiled at me. "All your father and I did was come to a mutual understanding for your benefit, Mel's, and hopefully, the team's."

Okay, but if I'd known, I wouldn't have looked foolish when someone twisted it.

"My daddy felt he had to bail me out of my mess with Jeff. He said he was going to go out and find me a crew chief."

"He didn't need to, though—because your daddy could never have gotten me on his own—you did."

After that, I found the courage to take on the eye of my emotional storm. As CJ drove me home, I grabbed my phone.

"Who are you calling?"

"One guess."

She lowered her hand onto my phone. "Don't. Not like this. Not as upset as you are—you're hurt and angry and you have a complete right to be—"

"Don't you think I have the right to be!" I yelled at my best friend and she flinched. I didn't yell—not at her. She pulled into an empty parking lot and threw the car in park before undoing her belt and turning to me, her back to the door.

Tears broke through—it was safe with CJ, but I now added frustrated to the list of other emotions flowing through me—humiliated, ashamed, disillusioned, hurt, and all those led to fury.

I clamped my mouth shut and stared out the window. My head in my hand and my elbow on the door.

"How do I salvage my reputation out of this? How do I— goddammit, I don't know how to sift through all of this. It hurts."

"Harper—" She grabbed both my hands and sat quietly for a moment as my crying was the only sound in the car. "Let's break this down into two different issues. Even if they are connected. First—the team—all these men did was help you with ingredients for this team—you made the cake."

I felt the tears flow quicker, but I didn't open my mouth because I knew there'd be a sob, and it would infuriate me to be crying that hard.

"Harper—I'm an ingredient, the sponsors, Rodderick's engines, Jacks, the crew, Amara, Mel, hell, even Cal and that idiot Spencer—we're all just ingredients. Don't you see that? You're the one who mixed them all together.

"Sadie came up with the idea, but you ran with it." She grabbed both my hands.

"You brought these people together, and you're the one who motivates and inspires them." She shook my hands to get my attention. "You were the one brave enough to start this—to put all these people together—to put together a vision."

"I'm still only a skirt and a pretty face. Everyone thinks I'm hiding behind—"

"Who cares? Fuck 'em. Seriously." She yelled at me and squeezed my hands. "I thought the whole point of this team was to ignore and defy 'everyone.' You knew this would happen—that haters like Dewey and Tyler—those who can't hack it—would be the first to criticize you."

It was such a CJ thing to say, I had a crack of a smile.

"Jesus, Harper, they would've found something else to pick on you about. What's the worst thing they had up there—that people helped you? Don't you think any of the top teams had any help or investors? Hell, don't you think any of the top entrepreneurs in the world got a boost from someone? Why is it different if a woman does?

"You've handled bullies like Tyler and Dewey before. You handled Tyler today—just as you always have—with sophistication and grace. You put his ass back in his rightful place. Behind you."

"And Mel, well…she just gave him a good shove off his throne for good measure. He was pushed down by a girl who wasn't even me—on national TV—and then given a verbal smack down by you, again!" Now CJ was the one with a smirk on her face. "The girl is growing on me, you know." She gave me a side-eye of amusement. "Don't you think he should be the one crying in his car?"

I thought of the scene from that perspective and my smile grew.

CJ added, "Hell, I think that's worth popcorn and a replay."

I let out a small laugh.

"Maybe we can play it on a loop in the garage just for fun. Over. And over. And over. "

We both chuckled a bit at the idea of a Merlo's funniest videos clip until I grew somber.

"One thing Tyler said was true, though, and I'm a bit freaked and pissed because I didn't think about it all those months ago—Cal owns half of Merlo. What happens if his father wants to sell it? Or what happens if he wants to replace me or you?"

"Can he?" CJ's voice was soft.

I shrugged, staring out the front window. "I'm not sure how it would work. But it could cause problems." I clasped my hands. "Do you think any of that was true? That Cal is going to try to take the team? Do you think he was trying to use me, was that why he was trying to mold me?"

"God, no." She was quick to answer, grabbing one of my hands, her voice decisive.

"Because," my voice hitched. "I don't know how I would handle it, if I found out another man I loved was trying to do that to me, again."

"You love him—you love Cal?"

Damn. Where did that come from?

I pulled out of her hands and wiped my fingers under my eyes, pulling down the mirror to see if there was any way to salvage my makeup. "That's not what I said…"

"Hell, yes, it is. You said—"

"CJ, focus—the man kept interfering the entire season and sticking his nose in things after I told him, over and over again, to leave it."

She looked ahead and sighed heavily. "You knew the type of man you were getting involved with…" she said quietly. "Cal is a good guy. Deep down you know that. But because of that, you knew he wasn't going to sit back and be quiet while he watched you struggle. However, that doesn't mean he was trying to change you—"

My jaw dropped. "Struggle? What. The. Hell?"

CJ held a hand up to me. "I'm going to remind you of something you said to me when I was all drama with Grady last year. I'll paraphrase, but it was basically, 'Oh, poor me. A sweet, hot, loyal man keeps trying to take care of me...how dare he...boo hoo...'" She gave me jazz hands to emphasize the sarcasm.

"Now, I agree, he may have been a dick; he's been intrusive and pushy and moody. But think about his intentions and go talk to him. Hand him his ass, tell him to go sit in the corner and think about what he's done, if you want. Let me call him. Give the man a chance to talk to you." I glanced over at my friend. "Then show him who's Boss Lady in the bedroom." CJ had the nerve to waggle her eyebrows at me.

"You are spending far too much time with Sadie." I let out a shaky laugh before pinching the bridge of my nose and taking in a deep breath. "I can't—not tonight. I need to go home and clear my head. I'll deal with the next level of drama tomorrow."

5 4

CHARLOTTE, NC

Harper

Home. It had been a long twenty-four hours since that shitstorm of a show and I was finally home—in my yoga pants, on my couch watching *Friends* with cookies and cream to soothe my nerves. I'd sent CJ home, which wasn't an easy feat. However, I couldn't deal with anyone right now. I begged her to give me the rest of the evening to be alone, and I would deal with the world tomorrow. I knew Cal was at the lake house, but she said she'd delay him.

When my buzzer rang, I was extremely disappointed, figuring she'd failed to follow my request.

I shoved a scoop of ice cream in my mouth and stomped over to the door, ready to ream anyone on the other side. "You had one job—"

The face that greeted me was a surprise. "Hey."

Spencer—with a plastic bag he held out as if it were a shield. "I brought you something to help take the edge off." Through the opaque grocery bag, I saw the outline of a pint of Ben & Jerry's.

I stood in the doorway, thrown by the unforeseen visitor. "Hey, um, thanks." And stepped aside as he walked forward.

"I saw the interview." He cringed slightly. "And you handled that prick brilliantly, but I knew you'd be fuming—so I took a chance and thought you could use something to cool off with." He brandished the ice cream as a lavish prize. "Ta-Da!"

I reached out and took the ice cream before walking back to the sectional where my nest was already arranged. He followed and chuckled when he spotted the cookies and cream already half-devoured.

"As you can see, I've already begun Operation Cool Down." I waved at the evidence of my indulgence.

"Good, I can tell, since your temper seems under control and your penthouse seems to be in great condition." He walked around through the dining area and into the kitchen. "It is a beautiful place. Very you—elegant, but not stuffy. Beautiful and uplifting."

"Thanks." I sat back on the sectional. Feeling a bit lost as to how to handle him being here, but deciding to go back to my ice cream. I'd let him tell me whatever he had to say and then I'd make a polite excuse about wanting to go to bed.

He walked back into the living area and around to sit next to me with a spoon in his hand. "Do you mind, I haven't eaten dinner yet, and I'm a bit starved," he said, with a soft tilt of the side of his mouth.

"Sure." I gave him the carton he brought.

"Let's share," he said and opened the Americone Dream—a flavor we both enjoyed.

We both took a scoop—the only sound was Ross and Rachel arguing in the background as we ate.

"So how was your day?" he said, completely deadpan.

And I let out a small laughed.

"Seriously. Are you okay?" he asked. "It was hard to tell because you handled him like a consummate professional when he was nothing short of a complete jackass. I hope you know that's how it played out." He dug his spoon in the carton. "It was exactly like you claimed. He looked like a jealous ass taking cheap jabs at you."

I shrugged. "I've settled down." I didn't want to get into the fact that I was more upset about Cal, and my feelings for him, than the darn interview.

He studied the carton. "Have you spoken to McBane?"

Here we go… "Spencer, I don't want to talk about him. What are you doing here anyway?"

He put a spoonful of ice cream in his mouth before answering. "I was in town on business. I had a meeting at Dupree. As I left, Dewey asked if I caught Tyler's show last night. When I said I had, he asked what I thought of it. I told him the truth…that the guy looked like an asshole. That didn't go over well. Dewey tried to spin it—claiming that Tyler was just doing his job as a 'journalist.'" He used air quotes around "journalist."

Spencer turned toward me, put down his spoon, and leaned forward a bit. "I'd bet money he was fueling this. Is he still causing you problems, Harper? Where has McBane been? Why is he letting all this happen?" Spencer inched toward me, the easygoing expression left his face as it hardened with indignation. "Did he really bribe Rodderick? Did he buy Merlo for you—is that the power he has over you?"

I pushed back from him and pulled up my legs. "No. He doesn't have anything over me." My shoulders sank. "Please, Spencer, I don't —" I stood suddenly and walked away—needing to move.

He followed me as I walked to the tall windows overlooking Charlotte. "Is that why he hasn't been around? Has he grown bored of his pet project and moved on? You can handle this, Harper. We can get other investors and cut him loose. Merlo has the sponsorships we need. CJ is doing well. By next year, you can get a different company to provide supportive services—"

I shook my head. "It's more complicated than that."

"What? Tell me and I can help—you worked your ass off for this team. You built this team. You don't deserve that heat. Why isn't he standing up for you and issuing a press release refuting any of this."

"Because part of what they said is correct—and I just didn't know it," I said. "It was my fault for being ignorant and naïve."

"And what about your father? Where's he in all of this?"

Tears pooled in my eyes. "It doesn't have anything to do with my father."

"Well, that would be a first," Spencer grumbled. He turned me, his hands on my shoulders as he tilted up my head to look at him. "Wish he would've done that years ago—then maybe things would've worked out for us. Maybe then I would be the one by your side."

I didn't have the brain capacity to deal with where I think he was going with that comment and pushed him aside. "Spencer, don't—"

"Harper, you'll get through this. I can help—"

The buzzer on my door went again. Annoyance flashed over Spencer's face.

"Excuse me," I said, and walked to the door.

I was straightening my ponytail as I opened it and was greeted with a not-so-happy Cal.

"Hey, what are you doing here?" I said. "I told CJ I didn't want to see anyone tonight—"

His gaze grew dark as it darted from me to Spencer, who stood behind me, leaning into the door frame. "It seems not everyone got that message."

Spencer smirked at him.

Oh jeez. I rubbed my hand over my face. I was becoming a cliché.

I turned, blocking the two men from each other. "Spencer, thank you for stopping by and for the ice cream."

Spencer's face was stone cold, but he grabbed his keys and wallet from where he left them on my counter and strode forward.

Before I could catch him, he bent over and kissed my forehead. If it had been Gus, it would've been friendly concern—but with Spencer, it was pure challenge. "Okay, I'll call you tomorrow."

Cal walked forward, into my home.

I acted as a barrier and pushed Spencer out the door, but not before he caught my hand and said, "Think about what I said and call me if you need anything or—"

"I'll be fine," I said, and gave him a pathetic half smile and closed the door before Cal could do or say anything.

I turned to find Cal leaned up against the back of the sectional, arms and legs crossed, his head down. "Why was he here?" It was a rumble from his chest.

"He just stopped by to check on me," I said, rubbing my temple. I needed some ibuprofen.

"He seems to be checking on you quite often for someone who doesn't even live in this city...and who has a girlfriend." The volume and tone of his voice rose.

"Cal, it's nothing. He's been—" I began. But really, why was he around so much.

"Every time I turn around, that man seems to turn up lately. Makes me wonder how often he really is here when I'm not." He glared at me.

Was he really accusing me of something? "Excuse me?"

"Why does he keep showing up, unless you want him around?"

I threw my hands up in the air. "Did you really come over here to start a fight with me about Spencer—because I think we have enough on our plate to discuss without dragging him into the mix."

He stood there—leaning against my sofa, arms crossed, legs crossed, and glaring at me.

"Why are you here?" I was so exhausted. I didn't have anything left in me.

"You wouldn't return my calls."

"I don't want to talk right now."

I walked into the kitchen because I needed to get away from him. I didn't want to talk to him, look at him, deal with him.

"Harper, I need to talk to you. I have things to tell you about—"

I froze. Because it was too much. I couldn't.

"When will it ever get through to you to just stop and listen. Dammit, Cal. I don't care what you need—not now.

"I've been hit with one thing after another the past few days. I need some goddamn space." Words poured out with so much intensity, I couldn't stop to contemplate what I was saying or their implications.

"I need to be able to breathe for a moment and get my bearings." I turned on him, and a frenzy ran through my body, filled with truth. "It's not about what you need right now. I don't care if you need to help, or you need to tell me something, or you need me to behave a certain way. *I need you to stop.*" My emotions leaked through and my voice broke slightly. "I need you to give me some damn space, and I need you to leave me the hell alone." I caught my breath as the pain lashed out and struck him like a slap to his face.

He stood and walked to the door, opened it, and whispered, "I'm sorry," and walked out. The door slammed shut, rattling my world.

55

CHARLOTTE, NC

Harper

The rain and wind hitting the windows in my office were nothing compared to the tempest that hadn't settled in my head. I walked in this morning with barely any sleep but determined to pull myself up today. Even though our show was live, clips of it were sent to online news outlets and went viral on social media, edited down to show three brash, unhinged banshees responding to Tyler's allegations, and nothing about our responses. Making Tyler look like an investigative journalist, and us look completely unprofessional.

Some entertainment news show even had an exclusive with Cal's ex-girlfriend, Vanessa, who claimed I violently attacked her at a restaurant in Chicago when Cal tried to speak with her. That one made me laugh, and I lifted my phone to call Cal before I realized what I was doing.

Amara was on damage control, and Spencer left a message to say he stayed in town and was on his way over to talk strategy.

I was Sisyphus, who pushed that stupid boulder up a hill, only to see it roll back down.

First, my father paid me a visit—the first one to my office. He marched in, came over, and gave me a hug—being my father first. And damn, if I didn't need that hug.

He closed the door and said, "Come on, Sugar. Sit down. We need to talk."

And just like that, I was a fifteen-year-old walking into *his* office and being called to the carpet for something he was going to make into a life lesson.

My father had the no-nonsense furrow to his brow and studied me. "You are having a rough time of it."

"You saw the show?"

He nodded.

I gave my father a side-eye glance, and he peered up at me from under his glasses. "And I've never been so proud of you." He squeezed both my hands.

"Let's get one thing out of the way...Jacks." He held up his hand. "Yes, I talked to Jacks. It was the first time in close to two decades I talked to that man, and it was because he saw something in you—in Merlo—that dragged his craggy butt off the sofa and made him want to get back in the game.

"I thought it was a good idea—that was all. I gave my blessing—yes, I thought it was a good idea to have a set of seasoned eyes on you and CJ, because Lord knows you two can get in some serious trouble. The two of you are lightning rods, and as asinine as it may be, it gave you more credibility. Also, even though we may have our issues, most of which are related to pride and good ol' fashion arrogance, I trust that man to keep CJ safe in that car."

I locked my fingers together and put them on the table in front of me, studying them. The side of my father's mouth tilted up at the deviance he saw in me.

"Now, Tyler—you handled him—not once but twice. I don't care what that man thought he was going to accomplish by blindsiding you with what he thought would be shameful information." He tossed a hand up in the air. "Of course, Cal gave a contract to Rodderick to partner with you—it's business. Everyone's done it before.

"And your relationship with Cal is no one's business. McBane being an investing partner would be easily found out as public information. You're the President and CEO of Merlo. You're both young and single—who cares?"

He reached over and grabbed my hands in his, tugging them closer and squeezing them. "Darling girl, don't you realize they are reaching for things to hit you with because you all are winning. They're picking on you because they know you have what it takes to be successful, and they—as angry men—have no other way to fight it."

I whispered, "I just wish it would stop."

He patted my hand and leaned back as he changed the tone of his voice. "Gotta toughen up. I taught you better than this. Keep doing what you're doing—ignore them and they will continue to look petty. Now," he clapped his hands on his lap, "What the hell are you doing letting Spencer squirm his way around you again? I thought he was engaged and safely tucked far away from here? I can't imagine Cal's too happy about that."

I gave my father a brief synopsis of my night, and he crossed his arms and shook his head before getting up. "Cal has a lot going on at home—boy's got enough to deal with because that father of his is a real piece of work. He's tried to subtly bribe me into letting Grady out of his contract, and when that didn't work, he offered to buy the entire race team from me."

I shook my head—The nerve of that man.

"I don't know how serious he was being, and I doubt Cal knows about it, but I can imagine what it's like to work with him." My father straightened his jacket. "My point is, I don't think it is a good idea to push Cal with letting a weasel like Spencer in the hen house right now."

"I get it—why you all don't like him. I have issues with him still too. But like you said before, it's business—and Spencer is good at what he does—he's helped us tremendously this year. He was responsible for the Gwen Friday interview and truthfully, I'm not sure how far I would've gotten with the partnership agreements without him—" I ran my hand through my hair.

"Have you stopped and wondered what was in it for him? I know enough about the type of man Spencer is—and so do you. He's ambitious and he only does things for a reason."

I sat back down.

"What's in it for him?" My father repeated. "Think about why you two broke up to begin with, darling? Was he ever supportive of you or your career? No—it was always about *his* ambition."

My father gave me a hug and left me staring off into space, rerunning my conversations with Spencer over the past few months and the arguments we had when we were together, and my father was right. Things didn't add up. I took what he offered because I was too busy and didn't want to question it. But Spencer wasn't that magnanimous. He never had been. So my dad gave me a lot to think about.

My next visit was from my best friend. The wind and rain pounding on my windows was nothing like the hurricane she resembled blowing in my office.

"I've been thinking about it…I won't get into how fucked up your relationship with Cal is just now because I think you both need a cooldown and to sit in your corners." She began pacing the length of my room. "But someone fed Tyler that information, and I don't think it was Dewey. I don't think he's the one with the social media blitz trying to make you look like Cal's arm candy. If Dewey wanted to damage Merlo, he'd still come after me and Grady. He'd try to get us off the track, one way or another."

She stopped and emphasized with her hands outstretched, "There is so much he could attack us with. I mean, come on, Grady and I are easy fodder. My record wasn't great this year—they could still harp on the thing with Jeff or any of the other crew members I had words with." She pointed at me. "But even if it was Dewey trying to discredit you, he's more blatant. He would've wanted to be the one on the show laying out the rumors, not giving Tyler the limelight."

I remained quiet, sitting in my executive chair, pushing it back and forth and playing with the pen in my hand—listening to her but staring past her.

"Harper? Are you listening to me? I don't think this is Dewey." She waved a hand at me.

I nodded. "I know."

Knock...knock

Amy popped her head in. "Sorry to bother you, Spencer is here... again. He came by before, but I told him you were in with your father and he said he'd come back. I forgot to mention it."

CJ started to walk out but stopped and turned around. She leaned over my desk and tapped her finger, saying, "Think of who else would want to discredit a partnership between you and Cal? Maybe someone who would want to fly in and be a hero? Maybe get his happily-ever-after with you and maybe, eventually, get Merlo to run? I know who I'd put my money on..."

She walked by Spencer without a word as he came through the door. At the last minute she turned and swiftly, dramatically pointed at his back as if handing down a sentence of which he was unaware. With thinned lips, a predator's eyes and practically jumping in the air with immense distaste, CJ made it clear who she meant. Subtly was not her forte.

It amused me enough to take the edge off. I relaxed my arms on the armrest, leaned back in my chair. The picture of relaxation, but not getting up from behind my desk to greet him.

He came in and straight to the side of my desk. "How are you today? I stopped by earlier to check on you—"

"Yes, my father came by to check on me. Seems everyone is expecting me to break apart today."

He grimaced. "How about I take you out to an early lunch?"

I looked at the folders spread over my desk. "I don't think I feel like going out anywhere."

He sat down, looking down at the floor and then up, crossing a leg over his knee—the picture of casualness. "What happened after I left last night?"

"Not that it's any of your business, but Cal's probably flying back to Chicago this morning." My voice was terse and flat.

He blinked. "Oh. I'm sorry. Really. I'm sure it wasn't something you wanted to deal with now with everything else going on."

Yeah, right.

"I saw the social sites this morning and really think it's important that you're seen out today. I think it would be good for you to be seen at lunch—especially the day after that story and all the media attention the clip from Tyler's show is getting." I stared at him as he spoke. "Let's let them see this isn't getting you down. That you're business as usual and not under McBane's thumb. Let's change the narrative and get it back on business."

"We are working on that."

"Good. One thing to do is draw attention away from your relationship with him and let the media think you dumped him and moved on. If you aren't dating him, if they think you aren't dating him, there'd be less to say."

"We aren't seen together often anyway—"

"No, I mean, let the media think you are seeing someone else." He leaned forward, elbows on his knees. "Maybe a new love interest?" He gave me a pointed look. "Maybe a former boyfriend...It will set everyone's heads twirling. It will take the wind out of everyone's sails—your father's, Cal's, the media's." I studied the man who used to be my world. The one who, as a young girl, I was ready to spend the rest of my life with. "Just think, there wouldn't be any validity to what that Tyler-guy was implying. I'm not associated with racing except for working with Dupree through my firm—we have a history of being college sweethearts, no less."

"Spencer, there's the small matter of Susannah..."

He held up a hand. "She's not speaking to me at the moment, so that's a non-issue." He waved it off. "She knows I'm helping out over here. I can handle it."

"I don't think that is a good idea. I'll just be cast into the role of the 'other woman' then—no, thank you."

"I'm just offering to be a decoy. We can debunk it, later. Tell Cal if you want." He shrugged. "It makes sense. You can be seen with me a few times, let this crap about McBane die down. Let people see

McBane doesn't pull your strings and we can figure out where to go from there. Surely, he'd want that for you."

We. When did this become a "we"?

He tilted his head slightly, rolling his eyes to the ceiling as if searching out the answer. "Listen, just think about it—talk to Amara if you want. For now, I'm starving; let's go to the deli up the street and get some coffee and maybe something to eat."

I decided playing along with Spencer was the only way I was going to get some answers and get to the bottom of what involvement he had in all this. My bullshit meter was off the charts. The lingering memories of the way I felt for this man turned sour as I inwardly apologized to the younger me, while I mentally castigated myself for the fact that I ever fell for him in the first place.

I leaned down, grabbed my bag, and said, "Alright, but I have to be back in an hour for a meeting."

He winked the way he used to when he wanted to see me smile. "Got it."

I threw him a fake one—It was all I could manage.

5 6

CHARLOTTE, NC

Cal

I was in the kitchen when Grady got back from his jog. "You look like hell."

He was the picture of perfect health and happiness—and I wanted to punch him. I didn't care if his brain just recovered from being rattled. I settled for glaring as he walked into the hallway.

Gus came in behind him. Great. It was a freaking party.

"Hey, man." he said, going to Grady's fridge and grabbing a bottle of water for himself and another one for Grady. Grady held two small towels and passed one over to Gus. As if this was a routine for them.

How cute.

Yes, I was in a mood.

"I take it from the dour expression, Harper's not happy with you," Gus said, falling into the chair next to me, his breath recovering from their workout.

I turned to both men.

"I told you not to go over there last night," Grady said, also sitting down. "CJ told you to give her some space and let her settle down."

Gus winced.

"Yeah, well, I did. And it seemed I wasn't the only one who had the idea to check on her. Spencer was there, supposedly offering his support."

"He's a prick," Gus said, pulling his lips back from his teeth in a grimace.

"Yeah, well, the prick was definitely showing his true colors last night. He actually preened like a damn peacock when I showed." I squeezed my fist when I thought of him kissing her forehead. I wanted to throttle him.

"And..." Grady prompted me.

"He left." I leaned back, rubbing my hands over my tired eyes. "But it went downhill from there."

"Did you have a chance to tell her about the company—about the move? Did you tell her about the conversation with Mom and what it all means?"

I shook my head. "It never got that far. I showed what a jealous, selfish asshole I can be, and she basically told me to leave her the hell alone." I stood up, not knowing what I wanted to do. My body was a mixture of exhaustion and emotion.

"You never told her that Mom was taking over McBane until Dad was better? Or more importantly, that she was signing over all of McBane's interest in Merlo to you—along with Fast Lane's operations?"

I'd talked with my mother yesterday. She told me not to worry about McBane. She and my dad had a chat. She told him she was tired of him driving her sons away with his damn prideful legacy. She also informed him that it was her money that stared McBane. It was also her blood, sweat, and tears that went into that company. And if he needed someone from the family to step up, she'd do it.

Suddenly my father was feeling much better, but my mom wasn't backing down. She is diving right in and enjoying every minute of it.

"So McBane Industries no longer has interest in Merlo?" Gus said, surprise in his voice.

I pulled out and held up the printed copy of the forms my mom had drawn up and signed, giving me full ownership of the interest. The official legal documents were in the mail. I wanted to tell Harper last night as part of my apology and tell her about my plan for the future.

Of course, after our confrontation, I realized my other mistake. I was going to tell her about my plans. Not discuss them with her. Again—I was trying to control everything. I was going to tell her what I needed to tell her, what I wanted to do.

I wasn't going to ask her what she needed or wanted from me—from our relationship.

I put my head in my hands and ran them through my hair.

Then, I turned to Gus. "What do I do?"

He leaned back and stared at his bottle of water. "Heaven above knows I'm not one to talk to about love. But I know Harper." He looked over at me. Studied me closely. My disheveled hair, worn jeans, t-shirt, and I knew I looked like I'd been through hell. "I know you probably love her—after being around Romeo and Juliet." He threw a thumb over his shoulder at Grady. "I know it when I see it, now."

He took a tug off his water. "Spencer broke her heart, and it took her a long time to recover. My girl is forgiving, but she learns from her mistakes. If you want her—Lord, help us, because you two will always push each other. But I think that's a good thing. Give her some time, she'll come around. There isn't anything that's been done or said that can't be forgiven."

"Holy crap," Grady said. "That was like some real Dear Abby shit there..."

Gus slapped the back of his head. "Shut the hell up."

Grady laughed. "You just wait until it's your turn."

"Not going to happen." Gus said, getting up to toss his bottle in the recycle bin and walking out. "I'll catch you all later."

"When he goes down, it will be hard," I said.

"Yep. It's going to be fun to watch," Grady said, smiling at the prospect.

Then Grady turned to me. "So you really aren't going back to Chicago?"

I shrugged.

"What are you going to do?"

I tapped the kitchen table. "No idea. But I know whatever comes next, I'm done wasting my life. If this past year has taught me anything —it's that I want more out of it."

<hr />

CJ found me on their back porch later that morning and said Sadie called to tell her that we were going to meet at Merlo at 1:30, and "We're going to get this crap sorted."

"She's not going to want me to be there."

"It's business and you're an owner…you have to be there," CJ said.

It was a little after 1:30 when I strolled past the reception and straight past Harper's office—which was empty. There were voices coming from the conference room, and I made my way down there. I walked in without pausing to see who was inside—figuring I would find Harper there. What I found was her was posse—CJ, Sadie, Amara, Amy, Mel, who I hadn't met yet, and…"Susannah?"

She smiled a brilliant, white, all-teeth smile. "Nice to see you again, Mr. McBane."

"Cal, is fine."

And she responded with a demure nod. I gave a hesitant wave to the other women and walked toward CJ.

All the women were holding a glass of champagne—except CJ, who sat down with a bottle of beer she began pouring into a champagne flute. When I gave her a confused, but pointed look, she tilted her head towards the women. "They're trying to be all fancy."

I stared at Mel and she toasted me. "Hello, you must be Mr. McAsshat." I stared at her. She nodded the champagne flute at me. "Don't worry, it's sparkling cider—unfortunately."

"No need to start contributing to your delinquency this early in your career," CJ said.

Sadie came over and sat at the head of the table, motioning to me. "You look like hell, my boy."

I rubbed my hand self-consciously across my cheek and looked

317

down at myself. I hadn't changed out of my jeans or shaved. Guess I should've cleaned up a bit.

"Yeah, I look about as well as I feel." I sat down at the table with them. "What are we celebrating?" I asked.

"We aren't celebrating anything yet. We are preparing to celebrate," Amara said.

"Why is that?" I turned to Susannah. "And no offense, because it's nice to see you again, but why are you here?"

Her smile got even bigger.

"Because Susannah just showed up in the spirit of sisterhood, and we're waiting for Harper to return so we can celebrate," CJ said.

"Okay—still don't know what we're celebrating..."

Mel lifted an eyebrow at me and, with the arrogance of a teenager, said, "So since you're a guy and have a dick, you need to leave."

"Mel. Please," CJ said. "You realize you are speaking to the major shareholder of the team? Just please stay quiet, while you're here. Things are about to get dicey, and while I know you're going to want to be here for it—this is Harper's moment. We aren't doing negative vibes today."

All there to support her. All there to lift her up. I was negative vibes.

It had been clear from the beginning. She tried to tell me. Maybe I had been turning into my father. Maybe my "help" was more about control, interference, micromanaging, because I didn't have faith in her to do it herself. Even from the very beginning, I wanted to be part of it, so I forced myself in—being arrogant enough to think she couldn't do it without me.

Sadie studied me. "Cal? Are you okay?"

"Cal, I didn't mean anything by it." CJ gave an unusual apology.

I looked between the two women. Decision made, I nodded at Sadie. "You have a dollar?"

Her brows drew down in confusion. "Huh? Why?"

"Do you have a dollar?" I repeated as I walked toward her, scouring the table for a piece of paper and a pen. I pulled an envelope out of my back pocket, opened it, and leaned over Amara, to grab a pen that was laying in front of Sadie.

Sadie put down her glass and reached into her purse, pulling out her bedazzled wallet, yanking out the bill. I finished, folded it, and handed it to Sadie. She opened it halfway, saw what was inside, put a hand on my arm, and softly said, "Cal. Honey…you don't have to do this… Just let her settle down—you know she's stubborn. Wait until she gets back. And wait until Susannah—."

It was the second time this week that with a few pen strokes I changed the direction of my life. I just didn't know if it would make a difference. I held out my empty hand to Sadie, who studied me with concern, and she handed me the dollar bill.

I held up my hand—both as a final goodbye and a surrender. "It's what she wants. I've only wanted to see her succeed and make her happy," I whispered to Sadie. I turned to the door, tucked the dollar bill in my jeans, and threw over my shoulder, "It was good to see everyone. Now, you have something else to celebrate."

57

CHARLOTTE, NC

Harper

Returning from lunch, I strolled into the conference room with Spencer following me. I stared at the gathered group of women and noticed an unexpected addition.

Before I could react, Spencer stepped farther into the room. "Susannah?" His tone was a mixture of tight politeness and unpleasant surprise as he started to approach her. "Wh-what are you doing here?"

The cold determination in Susannah's expression stopped Spencer in his tracks.

I stared at Sadie for an explanation, and back to Susannah, who looked like the cat about to pounce on the canary. I just wasn't sure who was the canary—me or Spencer.

CJ stood and walked toward Spencer.

Susannah sat perfectly still as she sipped champagne.

Why were they drinking my champagne? CJ and I had bought it at the beginning of the season when we were filled with optimistic, heady expectations.

"I decided to pay my good, ol' friend a visit and check on how she was doing after having her reputation and everything she's work toward almost annihilated on national television." She calmly put down her glass, blinked as she tilted her head, and said, "And how about you, Spencer? Why exactly are you here?"

He straightened, his focus darted around the room, taking in that everyone there was waiting for his answer. "The same reason. I'm here to support her, of course."

CJ nodded her head. "Hmm. Amara and Susannah had a chat late last night after the interview. See, Susannah heard about Tyler's interview from a mutual friend, and decided to watch it." She addressed everyone in the room. "She's also been watching things play out from a different perspective than the rest of us."

Susannah stood slowly, and as she did, she transformed from the saccharin sweet debutante she was comfortable being, into the woman whose glare was hard on Spencer. "Imagine my surprise when I figured out the Tyler Wilson on television was the same one who had been popping up on your cell phone for the last two weeks." She walked around the table and toward Spencer.

I was right. I shot a glance at CJ for answers. CJ's Cheshire cat smile was on Susannah, whose expression morphed into calculation, determination, and vengeance—she was pissed. "I came up here this morning, met with CJ, Sadie, and Amara and sorted this shit—your shit—out…"

Spencer took one step back.

Sadie gestured with her champagne. "It's been illuminating."

"You see, Harper," Susannah continued, keeping her venomous look on Spencer, "I was suspicious of the way he was buddying up to Dupree—he practically threw himself at that account. I told him I didn't think it was a good idea. I thought he was just trying to get back at you—because of the way you broke his heart?"

"The way I broke his heart?" I was jolted and turned to Spencer, who held up one hand to

Susannah and one to me.

"Oh, yes, I got quite the sob story about how your family didn't think he was good enough." She flicked out her hand at us while she walked around the table. "He said your family thought you could do better and ran him out of town—shattered him." She turned back to him, "Isn't that right, honey?

"I thought his interest in racing and him palling around with Dewey Dupree was about revenge." She turned to me. "I was furious at you; at the hold you had on him and tried to figure everything to keep him away from Charlotte."

She stepped behind Spencer, who was perfectly still except for his clenched teeth and the flush creeping over his face. He bit out, "Harper, this is ridiculous and I'm sorry any of you have to sit through this drama—but Susannah is a bit bitter about how things are going with us right now—"

She threw her head back and laughed. "Bitter. Hell yes, I'm bitter." She turned and lunged as if she would slap him. "You didn't love me. You didn't even want me." Her breath seized and my heart broke for her. "He was on my doorstep just a few weeks after leaving you. So sad and despondent—he's been kissing my father's ass, waiting for him to decide to groom him to take over his company. We'd talked about getting engaged and then—" She clapped her hands together. "Bam—my daddy brings up a prenup and then he hears about you. A better prospect. He dragged me down to Charlotte the first time, I'm assuming, to see if you'd be jealous."

"Susannah—enough!" Red mottled Spencer's cheeks. "Harper has enough going on right now than to deal with your jealousy."

She continued as if he hadn't spoken.

She stood next to a dumbfounded me, crossed her arms over her chest as if we were Spencer's firing squad, and took a deep breath before continuing. "Things were different for you now…you had your *own* company. You were estranged from your family, and I'm sure he had plans on separating you from CJ and Sadie. But you had McBane there with you, and Cal was both a hinderance and a challenge."

"So, he dug in. He found Dupree and he saw your original interview with Tyler Wilson. He knew where to hit you."

"You fed him that information." I turned to Spencer, who hadn't decided how he was going to respond yet. A mixture of fury and fake incredulous ran across his face.

"Harper, don't let her get to you—you're angry and looking for someone to blame, and she's taking advantage to get back at me..." Spencer sputtered. "I told you about Jeff and Dewey...for heaven's sake, I helped get you the interview with Gwen Friday!"

Amara stepped forward and held up a tentative hand. "Um, no. I got the interview with Gwen Friday. She hates you."

Susannah didn't break stride. "You told Dewey to bribe the crew chief. Jeff was his name, right? Yeah, I overheard that conversation too." Spencer flinched, but recovered. "To get someone inside the team —a red herring—wasn't that your advice? I overheard him on the phone." She nodded her head at him. "One of the ways he got that account was because he promised Dewey he could feed him information to hurt you."

Even though I suspected it, the actual words being spoken hit me hard and I flinched.

"I helped get you sponsors. Why would I do that if I was trying to ruin them?" Spencer said to the room at large.

"To look like a hero," I answered for him. "Then discredit Cal and get him out of the way."

His mouth gapped and he stepped back.

Spencer threw up an arm. "This is preposterous."

I thought about the glee in Spencer's face when Cal showed up last night and was furious at seeing him there.

Spencer stepped toward me, but CJ stood suddenly, cutting him off.

He reached out a hand toward me. "Harper this is ridiculous—we'd already discussed all of this—our past, our friendship...you know I just want to be there for you. I've never stopped caring about you—"

CJ began clenching and unclenching her fists, and the tilt of her lips told me all I wanted to know about what she was thinking.

Mel decided she needed to break it down for him. "I don't know you from Adam, bud," she said, still sitting and trying to reach for the champagne bottle. "But..." She flicked her finger at him and then pointed at CJ's hands. "I were you, I'd skedaddle out of here before CJ puts the Daytona lockdown on your balls."

Spencer dismissed Mel. "Who the hell are you anyway?"

"Dude, I'm not kidding." Mel just shook her head as she poured the champagne into her glass.

He stepped back and he exploded, "I don't know what the hell is wrong with you all. All I was trying to do was help her."

"Spencer, when we were together," I turned to him, my voice soft and nostalgic, "I was so in love with you." He also softened, thinking he may have a chance to change the course of things. "But I was so young and naïve." I turned and walked around the conference table. "It's not an excuse for allowing you to try to change me, or ignore what I wanted out of life." I emboldened my tone. "I was never meant to be anyone's accessory or prize."

Susannah looked away and I felt a twinge of guilt. "Now that I'm achieving something, you have the nerve to show up here and try to 'help' me?" I reached the other side of the table, my girls all in front of me. "I don't think I need your form of help—as you can see," I swept my hand over the room of women, "I've got all the support I need right here."

"Here! Here!" Sadie shouted.

"Damn straight." Amara stood and threw some attitude.

"Fuck, yeah." Mel shot her hand up in the air in a sign of defiance and solidarity.

"Goddammit, Mel—language!" CJ shook her head, spotted the champagne, and grabbed her glass away from her. "I swear, you're going to be the death of me," she muttered.

"You women are fucking nuts." His hair wasn't as perfectly coiffed as usual, and his face wasn't just red with anger, his features were hard and unattractive. His mask was lifted, and I saw the real Spencer, the one I'd only caught glimpses of over the years.

"Spencer..." With my hands on my hips, I straightened my back and stared at him without a trace of emotion, and said, "Get the hell out of my office. Get the hell out of my building and get the hell out of my town."

"Harper? Are you seriously going to—"

I gritted my teeth. "I'm giving you until this evening to get on a plane, train, or in a car, and then I'm calling my friend Davy, and his buddies from Carolina's offensive line, to escort you out of Charlotte." I stepped forward. "Got me?"

He stepped back, holding up his hands, putting him right in front of the conference room doorway. "Screw you all. I don't need this in my life."

Susannah stepped forward, shoved him—hard—and said, "Don't let the door hit your ass on the way out." Then she inhaled deeply, straightened her sundress, turned to me, and said, "So you can get me an introduction to Davy Johnson?"

"Girl, back off—that one's mine." Amara eyed her with a tinge of amusement. "But he's got a whole team for you to choose from."

"Right on!" Mel shouted out and fist pumped the air. "Party!"

CJ rolled her eyes heavenward. "God, help me."

We broke out into a contagious laughter—the kind of group laughter that turns into its own event, and by the time you're done, you aren't even sure what started it.

It was cathartic, and after the last few days, we all really needed it.

58

CHARLOTTE, NC

Cal

I was on my second glass of scotch when three men flanked either side of me.

"So, how bad is it?" my brother asked. I glanced up to see Gus, and Davy Johnson, running back for Carolina's professional football team and a longtime friend of their crew, had also joined him. This was going to be either an intervention, or a lets-get-the-poor-guy-drunk kind of support night. With these three men, it could go either way.

Davy came over, hand extended; even the defined muscles on his forearm hinted at the exceptional condition of the rest of his body. "Hey, man. Nice to see you again."

"I heard you're buying, so I thought I'd come drain your pocket, since it's still the off-season." He smiled, running his hand over his short, natural curls before lumbering onto a stool.

I tried to give him a warmer welcome, but there was sympathy in his eyes I didn't want to acknowledge.

Gus got the curvaceous bartender's attention, leaned over, and whispered something in her ear that made her blush. Her gaze flash at him before she slapped him playfully.

At another time I may have found that amusing. Gus turned his attention off the bartender's ass and back to us. "What?" he shrugged.

"And you think football players are dogs?" Davy smacked him upside the head. "We aren't here for you to find a bedmate this evening. My man here doesn't need to watch you prowling."

I held up my hand to indicate it was fine.

My brother sat next to me. "So—what's the damage? What are we left working with here tonight? Is it 'Angry Cal,' 'Plotting Cal,' 'Screw'em Cal'?"

I stared at my almost-empty glass before saying. "Well, I'm not quite sure." I put the glass to my lips, finishing my drink. "Within a span of a few days, I gave up my job, told my father to go to hell, lost my woman, and just sold my partnership with a Cup team for a dollar."

"Well, damn..." Davy said, clapping a hand on my shoulder, and Gus flagged down his new favorite bartender. "Shots, it is."

I held up my hand. "No shots. I don't need anything that may lead me to dig more holes for me to fall into."

The pretty, voluptuous waitress came over, long lashes batting at all of us, and I ordered myself a beer, and let the other guys tell her what they wanted.

We were getting a lot of attention, and I remembered I was with two popular Charlotte sports celebrities. Even with a ballcap pulled down on his head, my brother was recognizable, even by non-race fans. And Davy, well, you couldn't mistake a man with his physique for anything but a professional athlete. Even Gus was getting a bit of attention because there's a reason people call him *GQ*.

Women—and men—were summoning up the courage to approach us.

Gus motioned to the table over in the corner. We tried to work our way over there, but Davy got sidetracked for a few selfies and an autograph or two. We put the two of them in the corner as if they needed protection.

With a few more beers and some coaxing from my intervention crew, I caught everyone up.

Gus sat quietly, spinning his beer bottle, contemplating something.

"Spencer's a jackass," Davy said, and his glare was of a man who faced defensive linemen twice his size without blinking.

"I can't believe she's letting him still sniff around her," Gus said. "I thought she sent him packing."

"Oh, he's been sniffing around, and now he's marking his territory."

"He's not after just her. He's after Merlo," Gus said, still leaning forward on his elbows. "He's always seen Harper as an easy mark, as well as the fact that she's drop-dead gorgeous—"

I shot a scowl at Gus and he caught it.

"Don't look at me like that, I've never touched her." Gus's face was squinched up in disgust. "Jesus, she's like my sister—but I can admit she's beautiful."

Grady pulled out his phone as it rang, "American Woman" by Lenny Kravitz. "It's CJ." He stood and walked away from the table.

"Man, that guy is so tangled up in her," Davy said, his warm smile a blinding contrast to his tough-man image. "Good to see. I like him for her. That girl deserves some happiness."

I nodded. "They are good together—but sometimes they are so ridiculously happy it makes me want to punch him." I was speaking my truth tonight.

Davy chuckled. "Yeah—I know what you mean."

"Some of us had a front row seat through the courtship from hell—which is why I'm happy to keep my options maximized, and the drama in my life minimized," Gus said, coming back with another round of beers.

We all had time to take a pull or two off our beers before Grady came back, smiling from ear to ear. "Well, we can stand down. No need to kick Spencer's ass." I straightened as if to get out of my chair. "The women have it handled." Pride oozed out of my brother. "My only regret is I wasn't a fly on the wall to witness the prick's downfall."

5 9

CHARLOTTE, NC

Harper

"Pack it up. We're going to meet the guys." CJ came in, laying down the law and putting her phone in her back pocket.

"I'll take Mel home, I'm not up for a party tonight." I was emotionally spent. Also, I suspected Cal was still in town, and I didn't need another run-in tonight.

"Hell, no. I'm going too," Mel said, standing tall—all five-foot-nothing of her.

"I'm taking you back to Jacks'. I take you to a bar, and he'll strap me to the back of his bumper and drag me behind his truck as he leaves Merlo in the dust," CJ said.

Mel mumbled something about being old enough and not needing to be babysat.

"And you..." CJ pointed at me from across the table, "are the guest of honor, so you have to go. Davy and Gus are there too."

"Hell, yeah!" Amara chimed in.

"I know who you're leaving out of that lineup, and I've reached my quota of confrontations with men tonight," I said, and slumped in my chair. I didn't want to see him.

Sadie walked over and put an envelope down in front of me. Everyone stopped moving around and waited. "You need to see this."

I stared at it—it looked innocuous—plain, white, business-size envelope. But the way everyone else was still, you'd think there was a viper in it.

"What is it?" I opened it—I read it twice.

For everyone else waiting to hear, Sadie said, "Cal just sold me the remainder of Merlo... for a dollar." A Post-it Note was attached to the document that said, *All I've ever wanted to do was make you happy.* He practically shouted it at me earlier. The document was signing over the ownership of Merlo to both Sadie and me—but the note was just for me.

And that was it.

I'd been pushing him away. I cut us off. But with that paper, he severed the remaining piece between us.

I stared at the paper, not seeing it. I waited for the tears to come.

They didn't.

I stared and stared, seeing the stroke of his writing, studying it. Because I realized I hadn't seen his handwriting much—and the thought gave even more finality to things. I had more to learn about him.

I would've rather received sweet notes from him—not letters from him relinquishing the partnership that originally brought us together.

Sadness, frustration, anger—and, dammit—determination.

No. He wasn't getting away that easy.

He needed to learn how to deal with me—how to not coddle me. Deep down, I knew he respected me. Words he said to me earlier were finally settling on me.

"I help those I love—it's who I fucking am! I can't apologize for that. I may be an ass how I go about doing it—but fuck, Harper every-thing I ever did was to lighten your burden, not add to it."

I help those I love—it's who I fucking am...

I knew that. I knew it because it was something we saw in each other. I did the same thing. I flipped roles for a moment. Yes, I would move Heaven and Earth to help someone I love to succeed.

I may have done it first and asked for forgiveness after they had what they needed.

Hell, hadn't I done that with CJ several times—isn't that how Merlo even started. It was a desire to help CJ succeed that gave me the courage to go after Merlo. I hadn't asked her.

I just put the wheels in motion because *I believed* it was the best thing for us both.

He loved me.

I hadn't blinked as I stared at the note. A small tear formed on the edge of my lashes.

CJ cut through my thoughts. "You know he quit McBane, right?"

My head spun to CJ so quickly, I didn't even register doing it. "What?"

There was a chorus of "What?" around me.

CJ continued. "Grady said Cal had it out with his dad the day we were at Rodderick and then he quit. Walked right out. He planned to fly down here to see you—to tell you."

And then I laid into him.

"Harper?" Sadie asked. "What are you going to do about this?" She flicked a finger at the paper.

I stood up so quickly the chair behind me hit the wall. "I'm finding him and shoving this note down his throat. He doesn't get to be all chivalrous like that without me saying something."

CJ smiled triumphantly. "There she is."

After dropping off a very unhappy Mel, we drove to the bar where the guys were.

I threw open the car door, barely waiting for CJ's SUV to come to a complete stop. I didn't wait for the ladies to follow.

With the note in hand, I strode in—my long legs ate up the length between the front door and the back table where the men sat. CJ practically had to run to keep up with me. Davy's beautiful face broke into a huge grin, his smile a beacon welcoming the new entertainment. Grady focused on CJ, who was still trying to keep up with me as I weaved around patrons. Gus turned to follow their gaze, smirked, slapped the man next to him on his back. As I approached, Gus said, "Well this will be interesting…"

I zeroed in on Cal—his broad back, his thick hair, and just the way he sat in a chair, made my heart race. His profile as he turned and spoke to Gus stopped me in my tracks and had me second-guessing my intentions.

Gus eyed me and tilted his head in my direction. Cal turned and his eyes caught mine. They pulled me in—there was no turning back.

He rose from his chair as my high heels ate up the remaining distance between us.

I shoved the envelope at him—slapping his chest with it. He stood still, staring down at where my hand landed. "What the hell, Cal?"

Out of the corner of my eye, Grady had CJ in his lap, but Gus and Davy sat back, arms across their chest. All four were waiting for the show to begin.

As if afraid they'd miss anything, Amara, Susannah, and Sadie came running up behind us, my posse at my back. "We're here!" Sadie announced to the entire establishment.

Cal scanned the new arrivals, and the attention we were garnering from the surrounding tables.

He stared back down at me. I took the envelope I had against his chest and began waving it around. "You think you can skate of out of this so easily?" I started waving both hands around like a woman possessed. "Sign it over to Sadie and then, what? Ride off into the sunset—no looking back?"

"Maybe we should step outside—"

"No. I'm good. Explain to me what this is about?" I growled and shook the envelope at him.

He put his hands in his pockets and shrugged—arrogance personified. "You wanted to be free of me…I gave you your freedom."

"I just wanted you to stop interfering—"

Amara leaned close to us and spoke low. "Um, guys—you've drawn some attention…"

I glanced over my shoulder and saw all the cellphones out, blatantly recording this.

"Fuck 'em," I said, and the smallest twinge of a smile flashed over Cal's beautiful lips.

Amara spoke firmly, but with patience of a mother explaining something to a small child. "Yes, well, don't call me crying when you see what shows up tomorrow on social media and the internet."

I grabbed Cal by the arm to lead him outside. But he stood stock still, and it was like trying to move a tree trunk.

"What *do* you want, Sunshine?" His voice was just for me.

"I want you to—you…you…" I was at a loss for words, and Cal didn't wait for me to find them.

He stepped forward and wrapped his arms around me like a vise, lifting me onto the toes of my designer heels. "I want you," I whispered, realizing that was the end of the sentence—there was nothing else to add.

"Thank God." His hand moved up to cup the back of my neck and he kissed me. There, in the middle of a downtown Charlotte bar, with everyone having their cell phones trained on us.

6 0

CHARLOTTE, NC

Cal

The world faded away, amidst the catcalls and whistles. The thought of what would appear on social media were nowhere near my mind. Because I was holding her, kissing her, and my world was being rocked even as it shifted back on its axis. I dug my hand into her hair, marveling at how sweet her lips were against mine.

Something dropped from her hands and hit my foot—the envelope —before she wrapped her arms tightly around me, dragging me back down to her, deepening the kiss.

We came up for air when Grady kicked me. "You better take this somewhere private, or they may hose you down with the soda gun." He laughed as he bent over, retrieving the forgotten paperwork.

Amara chimed in, "Besides, you are quickly stealing the prize for most sugary-sickening sweet couple away from CJ and Grady."

Our foreheads touching, I said, "I really don't need that title."

"Why are we still here?" Harper's sexy tone whispered so only I could hear it.

"No idea—," I put my arm around her as I debated sweeping her up in my arms—but deciding that may be laying it on too thick.

"Don't you need to pay the tab?" she asked, looking over his shoulder.

"Let Grady pick it up—I'm the one who is unemployed," I said, as we walked out the door.

Stopping under a streetlamp, she turned to me, her face lighter than I'd seen it in ages. The smile she had was real—it was her. She grabbed me by the shirt, pulled me close, and gave me a quick kiss. "Did you really think I'd let you walk away?" She looked at me from under her lashes—flirtatious—and I realized just how much I needed it, that sunshine in my life.

I traced her jaw with my thumb, staring at the way her eyes were dancing. "The thing is, Boss Lady...I kind of need a job."

"Well, it seems that I may have an opening after all." She wrapped her arms around me, and whispered in my ear, "Because I also take care of the ones I love."

EPILOGUE

DAYTONA, FL

Cal

"CJ Lomax is on the verge of becoming the first woman to qualify for the Chase for the Cup. If she can just maintain her lead."

The announcer's voice made it through the cacophony of noise emanating from the track and our suite, while I bounced on the balls of my feet, excitement racing through my veins. I glanced over at Harper, who wouldn't tear her focus off the track. Her hands clasped together as if in prayer.

Surrounding us in the box overlooking the Daytona track, were family and friends, all on the edge of their seats—but no one approached Harper. Not now. Not as Merlo was so close to making it to the playoffs for the series championship. Only sixteen drivers would qualify, and this race determined if CJ was one of them.

Everything we'd worked for, everything we'd sacrificed came down to a little dynamo in a flash of steel.

My brother was following her close behind—having edged himself up through the pack for the last few laps on a fresh set of tires.

Grady was also on the bubble of making it to The Chase. And when they were on the track, the gloves were off. Until the day when Grady was under Merlo's banner, it was every man—or every woman —for themselves. But deep down, I knew Grady also had CJ's back.

Just like I had Harper's, as I stood silently behind her.

The announcer was the only noise that broke the silence in the suite on the last lap. *"Lomax is coming down the back straightaway and into turn three. She needs to win this race for her spot in The Chase...To make it a family affair, McBane has the number ten of Jared Mitchell to get past..."*

I caught a glimpse of my woman before fixating back on the track —it would be perfect if Grady and CJ were both in the championship —but it would mean a few more weeks of our hectic pace and would delay my plans to sweep her off to a remote tropical vacation.

Harper reached out and took my hand, holding it in both of hers and up against her body, as if it were a lifeline tethering her to Earth.

The unbelievable expression of pure joy and pride on Harper's face captured me in a vise grip. I wanted to take a photo and try to capture it for years to come. I was basking in the moment when the entire suite erupted, and Harper jumped into my arms.

CJ did it—she was the first woman to make it to the championship.

Harper did it—she got them both there.

Sadie and Harper both owned the team outright now.

I was an unofficial consultant who sat in on meetings and tried to keep my opinions to myself until we got home—we were still working on that part.

"Congratulations!" My mother came over for a group hug. My father still standing back, looking on. My father and I were back on speaking terms, but only after my mother had to play middleman. He was still having trouble accepting my decision not to return to Chicago.

I'd decided to take my mother's offer to run the expansion of Fast Lane's stores, as well as work on other acquisitions for that division. I opened an office in Charlotte and enjoyed focusing on one company and building it up. Of course, we were also a sponsor of Merlo's.

"Yes, congratulations. Well done," my father added. He was fully recovered, done with treatment, and in relatively good health. My mom hadn't backed down from running things, however. She had him, and the company, in hand, and everything seemed to be less intense that way.

"Now, get going—" My mom shooed us away. "We'll meet up later!"

Harper and I raced down the stairs from the suite, hand in hand, as if we were teenagers running away on an adventure—huge grins on our faces. I swung my woman in a large arc among the crowd of spectators and crew members, and then nuzzled her neck.

"We did it," she pulled back and yelled at me.

"No, Sunshine—you did it." I kissed her on the forehead, and then her nose, and then a peck on her sweet lips.

"Well..." Her eyes were alight and flirtatious, and I marveled over how I ever convinced her to be mine. She leaned up on her toes and whispered in my ear, "How about agreeing we make a good team?"

I locked my arms around her, attempting to rein in all the excitement, love, and pride running through me. I channeled it into the smirk I gave her and whispered back, "Whatever you say, Boss."

THE END

AFTERWORD

While I tried to stay as close to the sport as possible, and give readers a true experience, I intentionally didn't delve too deeply into technical aspects of stock car to keep the story from becoming too dated if the industry adjusts their format or makes other changes. I also played with the schedule of the races for creative reasons, and each year can also be different.

Since writing A FAST WOMAN, the industry has already started to change. It is an exciting time for the sport, and for women in the sport. Drivers, engineers, race officials, race announcers, track side reporters, tire changers, executives—the women are in every facet. So much inspiration for *Driven Women* to choose from!

Stay tuned and see who will be next...

ACKNOWLEDGMENTS

I wrote BOSS LADY during the pandemic, which was not an easy task but helped me remain sane. I wouldn't have been able to do it without my husband and kids who respected my need to work on this project—to maintain this piece of normalcy as we all tried to adapt.

Thank you to J L Lora and Cate Tayler for pushing me through the writing—again. Also, shout out to Jessie Harper and Shelly Alexander who always give me great critique notes and advice—and another shove through the process. Finally, Holly Ingraham and Elaine York help reel me in and polish me up. These are my *"Driven Women"* crew.

I found the amazing Lindee Robinson days before she worked with Brooke and Josh and she came through for me with this amazing photo for my cover. Deranged Doctors Design ran with it and I love it.

Most importantly, thank you to my parents for believing in me.

For my father to teaching me how to change my oil and put air in my tires, put a boy in an armlock, and encouraging me to never rely on a man to do things for me.

For my mom for being my biggest cheerleader and my strongest shoulder. My first call whether the news is good or bad and always the best piece of advice I ever get.

I wouldn't have had the ability or courage to get this far in life without you and I don't think I say that enough.

Laralyn

ABOUT THE AUTHOR

Laralyn is a proud special needs mom, and an autism and dyslexia awareness advocate. She lives in Maryland with her husband, three children and three dogs. She is a member of Romance Writers of America, Central Pennsylvania Romance Writers, Washington Romance Writers, and other affiliate chapters.

She loves to write about witty, strong women then throw sexy, charming men in their path and see the chaos it causes. It's a great distraction from everyday life and is usually done with lazy dogs at her feet, a chai latte or Diet Coke in hand, and the promise of a glass of pinot at the end the day if the writing is worthy. She is often distracted by chatting on social media.

Sign-up for her newsletter and learn what she's up to next by hearing about new releases, freebies, events, and more at www.laralyn-doran.com

You can also join my friends and me in our exclusive reader group, S.A.S.S. (Smart-Ass Scribbling Squad).

BOOKS BY LARALYN DORAN

Driven Women Series

A Fast Woman

Boss Lady

Made in the USA
Middletown, DE
30 June 2021

43424814R00197